Through a

Different Lens

A Pride and Prejudice

Variation

RIANA EVERLY

THROUGH A DIFFERENT LENS

Cover design by Mae Phillips at <u>coverfreshdesigns.com</u>

ISBN-13: <u>978-1-7751283-7-3</u>

Dedication

To my son and all the wonderful people
who see life through a different lens

Contents

Acknowledgements

This story has so many sources of inspiration, it's impossible to know where to start. Perhaps I should begin with Jane Austen herself, who gave the world these wonderful characters, beautiful and imperfect as they are.

My family also need their names in lights. I've talked at them and run ideas past them and made them read and reread this text too many times, and they still talk to me! And of course, I have to acknowledge the several amazing people I know who are on the autism spectrum, who see life through a different lens, and who have shown again and again that neurological difference is not necessarily a disability. It's just a different ability!

Thanks to Sophia Meredith for her insightful comments that reshaped the entire story, making so very much better. Also, thanks to my amazing beta readers, Donna Kraus, Mary Belle McClean, and Deborah Pearson, and to editor Marion Hoffmann for her wonderful advice and insight. I am infinitely grateful to Mikael Swayze for his excellent copy editing skills. Also, so many thanks to the wonderful community at Beyond Austen for their wonderful ideas and encouraging comments.

The beautiful cover art is by Mae Phillips of Cover Fresh Designs.

The cover art image is a detail from the watercolour and gouache **Henry Hill Hickman performing experiments on suspended animation**, by Richard Tennant Cooper, ca. 1912 The painting part of the Wellcome Collection gallery, part of the Wellcome Library, London.

Cover design by Mae Phillips at coverfreshdesigns.com

To my son and all the wonderful people who see life
through a different lens.

Chapter One

Ill Qualified to Recommend Himself

It was an evening much like many others over the past few weeks. The small party were gathered in the salon after an uncomfortable dinner, to amuse, delight, and take advice from the doyenne of the house. The meal had seemed endless, with one overly fine dish superseding another, testimony more to the expense of a fine French chef than to the consideration due to the palates of the assembled guests. Likewise, the conversation, more a series of interrogatory demands by the lady of the house than an exchange of light and pleasant thoughts to lend enjoyment to the meal. Now, the last of the dishes cleared away and the company retired to the salon, Elizabeth sat perched upon the uncomfortable sofa, seeking something amusing to say that would astound those gathered around. Beside her sat her dear friend Charlotte, whom she was visiting, and nearby, Charlotte's husband, Mr. Collins, who held the living at Hunsford, adjacent to the grand manor house of Rosings. Also in the room were the mistress of the house herself, Lady Catherine de Bourgh, domineering and fierce of temperament, her sickly daughter Anne, who seemed more intimidated than truly ill, Anne's companion Mrs. Jenkins, and Charlotte's timid sister Maria, who spoke hardly a word.

In all of these particulars, the scene had been repeated many times since Elizabeth first arrived at Hunsford for a prolonged visit with her friend; recently, however, two more members had joined their party, one adding to its pleasure, the other to its awkwardness.

The increased pleasure was due entirely to the newly formed acquaintance with Lady Catherine's nephew, Colonel Fitzwilliam, on a short leave from the army to visit his aunt and cousin and help tend to affairs of her estate. The colonel and Elizabeth had quickly formed a comfortable and easy friendship, for the gentleman was intelligent, quick-witted, and extremely good company. Elizabeth had taken an immediate liking to him and was pleased when he sought her companionship, either in the salon or whilst walking through the park.

His friend, however, was far less of a source of pleasure. Silent, stiff and brooding, the colonel's constant shadow was none other than Mr. Darcy, whom Elizabeth had come to know and rather dislike several months ago at her home in Hertfordshire, near the village of Meryton.

They had first met at the close of the previous summer. Everybody in town had gathered at a public assembly and ball, there to meet Mr. Bingley, the young—and single—gentleman who had taken Netherfield Park, a grand estate in the neighbourhood, sadly unoccupied for the longest time. The crowd was eagerly and impatiently waiting to see both the man himself and the rumoured gathering of his attendants, ladies and gentlemen aplenty from town, the exact number of each varying according to the teller. At long last, and to the relief of the anxiously curious townsfolk, Mr. Bingley arrived with only two other men and two women. The first set of dances had just come to an end, and in the moment of silence when the musicians set down their instruments to draw breath, and when the dancers had made their final bows to each other before leaving the floor, the doors to the assembly hall had swung open to reveal the anticipated party.

The sudden cessation of ambient sound immediately became a hush, and then, just as quickly, the noise resumed its previous levels as people began to comment on the newcomers. "How fine they are," "What elegant attire," "How handsome he is," were the words that filled the air. "Five thousand?" "Which is the new tenant?" "Who are the others?"

Within a short time, the questions resolved into answers, which did little to curtail the gossip. Mr. Bingley was the young man of medium height and a most cheerful disposition, dressed in the dove grey coat. The shorter man in green was his brother-in-law, Mr. Hurst, and the taller, in dark blue and black, was his good friend, Mr. Darcy. The ladies were his sisters, Miss Bingley and Mrs. Hurst. Mr. Bingley was uniformly pronounced most well-disposed, especially when his income was disclosed at somewhere near five thousand a year; his friend, Mr. Darcy, was judged even more handsome, as much for his features as for his reported income of ten thousand!

Of the newly arrived members of the community, however, only Mr. Bingley retained the good regard of his new neighbours beyond the first quarter hour of their presence. The rest of the party was quickly deemed rather too good for Meryton's poor society. Mr. and Mrs. Hurst talked only amongst themselves and their own party, and Miss Bingley, who was to keep house for her brother, deigned to greet the natives with a stifled curtsey and an upturned nose, only to subtly deride their manners, their country ways, and their unfashionable dress. As for Mr. Darcy himself, he spoke scarcely a word all night and would dance only once, with Miss Bingley. The longest speech anyone heard him make the entire evening was overheard by none other than Elizabeth herself when Mr. Bingley importuned his friend to request of the lady a dance.

"Come, Darcy," said he, "I must have you dance. I hate to see you standing about by yourself in this stupid manner. You had much better dance." Mr. Bingley seemed only too eager to return to the dance floor, where he had been promised a second set by Elizabeth's older sister, Jane. The young man's eyes kept flickering over to where the young lady was standing, and she in turn smiled demurely at him. But his friend would have none of it.

"I certainly shall not," Mr. Darcy replied in a stiff voice, flat and devoid of emotion. "You know how I detest it, unless I am particularly acquainted with my partner." At this he broke off for a moment to look around at the crush in the hall, and almost in alarm at what he saw, stepped back slightly. "At such an assembly as this, it would be insupportable. Your sisters are engaged, and there is not another woman in the room whom it would not be a punishment to me to stand up with."

"I would not be so fastidious as you are," cried Bingley, "for a kingdom! Upon my honour I never met with so many pleasant girls in my life, as I have this evening; and there are several of them, you see, uncommonly pretty."

"You are dancing with the only handsome girl in the room," said Mr. Darcy, following his friend's gaze towards the eldest Miss Bennet. Jane Bennet was widely acknowledged to be an unusually splendid beauty, and one would be hard pressed indeed to find a man who would deny this.

"Oh! she is the most beautiful creature I ever beheld! But there is one of her sisters sitting down just behind you, who is very pretty, and I dare say very agreeable. Do let me ask my partner to introduce you."

"Which do you mean?" and turning round, he looked for a moment at Elizabeth, till catching her eye, he withdrew his own and coldly said, "She is tolerable; but not handsome enough to tempt me; and I am in no humour at present to give consequence to young ladies who are slighted by other men. You had better return to your partner and enjoy her smiles, for you are wasting your time with me."

This unfortunate encounter had set the precedent upon which all others would be based. Mr. Darcy's cold demeanour made him no friends, and his haughty stance and unrelenting terseness only served to further convince the members of the local society that the man was proud beyond his considerable means and not worth the effort of friendship. It was for Mr. Bingley's sake, and his alone, that Mr. Darcy's presence was accepted at all by the denizens of the area, whether at tea or cards in the evening, or at the shops in the village.

Nor had Mr. Darcy improved upon closer acquaintance, Elizabeth recollected. For some three days, they had resided in the same house. Elizabeth's sister Jane had become ill whilst visiting Mr. Bingley's sisters at Netherfield, and Elizabeth had come to nurse her back to health. This, naturally, threw her into the path of the proud gentleman again and again, but always he drew back when in her presence. His eyes would narrow and his back would stiffen, and he would stare at her mercilessly, while never deigning to meet her eyes when she gazed back. He had always had little to say to her that did not carry the weight of disapproval, so evident in his cold tone of voice, and she had less still to say to him that did not sparkle with contrariness. She considered that they both took their amusement in disliking each other prodigiously, and thus she was pleased when he took his leave from the area after Mr. Bingley's ball late last November. She had not expected to see him again at Rosings.

However, Mr. Darcy, too, was nephew to Lady Catherine, and with his cousin the colonel, would be staying for some weeks to help the lady with matters of business pertaining to the estate. Elizabeth would have to do what she must to suffer his presence, for there was no escaping it.

And so, with the formidable Mr. Darcy staring accusingly at her from across the room, she cast about for something witty to add to the stilted conversation in the room. Lady Catherine, however, acted most uncharacteristically this particular evening and made a pronouncement that brought a smile to many faces, and relief to Elizabeth's. "We must have music," the grand lady intoned in her imperious manner. "Miss Bennet, you play a little. Whilst you will never have the talent that I might have possessed, I do hope you have taken it upon yourself to practice in Mrs. Jenkins' rooms, as I suggested you ought. You shall play for us, and we shall have music, no matter how unskilled you may be."

Not judging herself up to the task of replying graciously to this command, Elizabeth swallowed her retort, then stood and curtseyed with all the grace she could manage, then strolled to the pianoforte that sat in a small alcove at the far side of the large salon. To her surprise, Mr. Darcy silently followed her, and to her pleasure, Colonel Fitzwilliam offered to turn pages as she played.

Whatever the rest of the company thought of her playing, she did not know, for she could not hear their comments, neither did she care. She did, however, enjoy the book of country dances she found, many of which she knew and therefore could perform with some credibility. After working through the dances, she talked quietly with the colonel who was helping her select some new pieces; Mr. Darcy stood stiffly off to the side, not venturing to add his thoughts to the conversation, although he was near enough to overhear it most clearly.

Colonel Fitzwilliam asked teasingly after his cousin whilst he had been with his friends in Hertfordshire not so long before, and Elizabeth laughed. "Your cousin, Mr. Darcy, was not the darling of our village." She affected a mien of feigned solemnity which had the colonel chuckling as readily as her own smile returned. In her sombre tones, she explained how he had made little conversation at the assembly and would not dance, and had not endeavoured to endear himself to the community.

"What say you to that, Darcy?" the colonel smiled. He must surely know he was baiting his cousin. "Explain yourself!"

"I am," stated the grave gentleman as he stood so awkwardly by the pianoforte, "ill qualified to recommend myself to strangers."

Elizabeth heard these words somewhat distractedly, as she perused the selection of music being placed before her by the colonel, his friendly eyes matched by an engaging grin. Still, something in the more serious man's demeanour caught her attention. She had never liked him, but she had always found herself fascinated by him. She sat up a little straighter and listened as Fitzwilliam Darcy continued to explain himself. He spoke, as always, formally, somewhat stiffly, as if acting the part of himself in the grand production of his life.

"I certainly have not the talent which some people possess," said he, "of conversing easily with those I have never seen before. I cannot catch their tone of conversation, or appear interested in their concerns, as I often see done."

Suddenly, with these words, Elizabeth felt her world shift slightly. With every syllable that haughty man uttered, isolated facets to his perplexing character seemed to realign themselves and come into focus. She stared at him as if seeing him for the first time. He cleared his throat and stepped back an inch, standing quite still and averting his eyes from her curious gaze. A flood of recollections and half-formed ideas cascaded through her consciousness. She stared up again at the stiff and serious man half hiding in the shadows, wondering if her suppositions might be correct.

"Miss Bennet?" the genial colonel sounded concerned. "Are you well?"

Realising she had been distracted most grievously from her supposed task of selecting music, she uttered a rushed apology. "Indeed, very well, Colonel Fitzwilliam. Forgive my wandering mind, please. I have no excuse but that your cousin, Mr. Darcy, suddenly reminded me of somebody I know, and at that realisation, you might have knocked me down with a feather, it was so surprising."

The man under discussion drew closer, edging towards the pianoforte where the two were conversing with such easy repartee. "Knocked you down with a feather?" he asked in some confusion, "How could that possibly be? While you are by no means a large woman, your weight most certainly surpasses that of a bird's plumage, even that of an ostrich or a peacock. To knock you down would surely take something much more substantial than a mere feather!"

Exchanging an understanding smile with the colonel, Elizabeth replied evenly, "It is an expression, sir, meaning to surprise greatly. Is this, may I ask, but one example of why you feel discomfort joining others' conversations?"

The man nodded. "Indeed it is so. I seem, always, to miss the meaning of what is being said. Not everybody is as compassionate as you, to explain the nuances I do not catch."

"Perhaps more exposure to these undesired conversations would be of benefit," Elizabeth tried to keep her voice friendly, more for the colonel's sake than Darcy's, if she were correct in her musings. "My fingers," she intoned carefully, as she looked pointedly down at her hands, poised as they were over the ivory keys of the pianoforte, "do not move over this instrument in the masterly manner which I see so many women's do. They have not the same force or rapidity, and do not produce the same expression. But then I have always supposed it to be my own fault—because I would not take the trouble of practising. It is not that I do not believe my fingers as capable as any other woman's of superior execution." Her mind was whirling at the import of her newfound hypothesis as to the real import behind the proud man's confessions. She was hardly aware of her own words, and she needed desperately to think further on this unexpected insight. But Mr. Darcy was speaking once more.

He smiled then, a studied, careful smile, and forced his eyes to meet her own, now looking quizzically at him from beneath furrowed brows. "You are perfectly right," he said. "You have employed your time much better. No one admitted to the privilege of hearing you, can think any thing wanting. We neither of us perform to strangers."

At this, as he stepped away and retreated once more into the shadows, the final piece of the puzzle began to fall into place and the picture that had been forming before her coalesced into a cohesive whole, unfocused and need of a sharpening lens, but a whole nonetheless. All at once, Elizabeth believed that just maybe, she understood Mr. Darcy.

Elizabeth strove to find something to say in response to the man, and was relieved when the officious Lady Catherine interrupted this conversation, allowing her to reflect more fully on what she had discovered this evening. She resumed her playing, only half aware of the notes before her, and uncertain as to whether she had played a single one correctly. Her mind was too busy puzzling over the import of what she may have chanced upon that evening during the strange and short conversation.

It was later, much later, when Elizabeth had a chance to reflect on her astounding discovery. Lying in her bed in the parsonage, blinking against the midnight black of the smallest hours of the morning, the young woman cast her mind to her vexatious dealings with the proud and arrogant gentleman from Derbyshire. Each and every one of her conversations with him had been seared into her memory like a brand, but as she reconsidered them in light of her new realisation, the harshness of those memories eased and transformed into... something different.

She replayed, in her mind, her first meeting with Mr. Darcy at the Meryton assembly, recalling every detail as best she could, hoping to find some suggestions in her memories that might confirm her ideas. It was his words in reference to her that reverberated most strongly through her mind: "tolerable; but not handsome enough to tempt me." He had looked directly at her and offered these damning words before turning away.

Elizabeth had, at the time, been mortified and most horribly insulted, inclinations which she had hidden under her accustomed manner of derision and love for the ridiculous. But now, lying in her bed at the parsonage at Hunsford, so many months and so many realisations removed from that awful scene, she reconsidered her impressions. Before he spoke his final, cutting words, he had turned and caught her eye. But had he recoiled in displeasure, or in discomfort? Was that cold tone of voice really arrogance and superiority? Or did Mr. Darcy have more to hide than he might wish, withdrawing into himself and using an icy exterior as armour against the onslaught of the crowds?

Reflecting further, Elizabeth recalled the proud man's look as he had entered the hall. It had been a look of disdain, a look of aloofness.... Or had it? Had that look in his eyes, the slight widening of his eyelids, the almost imperceptible tucking in of his chin, been, instead, just perhaps, one of terror?

"I may," Elizabeth spoke aloud, her quiet voice melting into the silence of the room, "have grievously misjudged him."

It was a long while after her confession to the bedsheets that Elizabeth finally drifted off to sleep, the implications of the evening's events and her sudden understanding still running through her mind, and she awoke with the same notions playing upon her thoughts. She still had much to consider, and knew she would benefit from further thought on the issue, uninterrupted by her Mr. Collins' gratuitous mewlings or the polite but nonetheless irritating demands of Charlotte's sister, Maria. Of Mr. Collins himself, she held no great opinion. Though the man was her cousin and heir to her father's estate, she found him fawning and obsequious—in all, a ridiculous man whose only consequence in life was that he had managed to ingratiate himself into the favours of Lady Catherine, thereby to merit her condescension. More than a few moments in his company were enough to try the stoutest of souls, and hers, this morning, was feeling not at all stout, nor tending to any great degree of forbearance. Consequently she came to the pressing and not unexpected decision that a long walk through the woods and fields that surrounded Rosings was in order.

"Shall you really walk yet again, Miss Elizabeth?" Mr. Collins asked as she laced up her boots and sought her bonnet. "You walked yesterday, and the day before that. Her ladyship does not look well upon young women who are too robust. Consider her daughter, the lovely Miss de Bourgh: she possesses such a delicate nature, which can only be becoming in a lady. Perhaps she is a touch too delicate, but her fragile nature only emphasises her noble heritage. A fine lady should not be expected to bustle about doing things for herself when she has servants to do them for her."

Elizabeth tried not to harrumph at this statement, for the sickly Miss de Bourgh had not the constitution of a delicate flower, but rather of a wasting and dried up weed. Mr. Collins, however, was so wrapped up in his soliloquy, however that he paid little attention to Elizabeth's expression and continued his discourse.

"However," he considered, raising his eyes slightly and breathing reverently, "although being too robust may be seen as almost peasant-like in nature, when one considers the magnificence of Rosings Park, the great splendour and range of its woodlands and pathways, the beauty of its streams and glades, it is most understandable that you might wish to experience everything to the fullest before returning to Longbourn. That these grounds might have been yours to enjoy every day, we will not further discuss," he added pointedly. He was not above forever alluding to the topic that Elizabeth had refused him only days before the parson had offered for, and been accepted by, her friend Charlotte. Heedless again of any awkwardness, or perhaps, desirous of it, he continued, "I am most blessed in my patroness for allowing me such liberal use of her most pleasant parks. Did you know that the forest itself is nearly ten miles around, with countless fields and wilderness areas as well as part of the park?"

Taking advantage of the clergyman's need to draw breath, Elizabeth quickly replied, "Yes, indeed, Mr. Collins, Lady Catherine's holdings are most vast and prosperous indeed; I should be only too grateful to be able to partake of the natural loveliness that awaits me. Happy is the one who walks in the path of the de Bourgh family," she intoned seriously, awaiting the parson's rejoinder at her irreverent biblical reference. But the allusion fell on deaf ears and she was soon, to her greatest relief, outside and alone with her thoughts and her newly conceived suspicions about Mr. Darcy.

She had so many more recollections through which to sift, so many more conversations and interactions with the frustrating man to ponder, and yet, as Elizabeth strode purposefully away from the parsonage and towards the pathway leading through the wooded area to the stream nearby, she found her thoughts tending elsewhere, everywhere but on her intended topic. After trying in vain to rein them in, she decided to let these thoughts flit where they would, in the hopes that eventually they would alight upon some further revelations as she walked, letting the sights and sounds of her path guide her musings.

The gravel pathway led out of the back garden, through a small stile, and across a pleasant meadow, now a glorious carpet of fresh spring wildflowers. Pink, mauve, pale blue, butter yellow and white, the riot of new buds reminded Elizabeth of nothing so much as the pastel hues of ladies in a ballroom. All the scene needed were some stiffly formal men and a few overly solicitous mamas hoping for a brilliant match, and it would be complete. She imagined the conversation that might ensue.

"May I have this dance?" the raspberry bush would request of the buttercup. "Of course, sir, I was hoping you would ask."

Lizzy giggled at the silly notion and continued on her way, across the open field and into the wood that lay beyond it.

Here, the light was dappled and the air moist. Leaves had appeared on most of the trees, but they were small and fresh enough that the path was not in complete shade. Different insects buzzed through the trees here than had floated across the carpet of flowers, and every now and then a small animal—perhaps a rabbit—could be heard rustling through the brush away from the path. This section of the path was short, and within a few minutes Elizabeth emerged on the other side of the wood and took a deep breath. This was part of the park around Rosings, closer to the manor house than to the village, and if she tried, Elizabeth could see snatches of the house through the occasional gap in the foliage. And yet, right now, this space felt to her an isolated wilderness, her own kingdom, her personal realm, where she alone held sovereignty and where none might disturb her or vex her.

The path led now across a second small meadow to the stream that burbled in the distance, a picturesque landscape complete with the perfect arrangement of trees and low bushes, a stone bridge spanning the narrow rill, and even a bench on the other side. The bench, which Elizabeth could just barely see as it was mostly hidden behind a large and low shrub, already verdant with lush spring leaves, was an unpleasant reminder that she was not, in fact, monarch of these woods, and that others must from time to time visit them. But for now, she observed as she approached the spot, the bench was empty of occupants and this little kingdom was her own.

She sat on the bench, enjoying the view and the sound of the burbling stream, and withdrew from her reticule a small packet of letters. These she seldom was without, for they were from her dear aunt, whom she loved and respected most dearly. They travelled with her, although before today, she had never had occasion to reread them. Now, however, their contents seemed pertinent, and she carefully opened the earliest of them and began to read.

Chapter Two

Discovery

For much of their content, the letters were unexceptional, save for the dearness to her of their writer, her Aunt Gardiner. Mr. and Mrs. Gardiner lived in London, where her uncle was a prosperous businessman and head of a growing family, now numbering four energetic children. It was the eldest of these children of whom she had thought the night before, when Mr. Darcy had made his short speech. And it was of this same child, a boy named Samuel, of whom she now read.

The letter was dated several years earlier, when the boy was only about five years old. He had always been an unusual child, and her aunt was growing much concerned about him.

Oh, Lizzy, she had written, *I am much concerned about my sweet Sammy. As you know, he was somewhat late to talk, and we thought for a time he might be feeble-minded, although he seemed to understand us well enough at times. When he did start to speak at age three, it was sudden, and in full sentences, and your uncle and I assumed that it was merely his way. But now that the baby is growing—can you believe he is nearly three years of age himself already?—I see so clearly the difference between Sammy and his younger brother. Tommy babbles constantly, which is most endearing to hear, and orders us around with his grunts and gestures, like a little king commanding his subjects, and we are most willing to obey and he looks at us all the while, daring us to set a foot wrong. These things, Samuel never did, nor will he meet our eyes with his own, but he always glances away. Today I was visiting with my friend Mrs. Dyson, whose son is of a similar age, and I watched the two small children together. They play together, Lizzy. They point and talk and call for each other's attention, and build castles from their assorted toys and twigs and leaves they found on the ground. They relate to each other as you and I do, albeit in the way of very little boys. None of these things did I ever see from Sammy. Sammy just stares at the others and then wanders off to collect branches, which he lines up in ever-expanding rows, or stares at the waters of the pond as the ducks paddle by, leaving ripples in their wake. Other times he stands alone and flaps his hands ceaselessly, or spins himself around in circles until I think he will fall to the ground from dizziness. Is my dear boy broken, Lizzy? Are those horrible old women correct, that he is not of sound mind and must be sent to an institution? He is a good boy and I think very smart in his own way, for he reads so well and calculates arithmetic in his head, but when I see him by his younger brother, my heart wonders what my mind refuses to accept.*

A second letter from some months later reiterated this pain.

We have engaged a governess, for I am busy with the baby now and have less time to tend to Sammy's education. Miss Ellicott is happy enough with young Tommy, whom she says is learning as well as a boy of three might be expected to learn, but she expresses great concern about Samuel. He cries when there is too much noise, or when he gets dirty, and complains that his clothing is too rough on his skin. He does not smile at other children, and if his routine varies even one jot from the custom, he curls up and screams, or spins in his endless circles. His speech, too, is unusual, for he does not understand joking or teasing, and he hears every expression in only the most literal terms. He is not like other boys, she informs me again and again, all the while shaking her head sadly. What is wrong with my boy, Lizzy? Will he ever be right?

Another letter, dated shortly thereafter was more dire still.

Oh, my sweet niece, how I hate to burden you with my pain, you who are still so young yourself, although I feel a wisdom in you beyond your years. We have dismissed Miss Ellicott. We discovered that her manner of attempting to correct poor Sammy's behaviour involved locking him in a dark room and caning him for his weaknesses in understanding. She says the devil is in him, and that evil must be beaten out. She told us that when he spins in circles and flaps his hands when distressed, that is a sign of possession by wicked spirits. She was heard, even, to whisper about changeling children by one of the maids. For all of Sammy's faults, there is not one drop of evil in him. He is a child, little more than a babe, and bears no malice towards anyone. We are searching for another governess, but I fear greatly that none will treat my child with the tenderness he requires.

For the next year these letters continued in a similar vein, as Mrs. Gardiner came to realise that her son was very much unlike the other children. He did not make friends, and could scarcely be forced to acknowledge the existence of other children, let alone look them in the face and smile. Perversely, she commented, he seemed to wish for their friendship, but had no innate notion of how to get it. Then, a letter had arrived that was, at last, full of hope.

Lizzy, dearest Lizzy, you must come to visit. We have engaged a new governess, at long last, and we are most happy. Every other lady we met spoke similarly to Miss Ellicott, but not Miss Pierce. You will like her very much, Lizzy, for she has such a sweet nature and such a gift with the children, that they are eager to work to please her. Even the baby coos and gurgles when Miss Pierce enters the room with the boys. She is a charming girl, with a wit almost to rival your own, and very well educated. Her papa was a schoolteacher, it seems, and she learned with her father's students, much as I learned with my brother. But, her true value has been to Sammy. She understands him, she tells us, and has begun to work with him to help him, and to such success! He no longer flaps his hands when he is distressed, nor does he spin so much. He even engages in short conversations with his brother from time to time. She assures us that she has seen others boys like Sammy, and that she has every hope for him. Oh Lizzy, dearest niece, please come and visit us and see for yourself!

Elizabeth glanced once more at the date on this letter. It was some six years old, written when she was only fourteen years of age, still a child! Nonetheless, she had then considered herself as being almost a woman, with the good understanding and mature demeanour of one some years older, and had no little confidence in her abilities. She had begged her father for permission to spend some weeks in London with her family, and was granted her wish. Before many more weeks had passed, she found herself in London, where she soon made the acquaintance of the new governess.

Miss Pierce was, indeed, everything her aunt had said, and despite a difference in age of some years, the two quickly became friends. Miss Pierce, she learned, was the oldest of seven children, six of them girls! Her only brother was the youngest of the family, still only a lad of eight, and he was a different sort of child to what her sisters had been. He was, Miss Pierce related, very late to talk, and of an unusual disposition. "Whereas my sisters were most affectionate, Charlie would stiffen when hugged or held, even as a babe, and seemed more and more to live in a world all his own. He would not look into people's eyes, and cried at the slightest touch of water on his body, or at loud noises. He would speak, but in a flat and toneless voice, and would behave in a most rude manner whilst not knowing what he was doing wrong. But Papa, being most interested in education and on bettering his own knowledge, sought to learn what he might do for my brother. He learned of some men studying the new science of psychology and entered into correspondence with them."

One of these men was an American physician named Benjamin Rush, who advocated treating the insane with the kindness due to any human being. Although Miss Pierce's brother was not insane, her father decided that rather than punishing the lad for his unsociable behaviours—as was so often done to errant students in the schools—he ought to be gentle with the lad."

"Was it successful?" Even as a young girl still in the schoolroom, Elizabeth had a thirst for such information, and she was gratified when her new friend responded with a careful smile.

"It was not a failure." Miss Pierce's eyes grew unfocused as she thought. "Charlie is less afraid of noises than he was, and no longer cries and panics when he is in unfamiliar situations. Papa is working still on ways to encourage him to join in with the other children at the school, and the other students try to help and encourage him. In that respect, kindness has been a most effective path to take. I have learned so much from these young lads in my father's classroom."

"How interesting! How did you come to be governess here? I am so pleased you did, for now we may be friends, and I see how my cousins adore you!" Elizabeth had shuffled her feet in her enthusiasm, no matter how greatly she was striving to behave like a lady.

Miss Pierce had glanced at her young friend's feet, and to Elizabeth's relief and returned not a chastisement, but a warm smile. "And I am most pleased as well, Miss Elizabeth, for I am happy to be your friend!"

She continued her account, telling of how, though her father's correspondences, she met and became friends with another governess with a young student much like Charlie. Together the two women devised a series of games and exercises to encourage these lads to reach past their innate limitations. "When your aunt wrote to me about your cousin, I realised he sounded much like these other lads, and I knew that if nothing else, I could be kind to him. I did not realise how smart he would be, or how much I would grow to like him."

As the weeks in London passed by, Elizabeth had so enjoyed working with Miss Pierce and her cousins that when the allotted time of her visit had elapsed, she begged her father for yet a longer stay. She ended up living with the Gardiners for nearly a year, spending time in the nursery with the children by day and expanding upon her own education with Miss Pierce's guidance in the afternoons and evenings. The two would find new treatises on psychology and the treatment of the insane, and would devise new games that interested her cousin and helped him learn to interact with his brother and sisters, as well as with other children. It was both frustrating and fascinating, and by the time Elizabeth finally returned to Longbourn, she felt herself somewhat of an expert on working with children like her cousin Samuel.

As the seasons came and went, Elizabeth had returned to London for several subsequent visits to her beloved aunt and uncle. On one of these visits, she made the acquaintance of Miss Pierce's friend and that other lady's young charge, the lad so similar to her cousin. Although the two boys were very different in many ways, they also had had many characteristics in common. Glancing down at her letter now, written so long ago but with words so deeply etched into her mind, Elizabeth believed she had now met a third person with that same unusual nature: Mr. Darcy.

She sighed as she folded her letters and carefully replaced them into her reticule. Her mind was engaged and her feet wished to be put into motion as she thought. She stood and resumed her walk. After crossing the bridge, she found the path meandered gently through the lightly wooded fields and towards a small rise of land, on which she could see some sort of structure. Choosing this as her destination, she finally found she was able to force her thoughts into line, and began once more to ponder her interactions with Mr. Darcy.

Elizabeth cast her mind back, reviving all the memories of her interactions with that perplexing gentleman. After that first disastrous encounter at the assembly, the next meeting which imposed itself upon her mind was at a large gathering hosted by Sir and Lady Lucas, some short time after the ball. Elizabeth had been talking with Charlotte and Colonel Forster when she noticed Mr. Darcy approach the group, as if intending to join the conversation. He had stopped short, however, and stood somewhat awkwardly a few feet to the side, close enough to listen but not quite close enough to engage with the others. Elizabeth had noticed him staring at her, only to look sharply away every time she turned to catch his eye. "How rude!" she had thought at the time, and she had even dared speak of it to Charlotte when they had some moments in privacy.

"What does Mr. Darcy mean," said she to Charlotte, "by listening to my conversation with Colonel Forster? He approached, but seemingly with no intention of speaking. It is quite vexing!"

Charlotte had only laughed in response, "That is a question which Mr. Darcy only can answer."

Elizabeth gave a delicate snort as she turned her head to find the gentleman once more across the room, although his eyes were trained upon none but her with a most curious look. Shaking her head in bemusement, she said to her friend, "Look at him, always staring as if to find some fault. He may think it an amusement, but if he does it any more, I shall certainly let him know that I see what he is about. He has a very satirical eye, and if I do not begin by being impertinent myself, I shall soon grow afraid of him."

"You, Lizzy, should never be afraid of anyone, for I know you too well," Charlotte replied. "But I do have to wonder at the man. It is most intriguing!"

"Oh, no, Charlotte!" Lizzy had laughed, "You shall find nothing in that man but the harshest of critics, I believe. Keep your little suspicions for Jane and Mr. Bingley. Mr. Darcy surely finds nothing of any pleasure in me!"

And yet now, as she walked along the gently winding path, Elizabeth reconsidered what she had really seen that evening. Had she really observed derision in Mr. Darcy's eyes has he started at her across the room? His intentions in approaching her as she spoke with her friends had seemed, at the time, an attempt to intimidate, to let her know in no uncertain terms that her every word and gesture was being weighed and considered. But was there some other explanation for Mr. Darcy's strange behaviour?

Was the man, perhaps, desperately wishing to join in with the group as they chatted and playfully debated the topic at hand? She thought back to her aunt's accounting of Samuel, so keenly wishing for friends, but so lacking in the most simple social abilities needed to interact with his peers. Mr. Darcy's eyes, which had sought hers and then withdrawn almost in fear, his stiff stance as he hovered nearby, but unable to further approach, she both now reconsidered, and she found her earlier suppositions further confirmed by what she recalled in this new frame of mind.

Her feet had brought her now to the small rise of land, and the structure atop was now revealed to be a folly, which must command a lovely vista of the surrounding fields. She smiled at the prospect of enjoying the view and set forth up the hillock. Upon achieving the summit, she stepped into the folly and closed her eyes while she breathed in deeply, enjoying the coolness of the shade after her walk in the warm spring sun. Upon letting her eyelids flutter open once more, her sigh of pleasure became a small gasp of surprise, for there, upon a low bench hidden in the shadows, previously unnoticed by her sun-blinded eyes, sat the very man she had been considering all this while: Mr. Darcy himself!

As soon as their eyes met, Darcy leapt to his feet, a behaviour most clearly instilled in him from the earliest childhood. Lizzy stood as if frozen to the spot for a moment, eyes wide and mouth slightly agape. She had not expected to see him so soon, not before she had fully considered what she felt she knew of him. And yet, with him standing here, suddenly before her, it seemed for a moment as if she were being granted an opportunity to fully explore her hypothesis.

"Miss Elizabeth," Mr. Darcy greeted her, bowing a most proper bow. He caught her gaze, holding his eyes on hers as for a few moments if by the force of will, before letting them slide aside.

"Mr. Darcy." Lizzy gave a proper curtsey and then continued, "I did not expect to find anybody here. If I have interrupted your solitude, please accept my apologies. I will leave you if you wish."

"No!" The vehemence of his exclamation caught her somewhat by surprise. She had imagined he would be too much of a gentleman to ask her to leave, but now she stopped. Did he actually *wish* her to stay?

Before her revelation, she would have made another curtsey and found some excuse to depart. She had never sought out the gentleman's company, and had, rather, been pleased to avoid it, certain of their mutual dislike. If he had been in her company more than she believed he wished, she ascribed it to his carefully-taught manners and a societal expectation not to be too uncivil to one's company. At no point had she imagined he might have desired her presence. And yet, the strength of his assertion had surprised her, and in the new light in which she saw him, she found herself softening towards his stern demeanour.

He continued, "I would be happy for your company, although you know that I am not adept at small talk."

"Whereas I," she smiled, 'excel at it. But never fear, sir, I shall not torment you with mindless chatter about the weather and the lovely flower arrangement on the dining table."

"Should you wish to discuss flower arrangements, Miss Bennet? I had not supposed you to be interested in the art, but I must confess my ignorance as to your diversions."

"Mr. Darcy," she countered, "I believe the boot is on the other leg, for I know nought of your interests, so as to discuss them with you."

"Your boots, madam? Are you mis-shod? I shall turn my back should you wish to replace your footwear." The expression clearly had him confused.

She assured him with a gentle smile, "'Tis a common idiom, sir, to indicate the reversal of affairs from what was first stated." He nodded sagely, but Elizabeth suspected he only partly took her meaning.

"If you wish to tell me of your particular interests, sir, I should be happy to hear of them."

To this he made no reply, but stared at her, forcing himself at intervals to meet her eyes. *Ah,* she thought, *he does not wish to discuss his amusements, and understood my reply merely to be an offer to listen and not a request to speak. I am more and more convinced of my supposition.*

She paused for a moment, uncertain quite how to continue. If she were indeed correct, however, this man would better appreciate a direct approach, rather than some more subtle approach to the topic she wished to discuss. Taking a deep breath, she plunged into her speech like a soldier into battle.

"Indeed, Mr. Darcy," she said as calmly as she might, "I had wished to speak with you about exactly this subject."

Mr. Darcy's eyebrows rose. "About the flower arrangement? Why should you wish to discuss that?"

Elizabeth smiled. This was, she quickly ascertained, the best way into her inquiries. "Do you always take things so literally, Mr. Darcy?"

His quizzical expression answered her question before his words did. "I very often fail to find any other way of understanding them. In retrospect, when I have time to consider the words and context, I have a much deeper understanding of what had been said, but at the moment, these ambiguities of speech confound me." He frowned at the thought, and added, "I now understand your allusion to the boot being on the other leg. It is a metaphorical expression, one which really rather delights upon contemplation. However, at the moment of hearing it, as so often happens, I quite missed the meaning." He paused, and stared once more at Elizabeth's face, not quite meeting her eyes. She realised that her sympathetic expression would be unnoticed by her companion, and she invited him to continue, which he did shortly. "I find this is one of the many impediments I seem to have in catching the tone of conversations. People so often say what they do not, exactly, mean, or otherwise influence how they are understood by gestures or some subtle means which I cannot grasp, and I find I am left quite confused by how the discussions progress. I often find that it is to my advantage to remain silent. I would rather be thought aloof than a fool."

His words settled into Elizabeth's heart, each one stinging her with regret, for she had been one of those who considered Mr. Darcy's faults to be those of arrogance and pride, rather than pain and a feeling of inadequacy. She felt her emotions—the shame of her own past behaviour, the sadness she felt at his confession, and the pity that had suddenly sprung up in her breast for this man—settle upon her face. Not schooling her features, as she might otherwise do, she looked up at him most deliberately and asked, "Mr. Darcy, look at my face, at my expression. What do you see?"

The tall man peered at her most carefully, avoiding catching her eyes for longer than mere moments. He seemed quite perplexed by her question. "Miss Elizabeth, I am uncertain what you wish to know. I see your chin is receding slightly, where it is customarily thrust out a small degree. You seem to have caught your lower lip between your teeth, or perhaps you have otherwise manipulated it from within, for its centre protrudes ever so slightly, while the portions closer to your cheeks are withdrawn, as if being suctioned slightly into your mouth. Your nose... is perfect. I shall not comment on that, although I suspect it may have a tendency to freckle should you spend too much time in the sun without a bonnet come summer." He stood back, observing her closely, then continued.

"Your eyes—I have often admired your eyes—seem to droop slightly at the outer edges, an impression made more explicit by the angle of your eyebrows, and the centre of your forehead seems somewhat furrowed. Shall I examine your ears?"

"No, no indeed, sir, that shall not be necessary. You have given a most careful description of what you observed. I am most impressed at your observational skills and your ability to describe what you see. But I wish, rather, to know how you think I feel."

At this, Darcy's head snapped up and he took a short step backwards. "How you feel? Whatever can you mean?"

"I mean, Mr. Darcy," came the reply, "I wish to know if you can sense my emotions from my facial expressions."

This demand was met by silence. Then, eventually, "No, madam, I cannot. It is one of my great failings."

The sliver of pity in Elizabeth's heart swelled until she thought she might burst from the agony she felt on behalf of this misunderstood man, and she stepped towards him, being careful not to approach too closely. She imagined he would be most uncomfortable to have his immediate proximity invaded by one uninvited. "May we sit and talk, sir? Or would you prefer to walk? I have been rereading some letters from my aunt, and these recollections often leave me wanting exercise."

"How, if I may ask, do old letters require you to walk?" The question was serious, and Elizabeth answered in accordingly.

"The letters pertain to my cousin Samuel. He is now a bright young lad, full of promise, but his fate was not always so rosy. When I read again of his tenderest years, I feel agitated and cannot be still"

The gentleman did not object to the hearing of this account, and Elizabeth continued. "He was subject to a most unpleasant governess, who abused him most sorely, for all that he was five years of age, for his inability to read expressions, a characteristic that brings me in mind of you, sir."

At this, Mr. Darcy exclaimed, "Like me? How so? What sorts of abuses did this poor child suffer?"

"He was beaten, and locked in a dark room, in a misguided attempt to rid him of the devil." Even recounting this story after so long, Elizabeth's voice shook. Mr. Darcy did not comment on her voice, but echoed the sentiment.

"That is most grievous to hear. I, too, suffered at the hands of a nursery maid as a young child. I was not told the reason, but I still recall the beatings for doing no wrong that I could discern. But what evil could the governess see in your young cousin?"

Elizabeth thought furiously. She believed she might know some way to ease Mr. Darcy's comfort in society, but she could not offer herself as his tutor! His status was so much above hers, the association would be demeaning to him. And yet she was certain she might help. Would hearing Samuel's story let her enough into Mr. Darcy's confidence that she might attempt an offer of assistance? Steeling herself, she decided at once to try.

"As I have said, Samuel, like yourself, has trouble reading facial expressions." She paused, wondering how to continue. Then she started afresh. "Would you permit me to tell you a story, Mr. Darcy?"

"A story? How does that relate to facial expressions? Or are we still discussing flower arrangements?" Darcy's confusion seemed genuine, and he stared at Elizabeth openly, disregarding her returned gaze. For the first time, Elizabeth realised, she could clearly see the colour of his eyes. Before now, every time he had managed to hold her gaze for more than the briefest moment, his eyelids had fluttered or he had quickly glanced aside. She had held the impression of light eyes, but now she could see the colour for what it was, a misty moss green, verging on hazel. How easy it would be to dismiss the colour as light brown in the wake of his distracted glances, but how interesting and intense it was now, when his gaze was willingly bestowed. She ached to see his eyes in the light of the sun, and not in the deep shadow of this folly.

"Let us walk, then, Mr. Darcy," she offered, "and I shall tell you of my cousin. And then, if you permit me, I shall explain myself, for I see that you find my words most confusing." She smiled at him. "I find I am most adept at reading facial expressions—at least most of the time," she shook her head ruefully, "and yes, I believe my tale might be of interest to you. Come, sir, let us walk."

She waited for him to collect himself, and then stood aside. He might have been taught, from the youngest age, to offer his arm to a lady, but she would not expect it, and most certainly not demand it. She would let the gentleman determine how he wished to proceed, and she would act accordingly. She had learned this much, and so much more, with young Samuel.

To her surprise, Mr. Darcy did indeed offer his arm, and she took it lightly as they walked. He did not seem uncomfortable by the touch of her hand upon his forearm, and indeed, she thought his entire demeanour was more at ease than ever she had seen him. His shoulders were loose and his gait was easy and free. How different, she thought, from the stiff and rigid statue he seemed so often to be. They strolled in silence for some minutes and then Elizabeth began her tale.

"You have heard me speak, I am certain, of my aunt and uncle in London."

Darcy nodded. "The relations who reside near Cheapside, on Gracechurch Street. I heard your sister make mention of this once."

It was not a question and Elizabeth continued her explanation. "I care for them and respect them very much, and I have spent much time with them in the city. They might be in trade, but I am certain, should you ever meet them, you would not be ashamed to be in their company, for they are the finest people and most genteel.

"They have four children; the oldest is a boy, now twelve years old, named Samuel. He is a lovely child, and extremely intelligent, but he has also always been unusual. He spoke later than most children, and he did not seem to follow conversations well, even as he grew older. He would say things that did not flow naturally from the discussion at hand, and would interrupt with observations completely removed from the topic. He also exhibited some rather unusual physical habits. His father and mother despaired, at first, that he was feeble-minded."

"Unusual physical habits, Miss Elizabeth? What can you mean?" Mr. Darcy's interest was genuine.

"I mean, sir, that my cousin, when upset or agitated, feels the need to spin himself in circles and wave his hands in the air, or worry them together, as if rinsing them repeatedly. Other times, he rocks back and forth repeatedly, or makes strange high noises with his voice. He says that these motions soothe him."

Mr. Darcy blinked. "I see." He clearly did, for there was a flicker of recognition in his eyes. Elizabeth chose not to ask about this, but continued her tale.

"More importantly, young Samuel did not seem to understand things that were *not* said. If he were to misbehave, he did not understand gestures of reproof or angry voices. He did not react to the stern words, nor to the tone of voice used in issuing the reprimand. He did not seem to understand the relevance of an angry face, but would continue blithely on until he had to be punished quite severely for his misbehaviour. He could not read facial expressions or tone of voice, Mr. Darcy." She looked up at her companion and noticed once more the flicker of awareness in his unusual green eyes. As he remained silent, she continued her story.

"After his sister was born, my aunt and uncle hired a new nursemaid for the boys. This lady was the one who beat him and locked him away. She claimed that that as well as being somehow demonic, Sammy was an idiot and unable to learn, despite him being able to read complicated material and memorise a great amount of information. She suggested he belonged in an institution. You can imagine how distraught my aunt and uncle were, for they saw the fierce intelligence in their son. She was soon dismissed. Fortunately, they soon found a new governess who was quite different. This lady, Miss Pierce, became Samuel's staunchest ally. She knew of another young boy similar to Samuel, the charge of one of her friends, and she and her friend would discuss these boys in an attempt to learn how best to help them grow past their ever-increasing eccentricities."

Elizabeth watched Mr. Darcy very carefully. He gave no further indication of recognition, but nodded sagely, waiting for her to continue her recital. She tried to find another vignette with which she hoped to capture the forbidding man's attention.

"By the time he was four, Samuel had developed a passion for tin soldiers. He would not play with them as most children do, however, but would line them up in endless rows, stretching from one room to another in the nursery. Did you ever do that with your toys, Mr. Darcy?"

Now Darcy blinked most disconcertedly and sputtered, "But... how did you know? I do not recall this, but my own nurse told me stories of how I would treat my own playthings thusly."

"I suspected as much, sir, because the other boy Miss Pierce knew about did the same thing. Likewise, this boy—Henry, I believe is his name—would sit with his sisters in their schoolroom, but would not play with them as most children do. He would hover around them, but would not know how to engage them in a joint activity. And when Samuel was placed in a situation with other children, this is how he, too behaved. And he could not, without a great deal of anxiety, look at his playmates, parents or teacher in the eye for any length of time."

"As did I," Mr. Darcy volunteered. "My own nurse and governesses spent many, many hours instructing me on the necessity to maintain this eye contact. It is a habit somewhat ingrained in me, I believe, yet even now it is something I do only with difficulty." Reluctantly he admitted, "It seems I have a lot in common with your cousin and his friend."

"Indeed it does, sir." Elizabeth tried to keep her voice gentle and comforting, wondering if her efforts were of any avail to Mr. Darcy. "But let me also tell you once more, sir, young Sammy is extremely smart. He learned to read before he was three years of age, for no sooner had he begun speaking at that age, than he would alarm my uncle by reading the newspaper and reciting at breakfast the results of the horse races. He never developed an interest in the races themselves, but was fascinated with the numbers and times, and with the betting that took place around these events. My uncle, as you might imagine, was not so pleased when his child—still in leading strings—began suggesting which horses had the best odds in that day's races! He also has a ferocious proficiency with numbers, as well as a remarkable memory. And yet he still cannot understand a joke, or tell with ease when someone is happy, or angry, with his actions."

"You might be describing me in my own childhood, Miss Bennet. I admit to being fascinated by your young cousin. But what can you mean by imparting this information to me?"

"May I ask you some rather personal questions, Mr. Darcy?"

He nodded but the look on his face suggested some reluctance.

"When you enter a room full of people, what is your reaction?"

Without thinking the man replied most strongly, "I hate it! I cringe at the noise and at the chaos, and I dread the thought of being forced into close physical proximity with people I do not know. Having strangers touch me causes the utmost anxiety in me. I dread that almost as much as having to try to engage these people in meaningless conversation." He seemed comfortable with her own hand upon his arm, but she mentioned it not.

"And yet you persevere." This was a statement, not a question.

"I must. I was taught my obligations and the need to engage in societal affairs, as much as I might dread them. I find I manage somehow by withdrawing into myself, almost as if I build a wall around my consciousness to prevent the harshest of the sensations from assaulting me. I learned, partly by my own devices, partly from the relentless pressures on behalf of my parents, how to survive these events, how to give the appropriate responses to expected questions, how to bow and how to appear to be present. But all the while, my mind clamours for my body to leave the space, and I hide behind my protective wall."

Elizabeth chuckled. "For a taciturn man, Mr. Darcy, you have spoken most eloquently just now. That protective wall hides the soul of a poet."

"Words are not my enemy, Miss Bennet. Having to produce them without the opportunity to give each its due consideration is. I write much more gracefully and expressively than I speak. And yet, you still have not answered my question."

"Nor have I finished asking my own! But fear not: I will relieve your curiosity. Some months after Miss Pierce began her tenure in the Gardiner nursery, my aunt and uncle invited me to stay with them for a time. Because my parents had no governess for us at home, my aunt thought I might benefit from a year in London and from any matters Miss Pierce might teach me. I found in her a friend more than a teacher, although I learned so very much from her as well, matters both intellectual and social. What I did learn most especially from her, however, was how she dealt with Samuel. She had a special talent for reaching him where others were unable, and it seemed I had some of that ability as well, for Sammy responded so very well to me. With Miss

Pierce, we worked with him tirelessly, teaching him the skills that nature did not bestow upon him."

Mr. Darcy nodded in approval and she went on with her speech.

"We realised that whereas I had to struggle with French grammar, the nuances of the subjunctive were second nature to my cousin. However, he could not discern by his mother's scowl or crossed arms that she was upset that he had bitten the baby. But he is, as I mentioned, a prodigiously smart young boy, and we decided, Miss Pierce and I, that he could learn these skills, just as I learned French. It might take a great deal of time and effort, but we would succeed! And thus we devised a scheme for teaching him and we began our efforts."

They were walking now down a laneway that led through the park of the far side of the hillock, towards some of the crofters' cottages visible in the far distance, open fields on either side. The sun had begun to beat down quite strongly upon them, and Lizzy felt her head getting warm. She withdrew a handkerchief from a pocket to dab at the perspiration that was accumulating on her forehead. Mr. Darcy stared at her for a moment and then said, "I am sorry, Miss Elizabeth. I should have noticed the day was growing warm. Shall we return to the folly where it is cooler to continue our conversation? I admit I am most intrigued by all you have to say."

"Thank you, sir. That would be a wise idea. It also demonstrates, to some degree, how I might help you." Elizabeth caught herself too late. She had not thought to make her offer of assistance yet, before allowing the enigmatic Mr. Darcy to become more comfortable with her. It was, however, too late to take back the words, and she dreaded his reaction, for he had most certainly heard them.

At her statement, Mr. Darcy most suddenly stopped walking, and Elizabeth could see him return to the taciturn and unapproachable man she had first encountered.

"Help me?" he asked, incredulous, and dropped her arm as he stepped backwards.

She had spoken; she had no choice now but to continue. "Yes, sir. I believe I have the means and experience with my cousin to help you."

"You believe I am in need of help?" The voice grew stony.

"I believe I may assist you in being easier in society." It was growing more and more difficult for Elizabeth to keep her voice friendly and even.

Darcy's shoulders stiffened and his eyes grew cold. His interested and friendly demeanour from moments ago faded in an instant, to be replaced with the hauteur that had repelled all who had tried to befriend him.

"Thank you, Miss Elizabeth," he intoned coldly, "but I do not believe I require the 'help' of one such as yourself." His emphasis on the word "help" conveyed to her everything she needed to know of his opinion of the matter. He stepped back, bowed stiffly and managed a formal "madam," before striding away without a backwards glance.

Chapter Three

A Second Chance

Elizabeth stood where he had left her, amazed and mortified at his sudden change of mood and his abrupt and unqualified refusal to even consider what she might have to offer him. She had not expected his immediate and undying gratitude, or his complete unquestioning acceptance of her assistance, but to be so completely shut down and so insulted in the process had her on the verge of tears, and she stormed off down the path through the trees. "One such as I?" she asked the air around her incredulously as she marched. "One such as I?" Then, overwhelmed by a sudden rush of anger, she spat, "Oh, odious man! I was right the first time. Whatever else he might have to manage in his life, he is insufferable!" She snorted in a most unladylike manner as she turned to march back to the folly.

"Odious? Insufferable?" A voice came from behind a small copse of trees. "You can only be talking about my cousin." Two coat tails emerged from the trees, followed by the rest of Colonel Fitzwilliam, as he attempted to extricate his hound from whatever was buried in the pile of leaves and twigs the animal had found. "Come, Barghest," he commanded the dog, "Leave off! Come. Sit!" Having at last dragged the hound onto the path, he tied its lead to a tree and performed a gallant bow to Elizabeth, excusing his state of disarray and his uncommon entrance.

"We were taking some air when this hellhound smelled something in the wood and tore off, pulling me after him. I believe it is the remains of a squirrel or some other poor creature in that pile. We strive to be better gentlemen than you see before you, despite appearances. Is that not so, Barghest?" he demanded of his dog. The dog did not reply, but Elizabeth made the appropriate responses.

"I must apologise for my rudeness, but I could help but overhearing your angry words," the colonel continued. "What has my odious and insufferable cousin done now? He has a particular talent for vexing and annoying all who would befriend him with an ill-chosen word or an arrogant sneer. He is a good man, despite his hopeless manners. I shall not ask you to forgive whatever he said to you, but perhaps you might consider his unusual nature."

He offered his arm to Elizabeth, smiling his radiant smile at her. "Were you returning to the folly?" He glanced along the path to where the elaborate structure perched atop the hillock in the distance. "Please, allow us to escort you thither." He gestured to the hound, now lying calmly under the shade of a tree.

"Thank you, sirs," Elizabeth curtseyed to the dog and then to the colonel.

"Dare I ask, Miss Bennet," the colonel asked as they walked, "what my cousin did say to upset you so? Perhaps these are ruffled feathers I may be able to smooth."

"Alas, sir, I only offered him some history from my own family and a suggestion leading from that. More I dare not say, for I would not break Mr. Darcy's confidence, no matter that he did not demand I keep it. If you would know the nature of our disagreement—if such it was—I would importune you to ask him yourself, for this matter relates to him and not to me."

With all the social graces that his cousin lacked, Colonel Fitzwilliam quickly changed the subject to one more suitable for walking on a lovely spring day with a handsome young woman, and the morning's exercise concluded much more pleasantly than it had begun. But still, Elizabeth could not get Mr. Darcy and his similarity to her cousin from her mind, nor her conviction that, should he allow it, she might be of great assistance to him.

When she returned to the parsonage, Mr. Collins was out calling on some parishioners, but Charlotte was at home, writing letters in her sunny parlour. Spying her friend, she invited her to join her in the comfortable space. "Lizzy, where have you been? The sun is high already and you cannot have broken your fast. Let me call for some tea and bread."

This Charlotte did, and the two women sat in pleasant conversation. If Elizabeth had, for a time, resented her friend for making the choice to marry Mr. Collins, she saw now that Charlotte was not unhappy. Her friend had wed a man Elizabeth could not respect, and was committed to a lifetime suffering his inanities, but Charlotte had profited from the arrangement, and had a comfortable home and the prospects of a family and security, which she had not enjoyed before. Although it could never have been Lizzy's choice, it had not been a bad one for her friend. She sighed something to that effect and was surprised when Charlotte chose that direction in their conversation.

"I made my choice, Lizzy," she explained. "I knew what sort of a man he was, and saw that for all his faults, he was not a bad person. He has never been cruel or cross, and indeed, whilst he does not love me—nor I him—I feel appreciated and cherished, and there is a comfort in that which I cannot express in words. It is true that he often says things I wish he would not, but all his lack of sense and elegance cannot detract from his innate good nature and decency. Sometimes what we see on the outside disguises the truth that lies buried deeper down."

This gave Elizabeth great pause to think. Colonel Fitzwilliam had said something rather similar about Mr. Darcy just that morning, imploring her to see beyond the rough surface to the diamond that lay beneath. Could it be so? Was that rude and curt dismissal she had suffered at his denial merely one more reflection of his inability to sense what was appropriate in conversation? It had seemed so very deliberate and pointedly personal, but was that the true intention behind those cruel words? Or was this yet another example of his great discomfort at confronting new experiences and ideas?

The ladies finished their tea and turned to their separate tasks. Charlotte had some correspondence to complete, and Lizzy had promised to sew a doll's dress for one of the youngsters of the parish. Her thoughts returned again and again to the enigma that was Mr. Darcy when the door to the morning room flew open and Mr. Collins burst through, all in a fluster and waving a sheet of paper wildly through the air.

"Charlotte my dear! Cousin Elizabeth! An invitation! It arrived only now from Rosings. Lady Catherine has invited us all for tea only this moment! Hurry, for we shall be late!"

Charlotte leapt from her seat and began to put away her letters and papers.

"Is the invitation for today?" Elizabeth had to ask. "Surely Lady Catherine cannot expect you to be available for tea at her whim! Do you not have other tasks that need to be done? Parishioners who are awaiting your visit, or your duties in the schoolroom? And Charlotte has a house to manage, which cannot always be interrupted by her ladyship's demands!"

Charlotte stopped her sorting to turn to her friend. "But Lizzy, it is often like this. Lady Catherine cannot imagine that we have any duties more pressing than to attend her. She is our patroness, and our comfort depends upon her goodwill. My letters can wait. What will you wear? Oh, I must find Maria! Where can that girl have gone?"

Elizabeth looked down upon her dress, which she had worn that morning for her ill-fated walk. It was suitable for the fields and laneways of the area, but not for tea in a grand house. "I have not so many fine frocks with me, but I am certain I can find something suitable. Please excuse me." She gave a resigned sigh and returned to her bedroom to change.

The party from the Hunsford parsonage might be expected at once, but no carriage was put at their disposal and they were obliged to walk the short distance to the great house. Maria chattered on about whether there might be apple tarts or fruit bread, and Mr. Collins fussed over his coat, asking Charlotte again and again whether or not there were flecks of lint on the back, although uncaring of the detail that the coat was out of fashion by five years at least. For her part, Lizzy was concerned more for whom she might meet once seated in whichever grand room the Lady chose for her guests.

Would the colonel and Mr. Darcy be expected to entertain their aunt's guests at tea? Or would they be able to claim prior commitments that might excuse them from such a frivolous event? At the thought of Mr. Darcy and his curt words that very morning, Elizabeth's mood soured. How could she feign polite words and exchange pleasantries with a man who had so cruelly called her "one such as yourself?" Even a man with Mr. Darcy's social difficulties must know how insulting those words were. Would he have the gall to face her again after such abuse? She could well accept the notion of aiding a man with no ability to understand unspoken meanings, but a man with no conscience? That was impossible!

Suddenly the very notion of setting foot inside Rosings was horrifying and she wondered if she ought to beg off now, before the party arrived. Charlotte could claim some minor ailment on the part of her friend, surely! But Mr. Collins would disapprove, and whilst she cared little for his opinion, he would not hold it close to his chest, but would announce it widely, and Lizzy could not conscience bringing Lady Catherine's wrath down upon Charlotte in any manner. Further, if Mr. Darcy were present, the colonel would almost certainly be as well, and his company was pleasant enough that she might, for his sake, abide his cousin's. Thus, with a deep breath, she steeled herself for the encounter and forced her feet to move one before the other until they arrived at their destination.

The reception at Rosings was everything Elizabeth expected. They were shown to yet another ostentatious parlour by the housekeeper and asked to wait until Her Ladyship was ready. How like her! Elizabeth stewed. To invite people—nay, to demand their presence—and then to have found other occupations more important than greeting one's guests was the height of rudeness. That trait must run in the family, and not for the first time did Elizabeth wonder about the origins of some of Mr. Darcy's sentiments towards those he deemed lower than himself.

They had been sitting for about ten minutes when the door swung open and Colonel Fitzwilliam burst through. "Mr. Collins, Mrs. Collins," how bowed deeply, "Miss Bennet, and Miss Lucas! Please forgive our tardiness! I only heard this moment that my aunt had asked you to attend her for tea, else I would have been present when you arrived. My aunt sometimes forgets that other people exist outside of her experience of them."

What an interesting notion! Elizabeth had never before considered that one might even think that way, to assume that other people only existed when in one's presence. It was rather, she mused, similar to how the main character in a play only experienced the secondary characters when they were on stage with him. Was this something Mr. Darcy felt as well? Again, she wondered if whatever it was that troubled her cousin and Mr. Darcy might run in families, along the same lines as large noses or red hair.

The colonel was still apologising for his late entrance and begging the party from Rosings to be comfortable until the tea, which he had just now requested, arrived. "Ah, and here is my cousin!" Elizabeth felt her shoulders stiffen in preparation for seeing Mr. Darcy again, but to her relief it was Anne de Bourgh who entered the parlour. As usual, her face was pinched and her expression was one of distaste, but her words and her tone were all that was polite and welcoming as she echoed the colonel's apologies and asked whether tea was being prepared.

"Mother finds herself very suddenly and unexpectedly occupied, but she will join us shortly." She then set about engaging the group from the parsonage in conversation with a skill that Elizabeth had not expected. From her past visits at Rosings, she had imagined Anne de Bourgh always to be cross and sour, with little conversation, but now the young woman was everything charming, and when she smiled, her entire aspect changed. How extraordinary! Perhaps that habitual cross expression was not a reflection of her mood but merely of her physiognomy! And perhaps, having expected a sour personality to match a sour face, Elizabeth had imposed her own notions upon the woman.

With Miss de Bourgh and Colonel Fitzwilliam holding court, the entire gathering was rather pleasant and Elizabeth found herself enjoying the occasion rather more than she had anticipated, until the door opened once more and Lady Catherine sailed in with Mr. Darcy in her wake. Immediately the atmosphere in the room changed. In the moment it took for Lady Catherine to walk across the room and seat herself in the throne-like chair by the fireplace, Anne returned to the timid and sour creature Elizabeth had first encountered, and Colonel Fitzwilliam's easy smiles and effortless gallantry became stiff formality and cautious glances. The alteration was sudden, striking and most unpleasant.

Intrigued by the glimpse into Anne's character when not terrorised by her mother, Elizabeth attempted to continue the conversation the two had been having. Anne answered neatly enough, but it was evident that she was measuring every syllable by what she deemed Lady Catherine would approve. So fascinated was Elizabeth by this phenomenon that she nearly missed overhearing the colonel as he spoke to Mr. Darcy.

"You ought to apologise," the officer whispered. "I know not exactly what you said to her, but I am certain it was not polite." There was no response from Mr. Darcy, and as Anne had ceased speaking completely, Elizabeth had little difficulty in hearing the rest of the colonel's words. "At least walk over and offer her a polite greeting. You can be a boor and have a particular talent for insulting people. Take some initiative to be friendly."

Elizabeth was struck by the similarity of this conversation with the one she had overheard at that first assembly in Meryton so long ago. This time she did not see Mr. Darcy's eyes meet hers and then withdraw, but she felt his gaze at the back of her neck as he answered, "I cannot imagine what I have to say to her, and even less what she has to tell me. I am not one to make idle chatter with ladies in my aunt's parlour. Leave me, Richard, and return to your flirtations."

As these words dropped from those cruel lips, Elizabeth felt her shoulders stiffen and her entire mien shift, just as that of Anne de Bourgh had transformed with the arrival of Lady Catherine. Colonel Fitzwilliam must have observed this, for he now hissed at his cousin, "Darcy, we must speak. In the steward's office. Now!" The shuffle of boots across the marble floor told Elizabeth that the two men had left the room, and she resisted the urge to feel the back of her neck to ascertain whether her skin was burning from the intensity of Mr. Darcy's stare.

Horrid man! He was rude, cruel, uncaring, unthinking... he could not even be bothered to say so much as 'good afternoon' to her! Well, it was of little matter to her, for she resolved never to have another word with the arrogant man, just as she was certain he wished never to be in her presence again. That was settled, then. They should suit perfectly! She fretted and stewed as the tea was served, thankful now for Anne's lack of conversation and for Lady Catherine's claim on Charlotte's time.

As quickly as the Collinses and their guests had been summoned to Rosings, so they were dismissed. Between one sip of tea and a nibble of cake, Lady Catherine announced that the party was over and that it was time to depart. To her credit, Anne looked distressed at her mother's discourtesy, but said nothing, being reduced once more to a shell in the fierce lady's presence. Elizabeth's only regret as she took her leave was that she had not been able to converse with the colonel, nor to say good-bye to him. For the rest, she was more than delighted to be out of the house.

What a strange family this was! For all her grand gestures and her elaborate displays of noblesse oblige, Lady Catherine was nothing but a petty tyrant, ruling through fear rather than through respect. The mistress of Rosings might be obeyed, but she was also undoubtedly despised behind many a closed door. How preferable was Elizabeth's own father, with his middling estate and the goodwill of his tenants, than were Lady Catherine's great riches and the cowering or scorn of these beholden to her.

Of these, the most poorly done by was Anne, the lady's own daughter, to whom all the wealth and prosperity of Rosings truly belonged.

Although not blessed with fine looks or a hale constitution, those few minutes of candid conversation had proven Miss de Bourgh to have a fine mind and a pleasing manner, which were crushed under her mother's imperiousness. How the heir to Rosings might have blossomed if only she had been treated with a little kindness!

That word nearly stopped Elizabeth as she walked. Kindness: she had seen the outcome of its lack in Anne de Bourgh; she had seen its liberal application work wonders with Sammy. She had the choice of these, and she chose the latter. It seemed unlikely that Mr. Darcy would deign to be in her presence again—he could not lower himself to deal with one such as she after all—but should the occasion arise, she would strive to be kind. Perhaps one day that cold and cruel man might learn something of the idea and might try some kindness himself. To the unlikelihood of that occurrence, she could only give a bitter laugh.

Chapter Four

A Proposition

Nothing of any sort was heard from Rosings for two days. Mr. Collins fussed about his front garden hoping that Miss de Bourgh and her companion might drive by, and made frequent dashes into the house to inform his wife that nobody was seen driving down the lane. His despondency was almost amusing, but Lizzy knew how devastating a break with Rosings might be to his home and his future. To her, this silence was of little surprise. Anne was too much under her mother's thumb to issue her own invitations or to accept an invitation into the house, and must surely have been forbidden even to venture out with the phaeton. As for the gentlemen, Mr. Darcy surely had no wish to see the Collinses and their company again, and the colonel could have little recourse to visit on his own, were he not to be busy with his aunt's affairs.

It was, therefore, something of a surprise when, two days later, the doorbell rang and the parlour maid announced two gentlemen to see the ladies. Charlotte bade them enter, and Colonel Fitzwilliam strode into the room with a bright step and bowed in his elegant manner. He had every address of a gentleman, and both women smiled to see him.

"Mrs. Collins, how lovely you look this afternoon. That colour most becomes you. And Miss Bennet, have you been out enjoying Kent's glorious sunshine? Your eyes fairly glow! Yes I see you have already been out this fine day. Have you had your tea? My cousin and I would most enjoy your company on a short stroll if you are not too fatigued from your earlier walk. The sun is not so hot now and the breeze is most pleasant." With his lovely smile and inviting expression, it was hard to deny him such a simple and pleasant request.

The ladies put away their papers and embroidery and quickly found their walking boots and bonnets, and so soon were ready to leave the house. The men were waiting in the garden, passing the time in quiet conversation, and did not immediately notice the ladies as they emerged from the parsonage. To Elizabeth's surprise, Mr. Darcy was kneeling on the ground, careless of the stain it would bring to the knee of his buckskins, scratching the head of the same dog she had seen with the colonel two days earlier. She had not, she realised, imagined that the stiff and unbending Mr. Darcy might even be able to kneel! She laughed away the notion and decided to re-apply herself to finding forgiveness for the unwittingly rude man. The recent memory of his derisive "one such as you" still was fresh, however, and it required some effort to smile and approach him. Be kind, she reminded herself. You need not be a friend; only be kind.

Elizabeth greeted him, "Mr. Darcy. And Barghest, if I recall. I did not know, sir, that you were fond of dogs."

He rose to his feet quickly. "Miss Bennet. I did not hear you leave the house." He bowed as he had undoubtedly been taught to do. "I am much of an admirer of dogs, madam, and have several my own at my estate. My personal favourite resides right now at my house in London. Lady Catherine will not have him at Rosings..."

"Whereas I," the colonel interrupted, "care little for what my aunt says and bring Barghest, regardless. Although he does have to sleep in the stables with the horses," he added ruefully. "Hence my desire to walk with him whenever the weather permits."

Elizabeth watched Darcy bestow one last scratch on the great hound's head and noticed that he seemed more at ease than was his wont. She must ask him about this, she mused, but decided she would not renew the unpleasant topic of their previous discussion.

The colonel suggested a short walk down the lane towards the village, a mile or so distant. This was declared a most suitable objective, and the four set off. Colonel Fitzwilliam skillfully arranged to have some pertinent questions for Mrs. Collins about some matters relating to the parsonage and the parishioners she had met, leaving Elizabeth to walk beside Darcy. The dog ran ahead, turning every so often to ensure the safety of its people.

Elizabeth searched for some easy conversation, but Mr. Darcy pre-empted her. "Please allow me to apologise, Miss Bennet, for my words the other morning, and my rudeness at tea. My cousin demanded of me to account for what had upset you so, and when I confessed to the whole, he hauled me over the coals for my shameful behaviour." He paused and with a smirk, added, "That was an expression he used, and I had to think long about its meaning. I eventually discovered it relates to a mediaeval practice of torturing heretics, and thereby applies to my own situation in being a severe chastisement for unacceptable behaviour." Elizabeth stifled a chuckle, but said nothing as Darcy continued. "On reflection, I see that he was correct, and that I once again spoke without considering the consequence of my words."

"Indeed, sir, words have the power to hurt."

"How so, Miss Bennet? They may insult, but unless one is assaulted with a book being used as a weapon, words cannot cause physical pain."

"The hurt, Mr. Darcy, is not physical."

He thought about this for a while, then nodded. "Yes. I understand. The insult that is heard is perceived as some sort of psychic pain, not physical, but an injury to one's self-esteem nonetheless."

"You begin to understand, sir."

He nodded again. "Yes. Perhaps I do. I merely require time to analyse what I am hearing."

They walked in silence for a moment. Then Mr. Darcy asked, "Am I correct in feeling that you are not entirely pleased to be in my company?

What words did I say that most offended you? I would wish to withdraw them, or to explain my thoughts." It was difficult to maintain anger in the light of such a guileless admission.

"What, if I may ask," Elizabeth said pointedly, "did you mean when you refused an offer of help from 'one such as I?'" She had considered letting that day's conversation remain a matter of the past, but now felt that until she had deciphered what Darcy had intended by the cruel comment, she would never be able to look past his unfortunate comments and formidable expression.

He stared straight ahead, but his voice held a question. "If I offended you, it was unintentional. I meant only that your experience, however valuable, was with a young child. I am not a young child, but rather a grown man of nearly eight and twenty. These situations are surely too different for your experience to apply."

"The games we played with my cousin would surely be inappropriate for a gentleman of your standing and education, but the general ideas behind them might not be. The key to finding a suitable alternative is to adapt to the situation. Miss Pierce and I spent many hours studying treatises and latest news from preeminent physicians, and we were able to adapt their ideas to Samuel. And if I recall, Mr. Rush advocated—"

"Rush? Benjamin Rush, the American statesman and physician?"

This was surprising! "Yes, indeed, the very same. He has many interesting notions, not all of which sit comfortably with me. Still, his ideas around caring for those habitually taken with drink were most useful in the planning of our lessons with Sammy, as were his thoughts on caring for the insane. Of course, my young cousin is neither a drunk nor insane, but the principles which Mr. Rush espoused were nonetheless transferable to Sammy's situation, and that of the other lad I mentioned."

"I admit that I underestimated you, Miss Elizabeth. I had not thought your expertise so scholarly. I was wrong. Forgive me." His voice held as much contrition as his words, and Elizabeth accepted them.

They walked a few moments longer, and it seemed that Mr. Darcy had something still to say, but although his mouth began to open several times, he remained silent. After a while he stared into the far distance and added, "And I am uncomfortable with the suggestion that I require help. I have managed well enough for seven and twenty years without it."

Elizabeth could see his free hand clenching and releasing obsessively, thumb and fingers worrying against each other. She did not comment on her observation, but added evenly, "I had not intended to impugn your abilities, sir. You have, it is true, little need for my poor advice or experience. However, although you might not need it, you may wish it, not to compensate for any accomplishments that you may lack, but rather, to let you enjoy company more. Or, perhaps," she added wryly, "dread it less."

Darcy's easy gait began to stiffen once more, and Elizabeth once more sensed his imminent retreat behind his protective walls. Deciding to be bold, she called his attention to this.

"Are you feeling somehow threatened, Mr. Darcy? I see you adopting once more the face you wear in public assemblies. What has made you uncomfortable?"

They stopped walking for a moment, and Darcy took a deep breath from the warm spring air. "You are correct again, madam. I do have my pride. You mentioned the same at Netherfield, and you spoke truth. It is a difficult matter to accept one's failings. As well, I have become so set in my ways, the thought of entertaining some new venture is most discomforting. It provokes anxiety in my breast, and as you have observed, I do not deal well with anxiety. I withdraw, and often say something rude to discourage further discourse on the subject." He breathed deeply once again. "I feel you would not be putting your time to good use."

"We should walk again, sir," Elizabeth glanced at the path behind them. "Your cousin and my friend are approaching." Darcy offered his elbow, which she took. They walked a few steps further before she reminded him of an incident that morning when last they met.

"You noticed that as we walked, I was becoming heated by the sun, and that I needed to mop my forehead. You are a very observant man, and when you stopped to observe me, you found the clues that suggested that I was growing uncomfortable in the heat. Then you proposed the solution of returning to the folly."

"I could not permit you to become ill from the strength of the sun."

She bestowed a smile upon him. "You have demonstrated to me that you have all the abilities you require to become easier in society, and to learn some of the skills you claim you do not possess. You are very observant, as we have noted. I believe I can help you learn to interpret the small details you observe and use that information to ease your interactions with others. If you learn, for example, to ascertain whether your companion is excited or worried, for example, this can guide you in making the next appropriate observation in forwarding the conversation."

The tall man nodded his head most gravely. He thought for a moment before replying, "Yes, yes, I see what you mean. But... I am uncertain, Miss Bennet. Can it be done?" There was, fleetingly, a look of desperation on the proud man's face that brought Elizabeth almost to tears. For how many years had this man suffered an affliction that none could see or understand, one that made life so difficult for him? For how many years had he forced himself behind his protective battlements, leaving behind for the world to see only a veneer of pride and aloofness? And how dearly did he wish to be able to enjoy the life he saw others engage in, to laugh and joke and converse easily in company?

Carefully, slowly, aware of the consequences of what she was doing, she stopped and turned to Mr. Darcy. Charlotte and the colonel were a fair distance back and around a corner in the laneway, leaving Elizabeth and Darcy unobserved for a moment. Looking him in the eye, capturing his gaze with her own, she removed her hand from where it rested so lightly on his elbow and placed it more firmly on his forearm, close to his hand. Using her eyes and the physical connexion to force a new rapport with him, she replied in a calm and direct voice, "I make no promises, sir, but if you are prepared to make the effort, then so am I."

They walked on in silence, but it was not the silence of discomfort. Rather, Elizabeth sensed that Mr. Darcy had come to accept her as a presence in his life, for the time being at any rate. He had not flinched at the gentle but insistent pressure of her hand upon his arm and had accepted her direct gaze without turning aside his eyes. He was a most clever man, that she was certain, and unlike her young cousin, who had not understood why he was being subjected to these strange lessons by his nurse and his beloved cousin, Mr. Darcy was a willing participant in her schemes. He might never be completely at ease in company, but he could surely become more confident. His obvious comfort in her presence could only help them achieve their goals.

As they neared the village where they proposed to await their companions, Elizabeth also realised that her hand still rested on her companion's arm, and that—somewhat alarmingly, for she had hardly noticed when it occurred—he had tucked it slightly around and brought his arm closer to his body, so her hand was nestled between his arm and his side. It was not an unpleasant sensation, and not wishing to call attention to something which might cause distress, she made no mention of it.

How different this man was now from the one who had turned from her so abruptly only days ago, and even more so, from the one who been so cold and uncivil in Meryton not so many months before. His demeanour seemed to change at the tread of a foot, but it was not true incivility that underlay his icy facade, but rather, real discomfort and anxiety. His reactions to unknown and unexpected circumstances were unusual, perhaps, but not unique, and they could almost certainly be tempered into something more acceptable to society. With every word he uttered and every new glimpse into the true essence of the man, Elizabeth discovered new aspects to him. Perhaps his cousin was right, and he was, indeed, a very good man, lost in a world he did not quite understand.

Now she believed once again that he was certainly not the haughty and arrogant man she had initially supposed him to be! How every notion of him had been upended, how every prejudice had been quashed! She hoped her current assessment was the correct one.

Within moments, Charlotte and the colonel had caught up with them, and almost immediately upon turning back for the parsonage, Mr. Collins had espied them and called Charlotte over to visit with poor Mrs. Blake who was sickly. They waved Charlotte off and the three continued back to the parsonage. Darcy and his cousin now fell into a discussion about some horses their aunt wished to purchase, leaving Elizabeth to think over all she had been learning.

She thought back to one of their earliest encounters. What had Mr. Darcy said that evening all those months before in the drawing room, when Jane was ill at Netherfield? She had accused him of believing himself without defect, of having every aspect of his life under regulation. But he had countered this, saying, "I have faults enough, but they are not, I hope, of understanding. My temper I dare not vouch for.—It is I believe too little yielding—certainly too little for the convenience of the world. I cannot forget the follies and vices of others so soon as I ought, nor their offences against myself. My feelings are not puffed about with every attempt to move them."

Recalling each word he had uttered, Elizabeth now realised that he had as much as confessed to her his inability to yield to the whims of others, of his lack of skill at adapting to changing circumstances and capricious moods and tempers. Not being able to determine the motivations behind the actions of others without great thought and attention, each quirk of behaviour, each unannounced change in plan must assault him with the ferocity and incomprehensibility of a storm at sea. She had, once on a holiday, observed the punishing, crushing waves brought on by a summer storm at the seaside, and had heard tales from navy men of the awesome and gut-wrenching power of such a storm on the open ocean. Sammy had described to her his sensations, when a planned outing was suddenly changed to something quite different, in similar language to the old navy officers she had listened to. He described both torment of the mind as well as a real physical pain in his midsection.

And how would a sensitive man like Mr. Darcy react to those who knew him but took no care to accommodate his difficulties? He had confessed that as well. "My temper," he had explained, "would perhaps be called resentful.—My good opinion once lost is lost forever."

But instead of understanding the truth behind these words, these painful confessions from a man whose pride made admitting his failings most difficult, she had scoffed at him. Instead of compassion, she had cried, "That is a failing indeed! Implacable resentment is a shade in a character. But you have chosen your fault well.—I really cannot laugh at it; you are safe from me."

Had his voice been sad when he responded? "There is, I believe, in every disposition a tendency to some particular evil, a natural defect, which not even the best education can overcome." She sought desperately to recall his gestures and as well as his speeches, but she had been too lost in her own sense of importance. She had quite missed his explanation that even the education, which had given him the skills to read and write and manage his estate, as well as to bow and eat politely and dance well, had failed to help him learn the skills he needed to move smoothly in the whirlwind of a social universe he imperfectly comprehended.

Instead, rather than offering the friendship she now believed he craved, she had insulted him, replying, "And your defect is a propensity to hate every body."

"And yours," he had replied with a sad smile, "is wilfully to misunderstand them."

Oh, how this last remark had seared itself onto her memory, and how its remembrance now was bitter, bringing shame. For he was correct. She had not taken the time to understand what he was saying. Caught up in her notion that he found nothing but fault, she had failed to see the man for who and what he was.

They were now about halfway back to the house, and the gentlemen were discussing livestock, comparing what their aunt possessed to Mr. Darcy's herds and flocks at his own estate in Derbyshire. The mention of this estate brought to mind, quite suddenly, another conversation she once had relating to Mr. Darcy.

This conversation was not with Mr. Darcy himself, but another who had known him all his life. Mr. Wickham, a dashing young man recently associated with the militia stationed in Meryton, had claimed to have grown up with Mr. Darcy at the estate in Derbyshire. They had played together as children and had enjoyed a great friendship. But at some point a breach had occurred, leaving the two men at odds with each other. Mr. Wickham, now a lieutenant, had alleged that Mr. Darcy had grown too proud to maintain a friendship with the mere son of a steward, and had denied him the living he had been promised by Mr. Darcy's father.

But perhaps something else had occurred. Mr. Darcy, if he were anything like Lizzy's cousin Samuel, would be most conscientious about following rules and adhering to expected strictures. Denying a man his legacy lawfully granted would be as easy for a man like Mr. Darcy as would cutting off his own hand: possible under the most extreme of duress, but most unlikely under normal circumstances.

Assuming Lieutenant Wickham had been telling no falsehoods, what on earth might have moved Mr. Darcy to act thus? Was it merely implacable resentment, an irrevocably lost good opinion? Even for such a stiff and disagreeable man as Mr. Darcy this seemed doubtful. Had, perhaps, Mr. Wickham made the same mistake she, Elizabeth, had made, in judging the man without full awareness of his difficulties with social discourse? Improbable, since the two had grown up together, but perhaps Mr. Wickham's recollections bore the rosy glow of idealised childhood, and were unable to adapt to the realities of the grown man.

Or perhaps it was Mr. Darcy who had misjudged his friend's intentions. Surely Mr. Darcy had misunderstood his old childhood friend's request, due to ambiguities in wording or the loss of subtle language and gesture to his awareness, and had responded to the request he thought had been made, rather than the one that actually was. A misunderstanding could well have escalated from that point.

Yes, thought Elizabeth, this must be the case. Mr. Wickham had such an openness to him, such an air of congeniality and truth, that he must merely have misunderstood, and been misunderstood in turn. If I am able to gain Mr. Darcy's trust, Elizabeth thought, I shall attempt to speak of this to him. Perhaps I may be successful in smoothing this long-standing grievance to everyone's benefit. Perhaps Mr. Wickham did misjudge his friend as badly as I did myself!

Now, glancing at his face, half in the shadow of his tall hat as he talked with his cousin, she felt herself blush in remorse. And yet, she realised, she was most fortunate too, for she had the opportunity now to atone for her wrongs, and perhaps even repair a friendship gone bad. She had come to understand what she had missed before, and she promised herself that she would do what she could to pay recompense for her earlier lapses in understanding. She turned her head away to hide her pink cheeks, and in doing do, caught the gentleman's attention.

He cleared his throat and observed that they had nearly achieved their destination. Relieved at the direction of the conversation, Lizzy turned back to him and smiled. She could not invite the gentlemen inside, for the lady of the house was in the village with her husband, and so the three sat for several minutes on a bench in the garden.

"I find myself wondering, what has become of your young cousin? Have your efforts met with much success?" Darcy asked her. "I spoke of him to Richard," he indicated towards the colonel, "and he too was most interested in the lad and his progress. I am finding I wish an introduction to this young man, should circumstance ever allow it, but I also wish to know what to expect."

Lizzy smiled in satisfaction. "You will be pleased to know that Samuel has made great progress, sir. He attends a fine school in London, for my aunt and uncle have the means to support his tuition there, and he is, by all accounts, an excellent student. He is quite gifted in areas of mathematics and languages, and his tutors are all quite pleased with him. He retains some unconventional behaviours, I will grant you, and will most likely always be something of an eccentric, but he is happy and capable, and he has made some good friends. He will grow to be a successful man, able to make his way in the world."

"Your story encourages me," Mr. Darcy conceded. "But please, tell me, Miss Elizabeth, how this might relate to myself? I have managed well in life. I do not require the same guidance that so helped your cousin, for I have achieved what he strives for."

"Your capabilities, sir, have never been in doubt; it would seem that whatever so challenged my young cousin has touched you but lightly. Yet I might still help you to be easier in society, and to enjoy it more."

"Even should I agree," Darcy frowned, "I am late to these lessons, and am not some youngster to learn so quickly."

"Look at my face, Mr. Darcy," Elizabeth ordered. "Examine my expression. Tell me what you see."

As his cousin looked on in fascination, Darcy peered intently at her, his eyes perhaps lingering longer than a mere examination of facial nuance might necessitate. His remarkable green eyes traced her jaw, her mouth, then her nose, eyes, brows and forehead, before repeating their path in reverse. Eventually he spoke. "Your head is held in such a way that your face inclines upwards a small degree. Your chin, therefore, seems to protrude ever so slightly, although this might be a consequence of your head's position. Your mouth is fairly straight, although I see the corners tending upwards marginally. It is not a smile, quite, but I cannot say exactly what it is. Your nose, as I said before, is perfect. Your eyelids are somewhat closed, which again may be a result of your head's inclination upwards, and I see your eyebrows raised slightly on your forehead, which is smooth and not furrowed." He paused. "Shall I describe your ears now?"

"No, no, that will not be necessary. What do you find this collection of facial nuances to mean, do you know?"

He stood thinking for a moment. "I do not see any signs of tension in your face, so I will deduce that you are not angry, for anger creates tension. Nor do I see a smile, which denotes mirth. The whole effect is pleasant, but more than that I cannot say." Whilst unable to read her expression, his own spoke volumes, with its tales of curiosity, confusion and delight at this new game.

Elizabeth now allowed herself to smile fully. "I believe it is an expression of confident satisfaction, Mr. Darcy. Yes, I am certain that there is hope for you! I must confess, sir, that my challenge here is much less than with Samuel. By every measure of a man, you have attained success. You have gone to school, attended university and achieved a degree, you manage a large estate most competently, and you have friends, if your cousin the colonel and Mr. Bingley are anything by which to judge. And one need only glance at Miss Bingley to see that, should you wish it, you might easily find a bride should you wish to marry." At this, Mr. Darcy's expression clouded over briefly, but returned to its former state too quickly for Elizabeth to interpret his thoughts.

She hoped her smile was reassuring and then wondered if he would recognise it as such. His cousin would, to be certain. "You have managed to achieve by your own efforts what Samuel can hope for only with the diligence of his governess and myself. I may flatter myself and overstate the importance of our efforts with him, but I most sincerely believe that without Miss Pierce's excellent programme and our combined toil, Samuel would not be nearly as capable as he is. I fear he might even have ended up in an institution for the mentally unsound as his father and mother so dreaded. That is a fate that never threatened you."

"No, that would not be allowed the grandson of an earl; even the most feeble-minded have the care of a devoted servant and nurse. But I gather your meaning; this was never my lot, even should I have been the son of a labourer. My friends, whilst few in number, were great in devotion, and they eased my way with my peers. If you have the means to help me ease my own way, I should be willing to make the attempt." He pursed his lips and gave a decisive nod. "You have convinced me. I am most encouraged by your report of your cousin and am anxious to begin. How shall we start?"

With a smirk, Lizzy replied, "Perhaps we already have! But come, let us make a plan. Do you intend to tell your relatives of our endeavour?"

A horrified look came over Darcy's fine features. "Lady Catherine would likely forbid it. She does not take well to any suggestion that her family is not perfect. Even her own daughter's frailties and illness she sees as evidence of nobility and delicacy rather than a physical weakness. What think you, Richard?

"I concur: Lady Catherine should know nothing of this. But in all, I believe it is a fine course of action, Darcy. It will be a diversion if nothing else, and if it helps at all, it will be time well spent. Would you permit me to join your lessons, as an observer, Miss Bennet? Perhaps Anne would care to join as well, for she needs some reason to escape her mother's house."

Lizzy returned this request with a wide grin. "Indeed, colonel. You and Miss de Bourgh would be most welcome. But then we must not meet at Rosings." She frowned. "Your aunt would certainly discover us." She turned to Darcy. "The folly on the hillock where we encountered each other several days ago seems a pleasant spot to meet and sit. The colonel knows exactly what place I mean. It affords us some privacy and will shelter us from both sun and rain. Will this suffice, Mr. Darcy?"

"I was about to suggest it, Miss Elizabeth. I walk or ride every morning and come there to rest outside of the notice of my aunt. I can be found there every morning at the exact time you happened upon me. I am," he confessed, "somewhat of a creature of habit."

Very seriously, Elizabeth returned, "I should be quite amazed, sir, were you not."

Chapter Five

The Lessons

A nd thus the lessons began. Each morning, at the same hour, Elizabeth would meet with Mr. Darcy at the folly. If the weather was pleasant, both would walk or ride; if threatening rain, Mr. Darcy would drive by in Anne's phaeton, which had a canopy to protect the occupants from the sun or rain. Should the phaeton be needed, Colonel Fitzwilliam was always in attendance as well; on other occasions, he would join the lessons or not at his will, for it seemed he had other concerns that often kept him occupied of a morning. After the first few days, Elizabeth was charmed to see that Mr. Darcy had arranged for one of his aunt's servants to bring a basket to the folly, whereof they could partake of biscuits and a cool drink when they grew hungry.

"You are not a hopeless case at all, Mr. Darcy," Lizzy had teased the first time she noticed the basket. "This is a gesture of the height of social grace and ability. It shows that you are most able to think about the needs and comfort of others and that you are able to act the gallant gentleman you are born to be. I think you shall do quite well!" And her student had beamed at her praise.

As he bestowed upon her this radiant smile, Elizabeth realised that she had never before seen him with an expression of such undisguised joy before, and she was struck by the change to his face. Only now did she realise what a handsome man he was. His features, she admitted, had always been fine and more than pleasing to the eye, but it was when he smiled that the solemnity that often overshadowed his face lifted away, revealing a most agreeable visage. She would, she vowed, make him smile more often.

Lizzy began by introducing the topic most dreaded by her student: small talk. He understood the mechanics as a house painter understands the theory involved in mixing pigments. But Elizabeth wished to help him learn the art, so that he might become, if not a Gainsborough of chatter in the salon, at least a creditable imitator.

"You might wish to have one or two topics upon which you can converse lightly," she suggested. "Something of interest to you, but that also will appeal to your companions. Pray, sir, what are your personal interests, that amuse and occupy your mind when none other is there to disturb you?"

"My interests?" he furrowed his brow. "Why should anybody concern himself with that?"

"We seek not only to pass the time with small talk, but to form some small connexion between the participants in the conversation. By exploring whether you might share some common interests, you can create the illusion of getting to know each other without the risk of exposing your true self. You, sir, are a master at protecting your innermost essence, but without the effort of reaching out to others even with the most superficial of topics, you leave the room with only the impression of your pride and disdain. In short, upon first encounter you seem most disagreeable."

At this, Darcy started and huffed, "I? Disagreeable? I cannot believe that! I say nothing to offend people! Well, most of the time." He must have reflected upon his rude words only days before, for he turned a rather alarming shade of red. Then collecting himself, added, "I learned that much, at least, from my governesses and tutors."

"Sir, you say nothing, and THAT is what offends people!" Lizzy retorted. "You leave people with the impression that you have no interest in engaging them in conversation, that nobody is good enough for you. And I recall a conversation you had with your good friend Mr. Bingley, in which you insulted me most cruelly. 'Not tolerable enough to tempt me,' were your exact words, I believe!"

To his credit, Darcy bowed his head in remorse. "You were not intended to hear that. It was all I could think of to say to convince him to leave me in peace. You know how poorly I acquit myself with strangers. Dancing requires conversation, and whilst my feet can execute the steps of the dance, my tongue cannot execute the words I need to make myself an agreeable partner."

Trying very hard to school her thoughts and her tone of voice, Lizzy agreed rigidly, "That, sir, I can attest to."

Mr. Darcy may not have been at all adept in deciphering facial expressions, but when he was not hiding behind his protective walls, he was most eloquent in displaying them, and the look of contrition that washed over him was almost enough to bring about Lizzy's complete forgiveness. "I am most sorry you heard that," Darcy muttered. "It was not true."

With a breath to clear her thoughts, Elizabeth returned, "One never knows who hears one's words. That is why we must always be careful what we say. And, to our topic, it is the reason small talk is of such importance, trivial though it be by nature. It is how we display ourselves to best advantage with strangers, how we replace our impenetrable protective walls with something a bit... friendlier, which will allow those whom we might allow real friendship a safe entrance to our inner essence."

Darcy pondered these words for a few moments. He had risen, and was pacing the small space of the folly, from one Grecian pillar to the next, as he contemplated this little speech with the determination he might give to one of Sophocles' orations. "If I understand you, what you are saying is that we suffer through small talk so that we might have a means of selecting those whom we wish to admit as friends and intimates."

Suppressing a giggle, Elizabeth said, "Well, yes, in a way. You phrase it in a rather mercenary manner, but that is certainly a part of it. We also engage in small talk because it is more polite than staring blankly at people." Darcy stared blankly at her. Rolling her eyes and taking yet another deep breath, she continued, "And so, let us return to my original question: What are your personal interests? We need a base upon which we can build."

"Bridges."

Now it was Lizzy's turn to look incredulous. "Excuse me?"

"Bridges. I am most fascinated by bridges. I have several bridges on my estate, and I have always been fascinated by them. One tends to take them for granted, but so much knowledge and experience needs be pressed into use in order to construct a bridge that will be safe to carry a burden. There is so much to know and understand: How they are constructed, how long the span should be in comparison to the weight each might bear, how the width affects the equations, and how many supporting structures might be needed. Also, the span over which the bridge is built must be taken into account, whether it be over a dry gorge, or over roughly running water, which might cause the land around the supporting structures to erode. Also, I am fascinated in how the varying properties of different building materials can so alter how long or how wide a bridge might be. Did you know that London was built at the first place along the estuary of the Thames at which the Romans were able to span the river with a bridge? I am also most fascinated in the construction of the Iron Bridge in Shropshire, and I have studied it in great detail with the goal of recreating it across a gorge on my estate. Iron has many remarkable tensile properties, Miss Elizabeth, one of which is..."

Ah, so when the taciturn man was presented with a subject on which he knew much and which he found interesting, he grew most voluble! Like Samuel, Mr. Darcy clearly had some narrow areas of interest which grasped his imagination and which pulled him deep. Samuel had known more about the races and the horses that ran them from reading his father's newspaper, than most men betting their fortunes on them did, and he could recite from memory the most remarkable details and statistics, from where each horse was raised to what mixture of oats and hay it was fed after a race. Mr. Darcy's passion was, perhaps, more useful, but likely of little more interest to a casual acquaintance over tea than Samuel's recitation of the types of horse feed. Elizabeth fought to suppress another giggle.

"Oh, Mr. Darcy!" the lady threw up her hands in supplication. "I am certain this is all most fascinating indeed, but it is truly not a topic for the salon. No, no, this will not do for small talk at all. I'm afraid, sir, we must find you some other interests!"

At length, it was decided that travel and a general interest in new technologies would be suitable topics for the dreaded small talk. Having travelled extensively as a youth, including a trip with his family to the West Indies, Darcy would have a wealth of stories and tidbits that would provide interesting, but not challenging, additions to a light chat. Likewise, and particularly with other gentlemen, technology as a general topic was deemed suitable and most appropriate.

Mr. Darcy, it turned out, was also fascinated with the science of optics and lenses, and had amassed a fair collection of these curiosities, both ancient and modern, and in a variety of sizes and designed for a variety of uses. This collection could form the basis of conversations about science and technology.

"The simple magnifying glass," he informed her, "is an ancient device, and there are many extant examples from medieval scriptoria, where they enabled the artist monks to create their magnificent illuminations. Eyeglasses, too, are a fascinating invention, because of the need for precise grinding of glass, whilst seeking to minimise or eliminate chromatic aberrations. Other lenses have such great potential in the advances of industry, and parabolic lenses in particular have the unique quality of focussing light most tightly, and can be used to create a flame or to gather very dim light and concentrate it enough to render objects visible in the dark. And then there is the remarkable combination of lenses and mirrors, which let us create the telescopes through which we explore the heavens, and microscopes through which we explore the minutiae of our own world."

Discovering, to no surprise, that he would speak thus for hours, Elizabeth spent much time with her companion in learning how to use these areas of interest in conversation, without bewildering the listener or turning the social discourse into a lecture. Likewise, she guided her student, dissecting normal conversations and discussing where one should add a comment, and how to turn a conversation gently to a new topic, without the change seeming forced or unnatural. They wrote scripts, rewrote them, and practised them, and then practised the same skills without a script, for no one in a drawing room or salon conducts his social affairs from a prescribed set of notes and sentences.

When the colonel was present, Lizzy would command his participation in order to practise a three-way discussion, and on the rare occasion their cousin Anne joined them as well, having been made aware of the furtive lessons at the folly. Anne was indeed often sickly and of a miserable regard, but as on the afternoon of the invitation to tea, she was not an unpleasant companion. Once more Lizzy reflected that she suffered more from her mother's overbearing demeanour than of any real defect of character. Oh, how far a little kindness could go!

In addition to practising conversations, Elizabeth and Darcy spent much time analysing facial expressions. His own face, once freed of his self-imposed stony demeanour, was eloquent and expressive, and with the help of a hand mirror, he began to identify what he saw with what he felt. Deciphering expressions would always be an analytical exercise to him, Lizzy explained, but one which might become easier with time and practice.

"Your jaw seems tense, and your lips pressed together. Are you clenching your teeth? A small amount, perhaps? Your eyes have narrowed, from the bottom lid more than the top, and your brows are low and your forehead slightly furrowed in the centre."

"Good, good! And what do you think that suggests?"

"You seem upset, possibly angry."

"Excellent. Now observe and tell me what you see."

"Your jaw is more tense, your chin is firm and protruding. Your lips are tightly compressed, forming a line across your face. Are your lips pinched together at the centre? Yes, I believe so. Your nose... your nostrils are flaring ever so slightly and your eyes are narrower still. The furrow between your brows is more pronounced. You are still upset."

"Observe my body. What do you see?"

"Your shoulders are held tensely and your neck is very upright. Your arms are stiff by your side. There is no ease in your stance. I shall stand by my assertion that you are upset."

"This is not upset, Mr. Darcy, nor slightly angry. This is furious. You would be well advised to observe the differences and learn them again."

The colonel, who had been observing, now spoke up, "By gum, Miss Bennet, you are a fine actress. My cousin might be blind to the nuances, but I was ready to turn tail and run. You are more terrifying in your fury than the French! I should most wish to hide to escape your wrath! Either that, or drop to my knees and plead forgiveness, no matter that I have nothing of which to feel guilty."

Elizabeth laughed and explained her family's enjoyment of acting out scenes from Shakespeare on a winter's night. Darcy stood and observed, seeming both curious and only somewhat comprehending of the scene.

"Shall we return to our study, Mr. Darcy? Here is my upset face. Observe carefully and then let us see how it compares to the fury of heaven." She smiled at the colonel. "These exercises may also help you find some peace in crowded places such as assembly rooms, for if you can focus your attention onto people's expressions, like a game, it may help you to better manage the other stimuli to your senses. And so... upset: observe."

And thus they continued.

"Your fingers are twitching slightly. Your mouth forms a straight line, but perhaps your lips turn down slightly at the corners. Your teeth do not seem to be clenched but I believe you are holding them together. You are exhaling rather forcefully, and your eyes are narrow. Your brow is smooth, but it also looks slightly tense." He paused. "You do not look angry, but I sense dissatisfaction."

"Good job, Mr. Darcy. Dissatisfied, or rather, exasperated, is the impression I am trying to portray. Shall we try another?"

"Your face is relaxed, and your body likewise betrays no tension. Your lips curve up marginally in a slight smile, and your eyes are open naturally, neither unusually wide nor narrow. I would like to say you are happy, but your cheeks do not rise up to your inner lower eyelids as I see them do when you are genuinely laughing. I am confused, Miss Elizabeth."

"You are observing most carefully, sir, and learning well. This is a very pleasant face suggesting polite disinterest. When you see such a regard, most notably the smile that does not shine from the eyes, you may wish to consider changing the topic of conversation.

"This one perplexes me. Your face seems mostly neutral, although perhaps you are holding your mouth a bit firmly, as if willing it to remain neutral. Your breathing and forehead are unruffled, and yet your lower eyelids have risen slightly, giving your eyes the impression of glinting, as they do when you smile. And yet, your face does not betray a smile. Are you happy?"

"Most definitely, sir, but I do not wish to show it. This is the face of someone who desperately wishes to burst out in laughter, but dares not for embarrassing herself or somebody else in the room. It is barely concealed mirth. You are definitely improving and are a quick study! Observe my genuine, unfeigned and most willingly bestowed smile of pleasure at your progress!"

"Good morning, Mr. Darcy, how lovely to see you today."
"And you, Miss Elizabeth."

"Colonel Fitzwilliam, Miss de Bourgh, how lovely that you were able to join us this fine morning. My, but the weather has been lovely recently, has it not?"

The four were gathered, as usual, under the shade of the folly, with a basket of cakes and a flask of tea at their disposal. It had been Elizabeth's proposal to replicate the casual conversations at a tea party or informal gathering after a meal. They could begin as themselves, and then perhaps adopt other personae, so as to give Darcy the opportunity to practise his new skills in a number of similar, but different, situations.

"I understand your intentions, Miss Elizabeth," he had protested when she had first suggested her idea, "but I am already most comfortable in your presence; indeed, I am content and at my greatest ease in your presence. How shall this improve my skills?"

"Every repetition of a skill enhances its strength and efficiency, sir. Consider this the equivalent to practising scales. I know my scales on the keyboard, and yet I rehearse them regardless, so when I am forced to execute them in the course of a difficult sonata, I need not fret over fingering or rapidity. Conversely, should I stumble over the notes in the sonata, I may place the blame on my neglect of practising scales. We shall begin where we are comfortable and reinforce those basic skills. Now, do you prefer scones or jam biscuits when we have our tea?"

And thus the plan was formed and decided.

"The sun is awfully bright today, is it not, Miss de Bourgh?"

"Oh, definitely, Miss Bennet. I always struggle with headaches when the sun beats so strongly. Do you not find the same thing, Mr. Darcy?"

"Anne!" the gentleman retorted, "Since when do you call me Mr. Darcy?"

"Will, we are pretending to be strangers at a tea party. Surely you would not expect a new acquaintance to call you by your Christian name!"

"But Anne... Oh, very well. Yes, Miss de Bourgh," he rolled his eyes at Elizabeth, who tried to hide a chuckle, "I, too, find that excess sun can give me a headache." He glared at Elizabeth who was being only partly successful in her efforts. "Miss Bennet, I know that look. It is barely suppressed mirth. Please stop laughing at me."

"My apologies, sir. But you have learned much in interpreting facial expressions, and for that you ought to be proud. Please, sir, continue with your conversation with Miss de Bourgh."

"Yes, Mistress." Darcy narrowed his eyes, but returned to his dull and insipid conversation about the weather with his cousin Anne. Colonel Fitzwilliam joined in as well, at Anne's invitation, and Elizabeth pronounced the experiment a success. She then requested the colonel to assume his haughtiest imitation of the aristocracy—an easy task for the son of an earl—so they might continue with some variety in the company, and Anne quickly followed suit with a scathing portrayal of an imperious woman, whom Elizabeth recognised immediately as the woman's own mother, Lady Catherine.

Not surprisingly, Darcy was quite comfortable with the heightened formalities of these interactions, but seemed to flounder a bit when Elizabeth suggested they continue their tea with members of some of the lower classes.

"Not your servants, sir," she admonished him, "for them you surely order about and forget that they are people deserving of civility, but perhaps well-heeled merchants, whom you might meet at an assembly, or perhaps at an art exhibit."

"I, interact socially with tradesmen? Surely you jest! I am always most polite in my dealings with them in matters of business, but surely you do not expect me to pay social calls on shopkeepers and tradesmen!" His voice dripped with scorn, his eyes flashed with the deep cut of the insult.

But Elizabeth was not to be cowed. "Mr. Darcy, I am ashamed of you. Surely you must know that there is as much erudition and understanding among the sons of trade as among the high-born of the realm. These are men and women of elegance and good taste, and many of extremely well educated as well. Your own friend, Mr. Bingley, owes his wealth to trade. And yet you socialise with him most comfortably."

"It's true, Darcy," the colonel barked, "with the increasing importance of commerce and the changes on the landscape with these new factories and industries we are seeing cropping up all over, I believe we will be in the company of tradesmen more and more, and many of the ones I have met are far more sophisticated than old sots like my own father, who lives only to drink and gamble. I would rather take tea with a good intelligent shopkeeper than a self-important viscount like my brother any day of the week."

"Thank you, Colonel," Lizzy nodded her head toward the jovial military man.

"Please, think nothing of it, madam. And please, we are comrades in this endeavour and have been so for some time. My given name is Richard and you are welcome to use it, as do my cousins." He gave her a conspiratorial wink which earned him a dark look from Darcy.

"Be that as it may, I shall not socialise with those who rely on trade for their living. My finer sensibilities forbid it. I doubt not that there might be some of their number who are genteel in manner, but I can imagine no occasion in which I should converse with them as equals. No, I will not do it. I have my pride."

"Your pride, sir, does you no favours." Lizzy tried to keep the exasperation and hurt from her voice, although she knew he would not observe them.

"Really, Darcy!" Richard exploded at the same time. "You are too quick to mount your high horse! I can envisage many an opportunity to converse with intelligent and civilised men, regardless of their station."

"As can I," offered Anne. "I often take tea with the Blooms in the village, no matter that they rely on their shops for their wealth. They are as pleasant as anybody I have ever met, and more learned than most! Although," she grimaced, "Mother would forbid me to return if she knew of it."

"As she ought," Mr. Darcy replied, and neither of his cousins could talk him from his position.

"You have always been a pedant for convention," Richard rolled his eyes, "no matter how foolish it may be."

With a sigh of resignation, Lizzy saw the truth in Richard's words. Her cousin Sammy was similar in that respect, holding fast to rules both sensible and arbitrary. She imagined he saw them as concrete guideposts in a world of amorphous and intangible expectation and knew that argument would be unsuccessful. With a deep breath she suggested instead, "Then would you condescend to take tea with a family from the lower ranks of the gentry?" A family such as her own, although this she did not state aloud.

"Of course I would. They are gently born, as am I. They are my equals."

The so the role-playing lesson finally continued.

It was quite late by the time Elizabeth finally returned to the parsonage that afternoon. When Darcy had finally eased into his new role as play-actor, he had confessed that he really quite enjoyed the activity. In the end, the group had been enjoying themselves so much at play-acting through various, and increasingly ridiculous social situations, that they had quite lost track of the passing of time, and Elizabeth was rather taken aback to find her friend Charlotte bustling anxiously about the house. Charlotte's voice betrayed her agitation as she asked, "Where have you been all day, Lizzy? There is so much to do, so much to plan!"

"What is it Charlotte?" her friend asked, "Is everything well?"

"Oh, there you are, my dear," Mr. Collins shuffled into the parlour where the women stood, "we must make haste, lest we lose too much time! Cousin Elizabeth, are you not most honoured by this momentous occasion? Oh, the gracious condescension bestowed upon us by my patroness! How fortunate we are, and how many glorious stories you shall have to relate to everybody when you return, at last, to Longbourn. They will never tire of hearing of the splendours of Rosings—"

"I am most sorry to interrupt, Mr. Collins, but what am I to tell them? I have not yet heard what this wonderful event shall be!" Elizabeth declared, cutting off her cousin's tiresome speech.

"Charlotte, my dear, did you not tell her?" the parson asked. "Why ever not?"

"I was about to, husband, when you came in, so full of your excitement that I had not time to utter the words," his wife replied in a very matter-of-fact tone of voice. Then, to her friend, Charlotte explained, "It seems that Lady Catherine is to host a gathering tomorrow evening. She has invited all the principal families in the area, and I am certain that everybody will be in attendance. No one dare refuse an invitation from Lady Catherine!"

"I am certain," Lizzy replied coolly, "that few people are to refuse her anything at all!"

"Yes, yes, indeed, Cousin Elizabeth," Mr. Collins gushed. "And that is why we must start our preparations. You shall have to do what you can with your gowns, for I am certain Lady Catherine will expect you to be suitably attired, even if you will never quite aspire to her own elegance, and you shall have to repair to the great house to practise upon Mrs. Jenkin's pianoforte, in case you are asked to exhibit. Do you have suitable music? Oh, and what shall Maria wear, my dear?" he turned to his wife. "Oh, so much to do, so very much to do!" And he ran out of the room, reminding Elizabeth of nothing as much as a very confused rabbit.

"Well, then," Lizzy exhaled, "I suppose I had best go and examine my wardrobe, and see what of my dresses can be made serviceable for tomorrow night." She imagined her face as Mr. Darcy might see it, with eyes rolled heavenward and a grimace for a smile. "Did you only now receive the invitation, Charlotte?" She did not mention her sessions with Mr. Darcy, for Mr. Collins would certainly not approve, and neither the gentleman himself nor either of his cousins had mentioned a word of the gathering that morning.

"Yes, yes, only an hour ago," Charlotte nodded her head. "A messenger from Rosings came past, on his way to deliver the invitations to the other families. It all seems quite sudden, but I have come to learn that when Lady Catherine sets her mind on something, it happens quite immediately!" Elizabeth recalled the sudden invitation to tea not so long ago and stifled a huff of exasperation.

At this moment, Mr. Collins dashed back into the room and cast an accusing eye on his visiting relation, still flushed from her morning excursion. "Cousin Elizabeth, I hope I need not remind you to keep a civil tongue tomorrow night at the gathering. It is my belief, although her Ladyship has, of course, not confided in me, still, I have an ear for her true meaning and believe I know her heart, that Lady Catherine has decided to use this gathering to finally announce the engagement of her most lovely daughter to Mr. Darcy. You will be polite, will you not? Good, I shall expect nothing less. Now where is my best hat? I must find my hat!" And off he ran once more.

The words flew from his mouth as if secondary in importance to the location of his hat, but they settled heavily in Elizabeth's ears. The room seemed to whirl about her as Charlotte excused herself to begin preparing for the gathering, leaving Elizabeth to climb the stairs to her room, her mind in a daze. Was Mr. Collins correct in his supposition of the purpose of the soirée? He seemed firmly to believe that Lady Catherine would announce the engagement of her daughter to Mr. Darcy! Could that possibly be true? It hardly seemed possible!

She had, over the past weeks, spent a great deal of time with both Darcy and Anne, and in that time had come to know them rather well, most especially due to the nature of their interactions and the importance placed on discerning unspoken clues about intention and relationships. She was most certain that she had not seen the first hint of special regard between them. Oh, they clearly loved each other as cousins do, with their comfortable and familiar interactions with each other, but there was nothing beyond that, nothing that might suggest their suitability as husband and wife. Indeed, Darcy treated Anne no differently than he treated Richard, other than a distracted concern for her physical comfort.

Not even that very morning, when they had been pretending to be dukes and duchesses, scullery maids and errand boys in their role-playing exercises, had there been the slightest suggestion of an arrangement. Not a word, not a gesture, had been given to hint at any upcoming nuptials. And Mr. Darcy, Lizzy considered, could surely not conceal such an eventuality from those he let into his circle of intimates. He was a reasonable actor, but only when he placed himself into that position. In his daily life, she was certain, he was nothing but forthright and open about his affairs.

And, if she was correct, based on her experience with young Samuel, Mr. Darcy was a terrible liar. He had admitted to her on several occasions that he found deceit and disguise most abhorrent, partly because he had such difficulty in determining the liar and lie. When freed from his stony facade, he was an open and genuine man, with no trace of artifice in him How he interpreted his experiences might differ greatly from how others around him might see those same events, but there was no prevarication or deliberate obfuscation in his accounts.

How, Elizabeth wondered, could he have disguised his engagement to his sickly cousin so completely and convincingly that she noticed nothing amiss? It was simply not possible, not based on everything she had come to know about the man. Mr. Collins' report must surely be in error! Mr. Darcy could simply not be engaged!

And, if Darcy were engaged to Anne, if the parson's unfounded supposition were true, why should the news be so disquieting to her?

Chapter Six

The Evening at Rosings

The next day passed in a flurry of frenzied activities. Anne de Bourgh had sent a note excusing the Rosings party from their regular meeting, since everybody was required to attend Lady Catherine as she prepared for the evening's event; in truth, Elizabeth would have had little time to devote to her student, for she, too, was needed at the parsonage. After her own dress was picked apart and resewn to the extent that her skills and time allowed, with the requisite bows and ribbons and bits of lace, she moved on to help Maria with her chosen frock. Then, together, they assisted Charlotte, before all retiring to their rooms to wash and begin the tiresome preparations for the visit. At last, beautifully attired, decorated with whatever jewellery they could find, and coiffed to the limits of the attending maid's skills with hair, they climbed into the carriage Lady Catherine had sent, and were on their way to Rosings for the evening's socialising.

They were amongst the first to arrive. Perhaps Lady Catherine needed the carriage for others of her guests; perhaps she did not wish the party from the parsonage to make a grand entrance. The attending footman led the party from the parsonage up an unfamiliar staircase to a room which none of them had seen before. It was grander in size than the drawing room and parlour in which Lady Catherine had entertained the Collins and their guests before, and—if possible—even more ornate. The room was not quite square, with a bank of windows and balcony doors along the long wall that formed the exterior of the mansion. Heavy dark maroon draperies fell from ceiling to floor, separating and framing each of the many windows, their weight and sombre hue contributing to an air of intense ponderousness. The remaining walls were richly papered in ochres and golds, which should have looked opulent against the purple-red of the draperies, but which were rendered merely overly ornate and cloying. These side walls were punctuated by a procession of arched niches that held a small army of marble statuary, each niche liberally swathed in more of the purple drapery, and separated by paintings in cumbersome frames, each depicting dark and forbidding subject matter, although, for the most part, skilfully rendered by excellent artists.

The fourth wall, in which sat the doors through which they had entered, faced the bank of windows directly. Instead of the paintings and statues, this space was liberally decorated with relics and ornaments from the Indies and China. In the far corner, two peacocks, their bodies stuffed, their tails at full plumage, stood guard against any who might venture too close to the lacquered japan cabinet that formed the centrepiece of that particular display. Around the doorway, a bewildering display of masks covered the wall nearly to the ceiling, and in the very centre of that wall, a massive fireplace claimed prominence, the mantel-piece glistening in gilt and crystal, each facet lit and relit by the roaring fire that burned in the grate. Each element of the room, taken alone, would be marvellous, Lizzy decided. In concert, the effect was overwhelming with too little regard for good taste.

"Oh, isn't it marvellous, Lizzy?" Charlotte's sister Maria stared about the space with eyes as wide as saucers. "I have never seen so much gilt in one place in all my life! Are those peacocks? I have so often seen paintings and illustrations in magazines and books, but never the bird itself! Oh, Lizzy! Is that statue there unclothed? Oh!" The young girl's eyes swirled around the room with the dizzying motion of a fallen leaf tormented by the wind, always darting from one place to another, never resting or ceasing its motion. She gasped aloud at everything she noticed until the party drew closer to Lady Catherine, whereupon her eyes widened even more and she stilled her voice, too terrified to utter another syllable.

In the centre of this needless finery, the lady of the house and her daughter stood, receiving a party of guests as they arrived. The newly arrived couple with their son—a young man about Maria's age—were greeted most lavishly and with curtseys and condescension. Elizabeth was not expecting such effusions of hospitality for her party, but even she was amazed at Lady Catherine's curt welcome. Instead of even the barest hint of welcome, the Collins, along with Elizabeth and Maria, were admitted with little more than a nod of the head and an, "I see the carriage is now available." Anne, to her credit, looked embarrassed at her mother's ill manners, but said nothing as the party from the parsonage moved into the cavernous space.

Elizabeth scanned the sparsely populated room as she was led around by Mr. Collins to be introduced to the two unfamiliar couples standing by the tea table. She made a pretty curtsey and spoke the appropriate pretty words, and then as quickly as good manners allowed, made her excuses and slid across the room to where a familiar shape loomed stiffly against the dark curtains.

He wore the same dark blue coat he had worn to the Meryton assembly all those months ago. Elizabeth wondered why she recalled this detail with such clarity, before realising that even then, she had been quite keenly aware of the tall, taciturn man who stared stonily at people before averting his eyes in what everyone had assumed was disgust. Now she knew better, and she realised how uncomfortable he had been. And how uncomfortable he was now, despite the greater familiarity of the setting. Whether or not Mr. Collins was correct in his assumption of the *raison d'être* of the evening, Darcy would be made the focus of attention of a large gathering of people whom he knew only a little, if at all, and Lizzy could tell that rather than disdain, his true sentiments involved a deep desire to flee, coupled with the sure knowledge that he must stay and face the torture set for him. A firing squad, she suspected, would be of greater comfort to him than the evening ahead.

She approached him with measured steps and an expression of quiet pleasure. "Mr. Darcy." She curtseyed formally but her smile was much more than what was required for politeness.

"Elizabeth!" He blurted out her name in relief before recollecting himself. He then cleared his throat and repeated, "Miss Elizabeth, it is such a delight to see you this evening. I trust the arrangements my aunt made for your transportation were acceptable."

"You are chatting at inconsequential nothings very well, sir." She gave him a reassuring smile, eyebrows quickly floating upwards, before resuming their natural position. Darcy started at the expression, but said nothing. Elizabeth spoke again, "I wish we had been given some time to prepare for this evening, but I believe you may consider this your first examination in the Miss Bennet School of Social Comfort. I have faith in my student and believe he will pass the examination quite admirably."

"Thank you for your confidence, E.. Miss Elizabeth. I admit to some trepidation at the thought of this evening, but I also wish to put to the test some of the matters we have been discussing. I shall attempt to pay attention to tone of voice and gesture, in the hopes of better understanding the nuances of the conversations that swirl around me. I also hope that such concentration will help me should the noise of the evening grow too loud for my comfort."

"I have faith, sir. Try to enjoy yourself. And...." she broke off, not quite knowing how to ask her next question.

"Yes, madam?" Darcy was looking at her in some alarm. It was not like Elizabeth Bennet to be at a loss for words.

She paused and collected her thoughts, taking deep and regular breaths to dispel her discomfort. She became conscious that Darcy was aware of her every action and she briefly cursed herself for encouraging such behaviour on his part. She could see him assessing her face, and could almost hear his slow, measured voice, deep and sonorous: *your chin is quivering slightly, your cheeks are white, you are breathing most deliberately, as if to calm yourself and control your emotion, and the inner parts of your eyebrows are slightly raised where your forehead is pinched together.* Even with his difficulty in reading facial expressions, he would surely know she was distressed. She spoke slowly, as if delaying the knowledge of an event might delay its implementation. She did not wish to hear that Mr. Darcy and Anne were engaged to be married, and yet she had to know! Her emotions roiled at the thought of this, but she refused to consider the import of this disturbance. *I shall miss working with him,* she repeated to herself again and again. *That is all.* She would not allow for further rumination.

"My cousin was curious as to the import of this evening's gathering, since it was all arranged so quickly. He wondered if, perhaps, it had something to do with your presence here at Rosings, some special occasion, perhaps?"

Darcy was still staring at her, obviously alarmed at her expression and appearance. "Miss Elizabeth, are you well? You seem rather pale." She shook her head, assuring him she was well. "The gathering is, I believe, somewhat in my honour. My aunt claims it is to give the neighbourhood the opportunity to visit with my cousin Richard and myself before we return to London and our homes, but I believe her ulterior motives are to demonstrate to me how superior the local society is to what I enjoy at Pemberley. You must know that my aunt wishes me to marry cousin Anne..."

So it was true! Elizabeth found the room beginning to swirl around her, and she had to fight to regain her balance. She felt the pulse in her neck throbbing as her head grew light. The heat from the fireplace burned into her back whilst the cool air from the window by which they stood assailed her with its icy touch. *It is just that I shall miss working with him,* she repeated to herself. *He is becoming a friend, and once he marries, our acquaintance and our lessons must end. That is all. That is all.* She was concentrating so intensely on maintaining her balance and breathing that she was scarcely aware that Mr. Darcy was still speaking.

"Are you certain that you are well, Elizabeth? You really have become quite pale. Come, you must sit, and I shall call for some wine!" He summoned a serving girl and requested a glass to be brought over immediately. "Here, please drink. You are not well at all!"

"Forgive me for my weakness, Mr. Darcy," Elizabeth managed at last. "I am indeed well. I was merely caught unaware..." She turned aside to stop tears from forming in her eyes. "I must wish you..." she stopped again to breathe back the tears.

"Caught unaware? Everybody knows that Aunt Catherine hopes that Anne and I will marry. But she is the only one who will not acknowledge that neither one of us wishes it. She is destined to be most sorely disappointed. She will not listen to us, but in time, events will necessarily occur to convince her of the futility of her schemes."

At once, the looming darkness lifted and blood flowed back through Elizabeth's veins. She fell back into the chair as she stared up at her concerned companion. "You are not marrying Anne?"

"No, no indeed! It would be fair to neither of us, since we do not love each other that way. Our union would merely unite two estates, and not two hearts. As much as I have difficulties in deciphering the emotions of others, I feel my own quite acutely, and could not sanction a marriage where there is no affection. I know these are almost expected amongst my class, but such would be like deceit for me, and I abhor deceptions."

"So you have told me." She struggled up from her chair and blinked away the last of the tears. She would have to examine the wave of emotions later on, but right now she must present a pleasant and calm social face. Indeed, she must adopt a facade as impenetrable as the one Mr. Darcy so often employed, albeit that hers was one of genial interest and companionship rather than stony aloofness. "Your aunt is watching us, and more guests have arrived. I hope we shall talk later, at which time you may apprise me of your progress this evening."

Darcy took her hand and bowed deeply over it before bestowing a kiss on her gloved fingertips.

"Indeed, I look forward to it. Madam." As they had been speaking the room had become quite filled with the invited guests, and Lady Catherine was now glaring at her nephew, an expression which even he had little difficulty deciphering. "I see that I have duties to fulfil. Pray excuse me." He executed a perfect bow and walked off to discharge his social obligations whilst Elizabeth looked on as her turbulent emotions began to settle.

"Are you well, Miss Bennet... Elizabeth?" Colonel Fitzwilliam walked up to her and gave a perfunctory bow before adding one of his accustomed good-humoured grins. "You look somewhat unsteady. Is the room too warm, perhaps? My aunt insisted on a roaring blaze, despite the temperate weather. A good fire will call attention to the fireplace, for the chimney-piece alone cost—"

"Over eight hundred pounds!" Elizabeth finished for him with a laugh. "Oh, how many times have I heard my cousin wax poetic upon said fireplace? He must surely have regaled the whole village of Meryton with intimate descriptions of every room in this grand house!" Relieved to have something else on which to think, she curtsied to the colonel and greeted him properly. "Colonel Fitzwilliam—Richard—how do you do this evening, sir? I hope your day was spent more profitably than leading your poor cousin through one ordeal after another."

"Oh, Anne enjoys your lessons very much," he joked, "and they are no ordeal to her at all. Poor Darcy, on the other hand..."

"You always lighten my mood, Richard! Yes, I am well. I was merely overcome by a moment of disorientation. A sip of wine has revived me quite well." She gestured to the room, which was beginning to fill up with guests. "Your aunt has commanded a good attendance this evening. Do you know everybody?"

"Indeed, we have been paraded before them in years past. Come, let me introduce you to some very pleasant people!" He offered his arm and led her across the room.

The evening passed much as expected. Lady Catherine reigned supreme over the assembly, whether enthroned in her chair at the centre of the large drawing room, where she commanded her subjects to bow to her will, or whether strutting around the periphery of the space, intruding upon conversations and interjecting her opinions into matters, whether her thoughts were wanted or not. *If I had not known better*, Elizabeth mused, and not for the first time, *I would think Mr. Darcy's lack of social aptitude something learned and not innate!* Catherine de

Bourgh was certainly no model of the social graces, no matter her noble lineage.

"No, no, Mrs. Rothmere," the grand dame pronounced to one unfortunate lady, "you must tell your cook to use the gizzards in the broth. It would not do for her to be discarding useful food. And when you have your biscuits with tea, be certain that you avoid butter until after you have finished the fruit, for that will guard against stomach upset."

"Lady Grover, I do hope you have advised your daughter not to wear that shade of mauve again. It does not become her, with her colouring. Of course, not everybody can be like my Anne, who can wear every colour with equal grace. No, no, you must tell her maid that she should not wear that shade again. Oh, Darcy, there you are, Nephew. I was just telling Lady Grover how my Anne looks equally radiant in every shade of clothing. Do you not find it so, Darcy?"

"Sir James, have you implemented the system of categorising your poultry yet? Your farmers must have noticed an improvement in their numbers, for my way has yet to fail anybody. Of course, it only works with fowl. To keep account of your flocks, you must use the other method I taught you."

And so the great lady paraded around the room, dispensing advice where it was not needed and her thoughts where they were not wanted. Elizabeth succeeded in stifling her amusement at the display only by recalling how her friend Charlotte was subject to these same admonishments and instructions on a daily basis, with no recourse but to obey with a cheerful and gracious smile. What might be amusing for an evening could be nothing but grating when received so regularly.

Eventually Elizabeth's peregrinations from one conversation to another landed her by the tea table. She had to admit that she had rather liked many of the people she had met that evening, and wished only for more congenial circumstances in which to come to know them better. Mrs. St. Ives, the wife of another major landowner in the area, was particularly pleasant. A young woman, only some five or six years Lizzy's senior, she was handsome and intelligent, with an excellent understanding and a lively wit. Lizzy could well imagine her becoming a good friend, were the circumstances to be right. Mr. St. Ives was somewhat older—the current Mrs. St. Ives was his second wife, Lizzy believed—with a pleasant if unremarkable face, and a soft manner that concealed a keen mind and a ferocious interest in music, as she discovered upon making mention of the pianoforte in the other drawing room.

As she stood contemplating her new acquaintances, Elizabeth sensed a presence at her side and looked up to see Mr. Darcy approaching. "I would like some tea," he explained. "I have been making a great effort to converse, and I find my throat is rather dry." He looked around and, assuring himself that he was not being overheard, confessed, "Remembering all your advice is more exhausting than I would have imagined. I find it challenging to keep abreast of the rapidly changing expressions on people's faces as they talk, at the same time as making a note of the tone of voice and the actual words they utter. I do not know how people manage with such ease, pleasure even!"

He accepted the tea that Elizabeth had prepared for him as he spoke and took a sip as she offered some more advice.

"Think on this, Mr. Darcy. Ask questions of your companions in an area which you believe to be of great interest to them. Ask them of themselves, or their families. And as they speak, think of more questions to ask. Most people love nothing so much as to talk of themselves, and if you prove to show an interest and are willing to listen, they will pronounce you the world's best conversationalist, even if you say only ten words the whole evening. It will also save your voice, should you find it strained."

He gave her a sweet and grateful smile. "I shall take this advice to heart, Miss Elizabeth, and shall put your theory to the test. I believe my aunt approaches with the duchess. Madam." He bowed politely and made his departure, leaving Elizabeth to finish her own cup of tea in blessed, if momentary, solitude, before joining a small group gathered around the whist table.

Chapter Seven

Surviving the Onslaught

As the evening progressed, Elizabeth was kept busy talking with one group of new acquaintances or another, but she was diligent in keeping track of Mr. Darcy's movements and demeanour. She had been pleased to note his willingness to put his lessons to the test, despite his discomfort at the thought, and at first, after their first short conversation, his whole manner and bearing had been much easier than ever she had seen him in company. She had noticed him sitting quite comfortably in an armchair, listening to the Duchess hold forth on her chosen topics, and later on, he had seemed genuinely interested in the conversation he was having with Mr. St. Ives. He had stood stoically by his aunt as she dragged him from group to group, and had even smiled at his cousin Anne as she approached at one point to join the small assembly of which he was a part at that particular moment.

However, as the evening drew on and the noise grew greater as the conversations throughout the room swelled, she noticed Darcy begin to withdraw from conversations and retreat more and more behind his accustomed stony facade. His whole body seemed to change. His face became less mobile and expressive and his fascinating moss-green eyes seemed to grow dull as they stilled behind stiffened lids and stony cheeks. His posture also altered; no longer were his motions smooth and without tension. Now he stood stiff and tall, perfectly correct and elegant, but also distant and unwelcoming. If he had turned his back on the room, he could not have projected a less approachable persona to those in attendance. He did not shuffle his feet, nor fidget with his fingers, nor move his head to the other members of the party, but he stood stiff and remote, so disconnected with the fuss and ado that surrounded him that he may have been one of the statuary that lined the walls of the salon.

The metamorphosis from the friendly man at the evening's start to this living statue had been gradual, but Elizabeth was alert to Darcy's moods and she had noticed the slow change with concern. He had been at his most uncomfortable—exhibiting the same cold and distant hauteur that had so displeased the society at Meryton—for about a quarter hour before she was able to excuse herself from her companions to see if she might help him. He seemed hardly to notice her approach although the slight flicker in his eyes let her know that she was not taking him unawares. Slowly she walked up to him and murmured, so as not to be overheard, "Mr. Darcy, I fear the events of the evening have grown too much for you. The noise is high, and I believe I heard your aunt make mention of removing the carpets so there may be dancing. It is also warm in here, too warm for the night, and the lights reflecting off the crystals are bright on my welcoming eyes. For you, this must feel like a form of torture."

At these understanding words, the frozen facade momentarily melted away, revealing a very vulnerable and unhappy face, before congealing once more across those handsome features.

"Indeed, Miss Bennet, I feel myself the target of a siege, my senses the victims. The light and heat are troubling, but you are correct that the noise is my main enemy right now. I am unable to concentrate on the lessons we conducted, and I feel my only recourse is to barricade myself away. I fear this is how I presented myself in Hertfordshire last autumn. Now that I am more aware of my response, I suspect I was most rude."

"Indeed you were." Her sympathetic smile softened her chastising words, although she knew he would likely miss her kind expression. She paused to regard the activity that swirled around the massive room and to listen to the chaos of the many conversations that echoed from wall to ceiling and back again. No wonder the poor man was distracted. "I believe, Mr. Darcy, that it is growing warm in here. I should be grateful for a few moments on the balcony which, if I am correct, lies beyond those glass doors." She gestured to the bank of windows and heavy maroon curtains. "Dare I ask you to accompany me?"

His eyes spoke of his intense gratitude at the opportunity to escape the chaos of the drawing-room, even for a short time. But then, just as quickly, he began to shake his head. "It is not appropriate for us to be alone on the balcony. There are rules of propriety that cannot be ignored."

Ah yes, she realised. He would, of course, be most concerned about the unwritten rules of social engagement long before cares of her reputation or his own comfort and peace of mind. Her cousin Samuel, too, was driven by the rules; they created a framework on which he could base the rest of his experiences, and they governed his behaviour in a world in which so much of what he observed made little sense. Just as he could not imagine conversing with tradesmen—which could contravene the rules of his class—he could not consider breaking the bounds of propriety. Even though Mr. Darcy was much more flexible in his thoughts and behaviour than Sammy, Elizabeth was certain that he too would by instinct find and adhere to whatever rules and strictures might exist to define any given situation.

She suddenly found herself recalling her interactions with poor Mr. Wickham and that officer's tale of woe about his poor treatment by Mr. Darcy. At the time, she had fully accepted Mr. Wickham's tale and Mr. Darcy's culpability, but as she had come to know the latter, the matter seemed less and less clear. Mr. Darcy's existence was likely driven by the rules he deemed were set by society; one of those rules was to be forthcoming and scrupulous about every encounter. As he had mentioned on so many occasions, deception was anathema to him. With this in mind, whatever had occurred between him and Mr.

Wickham must not have been crystalline in nature, and certainly not as clear as Mr. Wickham had intimated. Elizabeth was now quite convinced that Mr. Darcy could no more deliberately countermand his father's wishes than she could sprout wings and fly. It was completely contrary to his nature. She must ask him about that at some point. It was most perplexing and troubling. But now, looking up at his desperate eyes, craving relief from the chaos of the room, yet resolute in not yielding to his desires in the face of a raft on unspoken rules, she could feel nothing but sympathy for the man.

He was, she was certain, bound by a strict moral code, and the rule of Acceptable Behaviour Between Unmarried Men and Women declared that the two parties should never be alone together without a suitable chaperon. Nevertheless, Elizabeth could see that unless he had some respite from the party, he would withdraw completely behind his protective battlements, not to emerge again for hours, possibly days. "Nonsense, sir!" she reprimanded him. "This is no time to dicker with fribbles and fluff. I consider myself throwing a drowning man a rope. I know you will understand the metaphor. Now, for you own sake, grab the rope and save yourself. I shall inform your cousin of our whereabouts, so she may serve as a suitable chaperone should she feel it necessary."

The stern serious look on her sweet face, coupled with her curt and unexpected words, was so incongruous that Darcy looked as if he were about to laugh. Instead, he nodded his head, quickly swept aside a portion of the heavy draperies and ducked through the resultant gap. A very short time later, having informed Anne of her mission, Elizabeth followed in his wake.

Within moments they were outside on the large balcony, breathing in cool fresh air. The door closed, shutting behind it the hubbub and cacophony of the soirée, leaving the two solitary figures in blessed quiet. Darcy did nothing for a few minutes but breathe deeply of the crisp evening breezes, eyes closed against the flickering light, hands on the balustrade as if supporting every ounce of his weight. Elizabeth stood to the side, still and quiet, letting him absorb the calm of the night, watching as his body relaxed and his breathing eased, shoulders losing their stiffness and his jaw its tightness. For five full minutes they stood there in silence, not talking, neither turning to regard each other, but partaking of the blessed silence and quiet dim light of the moon-filled sky.

Eventually the tall gentleman breathed deeply once and stood straight, reaching to his full height, before turning his eyes to Elizabeth, who had remained so calmly by his side. In the darkness of the spring night, his features were mostly lost in shadow, with only his profile picked out by the distant moon, his hair gently gilded in that faint silver light.

"Thank you, Elizabeth. I never would have thought to remove myself from the room, no matter how desperately I might have wished to do so. I had thought my duty to remain, my obligation to my host, superseded my need to escape the assault. The noise, the echo of each and every voice, from every surface... the bright lights piercing my eyes, boring me to the quick.... The odour of all those bodies, so close, threatening to overrun me and crush me... how could you know how gravely I was suffering? For I have asked my friends and am told once and again how most people do not feel the attack on every sense as I do. And yet you knew, somehow, and yes, you threw me that rope and I grabbed it like a drowning man, for drowning I was. I comprehend your simile, madam, and find it most apt." His voice was so quiet, she scarcely could hear it in the calm silence of the night.

Matching his tone, barely breathing, she replied. "I did not know, Mr. Darcy. I merely surmised. I know my cousin Samuel, and I observed you, and saw you in pain. And since I had it within my means to offer aid, I did so. Are you recovered, sir?" Tentatively she reached out for his arm, meaning only to reassure him of her support and presence with the lightest and briefest of touches, but no sooner did her gloved hand alight on his coat sleeve, his free hand reached over and clasped hers, the drowning man still clinging to the rope, even after being pulled safely to shore. "We need not go back inside," she whispered.

"We will be missed."

"Then let them miss us."

"You will be tarnished. Your reputation—"

"Means nothing to the people here tonight. Only my friend Charlotte and Mr. Collins will have any concerns about me. No one else will even recall my presence, let alone my name. Charlotte knows me too well to worry, and Mr. Collins is undoubtedly too busy fawning over your aunt to give a thought to my whereabouts. If I have helped you abide the evening, I have nothing to regret." She gathered her wrap about her shoulders and hugged it tight against the cool night air.

"You are cold. I should have noticed. I was too busy thinking of myself."

"You were recovering. How do you tolerate the noise and activity for as long as you do? You seemed comfortable at the beginning of the evening."

"The sensation of being overwhelmed by the noise and lights and other sensations does not occur immediately. Rather, it grows imperceptibly, starting from nothing, changing into a minor and unimportant irritation, then gradually becoming more and more present until it is all I can feel. I am so accustomed to this descent that I enter every social situation with such a feeling of dread that I immediately barricade myself. Tonight, I had hoped to put to practise those skills we have been discussing, and indeed, I was easier than I have been in a very long time. But even so, the sensation of being crushed by the activity came upon me at last. I am a lost cause, it seems. I am sorry, Elizabeth."

"Nay, do not be sorry! If you began the evening at ease, you have made great progress. And I believe I observed you enjoying some conversations. You seemed quite comfortable with Mr. St. Ives, and genuinely interested in his discussion. Do you share similar interests? Bridges, perhaps?" She joked.

Darcy laughed and shook his head. "I did not ask him about bridges, for I know my interest there is unusual. Rather, we discussed music. He is most knowledgeable and professes to play the violin rather well. I, too, have a deep interest in music, for it seems to express the thoughts and feelings that I understand so imperfectly at times. He has come upon some new compositions by a young Italian violinist named Niccolò Paganini. He is still unknown—St. Ives only heard of him from a musical friend who travels for his business—but his works are, apparently, quite fine, and fiendishly difficult. St. Ives and I may attempt them at some point during my stay here. Perhaps you would join us.... You and Richard, and Anne if she will come."

"You play music?" This was the first Elizabeth had heard of any musical inclination on the part of her companion.

"My mother was a great lover of music. My sister plays very nicely, and I was forced to learn the pianoforte as a child. In truth, I was not forced, for I loved it, even if I did not practise as much as I should." He looked solemnly at Elizabeth. "In that, we are equals." Then his gaze softened and he repeated his question. "Will you join us?"

She smiled, recalling her conversation with the man's wife. "I should be happy to, sir. I enjoyed meeting Mrs. St. Ives and should be delighted to continue that acquaintance. Tell me more, please, about the music you love the best."

At this, Darcy grew animated, and cast off the last of the weight of the evening's tortures. He expounded upon his thoughts concerning Mozart's symphonies and operas, about Beethoven's piano sonatas, and about new musical styles and compositions coming from parts of the continent. Not even Napoleon could stop the dissemination of music, and Beethoven, the great symphonist himself, had recalled the dedication of his third symphony when the tyrant proclaimed himself emperor. Elizabeth, a music lover as well, found herself enjoying the conversation, and her present company very much.

As much as her musings of late had revolved around Mr. Darcy, they had almost all concerned his difficulties and how these had caused him to be so misunderstood; she had given little thought as to whether she liked the man. Once she had divested herself of her initial prejudices after his behaviour at the Meryton assembly, once she had come to understand his behaviour stemmed from severe discomfort and not innate arrogance, she had ceased disliking him. Other stimuli to her dislike, such as Mr. Wickham's tales, she too had begun to think of in a new light, and she did not object at all to the hours she had spent in his company as they examined and analysed facial expressions, listened for vocal inflections of meaning, or play-acted imaginary conversations.

She had even, she realised, begun to look forward to their daily meetings. It was not a hardship when Richard and Anne were unable to join them. On those days they might talk as much as they worked, and she found that she really enjoyed those moments. Her feelings towards the man had progressed from loathing to comprehension and acceptance, and even sympathy. But now, there was something else, something even warmer: there was the beginning of affection.

She really liked Mr. Darcy! How had that come about? She could hardly imagine it, but she had come to think of him quite warmly, and counted him as a cherished friend. Surprised at this realisation, she looked up at him, and her golden eyes caught his moss-green ones and neither looked away.

She had, she discovered, found something she had not been expecting when she made the journey from Hertfordshire to Kent to visit Charlotte. She had envisaged an awkward, difficult visit with her dear friend and her husband, whom Elizabeth had rejected scant hours before Charlotte had accepted him. She had dreaded many a tedious hour sitting listening to Mr. Collins as he sermonised painfully on passages of scripture he only weakly understood, or as he fawned and scraped over Lady Catherine's every condescension. She had imagined herself sitting in pained silence over useless embroidery, trying to keep civil company with Charlotte's sweet but childish sister Maria, or forcing pleasant conversation where she wished to scream at Charlotte for a decision she could ill comprehend whilst her friend likely wished to scream that Elizabeth truly did not know her at all for thinking her choice to marry Mr. Collins so dreadfully foolish.

She had not once imagined finding a purpose in Kent, finding companionship amongst the younger residents at Rosings, finding friends. But it was true. Richard, Anne, and even Mr. Darcy himself had worked their way into her affections. Richard was the joker, the one always ready with an easy laugh, the perfect word, a conspiratorial smile. His manner was all that was pleasant and he was the most congenial of the cousins. Anne, quieter and more serious, due perhaps to her weak constitution, was nonetheless a sincere and honest companion, kind and patient, ready to listen without passing judgement, well-read and remarkably well-informed considering her near-imprisonment in her mother's home.

And Mr. Darcy... why could she not think of his by his given name? There was something so formal and correct about his every gesture, from the perfect pleats in his cravat to his carefully cultivated and practiced bows, that forbade such familiarity. And yet, of the three cousins, he was the one she realised she was most drawn to. His formal mien was his method of functioning in the world; perfect manners and a strict code of conduct served as the framework that let him interact with others. But beneath that sober and forbidding exterior lay a sweet and kind man, with a quick mind and a dry sense of humour, never mind that he so seldom let it be observed. He felt things deeply, but hid behind his assumed facade of hauteur and pride, protecting himself not only from the physical sensations that he felt so keenly, but from the emotional pain that came from floundering in a world he poorly understood, and that understood him not at all. He, of the three, was the one Elizabeth now knew, with whom she most wished to continue her acquaintance.

She had been staring at him while these thoughts flooded her mind, and he had been looking directly back, not flinching, neither diverting his gaze. He cleared his voice, as if he, too, had been contemplating something, and now wished to speak.

"Elizabeth, sweet Elizabeth..."

But he got no further, for at that moment his cousin Richard burst through the balcony doors, proclaiming, "Will, where in blazes have you been hiding? Our aunt has been breathing fire wondering what had become of you!"

Chapter Eight

An Unpleasant Walk

S leep did not come easily to Elizabeth that night. As much as she strove to clear her mind and get some rest, she could not help but replay and think upon the events of the evening.

After Richard had interrupted them on the balcony, he and Mr. Darcy had quickly returned to the drawing room. Darcy had assured her that he was much recovered and felt capable of surviving another hour or two of the chaos within. "Should I begin to be overwhelmed again," he had promised, "I will excuse myself for some air." A few minutes later, Lizzy herself had slipped back into the crowded room. As she had opined, no one had missed her, and if they had, had not considered her important enough to worry about.

"There you are, Cousin Elizabeth," Mr. Collins had uttered at one point, some quarter hour after she had returned to the room. "Have you complimented Lady Catherine on her gathering yet? Surely, you must have some words to offer her to adequately convey your deepest appreciation at being granted the most felicitous opportunity to socialise with members of a society ordinarily so far above your own. Come, Her Ladyship is just there, let us go together..."

She had had no further chance to talk with either Mr. Darcy or his cousins, and when the Collins party had left soon thereafter, upon Lady Catherine informing them that the carriage was ready, she was able only to bow her head to Mr. Darcy, who was trapped in a conversation with the duchess on the other side of the large room.

In all, the evening had been a great success. From what Elizabeth observed, Mr. Darcy had found himself able to engage in conversations with strangers, had begun a new friendship with the meek but interesting Mr. St. Ives, and had seemed fairly well at ease in the crowd. When he had begun to feel the sights, sounds and other sensations of the gathering becoming too powerful to withstand without withdrawing behind his protective wall, she had shown him the simple solution of withdrawing from the assault. He had revived on the balcony and, once removed from the hubbub of the society in the drawing room, he had regained his balance and was able to rejoin the group inside with some degree of equanimity.

As she lay in bed, hoping to sleep, her mind returned again and again to her conversation with Mr. Darcy on that cool, quiet balcony. Although, in their lessons in the folly, they had often strayed to topics removed from their exercises, never before had they engaged in a free and extemporaneous discussion, on a topic of interest to both, but that had nothing to do with Mr. Darcy's social difficulties. Without the self-imposed restrictions of feeling the need to return to their studies, Elizabeth had found she enjoyed their discussion on music more than she would have imagined. In that serene, private space, conversing on a topic that inspired him, no one would have thought Mr. Darcy's social skills lacking. It was as he had once said: when completely comfortable and at ease with people whom he knew well and liked, he was as friendly and pleasant as any man, and certainly more intelligent and insightful than most. He had some fascinating thoughts about the music they had discussed, and he was much more knowledgeable than any man she had ever met about the art. She had truly enjoyed every minute she had spent with him last night.

And, just before Richard burst through those doors to find him, Mr. Darcy had been about to say something to her. Had he been about to thank her for her advice? For her endless hours of practise and instruction? Was he hoping to extend, once more, the invitation for her to accompany him to the St. Ives's residence to hear the music of that young Italian violinist Paganini? Why, oh why, could Richard not have waited another two minutes? At long last, with these questions and thoughts swirling through her mind, she finally succumbed to the arms of Morpheus.

It was mid-morning by the time Elizabeth reached the folly. Uncertain as to whether Mr. Darcy would expect her to resume their sessions the day after the gathering, Elizabeth nevertheless took pains to arrive as previously planned. He had said nothing about their arrangement the previous evening, but he really had neither the time nor the opportunity to confer with her about the status of their accustomed meetings. Consequently, it was with some disappointment, but not surprise, that Elizabeth found herself alone at the folly when she arrived. The morning was warm and she was tired after her fitful sleep, and thus instead of walking further down the laneways, she took a book out of her bag and settled down on a cool marble bench under the shade of the cupola to read.

She had been at her task for no more than ten minutes when the sound of hoof beats caught her attention and she looked up to see not Darcy, but Richard riding up. He dismounted and tied up his horse in a shaded area near the water and quickly strode up the hill to the folly where Elizabeth sat. "Good morning Elizabeth," he bowed politely.

"Richard, it's always a pleasure to see you!" She replied. "I trust your aunt deemed her rout a success?"

He laughed, his easy jovial nature making itself known. "Aunt Catherine would not allow anything in which she had a hand *not* to be a success. Yes, she is happy, and would only be happier if Will and Anne would finally accede to her wishes, ignore their own and announce their engagement. But fear not, Elizabeth, that will never happen."

She looked at him with confused eyes and he blinked as if coming to a sudden realisation. Deftly changing the subject, he continued, "You have done excellent work with my cousin. He seemed almost pleasant in company last night, certainly happier than I would have ever expected. I do not believe I have ever seen him engage in such long conversations with people he knows so little, and he owes it all to you. In fact, Will sent me with a message for you, apologising for not being able to greet you himself this morning and begging your forgiveness. For all his ineptitude in the salon, he is a wizard with numbers and Aunt Catherine has commanded him to give her some time to peruse the account books for Rosings. He does this every year and is most adept at whatever it is he sees in them. He really ought to teach Anne, and indeed she has asked to learn, but our aunt will have nothing of that. It is her way, I do believe, of ensuring his return each year until he realises that if he only marries poor Anne, the estate will be his."

"Does he wish that? To unite the estates of Rosings and Pemberley?"

"No, not at all. Pemberley provides him with more than sufficient income, and enough of his time is taken in its management. He has no desire for a second commitment, which is how he sees the situation. In fact, he has suggested that I marry Anne for that reason: It would relieve him of Aunt Catherine's constant badgering and provide me with a comfortable situation once I leave my position with the military." At Lizzy's raised eyebrows and cocked head, he added, "But I do not care for Anne in that way either, nor she me. We are cousins, not lovers, and I do not wish for the responsibilities that go along with such a large estate. Something small would suffice for me!" He gazed out over the fields and pathways and asked, "Would you care to walk? The lane over yonder is in shade and leads to a most attractive mill and pond." Smiling, Lizzy accepted as she stood and took his arm.

"I see that Mr. Darcy takes his responsibilities seriously," she said as they strolled. "He certainly does not seem as carefree as so many young men of his wealth."

"That is true. I am his senior by two years, but all too often, I feel that he is the older. He has a very strict sense of duty and he will work tirelessly when he feels something needs doing. He is a good man in that sense." There was something about Richard's words that struck

Lizzy as suggesting something, but she could not quite follow his thoughts.

Instead, she asked, "Has he many friends, then? It must be hard for him to maintain friendships when he is so serious and reluctant to engage in social activities."

At this, Richard chuckled, "As you must know, and as I noticed last night, you seem to find his friendship pleasant enough! But it is true, he has not many friends; however, those he has are most dear to him, and he is unfailingly loyal to them. I know I would trust him with my life, and his small group of intimates will hear nothing bad about him at all. To know him is to love him, but very, very few people are granted the opportunity to truly know him." Richard paused for a few moments, then continued his monologue.

"Indeed, there is one young man whom he met at their club, who claims he owes our Will everything he has. Bingley, the man's name is. He is a pleasant gentleman-like fellow—he is a great friend of Darcy's." He was looking straight ahead into the dappled light of the laneway and did not react when Elizabeth's head jerked up at the mention of Mr. Bingley's name. He continued blithely.

"Ah yes, of course, you know Bingley, and his terrible sisters. Caroline set her cap at me for a while, hoping that my older brother might die and leave me heir to my father's title. When my nephew was born, relieving me of that possible inheritance, she took further note of my impecunious state and looked, instead, to Will's fortunes. He may not be titled, but his pedigree is impeccable. She has as her greatest ambition the desire to remove from herself any taint of trade."

Elizabeth nodded, "For one whose father was a merchant, she is indeed quick to scorn those who still rely on trade for their living."

The colonel agreed. "Bingley's fortune does indeed come from trade. His father owned several prosperous business ventures in the north, and sold his interests at an exceptional price, leaving the family extremely wealthy. But despite Bingley's admirable income, his tainted background made him a target for some less savoury types. One night, so Will tells me, Bingley was the intended victim of a crew of drunken reprobates. They have the moral fibre of the lowest of the low, but their bloodlines are pure and thus are admitted to the finest establishments. Well, Will heard their scheming and stepped in at the last minute to rescue the pup from a fleecing at the tables, and a beating afterwards.

"Rising up like a hero from a novel to save an innocent victim is quite Will's style; as I mentioned, he has a very strong sense of right and wrong. What was most out of character for him was asking the poor youngster to join him for a drink afterwards. From there, the friendship was formed, and Bingley now dotes on Darcy's every word, while Darcy feels it his God-given responsibility to see the young pup right and keep him out of trouble."

"Oh! yes," said Elizabeth drily, thinking back to how Mr. Bingley had abandoned Netherfield in such haste, and left poor Jane's heart in the dirt behind his carriage, "Mr. Darcy is uncommonly kind to Mr. Bingley and takes a prodigious deal of care of him."

`Care of him! — Yes, I really believe Darcy does take care of him in those points where he most wants care. From something that he told me in our journey hither, I have reason to think Bingley very much indebted to him. At least, I believe it was Bingley of whom he spoke; he told me no specific information, for It is a circumstance which Darcy, of course, would not wish to be generally known, because if it were to get round to the lady's family, it would be an unpleasant thing."

Now Elizabeth's curiosity was most piqued; whatever could he mean? Most certainly, Mr. Darcy had been quite unpleasant during his visit at Netherfield, but that was all due to his discomfort with people unfamiliar to him—was it not? What might he have done, and who was the lady?

"I am most perplexed, sir," she whispered. "Was Mr. Bingley in some sort of trouble?"

"Please remember that I have not much reason for supposing it to be Bingley," Richard replied. "For I really have only my guesses upon which to rely. What he told me was merely this; that he congratulated himself on having lately saved a friend from the inconveniences of a most imprudent marriage, but without mentioning names or any other particulars, and I only suspected it to be Bingley from believing him the kind of young man to get into a scrape of that sort, and from knowing them to have been together the whole of last summer."

No! Surely it could not be... Surely Mr. Darcy did not separate Mr. Bingley from her sister Jane! She had to inquire further. With a tremulous voice she asked, "Did Mr. Darcy give you his reasons for this interference?"

"I understood that there were some very strong objections against the lady."

These words, uttered with such carelessness, turned Elizabeth's world dark. Every hope she had still held for her sister's future happiness vanished, and every charitable thought she had held for Mr. Darcy disappeared as quickly.

So it was true. Mr. Darcy, who openly entered into a close friendship with a family just one generation from trade, would dare to think that a country squire's daughter—the child of a gentleman in possession of his own estate—was not good enough for that friend! Or perhaps it was her mother, her uncouth mother, always going on at full voice about marrying off her daughters to the richest man willing. And her sisters, silly, thoughtless, flirtatious Lydia, and dour, stern Mary with her weak voice and endless concertos. They were not, perhaps, the people one would choose for a family, but sweet, charming, and beautiful Jane was all but perfect. This was terrible! All the time she had been imagining herself to have misunderstood Mr. Darcy, he had been the proud, officious and arrogant man she had initially supposed him to be.

"Elizabeth, are you well? You are suddenly so silent." Richard guided her to a bench in the shade where she might sit, concern etched in each syllable and gesture.

"I am well, but this story alarms me," she replied quietly. "I am thinking of what you have been telling me," said she. "Why was he to be the judge?"

"You are rather disposed to call his interference officious?"

Sitting up stiffly, she announced, "I do not see what right Mr. Darcy had to decide on the propriety of his friend's inclination, or why, upon his own judgement alone, he was to determine and direct in what manner that friend was to be happy. But," she continued, recollecting herself, "as we know none of the particulars, it is not fair to condemn him. It is not to be supposed that there was much affection in the case."

"That is not an unnatural surmise," said Colonel Fitzwilliam, "but it is lessening the honour of my cousin's triumph very sadly."

"Yes, his triumph." She sighed. "I'm afraid, Richard, I am suddenly feeling unwell. Perhaps this heat is stronger than I had expected. I had best return to the parsonage. I am well enough to walk alone," she added, feeling unfit to continue any conversation with him. She waved off his entreaties to accompany her with the most civil words she could manage and stormed off back down the laneway in angry solitude.

How dare he! How dare Darcy have had the impertinence to separate Bingley from sweet Jane? And after giving the neighbourhood every suggestion of a forthcoming attachment, he had not only broken Jane's heart, but left her embarrassed in front of their society and the object of everyone's a pity. The Bennets, the lowly Bennets, might not be suitable for the high and mighty Darcys of the world, especially with the lower connexions on her mother's side—one uncle a country attorney, another in business in London—but surely, for Mr. Bingley to marry into the gentry was a social improvement; he clearly admired Jane almost as much as she liked him, and a marriage between the two could only be seen positively on both sides. What possible sense of superiority could have induced the man to divide two such well-suited people as he did?

Could it possibly be that Miss Bingley was correct, and that Darcy had Bingley in mind for his sister? Was there some previous attachment between the two? But if that were so, Bingley would not have favoured Jane as he did; as much as his genial and lighthearted nature seemed at great odds with Darcy's stern and dour mien, he was, by all accounts, an honourable man and would not have toyed thus with a young woman's affections.

Every positive thought that Elizabeth had entertained about Mr. Darcy vanished as a puff of smoke. He was uncompromising and perplexing, with difficulties engaging in social activities, to be sure, but had she merely misunderstood the root behind his behaviour? No, in essence, he was still the unpleasant and arrogant man he had always appeared to be. She was disgusted with him, and with herself for her efforts to help a man whom she had much rather despise! And as to that uncomfortable, unsettled feeling that troubled her soul, the sensation of a leaden block replacing her heart, what should she make of that? That must be the weight of the sorrow she felt for her sister. Surely, that's what it was.

With these roiling emotions of dismay, anger and disappointment vying for primacy in her breast, she stormed back into the parsonage and, claiming a headache, retired to her room.

Chapter Nine

A More Unpleasant Visit

Lizzy's headache had not much eased by the time the Collins planned to leave for the dinner to which they had been invited at Rosings, and Charlotte, seeing her friend's pale face and obvious discomfort, reluctantly agreed that Elizabeth should remain at the parsonage to rest. Mr. Collins was decidedly unhappy with this decision—"Lady Catherine, my esteemed patroness, specifically indicated that we must all attend!"—but ultimately he too was convinced that little good could come of bringing an ill guest to faint, or worse, before the magnificent Lady Catherine.

The Collins and Maria soon departed, and Elizabeth was left in the welcome silence of the house. She soaked a towel in cool lavender and mint water and slept for a short time with the soothing cloth draped across her forehead in the hopes of easing her head. When she awakened, she was much improved and she rose from her bed and moved to the window to survey what was left of the day. The sun was now low on the horizon, bathing the surrounding gardens and distant trees in a warm and gentle golden and gilding the leaves and rooftops of the village, just visible from her room. Exhausted by her tumultuous morning and consequent headache, and revived by her rest, Elizabeth was feeling hungry and she dressed quickly before descending the stairs to seek what she might find in the kitchen.

Satisfied with her simple meal, she retired to the small morning room where Charlotte was wont to spend her time, there to peruse once more the package of letters she had been receiving from Jane. Every letter she reread brought her thoughts back to the morning's awful revelation by the colonel, every word further inculcated in her mind the certainty of Mr. Darcy's arrogant hand in causing Jane's melancholy. The letters, Elizabeth observed, contained no actual complaint, nor was there any revival of past occurrences, nor any communication of present suffering. But in all, and in almost every line of each, there was a want of that cheerfulness which had been used to characterise her beloved sister's style. The poor girl was heartbroken, and Mr. Darcy was the devil at fault.

Her thoughts on this matter were interrupted by the door bell, and within moments, instead of Richard, whom she had half-expected to pay a visit to inquire after her health, in walked none other than the object of her unhappy ponderings: Mr. Darcy himself.

He walked in stiffly, almost unseeing, his gaze brushing over the room, but settling nowhere, as if his eyes were looking at but not seeing the objects they beheld. His gait was rigid, and he paced the room for several moments, shoulders stiff, arms inflexible by his sides. His face was almost blank, holding only a hint of that same arrogant regard that had so quickly earned him the dislike of every member of Meryton society. In short, there was nothing left of the friendly, engaging man with whom Lizzy had spoken so enjoyably just the night before; in his place was the proud, haughty and disdainful statue of their first unfortunate meeting. If Elizabeth had been less angry at him for his imperious and cavalier hand in separating Jane and Mr. Bingley, she might have found some sympathy for him and inquired after his state of mind. As it was, in her cold fury, she merely felt justified in her judgement that her more recent opinions of him had been the true mistake, and that her initial impression was, after all, correct.

"Miss Bennet," he stated at last, all recent informalities forgotten, "Mrs. Collins informed us that you were ill. I hope you are improved." His words were polite enough, but his voice suggested indifference. He hardly looked at her face, his eyes refusing to meet her own.

Manners necessitated a civil response. "I am much improved, thank you." Her voice was as cold as his, and she made no effort to hide her anger from her expression. But Darcy seemed to notice none of this. He paced the room again, sat down in a chair by the fireplace, then almost immediately rose again and resumed pacing.

At length, he moved towards her and spoke once more, in that same inscrutable voice. "In vain have I struggled. It will not do. My feelings will not be repressed. You must allow me to tell you how ardently I admire and love you."

The words, at first, made no sense to her; her astonishment was beyond expression. She had never solicited his good impression, never hoped for or even considered his affection. If they had developed a particular friendship, that, she supposed, was only to be expected between a capable tutor and a willing student. She had, at no time, even entertained the possibility of anything more. The pain she felt was surely just in sympathy for dear Jane, and anger at having been so misled by Mr. Darcy's appearance of good. Further, in light of her discovery about his true nature, she was quite satisfied not to have encouraged any such affection. But now this odious, prideful man was speaking of his love and passion. She could scarcely believe what she was hearing. Mr. Darcy was asking her to marry him!

Mr. Darcy spoke well, but without emotion, most strange considering the content of his speech. He must, some part of Elizabeth's mind realised, have prepared and memorised his presentation, knowing that he would find the words eluding him should he try to offer them spontaneously.

It was clear that he had also not considered the emotional response of his audience whilst preparing his speech, for there were feelings besides those of the heart to be detailed, and he was not more eloquent on the subject of tenderness than of pride. In his wonted manner of categorising the world as he observed it, he enumerated the objections to their union, which he sought to disregard.

"I have long considered the chasm which separates our stations in life, and whilst my own societal prestige will assuredly be lessened by the connexion with your family, I am prepared for the disapprobation of society. Likewise, I have considered the lamentable behaviour of your younger sisters and your mother's lack of decorum and genteel manners—and even your own father's lapses in managing his estate and dealing with his family—and have reflected on the consequent disruption of the expectations of both myself and my family. Most troubling are the unwelcome connexions with relations in the merchant class, which is a lowering of everything to which I have been raised to aspire. And yet, despite all of these disadvantages, I find I have come to love you and wish to have you as my wife."

Elizabeth listened in shock, unable to accept what she heard as he listed these obstructions to his goals, over which he had triumphed, and which ought therefore to be remarked upon with horror, and his victory over them lauded. Worse, he seemed quite unaware that such emphasis on the faults of his beloved was unlikely to recommend his suit. How very like him, in all his arrogant superiority, to think so entirely of his own situation and nothing of that of the woman he was attempting to woo.

To offer such insults would be reason enough to refuse him; when added to her fresh ire at his meddling in the affairs of Jane, and even Mr. Wickham, they removed from Elizabeth any desire to even soften the blow of her rejection. The full fury which had grown within her breast since the colonel's unwitting revelation that morning expanded even more, and soon she was unable—and unwilling—to contain it further.

At last, when he stopped to draw breath, she stood and strode purposefully towards him. "Stop now, Mr. Darcy. It is customary, I believe, to express gratitude at such a declaration and offer, but I cannot—I have never desired your affections, and you have certainly bestowed them most unwillingly. I must deny your wishes. I shall not marry you." Her voice was icy, and she barely was able to control the tremor produced by her rage. She turned to leave the room, but Darcy's horrified voice stopped her. It was the first sign of emotion she had heard from him since he had entered.

"Not?" The very notion of being refused seemed quite unexpected, and he actually stepped back in shock. "And this is all the reply which I am to have the honour of expecting! And yet—I had thought we were friends. I believed your behaviour towards me to be encouragement. You must have been aware of my intentions!"

Elizabeth turned towards him and glared into his moss-green eyes, which she refused to allow to turn away. "Look at me, Mr. Darcy. Listen to my voice. What do you see? What do you hear?"

He blinked, surprised at her demand. After a moment, he spoke. "Your voice is hard, each syllable clearly enunciated, almost clipped. There is no gentle elision between sounds, and I hear the result of tension in your vocal cords. Looking at your face, your whole stance, I see you are tense in your entirety. Your posture is inflexible and rigid, your shoulders held slightly higher than usual. Your chin protrudes slightly, and your jaw is tense. Your eyes are narrow, and there is a furrow between your brows and high on your forehead." He shook his head slightly as if unwilling to accept what he was seeing. "You are angry!" The revelation was clearly a complete surprise to him.

"Not angry, Mr. Darcy. Furious. You would do well to recognise the difference." The words fell like hailstones between them. "Now please do me the favour of removing yourself from my presence."

Darcy did not move for a moment, but quickly regained some of his control and dignity. "I might, perhaps, wish to be informed why, with so little endeavour at civility, I am thus rejected. But it is of small importance."

"I might as well enquire," replied she, her anger radiating through every word she spoke, "why, with so evident a design of offending and insulting me, you chose to tell me that you liked me against your will, against your reason, and even against your character? Was not this some excuse for incivility, if I was uncivil?

"But I have other provocations. You know I have. Had not my own feelings decided against you, had they been indifferent, or had they even been favourable, do you think that any consideration would tempt me to accept the man, who has been the means of ruining, perhaps forever, the happiness of a most beloved sister?"

At this, Darcy froze in his place, his face drained of colour, but he quickly regained his composure, returning once more to the unfeeling and imperious man of her first acquaintance. Elizabeth paused and saw with no slight indignation that he was listening with an air which proved him wholly unmoved by any feeling of remorse. He even looked at her with a smile of affected incredulity.

"Can you deny that you have done it?" she repeated.

With assumed tranquillity he then replied, "I have no wish of denying that I did everything in my power to separate my friend from your sister, or that I rejoice in my success. Towards him I have been kinder than towards myself."

So it was true! Elizabeth felt her knees weaken. She had not understood this as yet, but until this moment, some part of her had hoped that Richard had been mistaken, that Mr. Darcy was, in fact, innocent of any misdealings between her sister and Mr. Bingley. Upon his confirmation, not only of his hand in the matter, but of his satisfaction with the results of his unwarranted meddling, proved to be a betrayal of Elizabeth herself as much as of her sister.

"Obnoxious, insufferable man!" she huffed beneath her breath. It would have been bad enough had Darcy stepped in where not wanted in order to bring his friend to his senses about his duties, about engagements in Town where he might be needed, or about other social responsibilities that precluded his remaining in Hertfordshire. But to so calmly and smugly take pleasure in the act of destroying an amour, with no real incentive that Elizabeth could decipher other than removing his friend from a poor alliance—that was beyond cruel. It was heartless.

If she had not been furious before, she now felt herself almost swept away by that emotion, and she fought to retain any sense in her words and clarity in her thoughts. "Kinder than towards yourself? How can you possibly think that you showed your friend any sort of kindness? You have a strange notion of friendship, sir, and it is one I wish little to experience. Jane loved him, and you broke her heart as readily as his! That, sir, is not what I think of as kindness!"

To his credit, Darcy blanched again briefly, then went red. He is angry now at my recognition of his true nature, Elizabeth decided. He had hoped to dupe me, to sway me to his favour. This knowledge of what he really thinks is beyond what he expected from me.

But to her surprise, Darcy responded, "I saw no such affection in her manner. Your sister is lovely and all that is charming, but I detected no special regard for my friend. I did not wish him trapped in a marriage to one who did not truly love him."

"You, sir, detected no special regard on the part of my sister? How dare you even suggest such a thing? You, who by your own admission, have no easy time in discerning the emotions and feelings of others? You, who were unable to see, upon walking into this room today, that I was in a state of great anger, directed towards you? You took it upon yourself to determine whether my sister, whose manner and nature are so composed and reserved, felt more towards your friend than towards his income? How dare you even think it?

"And then, to work so actively to separate them, as if they were toys at your disposal, to manipulate to your wishes? Is that the behaviour of a true friend? At any time, did you seek to discern the true feelings of your friend, to learn his thoughts and inclinations towards my sister? Or did you even once speak to her? How could you possibly think you should know better than those who have loved Jane all their lives how she feels towards your friend? You are a cruel man, and should be heartily ashamed of yourself!"

The ire that had previously turned her voice to ice was now a veritable flood of fury, and she stormed around the room, the aura of anger that surrounded her almost physically palpable.

Darcy cleared his throat as if wishing to speak, perhaps to justify his actions, but Elizabeth would hear nothing from him. Raising her hand, one finger pointed, she effectively silenced the words he was about to utter, before proceeding with her list of accusations.

"But it is not merely this affair," she continued after a few moments, "on which my sentiments are founded. Long before it had taken place, your character was unfolded in the recital which I received many months ago from Mr. Wickham. On this subject, what can you have to say? In what imaginary act of friendship can you here defend yourself? or under what misrepresentation, can you here impose upon others?

"I had recently begun to think myself misled by Mr. Wickham: I had considered my earlier opinions of you mistaken, as we worked together to ease your conduct in society. You are a fine actor, Mr. Darcy, for one who claims to eschew deception. But whilst you may abhor deceit in others, you seem to have no difficulties in executing it yourself. When I considered the hours we spent together, you and I, deciphering and analysing social situations, I had truly come to think that you were a decent man whose only true faults lay in understanding how you presented yourself to others. In that light, Mr. Wickham's words seemed ill-considered and unjust, seeing that you were unable to defend yourself against them. But I was correct in my first impressions, I fear. I thought we might be friends, but now I find myself sorely disappointed. Alas, Mr. Darcy, you are the last man in the world I could be prevailed upon to offer my friendship now, let alone marry. Now please, leave me be."

"You are truly angry!" Darcy was bewildered. His words were a combination of a question and statement. He inhaled, a deep shuddering breath, seeking the gentlemanly behaviour he knew must be required at such a time. "I am most deeply sorry to hear of your sentiments. Forgive me for having taken up so much of your time, and accept my best wishes for your health and happiness." And without a further word, he turned and left the room

The space in which he had been standing seemed cold and empty, the air vacated by his commanding presence an endless void, and Elizabeth stepped forward into it, almost as if hoping to be comforted by the man she had just dismissed so abruptly and with such harsh words. Tears welled in her amber eyes and she wrapped her arms around herself, unheeding of the wet trail that led down her cheeks. She staggered backwards and fell onto the nearby sofa, the tears now streaming unchecked, and she wept for a good many minutes.

"Oh, Jane," she cried into her arms, "how you have been maligned. How poorly treated! Oh, that I could return in time to at least make your situation known to that odious man. You might be happy now, perhaps even married." She sobbed some more. "How dare he have mistaken your regard for Mr. Bingley? To think that you, of all the people in the world, would care only for a man's riches, is unfathomable. 'Tis true, you display your sentiments but little, but could he not have seen enough even to inquire? It is too sad, too awful to contemplate!"

And yet, even in this melancholy and accusatory frame of mind, Charlotte's words from so long ago reverberated through Lizzy's mind. "It is sometimes a disadvantage to be so very guarded," Charlotte had said to her, near the beginning of their acquaintance with the party from Netherfield. "If a woman conceals her affection from the object of it, she may lose the opportunity of fixing him. Bingley likes your sister undoubtedly; but he may never do more than like her, if she does not help him on."

"Oh, Jane," Lizzy repeated. "Was Charlotte correct? Did Mr. Bingley truly see no real evidence of your regard for him? Mr. Darcy was undoubtedly wrong in his actions, for he is only newly come to understanding the interpretation of feeling, and even that he does poorly, but did Mr. Bingley himself see so little in your placid countenance?" She moaned and the tears flowed afresh. "Oh, poor, poor Jane!"

She sat thus for a very long time, crying and helplessly recalling every instance of interaction between the various parties involved, until the sound of Lady Catherine's carriage intruded upon her woeful ponderings. Feeling ill capable of meeting the party with any degree of calm, or of encountering Charlotte's observation, she fled the room and hurried upstairs to her bed.

Chapter Ten

Explanations and Ruminations

The morning dawned bright and sunny, promising a beautiful day ahead, but Elizabeth felt as if storm clouds were all that waited on the horizon. She had slept ill, and awoke with a headache, the same meditation that had tormented her the night before still plaguing her every thought. She could not sit still to read, nor to sew for the poor of the parish, and when she sought to aid Charlotte in the still room, she spilt the lavender water and nearly put the wrong herbs in the liniment. "Lizzy, you are not yourself today," Charlotte had chastised her, "and are not helping me! Much as I love you, perhaps you should take yourself elsewhere lest I make mustard preserves and berry compresses for little Jenny Mullin's cough."

Thankful for a respite from the day's planned activities, and hopeful that the fresh air and sunshine might ease her mind and sore head, she grabbed her bonnet and was soon outside and walking towards the folly.

Why she made that her destination, she was uncertain; her feet seemed to carry her there of their own accord. "'Tis the cool shade in the fresh air of the outdoors," she reasoned as she approached the hillock on which the structure stood. She found purchase on one of the cool marble benches and took out her book to read, but her mind would not remain still enough to concentrate, and after reading the same words for the fifth time, comprehending not one of them, she resumed her exercise, heading now down to the lanes where she had walked so many times with her supposed friends.

A shadow beneath one of the trees caught her eye, and recognising its shape, she turned back abruptly, hoping to make her way out of the shadows and light before the owner of the shadow took note of her presence. But she was to be disappointed, for the shadow moved and called out in a rough voice, "Miss Bennet."

A lifetime of enforced civility coerced her to turn and reply in a suitable greeting, "Mr. Darcy." He was holding out a letter, which instinct required her to take, without thinking of the import of the action.

In the same rough voice, laden with emotions she had never heard from him before, he announced, "I have been walking in the grove some time in the hope of meeting you. Will you do me the honour of reading that letter?" And without waiting for a reply, he spun around and disappeared back into the shrubbery.

Elizabeth stared at the letter in her hand. The seal was soft, the wax fresh, and it was imprinted with the insignia from his ring: FD. She should not read it. She should take after him and return it, or better, cast it into the river where it would be rendered into rags and tatters, the ink forever ruined by the rushing water. But her fingers were already fumbling with that fresh wax seal, and before her mind came to a rational decision of how to proceed, the letter was open before her and her eyes flickered down to take in the first few words. It was dated that morning at eight o'clock, from Rosings.

Be not alarmed, Madam, on receiving this letter, by the apprehension of its containing any repetition of those sentiments, or renewal of those offers, which were last night so disgusting to you. I write without any intention of paining you, or humbling myself, by dwelling on wishes, which, for the happiness of both, cannot be too soon forgotten; and the effort which the formation and the perusal of this letter must occasion should have been spared, had not my character required it to be written and read. You must, therefore, pardon the freedom with which I demand your attention; your feelings, I know, will bestow it unwillingly, but I demand it of your justice.

Such was her surprise at Mr. Darcy's concern about his character that she found her eyes moving on the next few sentences.

As we have often discussed, I express myself much better through the written word than through extemporaneous speech. My nature renders me ill-equipped to acquit myself in person; these, therefore, are the true expressions of my thoughts, my incentives, and my intentions. I can only trust you to consider them with the fairness of nature which I know is fully resident within your being.

Before she knew what she was about, Elizabeth found herself back at the folly, sitting once more under the deep shade of the cupola, shielded from the strength of the morning's sun. Her earlier agitation was now stilled to deep curiosity, and whilst expecting no pleasure at what she was about to read, found herself most unwilling to discard this last opportunity to learn something of Mr. Darcy's nature. She had thought him a friend once. She owed him this one last chance to explain himself, even if she could never forgive him for his actions. She read in silence:

Two offences of a very different nature, and by no means of equal magnitude, you last night laid to my charge. The first, that, regardless of the sentiments of either, I had detached Mr. Bingley from your sister, we discussed, nay, fought over.

In reflection, you were correct. Until your kind offer of assistance with my social inadequacies, I had only lightly considered the impact of my words and actions upon others, and most especially in the realm of the emotional. Having been lauded from early childhood for my intellect and skills at solving problems, I have never learned to think about the feelings of others, which I am, as you well know, so poorly able to determine. Contrary to the nature of our discussions, I have until now always taken pride in this ability to remove myself from a situation and regard it analytically, and this I did with regard to my friend and your sister.

Mr. Bingley is a good friend and he accepts me as I am, and I him. But I have often seen him in love, for he is not a man to keep the exuberance of his emotions silent, and despite the preference I saw him show towards your sister, I did not perceive any regard beyond what I have so frequently seen him display towards his latest amour. But it was not until the evening of the dance at Netherfield that I had any apprehension of his feeling a serious attachment, when I heard talk that Bingley's attentions to your sister had given rise to a general expectation of their marriage. Until that moment, when it was so explicitly explained, I had not taken notice of my friend's inclinations. It was only then that I could perceive that his partiality for Miss Bennet was beyond what I had ever witnessed in him. This blindness on my part, I partly attribute to my inability to understand the emotions of others; I now also blame myself for not having paid the attention due to one whom I call a friend.

If I was so blind to my own dear friend's affections, he whose open nature I know so well, it should be little surprise that I was quite unable to observe any special regard on the part of Miss Bennet. She, I also watched. Her look and manners were open and cheerful, as engaging as ever, but without any symptom of particular regard that I could determine. It appears I was mistaken. I was in error. I did not believe her to be indifferent because I wished it; —I believed it on impartial conviction, as truly as I wished it in reason, which, as we have long determined, is a poor judge of the affections that roil within men's hearts.

Now Elizabeth felt the stirrings of emotion other than rage and hatred for this man. He had been confronted with his shortcomings and had confessed to them fully, acknowledging his error, even admitting some degree of regret. She had to read more.

But my purpose in coming between the two was altruistic; my objections to the marriage were not merely those which I last night acknowledged to have required the utmost force of passion to put aside in my own case; the want of connexion could not be so great an evil to my friend as to me. (How dare he bring this up once more?) But there were other causes of repugnance; foremost among these was the great emphasis your mother placed, in the hearing of the principal members of the community, on the monetary value of a union between your sister and my friend. If I had been concerned based on my own observations as to your sister's motivations, hearing the words from your mother convinced me that Miss Bennet was encouraging him more to satisfy your mother and her quest to marry off her daughters well. Any other objections regarding your mother's family and the want of propriety displayed by others in your family—I shan't dwell on your father's indifference or your youngest sister's unseemly flirtations—paled before what I believed to be a mercenary action on your parent's part, if not your sister's.

But amidst your concern for the defects of your nearest relations, and your displeasure at this representation of them, let it give you consolation to consider that to have conducted yourselves so as to avoid any share of the like censure is praise no less generally bestowed on you and your eldest sister, than it is honourable to the sense and disposition of both.

I will only say farther that, from what passed that evening, my opinion of all parties was confirmed, and every inducement heightened, which could have led me before to preserve my friend from what I esteemed a most unhappy connexion.

Elizabeth hung her head in shame. It was true. Her mother's unthinking words, her constant crowing about Mr. Bingley's five thousand pounds, her brazen shouts and obvious comments about how well Jane would do as the mistress of such an estate, coupled with her sister's placid nature, could only give a man such as Mr. Darcy—he who admitted to a scientific and unemotional analysis of the information most obvious to him—that Jane was nothing but a fortune-hunter, spurred on to her prey by her mother. Blind he might be to his friend's true feelings for Jane, and even more so for Jane's towards him, but in truth, Darcy had nothing in mind other than Bingley's ultimate happiness at heart, even if he had blundered so very badly in the management of it. Her anger towards him remained, but some small threads of sympathy, some minute filaments of understanding, now began to influence her rage and upset.

Mr. Darcy's letter next enumerated his actions, in concert with Bingley's sisters, to remove the man to town, with little thought of returning. How easily Bingley had been convinced of Jane's faint regard for him; how easily he let his friend and sisters persuade him that he had deceived himself as to her true feelings. Darcy himself admitted that had Bingley been stronger in his own sentiments, he should never have allowed himself to be this convinced; perhaps it was Bingley, and not Jane, who did not feel as deeply as he should. Darcy's letter continued:

There is but one part of my conduct in the whole affair, on which I do not reflect with satisfaction; it is that I condescended to adopt the measures of art so far as to conceal from him your sister's being in London for the winter. I knew it myself, as it was known to Miss Bingley, but her brother is even yet ignorant of it. Perhaps this concealment, this disguise, was beneath me.—It is done, however, and it was done for the best, according to my weakness of understanding at that time. On this subject I have nothing more to say, no other apology to offer. If I have wounded your sister's feelings, it was unknowingly done; and though the motives which governed me may to you very naturally appear insufficient, at the time I had no cause to condemn them. However, with my newfound understandings of the true workings of the heart, I may have made other decisions.

With respect to that other, more weighty, accusation, of having injured Mr. Wickham, I can only refute it by laying before you the whole of his connexion with my family. Although my supposed treatment of this man was the lesser part of your complaints against me, they comprise the larger part of the insult to my character, for in this case I am absolutely certain I have done no wrong.

"Done no wrong?" Lizzy snorted in exasperation. "He dares claim he has done no wrong? He, who openly admits his blindness? We shall see, Mr. Darcy, we shall see. But," she reckoned, "at least he fully admits his error in regard to my poor sister."

Of what he has particularly accused me, I am ignorant; but of the truth of what I shall relate, I can summon more than one witness of undoubted veracity.

Over the next page and more, Mr. Darcy proceeded to explain his whole history with Mr. Wickham, from the time they were both very young children to the present.

Mr. Wickham is the son of a very respectable man, who had for many years the management of all the Pemberley estates; and whose good conduct in the discharge of his trust naturally inclined my father to be of service to him; and on George Wickham, who was his god-son, his kindness was therefore liberally bestowed. My father supported him at school, and afterwards at Cambridge. My father was not only fond of this young man's society, whose manners were always engaging; he had also the highest opinion of him, and hoping the church would be his profession, intended to provide for him in it.

But, Mr. Darcy wrote in his letter, Wickham had not proven himself to be suitable for the church, being of a more dissolute nature than one wants in a clergyman, and when first Darcy's father, and then shortly, Wickham's, died, the young Mr. Wickham pronounced himself resolved against taking orders. In addition to his legacy of a thousand pounds from the late Mr. Darcy, Wickham had requested of his former playmate a sum of three thousand pounds in lieu of the living offered to him; this, he claimed, would enable him instead to study the law.

All connexion between us seemed now dissolved.... For about three years I heard little of him; but on the decease of the incumbent of the living which had been designed for him, he applied to me again by letter for the presentation. His circumstances were exceedingly bad. He had found the law a most unprofitable study, and was now absolutely resolved on being ordained, if I would present him to the living in question. You will hardly blame me for refusing to comply with this entreaty, or for resisting every repetition of it. His resentment was in proportion to the distress of his circumstances—and he was doubtless as violent in his abuse of me to others, as in his reproaches to myself.

Lizzy read those preceding words several times, berating herself again and again for her quick readiness to accept what Mr. Wickham had told her. "Even when I began to doubt him, I did not doubt enough to ask Mr. Darcy for his side of the tale. I was so willing to believe the lies against a man I disliked that I was wilfully blind to the truth. In this way, I am no better than Mr. Darcy himself, with respect to his hand in detaching my sister from Mr. Bingley. Oh, I have been as unseeing as he, but without his excuses."

The tears she had been holding back now flowed freely, threatening to mar the letter as surely as the stream into which she had thought to throw it upon its receipt. Holding the pages away from her wet face, she mopped the betraying tears with her handkerchief, and only when confident of controlling their fall a while longer, did she return to the missive.

Last summer he was again most painfully obtruded on my notice. I must now mention a circumstance which I would wish to forget myself, and which no obligation less than the present should induce me to unfold to any human being. Having said this much, I feel no doubt of your secrecy.

Oh, how she had been mistaken! The tears did fall, and freely, but now not at her own poor judgement, or at Mr. Darcy's high-handedness, but at the heartbreak and near-ruin of an innocent child. Mr. Darcy had written of the planned elopement of his sister—only fifteen years of age at the time—with none other than Mr. Wickham! The scoundrel had schemed with Mrs. Younge, a woman previously known to him, and now Miss Georgiana Darcy's companion, and in the course of a vacation at Ramsgate the previous summer, he had come upon the girl—accidentally, so he had said—and proceeded to woo her and convince her that she was in love with him!

It was merely by chance that Mr. Darcy had decided to come to Ramsgate himself mere days before the intended elopement which Georgiana had confessed to him, a most beloved brother.

You may imagine what I felt and how I acted. Regard for my sister's credit and feelings prevented any public exposure, but I wrote to Mr. Wickham, who left the place immediately, and Mrs. Younge was of course removed from her charge. Mr. Wickham's chief object was unquestionably my sister's fortune, which is thirty thousand pounds; but I cannot help supposing that the hope of revenging himself on me was a strong inducement. His revenge would have been complete indeed.

Now Lizzy's tears were for herself. To think of the girl—barely more than a child—heartbroken, embarrassed, grist for every scandal mill Society might have in its stores, that was cause enough for the most severe of anguish. The cad had as much as told her that she was worth no more than her dowry, and that revenge against her brother was of greater import to him than was her young and tender heart. No wonder Mr. Darcy was so concerned about his friend Bingley. Having, by the merest glance of good luck, saved his sister from a heartless fortune-hunter, he must see them everywhere. Coupled with the narrative and explanation he had given above, it was no wonder he had perceived Jane, and worse, their mother, to be less polished country versions of the same.

This, madam, is a faithful narrative of every event in which we have been concerned together; you will, I hope, acquit me henceforth of cruelty towards Mr. Wickham. You may possibly wonder why all this was not told you last night. But

I was not then master enough of myself to know what could or ought to be revealed. For the truth of every thing here related, I can appeal more particularly to the testimony of Colonel Fitzwilliam, who from our near relationship and constant intimacy, and still more as one of the executors of my father's will, has been unavoidably acquainted with every particular of these transactions. If your abhorrence of me should make my assertions valueless, you cannot be prevented by the same cause from confiding in my cousin; and that there may be the possibility of consulting him, I shall endeavour to find some opportunity of putting this letter in your hands in the course of the morning.

I have one final statement to add. Whilst I might have difficulties in ascertaining the emotions of others, as we have worked together, I have become most aware of my own. To that end, I must tell you that I love you, and shall treasure the memory of our brief acquaintance all the days of my life. God bless you.

She folded the now-tear-stained letter most carefully and placed it into her reticule, between the pages of her book to protect it. She had thought before that she had misunderstood Mr. Darcy. How much more so, now, did she ponder on this topic, and she wandered the laneways and trails in the park for many hours until, at last overcome by fatigue and hunger, and finally feeling enough in control of her expressions to face her friends, did she return to the parsonage.

Chapter Eleven

Journey

The next two weeks of the stay at Hunsford passed both remarkably swiftly and excruciatingly slowly. The day after handing her his letter, Mr. Darcy and Colonel Fitzwilliam had stopped by to pay a parting call before returning to London, but Elizabeth missed their visit. She was sorry not to have had one last conversation with Richard, but felt most relieved at not having to endure Mr. Darcy's company. What could she have said to him? The words were too fresh, the accusations against her family and even her character too acute.

Oh, he had not directly cast aspersions upon her, or upon Jane. But his comments about her mother—brash, loud and without refinement—about her intemperate family—these she meditated upon and came to the uncomfortable realisation that they cast no positive reflection upon herself. Worse, his confessions about his dealing with Mr. Wickham had thrown her into great self-doubt. She knew now that even when she had been most positively disposed towards Mr. Darcy and had begun questioning the purpose behind Mr. Wickham's cruel slander of his old childhood friend, she had not quite believed the stories to be untrue. She had questioned neither Mr. Wickham's motivations in telling such tales, designed only to injure, nor the impropriety of disclosing such intimate, personal information to such a recently formed acquaintance.

"How despicably have I acted!" she had groaned in the privacy of her room that first night. "What hubris I have shown! I, who have prided myself on my discernment, who have valued myself on my abilities, who have often disdained the generous candour of my sister, and gratified my vanity, in useless or blameable distrust!" No amount of pacing could dispel the shame she felt creeping its rosy way across her cheeks. "Oh, poor, awful me! How humiliating is this discovery!" She thought back to how her every interaction with Mr. Darcy had been coloured by that first awful night when he pronounced her merely tolerable, and how quick she had been to accept Mr. Wickham's cruel words, which she accepted blindly because they confirmed her dislike of the man who had wounded her pride. Pleased with the preference of one, and offended by the neglect of the other, on the very beginning of their acquaintance, she had courted prepossession and ignorance, and driven reason away, where either were concerned. "Till this moment," she moaned, "I never knew myself."

Yet these were not thoughts she could share with the author of her discovery, not yet. She must stew over them, come better to know herself. To meet with him now would bring her no solace, only the deepest humiliation. And later... she knew well there would be no later. She had spurned the man she had reluctantly grown to like, and who had confessed his love. He was proud, indeed, and would not renew his addresses, not after the manner in which she had abused him.

Consequently, as much as her sense of justice demanded she offer an apology, she was even more relieved at not being required to offer it quite yet. Mr. Darcy had taken the risk of writing her a letter; perhaps, once she had made peace with her embarrassment, she might take an equal risk and reply.

But for now, there were the necessary visits to Rosings, to condole with Lady Catherine on the loss of such fine young men from their company, trips into the village to procure small gifts and tokens for family members who would no doubt be expecting such, and, of course, packing, and (after Lady Catherine's censorious lecture on the correct way to go about it) repacking of trunks.

"Maria," Elizabeth had consoled the young girl after her third attempt to carry out Lady Catherine's instructions, "do not take her words so much to heart. She will not know how you have packed your trunks, and indeed, I do believe she has never so much as placed a handkerchief in one herself. She merely orders her maid around, and most likely arrives at her destinations with a trunk full of hopelessly creased frocks, which her poor maid must then seek to repair. Pack as you were wont to before!"

But Maria, terrified of disobeying her ladyship in any manner whatsoever, refused to take Lizzy's advice and proceeded to attempt, for a fourth time, to do exactly as she had been instructed, much to the detriment of her garments.

At last they arrived at their final evening in Hunsford, which necessitated a last dinner with Lady Catherine and Anne de Bourgh at Rosings. The meal was everything Lizzy had expected, and if there was no pleasure in it, this was nothing of a surprise. It was only at tea in the aftermath of the long and drawn-out meal, after Lady Catherine had tried, to no avail, to convince Elizabeth to remain some extra few weeks, that Anne managed to remove herself from her companion's stern company for a few moments to speak some words with her.

"I have hardly seen you these last weeks, Elizabeth," she said, holding a delicate plate of sweets in one frail hand. She stared at the pastries as if she were uncertain what, exactly one should do with them; certainly it seemed she had no intention of eating them and only took them as an appeasement to her mother. "After Richard and Will left, when we had no further cause to visit the folly, I had hoped to invite you to my suite for tea. But I had only been allowed out before because Mother thought Will was courting me and using Richard as a chaperon." She laughed quietly in her sad, brittle manner. "She will never understand that we have no intention to marry until such time as one of us weds somebody else."

Not knowing what to say in response to that, Elizabeth merely nodded and waited for Anne to continue. The young woman clearly had something to impart to her.

After a moment spent staring at the plate before her, Anne did indeed speak further. "My cousins left so suddenly. They had, at first, intended on leaving some weeks past, but Will kept delaying their departure. Mother, of course, believed it was because of me, but Richard and I knew better." She looked up at Elizabeth, her eyes full of meaning. "And then, without warning, they were gone. In the course of a day, less even, Will changed his plans from remaining at least another two weeks to packing and calling for the carriage immediately." She toyed with her sweets. "What happened, Elizabeth? I have never seen him so upset as after that last evening."

Elizabeth felt her face flush, and she found herself unable to meet Anne's eyes, which saw so much more than Elizabeth wished to show. So this is what it feels like, she suddenly realised. "We... we had a disagreement, over some matters relating to our earlier acquaintance. That is all I am at liberty to say."

Anne's eyes bored into her own with an intensity that left Elizabeth wondering if the other woman were able to read her mind. "I have seen Will confused, angry, frustrated, ill-at-ease, and as silent and unmoving as those awful statues in the upstairs drawing room. But I have never seen him so despondent. When he finds matters too difficult to take, he usually withdraws behind his stern facade, but upon my word, Lizzy, the night before he left, I thought he might be about to break into tears. Will you tell me what happened? I will never marry him, but he is my cousin and in that regard I do love him dearly."

Breathing deeply and blinking back unexpected tears of her own, Elizabeth replied, "It is not my story to tell, for it pertains to others who are not here to defend themselves. But we were both wrong, and we parted on unhappy terms because of it. I am sorry to have caused your cousin distress; I am certain he is rueful of the distress he caused me. But I doubt we shall ever meet again. When you next see him, please tell him I deeply regret any pain I caused him. I do not expect his forgiveness, but I have forgiven him."

Shaking her head with small, almost unnoticeable motions that nonetheless left the young woman's ear bobs swinging slightly, Anne sighed. "I shall do as you ask. But one thing I must let you know: Will does not resign easily from a challenge. Perhaps this is a positive aspect of his unusual character, for he does not always recognise when a situation is hopeless, and in refusing to acknowledge defeat, he often succeeds where all others might fail. Should he act thus, should he attempt to speak with you once more, please—for my sake—be kind. He is not an easy person to know, but he is the best of men."

Kindness. That was all she had now to offer. Perhaps one day it would be enough. "Yes," Lizzy whispered. "I have come to know that."

Any further discussion was thereupon ended by the imperious tones of Lady Catherine, demanding to know what her daughter and Miss Bennet were talking about. Lizzy was reminded so forcefully of those same words, uttered some weeks before, as she, the colonel and Mr. Darcy sat at the pianoforte. She glanced to the side room, where the instrument sat, silent and gleaming in the abundant light of too many candles, and let the flood of memories overtake her, saying only the necessary niceties for the benefit of her hostess, and desperately wishing to be gone.

The morrow dawned cloudy and damp, but with the hustle and ado of loading the trunks onto the chaise sent for them, along with the fuss of readying for the departure, the weather was forgotten.

"Have you had enough for breakfast, Lizzy?"

"Maria, you have forgotten your green pelisse. And where is your bonnet with the mauve flowers?"

"Cousin Elizabeth, I am certain you will relate to ALL your relatives how well we get along here in Hunsford, how fine our position, how great the condescension of Her Ladyship."

"Don't forget this basket of food for the carriage, and be sure to offer ale to the driver and manservant when you stop to change horses."

At last, with final farewells, stiff curtseys and—where appropriate—loving hugs dispensed with, they were off. Maria chatted aimlessly for a while: How grand their visit had been, how marvellous Rosings, how lovely the countryside. Elizabeth listened for some time until the girl grew tired of recounting every visit to the manor house and every detail of Charlotte's home and drifted into silence.

Maria's chatter about her sister Charlotte's happy situation left Lizzy thinking less sanguinely about her own sister's. As desperate as she was to see Jane, to hug her and hear all about her time in London, how could she look upon her without her face revealing every painful thought that had passed through her mind these last two weeks? Could she gaze with any equanimity at that beautiful and serene face whilst knowing that her placid and unruffled nature was the exact cause of her current distress? Should Lizzy tell Jane about the circumstances behind Mr. Bingley's unfortunate removal from Netherfield? No, surely not! For even had he remained, there was no certainty that an engagement would have ensued! Nor would it do to cast aspersions upon Mr. Bingley's admittedly weak nature. Would a man who was truly in love have been so easily convinced to leave the object of his affections? Or, perhaps, was Bingley merely infatuated, as Mr. Darcy suggested he had been so often in the past? No, she decided at last, there was no possible manner in which she could mention Mr. Bingley and his departure from Meryton without adding to Jane's low spirits and renewing her heartbreak.

But what of Lizzy's own tortured heart? Did she dare tell Jane of her discovery about Mr. Darcy? Jane loved her cousin Samuel as much as Lizzy did, and knew about the challenges the young lad faced in his dealings with others, but to have such intimate knowledge of a loved family member was so very different to sharing similar knowledge about a stranger. It did not require much contemplation for the decision to be made: Mr. Darcy's secret must remain his own, and must not be shared, even with Elizabeth's greatest confidante.

That decided, Lizzy then pondered what, if anything, to reveal about the strange courtship that Mr. Darcy had been carrying out without Lizzy's knowledge, and about his proposal, her refusal, and of course, that letter. Her fingers worked their way into her reticule, where they met the edges of that cherished and scolding letter, now protected by the hard covers of her book.

She had to tell Jane something of the matter; if she did not unburden her heart to someone, she felt it might burst from keeping so much inside it. But not yet; not until she had further time to contemplate her own feelings on the matter, feelings which were still most unsettled within her breast. She could not yet regret rejecting Mr. Darcy, but she was most distressed at the pain she had caused him—pain which at the time was given with full intention, but which she now realised was undeserved. And what of Mr. Wickham? How would Jane accept that information? It had been Jane, after all, who had counselled Lizzy not to form too rigid a dislike of Mr. Darcy, not to accept too blindly Mr. Wickham's words of the gentleman's supposed perfidy, to find, perhaps, a way in which both men might be vindicated. Jane could scarcely think ill of anybody; to learn of Mr. Wickham's lies and deceptions would be a hard blow indeed. That too, Lizzy decided, must wait.

By now, the carriage was rumbling over the cobblestone streets of London, and within a few minutes they would arrive at her aunt and uncle's townhouse. She was desperate to see her sister again, and longed for the comfort of her dear aunt's undemanding but intelligent conversation and her uncle's good humour and good sense. Summoning up a cheerful expression, she quickly rehearsed all the amusing and interesting anecdotes she might relate about her six weeks in Kent, without disclosing any unpleasant information about her visit.

Before much more time had elapsed, they had stopped, and a flurry of pastel skirts and cheerful faces tumbled from the front door to the house as Jane, Aunt Gardiner, and various and assorted cousins rushed out to greet the travellers. Almost before she had a moment to step foot onto the street beneath the chaise, Lizzy was in Jane's arms. "Oh, I have missed you!" Jane cried into her sister's ear.

"And I, you, Jane! Oh, how I could have used your kind heart and ready ear! But look, my cousins!" She pulled back from her sister's embrace to regard the four children clamouring for her attention.

A little girl with golden ringlets not quite held back by a ribbon at her nape was tugging at Lizzy's skirts. "Wizzy! Pick me up! Up!" she called in a high voice. Elizabeth scooped the three-year-old into her arms and nuzzled her soft neck. "How is my sweet Julia?" she cooed back at the little girl and was rewarded by a wet and somewhat sticky kiss on her cheek before Aunt Gardiner stepped in to the rescue.

"Julia, let Cousin Lizzy put you down now. I'm certain she wishes to come inside and rest after her journey."

"Up, up!" was Julia's reply, and Lizzy reassured her aunt that carrying the youngest of the Gardiner children was a pleasure and not a burden.

As she walked, she was careful not to trip over Helena, who was nearly seven and only slightly more aware of her behaviour. The two boys stood back slightly, but were clearly just as eager to greet and play with their favourite cousin. Jane was, of course, loved dearly by all, but she was a bit too serene and proper for these energetic children. Lizzy, they knew, would happily sit down on the floor with them, or fold paper boats in the back garden to release in the bird bath, or jump rope or make mud cakes. Ten-year-old James grinned a toothy smile that spread sunshine across his freckled face, and Samuel, more serious and feeling almost a man at the advanced age of twelve stood as still as a statue, only the slight twitch of his fingers betraying his excitement at being reunited with the cousin who had worked so hard with him, and whom he loved almost as much as his mother.

The party made it up the stairs to the entry hall with no incident, and formal introductions were made between the Gardiners and Maria Lucas, who immediately took to the little girls. Before they had a chance to sit down to tea, the girls and Maria had already made plans to decorate a bonnet that Helena had recently received as a gift.

Tea was accompanied by light conversation and general inquiries on the part of Mrs. Gardiner and Jane about the travellers' visit to Kent. Mrs. Gardiner had known Charlotte well, for on several occasions Charlotte had accompanied Lizzy to town for a visit, and she was most anxious to hear about her niece's good friend. She had not really known Maria, the girl being some years younger and not part of Lizzy's group of friends, and she also was most attentive and desirous to know the wide-eyed girl.

Once she had lost her natural trepidation at being in new company, Maria was happy to speak and expound on all her experiences and observations about her sister's new home, giving Lizzy the opportunity to sit back and observe the room. The little girls, her sweet young cousins, were exactly as she had expected, having seen them only recently at Christmas, and James was just what a ten-year-old boy should be—keen, learning his manners, and only sometimes inappropriate with his words and actions.

But now she looked at Samuel with new eyes. She adored this young man, so quiet and serious, but possessing a keen intellect and, when comfortable, a biting wit. Recalling all the weeks and months she had spent with him and Miss Pierce, all the frustrations and successes, she celebrated his victories, and thought anew of what might become of him. He would, she decided, be remarkably successful in his father's business, should he chose to take that line of living. He knew his strengths and weaknesses and would know how to surround himself with people who might balance out his shortcomings. But more than that, Lizzy now knew how he might present himself socially. Having seen Mr. Darcy and having watched that man battle with such similar troubles as young Samuel did and emerge victorious, she felt an optimism that was new to her. Mr. Darcy was, all his difficulties aside, a good man leading a good and useful life, with friends and family who cared for him, and Samuel would as well.

"You are wool-gathering, Lizzy," she heard her aunt exclaim. "What has you daydreaming so?"

"Oh, Aunt," Lizzy prevaricated, "I was merely enjoying watching the children. They are growing up so beautifully. And, I admit, I am somewhat fatigued from the journey. Oh no," she added quickly as she saw her aunt about to rise to call for a maid to lead Lizzy to her room, "I do not need to rest. I only let my mind wander for a moment as I let my weary bones settle into the chair. Do not be alarmed!"

"Well, my dear," her aunt countered, "you may wish to rest before dinner. We are expecting a guest, a most unusual young man, who brought himself to our notice about two weeks ago. He very presumptuously knocked at the door one day and introduced himself, and has become most good friends with our Sam. Despite my initial misgivings, I must now say that I approve most heartily of this budding friendship, and if you have no objections, Sam will join us at the dinner table, rather than eating in the nursery."

Lizzy smiled. "I would be honoured to dine with my cousin. Some of my wool-gathering dealt with how grown-up he has become since last I saw him. Tell me more of this new friend of his, if you will."

"I believe you know the gentleman," Aunt Gardiner said with a sly smile. "You know him quite well, if I am not mistaken. Sammy," she called to her son, "Would you tell Cousin Lizzy the name of your new friend?"

"I would be happy to do so, Mama," the lad replied. He turned to Elizabeth and intoned in his most proper voice, "His name is Mr. Fitzwilliam Darcy."

Chapter Twelve

Unexpected Company

I t was not until the children had been sent up to their rooms, and Elizabeth was in her own chamber chatting amicably with her dear aunt and beloved sister, that she finally broached the topic of the evening's dinner guest. "Aunt, you must tell me how he came upon your notice! I can scarcely believe the gentleman I know would comport himself thus!" She thought of his discomfort in new company and his expressed disdain at the very notion of interacting in social discourse with people he deemed below his rank. The role-playing activity with Richard and Anne, when she had suggested an interaction with a wealthy merchant came immediately to mind. How he had disdained even the suggestion of pretending to fraternise with his social inferiors! Likewise, his proposal, that odious and ill-advised proposal, had dripped with shame and contempt at the abasement of allying himself with the merchant class. Why, even she—the daughter of a landed gentleman— was deemed a threat to his status. Was this some joke? Surely the man she knew would not have stooped to come within a mile of Cheapside.

Elizabeth's hands flew as she talked and her eyes were bright. Her aunt, she knew well, was as perceptive as she herself, and had honed her natural abilities in the care of her son. This beloved relation would almost certainly notice her agitation, and would determine to ascertain its source. Too late did Elizabeth attempt to settle her agitated hands and calm her expression, for she could see her aunt's eyes flicker across her countenance and could nearly hear the thoughts in that lady's head as she imagined undisclosed affection, some manner of turmoil, or more likely, a combination of the two. Neither could Elizabeth miss the glance between her aunt and Jane, whose mild expression belied her most intense curiosity, and she just barely managed to suppress a groan. She was found out!

With a final and futile attempt at equanimity, she asked, "However did he present himself to you in such an alarming and unaccustomed fashion?"

Turning her pale eyes on her niece, Mrs. Gardiner calmly recounted the first meeting. She seemed to recognise that questioning Elizabeth now would only serve to heighten the young woman's agitation and so spoke without elaboration. "He came around late in the afternoon some two weeks ago, whilst Jane and the children were at the park with Miss Pierce. I was alone in the salon tending to my correspondence and your uncle was in his study. I believe Mr. Darcy had made inquiries as to when your uncle would be at home, so as to set forth his reasons for the visit and to plead his case. I had been half-expecting my dear friend to visit at that time and upon hearing the door bell, I readied myself for her. You can only imagine my surprise when instead of cheerful and laughing Gwendolyn Dyson at the door, I should be greeted with the sight of tall and taciturn Mr. Darcy!" She chuckled at the memory. "He stood there at the threshold as if waiting to face a firing squad, so stiff and silent, with such a look of terror on his face."

"Oh, Aunt, I can imagine it," Lizzy interjected. "I have never seen him terrified, but have had cause to observe him when he is discomfited, and I know well that rigid stance of his, like a statue not quite come to life."

Jane added in her quiet, calm voice, "He would stand thus at assemblies in Meryton, both terrified and terrifying. I pitied him, knowing there must be something that troubled him so."

Elizabeth turned to stare at her sister in amazement, whilst Mrs. Gardiner shook her head sympathetically. "Poor man. Perhaps I am more accustomed to such behaviour than many, because of dear Sammy, but my first instinct was one of compassion. I could see the poor man was so uncomfortable, standing in a strange house, introducing himself to people whom he had never before met, or whom he was never likely to meet in normal circumstances. Well, Mrs. Danforth announced him and rushed off to summon your uncle, and it was all I could do to get the fellow to come inside the parlour and sit. Indeed, I thought he might pace a hole through my new carpets before your uncle arrived, poor lad." She clucked like a mother hen, although Elizabeth realised that her aunt was closer in age to Mr. Darcy than was she, herself. Indeed, Mrs. Gardiner was scarcely ten years Jane's senior, leaving her only three or four years older than Mr. Darcy.

"Well," Aunt Gardiner continued, "by the time your uncle arrived, the carpet was still intact, and we convinced our visitor to be seated. He introduced himself as Mr. Darcy of Pemberley and seemed ready to set himself upon a speech which he had clearly written and memorised. I hated to interrupt him, but I had to comment on his estate, for Pemberley is only a few short miles from where I lived as a child, and as we conversed about the area and those whom we might know in common, I felt him begin to be somewhat more easy.

"At length, he stated his reasons for intruding himself upon our notice. He remarked that a particularly kind and lovely young lady of his acquaintance had been guiding him in his quest to become more comfortable in social situations, having disclosed to him her previous success with a nephew." She looked pointedly at Elizabeth, whose eyes widened and whose fingers began worrying the tassels at the edge of a large pale blue cushion.

"Oh, Aunt, should I not have made mention of Samuel? I meant no harm, only to assure Mr. Darcy that I had some knowledge of helping people ill at ease in company." Worried now that she had somehow wronged her cousin she found it hard to meet her aunt's eyes, and wondered if this was how Mr. Darcy felt at every encounter. But her aunt quickly put her at ease.

"Fear not, Lizzy! I was not angry, only curious. It seemed an unusual topic to discuss with a stranger—rather intimate for one with whom you have only a short acquaintance."

Elizabeth blushed even more deeply now, recalling how readily she had accepted Mr. Wickham's confessions almost upon their first meeting, and how she had scorned Jane's attempts to excuse Mr. Darcy's reported behaviour. She forced her thoughts away from her shame and back towards her aunt, who had asked her how she recognised that Mr. Darcy had similar difficulties to Samuel.

"That, Aunt, was easy, for he admitted it himself. The moment he explained that he had difficulties catching the tone of conversations, my mind went immediately to Samuel, and the more Mr. Darcy talked, the more I was certain of what plagued him. I had in mind that I might be able to assist him somewhat, and I spoke my thoughts rather more quickly than I ought. But I had to mention my cousin, else why ever would a man like Mr. Darcy accept my guidance?"

A sly smile on her face and with eyebrows raised, Mrs. Gardiner posited, "The gentleman seems rather well-disposed towards you. He might have accepted regardless."

"Charlotte did always suggest that his glances were admiring rather than scornful, Lizzy," added Jane.

Now Lizzy's blushes stemmed from a different source, but she kept her voice even. "Pray tell, what did Mr. Darcy want here?"

"You had mentioned our name to him and he discovered our direction through some rather determined searching, and despite the great unease it caused him, he forced himself to walk up our stairs and ring on the door bell. I believe that took more determination and bravery than many soldiers face going into battle."

"Oh, I can well believe it!" Elizabeth breathed, before gesturing her aunt to continue.

With a chuckle, her aunt explained that Mr. Darcy had been so fascinated by all he had heard of young Master Samuel Gardiner that he wished to make the lad's acquaintance. He assured both parents that he would be more than satisfied to always have another person present—as much for Samuel's comfort as for his own—and after some consultation between them, the Gardiners accepted Mr. Darcy's request and invited him for luncheon the following day, which would give them time to introduce the idea to their son.

"To our surprise, Sammy took to Mr. Darcy immediately. We are so accustomed to him being most cautious around strangers and being highly agitated in conversing with anyone not very well known, but within moments, the two were chatting like old friends. Miss Pierce and I were both in the room, as the other children were in the park with Nellie, but at no time did Sammy display the first sign of distress. It was almost if he recognised something of himself in his new friend. Before the afternoon was out, Mr. Darcy was indeed a friend."

Mrs. Gardiner looked once more at her niece. "And he is, indeed, a rather charming young man once he becomes comfortable with his company. And quite handsome, if you have not noticed," she added with a sidelong glance and a smirk as Lizzy felt herself blush yet again.

She continued, "I wondered, at first, at such a great man as Mr. Darcy deigning to be seen in our less exalted part of town, but that seemed not to bother him at all. Indeed, all of his discomfort seemed to revolve around the social niceties of making new acquaintances and attempting to make light conversation, and our different social status has been less than insignificant."

Elizabeth nodded. "I had wondered about that. I know he thought little of me when we first met and considered me far beneath his notice. He has also had less than complimentary matters to say about my mother..." she let her voice drift off, embarrassed at the memories her words evoked.

"But he has only the warmest words to say about you, Lizzy," Aunt Gardiner's eyes spoke more eloquently than her words.

"Oh, Aunt, I can hardly imagine so! Not after I abused the man so violently to his face. I should think that if he knew I were in town, he would find some reason to excuse himself from your planned dinner."

"What on earth do you mean, Lizzy? Mr. Darcy made no mention of any disagreement between you, and he certainly seemed most eager to attend to the conversation when your name was mentioned. He only had kind words, dearest, and his face would light up when he told us about your lessons together. What happened that you should have abused him thus?"

Thus, shamefaced and with tear-bright eyes, Elizabeth found herself relating almost the entirety of the circumstances around Mr. Bingley's removal from Netherfield and Mr. Darcy's proposal to her aunt, omitting only the tale of Miss Darcy's near-elopement with the wicked Mr. Wickham. "Oh, Jane, Aunt, the words with which I accused him! I, who thought myself so observant and sensitive to every nuance of thought and emotion! I, who prided myself on making such unerring judgements upon short meeting! I, who had the audacity and hubris to claim to teach these skills, which I seem not to possess myself. Oh, how can I ever face him? Surely he will never wish to see my face again in his life!" She reached to the dressing table for a handkerchief to wipe away the tears that her wavering self-control had failed to stop from flowing and turned her head towards the window.

Jane brought her sister into her arms for a fierce embrace and Mrs. Gardiner clucked; she surely recognised the reason behind her niece's agitation. She placed a cool hand upon Lizzy's restless ones and spoke quietly.

"Dearest, I am most confident that when Mr. Darcy sought us out, he was quite aware than any connexion with our family must, at some time, throw him into company with you. And," she paused slightly to capture her niece's full attention, "when mention was made of your coming visit, he most specifically requested to be able to join us so that he might enjoy your company once more." She pulled the now sobbing younger woman into her arms and held her as she wept.

"Oh, Lizzy, dearest, here is another handkerchief. Cry it all out. Mr. Darcy might not have the greatest innate skill at deciphering expressions, but when he is comfortable, his face betrays his to the world, and when he speaks of you, his visage does not suggest disdain or dislike. No, rather, it glows in admiration. Lizzy, he likes you so very much, and not even your abuses and cruel words have been able to change that. Come and meet with him at dinner, and be not sad or ashamed."

Eventually Elizabeth brought herself under better regulation and promised her aunt that she would behave herself most properly at dinner. As she wiped her face, she asked how Samuel had reacted to this new friendship. Mrs. Gardiner's lips curved into a soft and grateful smile as she spoke more about her oldest son.

"Lizzy, you will be all amazement when you see him tonight. I know the time of their friendship has been short, but already I see in Sammy a new confidence and maturity. Oh, no, fear not! Mr. Darcy is not trying to make my boy grow up before his time—I can assure you that I, your uncle, or Miss Pierce has been in the room with them so we know fully what they discuss. Mr. Darcy lets Sammy direct their conversation or activities. Sometimes they play chess, or discuss the races and calculate the probability of a certain horse winning. But they have also built paper boats and seen which floats the longest or travels the furthest out on the Serpentine, or they exercise in the back garden or the park across the way, at running or cricket or football."

"Mr. Darcy plays football? I should imagine such a thing far below him!" Lizzy snorted.

"You still have such preconceived ideas, Lizzy dearest. He is proud, to be sure, but it is the pride of dignity and not the arrogance of superiority. He runs with both of my boys and teaches them to kick the ball to best control its direction and speed, as any active man would do, as their own father does when he is not needed at his place of business.

"I believe that Mr. Darcy has let our young Sammy see how a lad such as himself might indeed become a most genteel and capable man; this is the new confidence I see. It is the confidence of knowing that all the work my boy has done, with your most vital help and Miss Pierce's, will allow him to prosper and live a good and satisfying life. His efforts are to a good end, and as he sees the evidence of this, he becomes a happier child. And as his contentment increases, so does his progress and success. Even his school master made mention of this just yesterday when he came to call upon walking home with Sammy after the day's lessons were over."

"Then I am most happy, Aunt, and shall do nothing to jeopardise this budding friendship. You know how I adore my cousin, and how I rejoice in the success of his hard work; I could never harm him." She wiped the last of the errant tears from her eyes and affected a cheerful grin. "Now, pray tell, what shall I wear for dinner? Shall we empty my trunk and examine whether any of the dresses not quite good enough for Lady Catherine de Bourgh of Rosings might possibly be adequate for Mr. and Mrs. Gardiner of Gracechurch Street?"

Despite her assurances to her sister and aunt, however, Elizabeth was more than slightly ill at ease at the thought of seeing Mr. Darcy once more. Of course he would be too well-bred to speak ill of her before her aunt and uncle; but did he really wish to see her once again? Surely not, after those horrid things she had said to him, and after she had so conclusively proven her own blindness! And yet, he had sought out an introduction with a family so far beneath him socially, and initiated a friendship with a boy just beginning his journey towards manhood, purely on the grounds of her information of them. What on earth could Mr. Darcy have hoped to gain from meeting young Samuel? There could be no material advantage to him, but from all her aunt had intimated, the friendship was genuine and of pleasure to both man and boy.

More amazing, Mr. Darcy had taken such a bold step and had exerted himself so greatly to risk the censure of his society by seeking the company of tradesmen and by denying his discomfort in unknown situations in so doing. He introduced himself to strangers! He fought to free himself from his protective walls in order to seek a new friend. In the midst of her mortification and anxiety, Elizabeth felt a strong thread of pride in her student!

These ruminations filled her head as she descended the stairs to the salon where she would await her relatives in anticipation of their dinner guest. As she entered the comfortable room, she noticed she was not the first to appear. Samuel was seated on the sofa with a book in his hands. He noticed her arrival and leapt to his feet. "Cousin Lizzy!" He was torn between greeting her as a gentleman should and his boyish inclination to run to her and wrap his eager arms around her.

She observed his internal struggle and satisfied both desires by curtseying most properly before walking over to him and bestowing a kiss upon his sandy head. She had to bend far less than in years past, and it would not be long before this lad would surpass her in height. He returned her kiss with a brief embrace before he bowed as a gentleman ought and returned to his book. His hugs and kisses had been hard-won, for as a young child, Samuel had resisted any physical displays of affection, and seemed quite bothered by any touch of another's skin upon his own. This, too, had been an obstacle to overcome, and whilst the boy would never be one to encourage the physical closeness sometimes seen between friends, he could now shake hands confidently and without betraying his discomfort.

Absently, Lizzy wondered if Mr. Darcy too shied away from all physical contact, before recalling his hand upon hers as they walked the lanes of Rosings, or as they sat quietly under the shade of the folly. She felt a wave of warmth suffuse her cheeks at the memory and breathed deeply to restore her equanimity. Before she could dwell too heavily upon these matters, she pushed the thought firmly from her head and addressed her young cousin, asking about his day and his studies, and about his friends at the school which he attended.

Although he looked everywhere but at his cousin's eyes, the boy chattered on about his experiences, requiring only the occasional question from Elizabeth to enable him to supply the information and details that any youth approaching his adolescence might be remiss in imparting. He had, he announced most proudly, been invited to spend the fortnight of the upcoming school holidays with his friend Robert Harwin, whose father owned a prosperous shipping company, and who was a good business associate of Mr. Gardiner.

"Papa has agreed, and we are to go to Margate!" Samuel announced with great excitement. He bounced on his chair and flapped his hands for a moment before glancing down and them in realisation of what they were doing. Stilling his recalcitrant appendages, he continued, "Is that not the most exciting news, Lizzy?" Then he paused, and added, "I do hope my new friend, Mr. Darcy, will not miss me too much. Do you think he shall?"

Elizabeth smiled to herself, but added in a most sincere voice, "I am certain he will, but he is also, by all accounts, a most busy man, and he will certainly find some activities to keep him engaged until your return." Samuel sat up a little straighter at this, and a proud and satisfied expression stole over his young face.

They talked generally of sea bathing and Margate, and of Samuel's studies at school for a few minutes until Mr. Gardiner strode into the room. He had been at his workplace when Elizabeth and Maria had arrived from Kent, and had yet to greet his favourite niece. He was Mrs. Bennet's younger brother, possessing all the refinement of character and common sense that his sister lacked. He was also a good businessman, owing as much of his success to his genial good nature and uncompromising honesty as to his business acumen, and was generally liked and respected in the community. His intelligence was clear in his bright eyes, both traits of which he had passed down to his son. The boy looked up as his father entered, and before Mr. Gardiner had a chance to open his mouth, Samuel cried out excitedly, "Papa, Papa, look who has come! It's Cousin Lizzy!"

Uncle and niece greeted each other as warmly as might be imagined, for they could not have doted upon each other more had they been given the choice of all the family in the world. Mr. Gardiner was genuinely delighted to have Elizabeth in his house. "Stay a few more weeks, Lizzy," he implored her. "Your aunt enjoys your company so, and I know your cousins adore you. You set a wonderful example for my little girls, and Jimmy pays so much more attention to his manners when you are here to chide him. And," he looked proudly upon his eldest son, "we all know how Samuel thrives in your company. Aunt Maddie agrees with me, and we shall write to your parents this evening if you will but agree. Think, Lizzy, of all the adventures we might have while you stay with us. How long has it been since you were last at the theatre or the museums, or the opera?"

And so it was decided, with very little convincing required on Uncle Gardiner's part, that Elizabeth would stay some further weeks with the family in Town. Within moments of this decision, Jane, Mrs. Gardiner and Maria entered the room, followed almost immediately by the housekeeper, announcing their guest. "Mr. Darcy of Pemberley has arrived."

Chapter Thirteen

Dinner at the Gardiners

If Mr. Darcy felt any discomfort being in Elizabeth's presence once more, nothing in his words or manner betrayed the fact. He looked comfortable in the Gardiner's salon, more so than at Rosings, or, in fact, anywhere outside of the folly or on the long walks they had taken through the grounds at his aunt's estate. He entered the room with an easy and friendly confidence and greeted his hosts in the manner of long-established friends well satisfied with each other's company. To Jane he bowed politely and inquired after her health. To Samuel, he inclined his head before shaking the youth's hand as he might an adult of his circle, which left a smug and proud grin on the lad's face. Neither seemed to mind the brief physical contact. He greeted Maria Lucas most cordially, asking after her sister with a look of genuine interest, and at last he turned to Elizabeth. He bowed to her, perhaps a touch more deeply than etiquette required, and when she curtseyed in return, he took her hand and brushed his lips over her fingertips. His actions were all that was polite and proper, but they left nobody with any doubts as to his intentions towards Elizabeth.

As they sat for a while before the meal was served, he reclined comfortably in the chair he was offered, conversing easily with Samuel and Mr. Gardiner, smiling freely and displaying yet another aspect of his fascinating character. Elizabeth tried not to stare at this stranger with the familiar face, this man who chatted with newly encountered social inferiors as if they were old and dear friends, who sought and cultivated the friendship of a youth, who taught children football and who smiled and laughed with the good nature of a natural socialite. She could scarcely reconcile what she saw now with the stony-faced and arrogant creature who had stalked the edges of the Meryton assembly rooms only a few short months before.

As discreet as she tried to be, Elizabeth's glances could not escape her aunt's keen observation. "It would be hard to believe that Mr. Darcy is not always so easy in company, that he and my Sammy share so many traits in this respect, had I not seen him with my own eyes upon his first visit," she whispered.

"Indeed!" came Lizzy's quiet reply. "I cannot account for this change, nor would I have believed it had I not seen it myself. It does you and my uncle great credit, Aunt, that he should be so very at ease here." Or, she considered in silence, that he should be here at all!

Suppressing a laugh and with kindly shining eyes, Mrs. Gardiner replied, "Perhaps, Lizzy, but I believe it does greater credit to you! For without your help, Sammy would not be the lad he is now, and Mr. Darcy would not have dared to make that very first visit. I believe we may all feel quite satisfied with ourselves in this result that we see before us." She now turned to Maria, who had been telling Jane all about Mr. Collins' closets, and entered into the conversation, leaving Elizabeth to join them or ponder the sight before her, as she desired.

Dinner was a pleasant and comfortable affair. It was Samuel's first meal with the adults, and he acquitted himself most admirably, seeking the approbation of both his favourite cousin and his new great friend. It was clear that Miss Pierce had spent much time with her charge, refining his manners for the dining room and ensuring he would be confident enough that the scrutiny of his company—even though they might be his loving family—would not shake his composure. Elizabeth resolved to spend a few moments with her friend Miss Pierce the following day to commend her on her solid instruction and to praise her student for his excellent execution of what he had been taught.

The conversation all around the table was light and most amiable, and the company small enough that all could participate in the discussion. Only Maria, unused to the Gardiners and half-terrified of Mr. Darcy, kept silent, although Jane, always kind and solicitous, strove valiantly to make the girl comfortable; the rest, including Samuel, participated fully, if sometimes disjointedly. Lizzy gazed upon her cousin and fairly glowed with pride at the fine young man he was becoming, especially when compared to the most awkward and uncommunicative child he had been not so many years before.

The topics of conversation ranged from the current selection of entertainments at the various theatres and private salons, to the weather, the latest news from the races (which garnered a frown from Mrs. Gardiner but no reprimands), to the newest advances in bridge-building. Samuel seemed fascinated with the topic, and when Mr. Darcy began talking about structural iron and the smelting facilities and factories in his home county of Derbyshire, Samuel all but begged for an invitation to tour some of these facilities.

To his credit, whilst Mr. Darcy was an expert on the smallest details about bridges, a fascination which bound him rather beyond the ordinary, he was able to keep the discussion interesting to all at the table and refrained from diverting into minutiae which would interest only other devotees. He enumerated some of the bridges near his estate and proved to have a gift for description, bringing to life the sights and sounds of the environs of his favourite structures, complete with animated recollections of the villages and the people who resided in them. His tales elicited sufficient oohs and aahs that by the end of the meal, the Gardiners had expressed an interest in visiting Derbyshire in the summer to see the neighbourhood and its bridges for themselves, and a corresponding invitation was issued by Mr. Darcy to stay with him at Pemberley whilst they were in his part of the county.

"You mentioned, upon our very first meeting, that you had once lived in Lambton," he directed at Mrs. Gardiner. "I am certain that should you travel north you will wish to visit your friends and relations there. The town is only five miles from Pemberley, and I would be most honoured to have you as my guests for the duration of your stay."

He continued so enthusiastically that the Gardiners could hardly refuse him. He then turned to Elizabeth and catching her eye and holding it, added, "It is my deepest hope that you might travel with your relatives, for I would like nothing more than to show you my home." He spoke with great meaning, once more leaving little doubt as to his feelings towards the lady. Mr. and Mrs. Gardiner said nothing but Lizzy noticed that they exchanged glances that spoke more eloquently than words. Maria stared at her plate and said nothing. Samuel, too, was oblivious to the unspoken conversation around him, and only asked more questions about iron bridges in the vicinity.

It was not until much later, after sweets had been served and the men had finished their port and rejoined the ladies in the salon, that Mr. Darcy at last approached Elizabeth to speak with her alone.

"Miss Elizabeth," he began, a strange look on his face, questioning and cautious.

"Mr. Darcy." She met his eyes briefly, then looked away, fighting a war of conflicting emotions that roiled within her breast, unable to identify any, let alone examine them. Was this how he felt when forced to meet another's gaze? Was this acute discomfort she felt now something he experienced with every encounter? The churning in her mind was almost unbearable, and she could hardly think what to say. Before she had the time to collect her thoughts, he came to her rescue.

"Your shoulders are pulled slightly forward, and your fingers are playing ceaselessly with the tassels on your shawl. You seem to find it difficult to maintain a steady regard, and your breathing is a bit more rapid than normal. Your chin is tucked in somewhat and you are worrying the inside of your lip, whilst your eyebrows are raised in the centre, with a slight furrow between them. Your nose, as always, is perfect." She could not help but look up at this recitation of her expression and stance, and now that he had captured her attention he continued, a small and satisfied grin stealing over his face. "All of that indicates that you are worried and ill-at-ease, and the way in which you cast your eyes towards me and then turn away as if burned suggests that I am the cause of your distress."

She inhaled quickly, embarrassed to have so poorly controlled her features. "Mr. Darcy, I...." Turning resolutely towards him she decided that an immediate apology was in order, both to right the wrong she felt she had committed and to help regain some measure of calm. He would accept direct words far better than obscure allusion and subtle suggestions. Fighting to keep her voice steady, she spoke quickly. "I am most heartily sorry, sir. My words to you in Hunsford were unpardonable. The things I said were most unwarranted and ill-considered, and my only excuse must be my pain at the knowledge of my sister's abandonment. If I had been more myself and had taken the time to listen to your words and your explanation—" she broke off, unable to formulate further thought.

His voice, when it came, was low and comforting, like rich honey on a wound. "Miss Elizabeth—Elizabeth—your words gave me much pause to think, and they were not, in fact, ill-directed. You were not wrong in your accusations, and I have taken what steps I am able to correct my errors. Allow me to apologise, too, for my gross misconceptions and missteps concerning your sister. I should never have interfered, knowing as I do my limitations, but having the hubris nonetheless to presume I knew more than my friend, whose heart and well-being were at stake. I admit I thought only of his welfare, but should have been more aware of my... unusual perspective in forming my opinions. I should have known that in matters of the feelings of others, I am not always right."

His voice now softened further and took on a *soupçon* of desperation. "It would please me greatly to renew our friendship. Please, if you will do me the honour, let us not think of our past wrongs towards each other, but forge forward, leaving these painful memories in the past." He looked down at his hands, only inches from her own, but refrained from reaching across that short space. Elizabeth felt her own hand being drawn to his, as if by a strong magnet, but mindful of the others in the room she maintained control over her limbs. Darcy continued, "I visit Samuel often. For the duration of your stay in London, would you allow me to call on you when I visit?"

Blinking rapidly, Elizabeth felt a flush creep over her cheeks as she heard these words. Mr. Darcy did not hate her! He had every right to think ill of her, to be repulsed at the thought of her company, but instead he wished to call upon her! She felt once again the mortification she had experienced each time she had reread and contemplated his letter, and she relived the desperate sense of loss that had washed over her when she thought she had lost his good opinion forever. She was still unwilling to think too deeply about what that loss meant to her, but she found herself delighted and relieved by this reprieve.

"Yes, you may, Mr. Darcy," she breathed. "I would like that."

She was rewarded with a smile and a look in his eyes that she once might have found intimidating, but now knew was something completely different. He admired her. Casting about for some topic of conversation more suitable to the family salon after dinner, she offered to fetch tea for him, and upon returning with a cup and saucer for each of them, asked how he had found her family. "Surely I never gave you their direction," she explained.

"No, I object," came the response, "for you did. You happened, during a conversation on one of our walks at Rosings, to mention your uncle Gardiner, and on another occasion mentioned the name of the street upon which this house sits. After that finding the family was a simple matter." He spoke as plainly as if he had been asked to find his newspaper upon the breakfast table.

"But I can hardly recall what I said, and we spoke so often, of so many matters," Elizabeth countered. "Surely you do not remember every detail of every conversation. Did the name and street mean so much to you that you fixed them in your memory?"

"Aye, there was that extra incentive to recall your family's name and street, but in truth, I do recall almost everything I see and hear. My memory is not infallible, but few details are lost to me."

"Oh!" Elizabeth reddened, horrified at the thought that at any time, Mr. Darcy could relive her horrid refusal of him in his mind. "All those things I said to you...."

"Are in the past. Elizabeth. Just because I have the ability to remember every detail does not mean I do. Do not fret about them. If I bring your words back to mind, it is only to remind myself of my shortcomings when I find myself growing too arrogant. But it is true that my memory seems to be better than most. This was a blessing in school, to be certain, and also when...." he glanced around to ascertain that their discussion was not being overheard, "When my sister was being wooed by Mr. Wickham. A detail she had mentioned in passing at one time brought me to her side short days before the planned elopement, and after the scoundrel absconded, I was able to find him by recalling from an overheard conversation the name of the street where a cousin of his owned a boarding house. It was there I confronted him and obtained his confession, which I used to convince my poor sister not to pine for the cad."

His voice had been growing tighter as he spoke, his shoulders stiffer, and the statue mask had slowly been sliding over his face. Aware of his reactions, he breathed deeply and consciously to return himself to his previously felt ease. "I apologise, madam. I should not have mentioned that dreadful event."

"No, Mr. Darcy, I am the one to apologise, for I am the one who brought these memories to the fore. But pray, sir, let us talk of other things, happier things. I, for one, would be most curious to know what brought you to seek out my cousin in the first place. Surely a man of your status and maturity has no need to befriend a twelve-year-old lad, the son of mere merchants!"

"The need, no indeed. The wish, however, is different from the need. I wanted to meet this lad, to see the child of whom you had spoken so tenderly, to learn from his own lips what you had done for him. And, I admit, I wished to do as you instructed and practise my social skills in new and uncomfortable circumstances. In short, Miss Elizabeth, I wished to learn to recommend myself to strangers.

"Your aunt and uncle, however, made this a most difficult—nay, impossible—task, for they refused to remain strangers and became, instead, people whom I would be honoured to call friends." He acknowledged her shy smile with one of his own. "They are truly good people, Elizabeth, and you have every right to be proud of your relations. Where I might previously have thought meanly of them for their lower status, I see now that they are elegant and sophisticated people, most likely better learned and of better understanding than many of the highest circles. I came to meet Samuel and to test myself; I returned out of genuine respect and growing affection. If I ever spoke ill of your family, I see how very, very wrong I was."

"Alas, sir, you were not wrong at all." Now Elizabeth cast her eyes away. "My aunt and uncle are the best of people, but would that I could speak so of some of my closer relations. Lydia in particular is most vexing, for she is an incorrigible flirt, determined to make a display of herself, and I feel that most deeply. Would that my father had taken a firmer hand with her, most notably where the officers were concerned...." she blushed now, and apologised for her lapse in bringing Mr. Wickham back into the conversation. "I was most relieved to hear that the militia will be removing to Brighton for the summer. It will only be good for my younger sisters to be out of that sphere."

"Oh no, Lizzy, haven't you heard?" Jane walked up from behind Elizabeth. She had clearly heard her sister's last thoughts.

"Jane, I did not hear you approach! What are you saying? Have you news from home?"

Her lovely face unperturbed and serene, Jane replied, "I had a letter from Mary this morning. Lydia has been invited to join Colonel Forster's wife as her particular friend, and will be travelling to Brighton with the officers. Mary was most worried about the possible trouble Lydia might find, and Kitty is torn between wails of fury at not being invited and torrents of tears at being passed over. Mary, of course, writes of the evils of temptation, but from what I understood, the only one who succumbed to temptation was Papa, in choosing the easier path of allowing Lydia to go, instead of exercising his authority as parent to preserve some semblance of dignity in the family."

Elizabeth's face drained of blood and she felt her knees weaken as she fought for composure.

"Miss Elizabeth?" Darcy was concerned. "You have gone white and your mouth and brows suggest you are in distress. Sit, sit, and I shall bring you some wine."

"Nay, sir, I am well. 'Tis merely the thought of my sister, exposing herself to all nature of possible vices, away from any control or family or rational thought...."

"Lizzy," Jane countered, "Mrs. Forster is young, but Colonel Forster is a sensible man, and will not allow our sister to come to harm. All will be well."

"Always the optimist, Jane!" Lizzy allowed herself to laugh. "Yes, I shall have to accept that and hope you are correct. I must write to Papa to ask him to change his mind, but," she caught Mr. Darcy's eye, hoping to convey her decision not to reveal his sister's misadventure, "I have no particulars to relate to convince him of this folly. I can only hope he comes to see reason. Now," she said with a determination to be cheerful, "let us go and see what young Samuel thinks of his first dinner with the adults!"

Chapter Fourteen

Conversations

O ver the following days, a schedule of sorts developed. Mr. Darcy appeared at precisely nine o'clock on Monday, Wednesday and Friday morning. "I have allotted my time accordingly," he explained, "and conduct the business of my estate and local affairs on Tuesdays and Thursdays." He took an early breakfast with the family and visited with Samuel before the lad left for his day at the local school, whereupon he spent the remainder of the morning with the Miss Bennets and Miss Lucas, and, when she was not otherwise engaged, Mrs. Gardiner.

They might sit in the morning room and converse easily over tea and the newspaper, discussing the latest tidbits from the society pages, or at times, news from the battlegrounds of the Continent. Or, they might debate the merits of some recent publication of poetry or the performance of some theatrical production currently on the stage. At times, they would all walk with the younger children and Miss Pierce in the park, taking in the fresh late spring air whilst the children were permitted to expend their energy under their nursemaid's careful eye. Mr. Darcy had attempted to discuss his own situation with Miss Pierce, since Elizabeth had spoken so well of her, but she assured him that she herself could have done nothing beyond what Miss Elizabeth had done.

"Nay, sir," she had informed him, "You have taken Miss Bennet's lessons to heart, and have succeeded far beyond what I might have imagined, had you begun like young Master Gardiner. I believe, rather, that Miss Bennet has been of greater use to you than I ever might have been, for she is of your class, not a working girl like myself, and can guide you through the nuances of gentle society in a way that I never shall. Look to Miss Bennet, sir, for she is your better teacher!"

He related this to the lady in question as they walked one morning in the park. The swans had come to the shore to scavenge for crumbs or seeds or whatever other treats might be offered to them, and the Gardiner children were delighted at the sight. Little Julia was somewhat shy of the large white birds, but Helena, so much older and braver, strutted around with her knees locked and her feet pointed outward, announcing that she wished one day to become a swan herself! Jane was at the house with Maria, who pleaded a head ache, and Mrs. Gardiner was visiting a friend, thus leaving Mr. Darcy and Elizabeth to converse in some privacy.

"Miss Pierce insists that you are best able to help me find comfort in the clamour of society," the gentleman spoke as they sat on a bench near where the children and waterfowl played. "She might well be right. But what thought you of that final soirée at Rosings? I had hoped to speak with you about this earlier, but..."

"But other events intervened," Elizabeth finished for him in subdued tones. "For that I am sorry."

"We promised not to speak of that. However I would be most appreciative to know of your thoughts concerning the gathering."

"My thoughts, Mr. Darcy, are nothing compared to yours. I am not the pianoforte master, letting his star pupil free before an audience, later on to judge the performance. I am merely your guide; you are you own master. What thought you of the evening? How did you fare after my party returned to the parsonage?"

"It was much better than I had expected," he replied frankly. "Whilst the assault on my senses did occur, it was much less brutal than is often the case, and it came upon me less immediately. I believe that having some confidence in my ability to converse on meaningless matters contributed to my overall comfort, leaving me less vulnerable to the excesses of noise. I also had something on which to focus my energies, rather than on the discomfort of my surroundings. When I began to feel lost, I drew upon your exercises and, to some degree, was able to regain my composure. Being able to observe and interpret the unspoken aspects of a conversation—the gestures, the facial expressions, the glances—both added to my awareness of what was being discussed and gave me a task to keep from succumbing to the barrage of sound and light and smell."

"Watching you, I thought you looked quite comfortable, at least at the start of the evening. I did not speak with you after we returned to the room after our rest on the balcony. Did you find yourself at ease once more?"

"I did indeed! I had never thought to excuse myself for a short rest and then return to the battle. How much easier that was than to wage full war with my aunt and excuse myself entirely for the remainder of the evening. There!" he chortled. "I have used a metaphor!" Elizabeth saw him watch her face for her response, which she offered by means of a wide smile. Only then did he continue. "To take a short stroll outside or get some air is hardly even remarked upon. This shall certainly remain a key weapon in my arsenal!"

Elizabeth laughed, her eyes crinkling at the corners and glinting in the dappled sunlight as she did so. "So it is a war, then, Mr. Darcy? And every social encounter a skirmish? Who is the winner in these battles you fight? Nay, who, sir, is the enemy?"

He returned her smile. "Ah, another metaphor. Let me think on it... yes, I understand your meaning now. The enemy, alas, is myself, and yes, I do feel as if I stride into battle. Or, perhaps now, merely a minor fracas! But tell me, Miss Elizabeth, what thought you of Mr. and Mrs. St. Ives? Did you like them? For I have learned that they are in town, and I should like to invite them to my home for an evening of music... if you might agree to join us?" The sentence ended as a supplication. "I shall, of course," he quickly amended, "include your aunt and uncle and sister in the invitation. And Miss Lucas. When does she return home to Meryton?"

"On Monday next. Jane and I were to join her..."

She was unable to conclude her sentence at the look of dismay that overcame her companion's face. "Pray, tell me you are not leaving London, Elizabeth!" he cried. "We have so recently renewed our friendship; I should be most distressed to say goodbye to you so soon!"

Without conscious thought, she placed a reassuring hand on his forearm. "Do not be alarmed, sir, for I am not leaving! You may thank my aunt for that, for she has convinced me to remain until the family travels north in the summer. She wishes me to spend time with my cousins, and I am not averse to doing so! Sammy will be away with his friend for a fortnight, but he will return before long. And I do love the little girls, though they be but babies still. You may also thank my aunt and uncle," she teased, "for convincing my father that he may do without me for some further weeks! Mama cares little whether I am home or away, but Papa does miss having someone sensible with whom to discuss local affairs. Jane, sweet soul that she is, has every bit the understanding that I may claim, but she is so good, so quick to absolve blame, that she can hardly be depended upon for a gossip."

Giggling, she turned to her benchmate and asked, "And to whom do you turn when you feel the need to disparage your neighbours? I should hardly imagine Mr. Bingley could answer that role, for he is too much like Jane, too quick to be satisfied and to impose the benefit of the doubt, even where there is none." Her eyes clouded over as she spoke, and she was unable to remove the wistfulness from her voice.

Gently, Mr. Darcy asked, "Does Miss Bennet then return to Meryton with Miss Lucas, or will she also remain in town?"

"She returns with Maria."

"Then," Mr. Darcy announced with some firmness, "I must invite the residents of your uncle's house to my own home tomorrow for dinner, before the ladies leave us. I shall prevail upon my cousin, Richard's sister, that is, to play the hostess." He shifted in place upon the bench, as if struggling internally over some decision he had to make. He stared out over the water, where the children were being gathered up by Miss Pierce despite their protests, and then, after a moment of silence and having come to a decision, he suddenly announced, "I have just had news that might be pleasing, if I may be so lucky as to redeem myself with one whom I hope to still call friend. To that end, Miss Elizabeth, I find I must seek out your uncle to extend the invitation formally, and then I have a duty to perform." He rose and bowed over the lady's hand before bestowing a gentle kiss on her fingers. "Pray excuse me. Ah, here comes Miss Pierce with the children. Until tomorrow, Miss Elizabeth." And with his long strides, he turned and vanished down the path.

The invitation to Mr. Darcy's house was duly proffered and accepted, and the following afternoon, Mr. and Mrs. Gardiner, Elizabeth, Jane, Maria, and Samuel, entered the Gardiners' rather crowded town carriage and found themselves being transported to the fashionable area of town where Mr. Darcy's abode lay.

Mr. Darcy himself was standing at the rather grand front entrance to the town home, rather contrary to common custom, and he personally assisted the ladies out of the carriage, letting his hand rest somewhat longer than necessary upon Elizabeth's. Mrs. Gardiner's eyebrows rose at this sight and she exchanged a glance with her equally observant husband, but since Mr. Darcy had made his intentions clear, she said nothing.

Waiting just inside the house was a grand looking lady, a few years Mr. Darcy's senior, whom he introduced as Lady Philippa. "Lady Philippa is my cousin, sister to Colonel Fitzwilliam, of whom you might have heard mention," he explained to his guests. "She has graciously agreed to act as hostess this evening." Suitable bows and curtseys were exchanged, before he continued the introductions, now speaking to Lady Philippa, "Miss Elizabeth has met Richard, and I do believe they and Anne conspired against me at Rosings."

"Indeed, Miss Elizabeth," the lady's voice was low and deep. "And how did you find my brother? If he was successful in helping you avoid the worst of our aunt, he must not have left you with too terrible an impression. Do, come and sit by me, and we may gossip about those we know in common." To Elizabeth's surprise, the lady bestowed upon her a smile quite like Richard's, linked arms with her, and led her through the grand doorway at the end of the entrance hall, beckoning the others to follow.

The party now filed into a well-appointed and comfortable parlour where they would be served with a selection of sweetmeats and tea and where they might converse in comfort for a time before the meal was served. A large dog, similar to the one Colonel Fitzwilliam had brought along to Rosings, lounged at the foot of what must be his master's chair. As the guests entered, the hound raised its sleek head and cast intelligent eyes on the newcomers, then shifted to its feet and trotted over to Mr. Darcy. The man absently reached down and scratched the large grey head, evoking a gentle whimper from the animal.

"Cabal," he intoned to the animal in a voice Elizabeth had never before heard, "Sit." He pointed to the small rug by the fireplace near the chair, and the animal obediently returned to its former position, where it might protect its master from all harm.

"My dog," he needlessly informed his guests. "I ought not to make a habit of allowing him to remain when I have company, but most of my guests are known to him, and he to them, and they make little objection. Indeed, you are the first dinner guests outside of my immediate circle whom I have entertained here since my father passed on five years ago." He patted his thigh and the dog was almost immediately by his side again. Darcy knelt and more deliberately scratched the furred head once more. Then he rose, saying, "I find myself somewhat uncomfortable being a host, and Cabal, as always, helps me find the calm I often so desperately need."

"Am I of so little importance, then Cousin," Lady Philippa laughed, "that you value your hound above me?"

"No indeed," his response was serious, "but whilst I rely upon you in your role, I am nevertheless the master of this house and the host, which entails its own responsibilities, and Cabal's presence settles my mind." He gazed down at the placid hound, then returned his eyes to his company. "But you are here now," his voice brightened somewhat, "and

I am less anxious than I had expected. I can have Cabal returned to the upper floors if you prefer it."

Having grown up on a country estate, Elizabeth was comfortable with personal pets, and Mrs. Gardiner began to speak of her own dog growing up. "It is difficult in the city," she explained, "for us to have a large hound, but I do miss the animals we had around the house. Miss Pierce has suggested a small lapdog for Samuel, saying that having such a companion can be an effective means of helping him concentrate on appropriate behaviour and of settling him when events become difficult for him to manage. We have been considering her suggestion..." She allowed her thought to fade.

"Indeed, I find Cabal to be thus for me," Mr. Darcy's voice grew more animated. "He is comforting and ever-present, and I know he does not judge me poorly when I am troubled. When he is near, I have an easier time in company, although I know not why. I must admit I had him with me in my carriage on that first day I came to call on you, Mrs. Gardiner. Without his solid and reassuring presence, I would have turned tail and fled long before arriving at your house."

"Then, for certain, sir, let him stay!" cried Elizabeth.

"May I meet him?" Samuel asked. "I should like to know him, if he won't bite me."

Darcy led the lad to where Cabal had returned to his carpet by the hearth and showed him how to speak calmly to the beast and stroke its soft head. Before long, the lad was settled most happily at the animal's side. Cabal withstood the boy's tentative ministrations with the utmost of canine patience, and Samuel's eyes grew bright and his smile open. When he raised his head to look at his mother, Elizabeth could see her aunt's decision written upon her face to give much serious consideration to Miss Pierce's suggestion.

Tea was soon brought in by a young maid, and light and general conversation ensued. Lady Philippa was adept at engaging all of her guests and even shy Maria Lucas seemed happy and at ease. "Are you comfortable in that chair, Master Samuel?" the lady asked. "It is so lovely to see young faces in this room once more. We await only one guest."

At that sentence, Mr. Darcy sat up straight with a stricken look on his face. He schooled his features quickly, but Elizabeth, who had been most attentive to his deportment in his own house, noticed. Under the pretence of helping her to some tea, Mr. Darcy pulled her aside and quietly but desperately said, "Miss Elizabeth, I must ask your thoughts quickly. I still have time to act."

"What on earth is the matter, Mr. Darcy?" she replied in alarm.

"There is nothing wrong, but I do wish to avoid a rather bad social faux pas. I have indeed invited another guest this evening..." He left off as if uncertain how to proceed.

"But sir, this is your home and you may invite whomsoever you wish. If your cousin has no objection to this guest, why ever should I?"

"Indeed, that is true, but this guest is known to you, and until this very moment, I had not given thought to how my actions might affect one of our company. It was intended well, you must believe me, but all of a sudden I have come to feel that I have made a terrible mistake. I fear that once again I have failed to give thought to how my actions might affect others." He paused, flustered, and Elizabeth heard herself calmly and rather loudly asking how Mr. Darcy took his tea in order to cover the silence and to dispel any curiosity on the part of others in the room.

Then, more quietly, she added, "What have you done, and how may I be of help?"

Mr. Darcy's face fell as he replied, "I am afraid I will once again do harm to... well, to your sister." He breathed in deeply to fortify himself and then blurted out, "I invited Charles Bingley. He is only recently returned to town from visiting his family in the North, and I wished to make reparations for my cruel actions of last autumn. I wished to reunite him with Miss Bennet. But once again, I thought not of how inviting him this evening might affect both him and your sister. Pray tell, what shall I do? Shall I have my doorman keep him aside whilst I explain my error?"

"Oh!" Elizabeth exclaimed. "This is a quandary, sir! I do wish I had known of your plans earlier, so I might ask my sister of her thoughts and feelings in the matter. But it is done now, and too late to ask the parties involved. Does Mr. Bingley know of Jane's presence here tonight?"

"No, no he does not," Mr. Darcy sighed. "I have failed them, and you, once more."

"Me?" She was astounded. "How, pray tell, have you failed me?"

"I thought only of myself. You have worked so hard to help me learn to think of how my actions affect others, and yet, at this time when so much may depend upon a single meeting, I neglected all your words and lessons and thought only of myself and my own actions. And, in doing so, I have brought about yet another occasion to hurt one whom you love. I am most sorry, Elizabeth."

"'Tis not too late, sir. Instruct your butler to remove Mr. Bingley to another room when he arrives. I shall speak with Jane now, and when Mr. Bingley is ready, you must then speak with him. What you say will, of necessity, depend on Jane's response to me. You have not failed, sir, for whilst you thought of others later than you might have otherwise done, you did think of them. And your intentions, once again, were good. Rest easy while I speak with my sister."

As Mr. Darcy quickly exited the room in search of his butler, Elizabeth took a cup of tea over to Jane, and explained Mr. Darcy's lapse. If the lady were at all discomposed by the news that her former friend might be joining the party, her serene countenance did not express it. Only the slightest change in the direction of her gaze let Elizabeth, who had known her longer than almost everybody else, see that she was feeling distressed by the information.

"Mr. Bingley is invited?" she repeated, her voice unnaturally even. "How pleasant it will be to see him again."

"Oh, Jane," her sister replied warmly, "this surely must distress you. He knows not that you are here, and we do not know his thoughts."

"I am well, Lizzy, truly I am!" came the reply. Jane's voice was as calm and reasonable as ever, but now a flush was delicately stealing over her pale cheeks. "We may meet as common acquaintances, and all will be well. Do not worry over my account."

"Mr. Darcy is still able to put off the meeting, dearest."

"No, I wish to see him. Yes, it is my wish. I shall remain calm, and we may continue as friends. I have no worries that his intentions are other than neutral, for otherwise he would not have left in such a hurry last November. No, he suffers no attachment to me, and I shall manage with poise and equanimity. Indeed," said she, "once this first meeting is over, I shall feel perfectly easy. I know my own strength, and I shall never be embarrassed again by his coming. I am glad he dines here this evening. It will then be publicly seen that, on both sides, we meet only as common and indifferent acquaintances."

"Yes, very indifferent indeed," laughed Elizabeth. "Oh, Jane, take care."

"My dear Lizzy, you cannot think me so weak, as to be in danger now?"

"We shall have to see how the gentleman himself responds, but I think you may be in very great danger of making him as much in love with you as ever."

As soon as she had uttered these words, Jane gasped and whispered, "If he were ever in love with me, he should not have left." But Elizabeth had no opportunity to question her decision not to inform her sister of Mr. Darcy's machinations in removing Mr. Bingley from Netherfield, for at that moment, a footman approached her, requesting her presence in the library immediately. Mr. Bingley must surely have arrived, and Mr. Darcy needed her assistance!

Excusing herself, and asking Jane to cover for her absence with the excuse of needing to attend to private matters, Elizabeth slipped out of the room and followed the footman through the house towards the library. She hardly had time to take notice of her surroundings, but was aware that the house was most finely appointed, with the most elegant of fixtures and furnishings, while still remaining restrained and refined. There was none of the gaudy and ostentatious display of Rosings here, and Elizabeth wondered how much of the current state of the house was due to Mr. Darcy himself and how much to his parents before him, or possibly his sister.

All too soon she was at the door to the library, which the footman opened without ado and ushered her inside. Mr. Darcy stood by a bank of shelves near the fireplace, anxiety etched in his entire being, his posture rigid and his face a relief carved in stone.

"You came!" he breathed in disbelief.

"You thought I would not?"

"'Tis unorthodox. You will be missed. You will, of course, be free to explain the circumstances if asked. Thank you." He took her hands in his and squeezed them quickly before releasing them. "Thank you," he repeated. He furrowed his brow for a moment, then asked, "What of your sister? Is she in agreement?"

Lizzy nodded. "So she tells me. Her face and voice are as unruffled and serene as ever, but she is distracted by the news. Nevertheless, she assures me she is happy to meet with your friend and allow him back into her circle as a disinterested acquaintance."

"Disinterested!" Darcy shook his head in disbelief. "If you knew the trouble we took to convince him of her own indifference! No, please... I would not repeat this argument, for I know how wrong I was. But I can assure you that my friend's affections were engaged. He admired her greatly. I imagine he does so still."

The pain of this revelation was as acute now as it had been upon the first hearing of it, and yet with the knowledge of Darcy's reasoning, it was less troublesome to bear. Lizzy let out a long sigh and then asked after Mr. Bingley himself. "Is he here?"

"Mr. Bingley has only now arrived and awaits me in my study. Will you come with me as I speak with him? I find I am more able to consider others' points of view when you are with me."

She did not quite know how to respond to that last statement, and, instead, asked after Mr. Bingley.

"I have not yet seen him," Mr. Darcy explained. "I wished to have you with me when I explain my thoughtless actions of this evening."

"But sir, will he truly respond honestly and candidly if he sees me by your side? Not only am I somewhat of a stranger to him—someone to whom he would never open his heart—but I am the sister of the woman under discussion. I believe he must be allowed to have his true feelings heard, and this would never happen were I to accompany you."

Mr. Darcy's face paled again. "Damnation!" he exclaimed, then quickly apologised for his foul language. "I had not thought of that."

Searching for a solution, Elizabeth chewed her bottom lip, then proposed, "Why do you not go and greet your friend, and explain the situation. I shall await you here, and can join you in a moment if I am needed. This will be my excuse, too, for my absence from the salon. I stumbled upon your library and found myself so entranced with the books that I lost track of time! Everybody will believe that of me."

Mr. Darcy smiled, although his hands were clenching and releasing, his thumb worrying against his fingers. "Yes. That will do. My study is through those doors," indicating a set of doors between two sets of shelves, leading directly into the room adjacent. "Wish me luck, Elizabeth. I may lose a friend in this, but I must attempt to right my wrongs."

With that, he pulled open the connecting doors and walked through, his stance as rigid as ever it had been.

Chapter Fifteen

Righting a Wrong

Even with the door closed between them, in the silence of the library, Elizabeth could hear the conversation next door. What should she do? To interrupt the tête-à-tête would be disastrous for Mr. Darcy; he had screwed up the courage and all of his newly learned skills to confess both his sins and Jane's presence to his friend; an interruption now would send him back to the realm of the stiff, impersonal automaton whose cold hauteur spurred the disdain of an entire community within minutes. That would help neither Mr. Darcy nor Mr. Bingley. And yet, in good conscience, she felt most uncomfortable overhearing the conversation. It was a breach of trust, almost a betrayal. Mr. Bingley had no idea that she was present, and his words would not be tempered for her ears.

However, it seemed she had little choice, as Mr. Darcy began speaking the moment the doors were closed behind him.

"Charles," he said, "it is indeed a pleasure to see you again. How are your family? I hope your aunt is well. Have your sisters remained in Scarborough or do they join you in town?"

"Darcy!" came the cheerful response, "The pleasure is mine to be here once again. That must be the most civil speech I have ever heard you make. And I do not believe I have ever yet heard you ask after my sisters. They are well, and thankfully remain in the North with my aunt. I appreciate the invitation to dine this evening, for I have only today returned to town, but what is this great secret you must discuss, that your butler shuttled me directly to your study? Is Georgiana here? Is she well?"

Elizabeth heard some shuffling, which she imagined to be Mr. Darcy's feet, before the man spoke once more. "Georgiana is well and remains at Pemberley. No, I have other guests, about whom I need speak to you. But before that, I must make a confession and an apology, and beg your forgiveness. Should you decide not to stay to dine, I shall understand."

"What on earth is eating you, Darcy? This is so unlike you. Pray tell, what has happened, for it is surely something of great import! Speak, man, speak!" Elizabeth could hear Mr. Bingley's tone of voice shift from abundant good cheer to apprehensive coolness, and thence to outright worry. His words grew louder and faster, his rhythm of speech clipped.

"Charles, sit. Please, let me speak my piece. Then you may scold and chastise me to your heart's desire." And with that introduction, he related the entirety of his misdeeds concerning Jane in the autumn of the previous year. His recitation was answered with absolute silence that lasted more than a minute.

When Mr. Bingley did, at last, speak, his voice was very quiet and still, as cold and as hard as steel. "If I understand you, you fully admit your inability to clearly observe and understand the feelings of others, and yet you separated me from the woman I admired more than any other based not on her words, but on something her mother said in passing?"

Mr. Darcy must have nodded, because there was another short silence before Mr. Bingley continued, his voice as cold as the grave. "And further, you knew of her presence in London these last months, but concealed this knowledge from me? You encouraged me to visit my aunt in Scarborough, not because you were concerned for my well-being, but because you did not wish me to meet Miss Bennet by some happenstance." Now his voice began to rise in volume and fire. "Darcy, how could you? I have been pining up in Scarborough, hoping to mend my heart like the leather in my father's factories, and she was here all the time? And she loved me all the time! Did you think so little of me that you could not let me decide for myself whether the woman cared for me? I thought she did, I thought I knew that she did, and I stupidly allowed you and Caroline to convince me otherwise. I am sore ashamed to have called you friend. Now, if you please, I must leave and determine the whereabouts of my angel, that I may beg her forgiveness and try to woo her back. If you have any information as to where I might find her, I demand it now. You may apologise to your gathered guests, whoever they may be, for my absence. Then I will be gone."

Mr. Darcy replied, "I see you are upset. No, I can see by the firm line of your mouth and the way you are holding your hands, and by the narrowness of your eyes, that you are more than upset. Your voice too, suggests to me what you are feeling. You are very angry, and rightfully so."

"Darcy...." The name sounded like a threat to Elizabeth's overhearing ears.

"Charles, please, hear me out. I cannot justify what I did, but I can explain myself to some degree. You will not believe me when I say it, but I really had your best interests at heart, no matter how very wrong I was in my conclusions. I have come to know myself somewhat better of late, and I am telling you this in part to right my wrong, and in part to further work towards bettering myself as a man. But my primary concern, and the reason I have risked your wrath and the loss of your friendship, is to reunite two people who should, by rights, make their own decisions regarding each other.

"Your angel—Miss Bennet—is in my house now. She is one of the company here tonight. I invited you with this knowledge, and only lately thought to alert you to her presence here. I am a poor friend, Charles, and a sorry excuse for a man at times, but if you will abide my company for this one night only, I would be pleased to introduce you to her family, who join her."

Elizabeth heard a soft exhaling sound, most likely Mr. Bingley throwing himself into a chair. Then his voice came again, but without the cold knife-edge of fury. "Here? She is here? I must see her! Does she know...?"

"Yes, Miss Elizabeth has informed her that you were also invited. She would be pleased to see you."

"She still wishes to see me? After I abandoned her... I mean, Netherfield? Well, take me up, man, take me up! I can vent my spleen on you later, but now I must see my angel!"

ᴥ ᴥ ᴥ ᴥ ᴥ

The rest of the evening was surprisingly pleasant. Despite Elizabeth's—and Jane's—fears, there was very little discomfort felt when Mr. Bingley entered the salon where the family were sitting before the meal. Mr. Darcy had collected Elizabeth from the library, "where she was pursuing my collection of modern poetry," he explained to his friend, and the three had then walked together to join the others.

Upon sighting Mr. Bingley, Jane turned red, then paled, and then offered him a tentative and shy smile, to which he responded with one of his beaming grins. Immediately after the necessary introductions and greetings, he walked right over to Jane, where he proceeded to pull her slightly away from the group and talk earnestly with her for the remaining time before dinner was announced. Mrs. Gardiner's raised eyebrows were met with an arch smile on Elizabeth's part, as Mr. Darcy observed this silent conversation with a slight and confused frown. "I shall explain later," Elizabeth promised him, before taking his offered arm to be led to the dining room.

Conversation over the meal was light and convivial, with the group being small enough that all could participate should they wish it. Mr. Darcy sat at the head of the table, and Lady Philippa at the foot, with no deference to rank or status in between. Samuel was given the extreme honour of sitting at Mr. Darcy's side, and the smile on the boy's face was reward enough for any minor shortcomings in his contribution to the general discussion. Elizabeth was correct in her assessment that

Samuel's social abilities, with all the help he had received, were not even equal to where Mr. Darcy's had been before she had begun the improvement exercises with him; Samuel would face a lifetime of struggle in this realm, no matter how far he had advanced. As much as the lad clearly wished to join in the discussion, it was evident that he was still unsure how to begin or what to say. This was, of course, his first foray into the bewildering world of adult dining outside of the comfort of his own home, and he was, in addition, the youngest at the table by some years. Maria, the next in age, was nearly five years older than he and for all her shyness, was accustomed to dining in company; this alone could explain his awkwardness. However, he was unable to find an appropriate entrée into the discussion, and would rather, in his attempt to join the conversation, utter whatever unrelated comments happened to be in his thoughts at the moment.

Despite these unsuccessful attempts, Mr. Darcy paid the lad great attention, entertaining his off-topic remarks with equanimity and giving all serious consideration to his comments, at no time seeming in the least condescending or dismissive. He did not seem at all perturbed to excuse himself from other conversations to hear what his young friend had to say and attempted most gently to draw the boy into the general conversation. Elizabeth was struck anew at how he genuinely seemed to enjoy the boy's company. Indeed, at times he seemed so interested in what her young cousin was saying that he neglected the rest of the company for some minutes.

This kindness and unexpected sensitivity was not lost on either Mr. or Mrs. Gardiner, and it was clear that Mr. Darcy rose even higher in their estimations that evening than the exalted regard he had enjoyed before. Elizabeth was most pleased to see her student excelling so greatly at determining the unspoken needs of one of his guests, and at the obvious pleasure her favourite nephew was deriving from the experience. She was almost ready to forgive the man his thoughtlessness at inviting Mr. Bingley with so little warning to any of the concerned parties!

As for Mr. Bingley, he displayed every evidence of his good breeding and better nature, and allowed none of the barely contained fury from his interview with Mr. Darcy to impose upon his demeanour. He was cheerful and loquacious, asking after all the Bennet family and Meryton society in general with every indication of sincerity. He offered no excuses for his precipitous departure from the village the previous autumn, but did drop several hints that he might well be planning a return to Netherfield.

"My friend tells me you are to return to Hertfordshire soon, Miss Bennet," he remarked to Jane as the soup dishes were being cleared from the table.

"Yes, yes I am. On Monday, Maria and I leave my aunt's house to return to our homes. But I shall miss London," she added quietly.

"Oh, I do hope you shall not miss it excessively!" cried Mr. Bingley warmly, "for I have heard Hertfordshire is most pleasant in the spring and summer. Most pleasant indeed! And should I wish to return, I would want pleasant company, and I know there is much of that to be found there!"

Jane did not speak, but her blush answered for her.

And thus the evening continued in as agreeable a manner as could be imagined.

There was little conversation in the carriage on the journey back to the Gardiners' residence, for Samuel at last forgot his reticence and spoke at length and endlessly about the marvellous evening he had had. He was clearly so proud at being considered one of the adults in his new friend's eyes, and recounted the most unexpected details from the visit, including the number of forks at the dinner table, the ratio of raisin tarts to lemon pies at tea after the meal, and the details of the great crystal chandelier that hung in the salon in which they had sat. From there, he diverted into a monologue on the intricacies of the crystals in said chandelier, although Elizabeth could not imagine when the lad had found the time to examine it so closely, and thence into a lecture on the uses of crystals and shaped glass in the science of optics.

"Mr. Darcy has a small study set aside exclusively for the study of lenses," he announced, "and before I leave for Margate with Robert, he has offered to show me his collection. He said that Cousin Elizabeth and Mama are welcome to come as well, as is Robert. He then reminded me to ask Robert if lenses interested him as well, for I should have otherwise just brought him with me. There are several different types of lenses, including some fascinating parabolic lenses, which can gather light and focus it within the curve of the lens..." And on he spoke, until at last the carriage arrived at its destination and the Gardiners and their guests descended the stairs to return to the house, and thence to their beds.

As they sat talking quietly in Jane's room later on, the Bennet sisters could not help but go over the events of the evening. "Oh, Jane!" Elizabeth paused while brushing out Jane's long hair. "How pleased Mr. Bingley looked to see you once more. Shall I consider his future actions with respect to my favourite elder sister? For I believe I know all too well my sister's thoughts towards him!"

"Lizzy, you must not do so." Jane turned her head, causing Elizabeth to pause in her ministrations. "You must not suspect me. It mortifies me. I assure you that I have now learnt to enjoy his conversation as an agreeable and sensible young man, without having a wish beyond it. I am perfectly satisfied, from what his manners now are, that he never had any design of engaging my affection. It is only that he is blessed with greater sweetness of address, and a stronger desire of generally pleasing, than any other man."

"You are very cruel," said her sister, "you will not let me smile, and are provoking me to it every moment."

"How hard it is in some cases to be believed!"

"And how impossible in others! But Jane, tell me, is he what you remembered? Is he as pleasant, his manners as friendly? His attentions to you unchanged?"

The elder Miss Bennet sighed and took the brush from her sister's hand as she turned her attention back to her long hair. "Oh, Lizzy, he truly is everything I might desire. But I cannot think of that, not now. He gave no indication of any special regard..."

Elizabeth laughed. "If I do not see him back at Longbourn within a week of your return, I shall be very surprised indeed!"

Chapter Sixteen

An Unfortunate Event

Jane and Maria departed the following Monday for home as they had planned, leaving Elizabeth as the sole guest in the Gardiner house. The children were particularly pleased that she remained, for as much as they loved Jane's sweetness and loving nature, Cousin Lizzy was, to be blunt, much more fun! Jane was the perfect person to introduce her young cousins to the niceties of tea parties and how to look lovely in every setting, but Lizzy would sit on the floor over two opposing armies of tin soldiers, or would don a smock and make mud pies and sail paper boats in the birdbath that adorned the back garden. Her cousins adored her and she them, and she was sufficiently helpful to both her aunt and Miss Pierce, whom she counted as a friend, that everyone expressed hopes that she might stay indefinitely.

Samuel was now off school for the holidays, and was awaiting only the break that his friend's father had arranged before he would join Robert's family on their seaside trip. This was to be a week hence, and knowing the plan, Mr. Darcy made a point of coming every morning to visit his young friend. That Elizabeth was to be present seemed only to increase his enthusiasm for the visits. As per his previous habit, he would visit first with young Samuel, when the two would discuss such matters of interest to them and them alone, before attempting to become more socially adept in order to visit with the ladies of the house.

"You had, before, taken Tuesdays and Thursdays for your own affairs, Mr. Darcy," Elizabeth teased as they walked in the park after tea. The sun was unusually bright this particular day, and Mr. Darcy was wearing an odd pair of spectacles with coloured lenses which she had never before seen. Miss Pierce and the children raced ahead to try the paper boats they had recently completed, with a promise to feed the birds and ducks afterwards, leaving Elizabeth to quiz her companion in some privacy. "And yet," she continued her question, "today is Tuesday and you are here. Is it only to make my young cousin happy?" Mr. Darcy had brought Cabal at the request of Samuel, and the addition of a four-footed member to their party had brought high spirits to all the children and had brought to Lizzy's awareness once again how much her companion's behaviour changed according to his levels of comfort in his society. The dog was certainly an asset in helping Darcy maintain his relaxed and friendly disposition. How the birds would respond to Cabal's presence was a question yet to be resolved.

The gentleman chuckled. "Master Samuel's happiness has a direct influence upon your own, Miss Elizabeth, and your happiness is of great interest to me."

"Very prettily said, sir!" she returned with a light voice. "But surely you have business that needs attending."

"Indeed, I do. However, I find that for short periods, I am able to discharge the most necessary of my affairs in the later hours of the day. I have planned my schedule, and if I adhere to it strictly, I am in no danger of neglecting my obligations." They walked for a few moments, enjoying the warm sunlight and the light breezes that stirred the verdant spring foliage around them, then Mr. Darcy continued, "But I admit I shall miss Samuel when he is away. You might think me strange for entertaining the friendship of a twelve-year-old boy, but the truth of the matter is, I enjoy his company. He is most intelligent and his youth reminds me that I need not carry the weight of the world upon my shoulders. I have never before known someone who thinks as I do, and who finds the same fascination in those areas that consume me. His facility with numbers is marvellous to behold, and his comprehension of statistical probability rivals my own."

"You are a modest man, Mr. Darcy."

"No, I do not believe I am... Oh, you are teasing me! There is no need for false modesty when one knows one's abilities are superior. It is not boastful, merely factual. But once more, I beg we return to the topic. He has become interested in my collection of lenses, which delights me, for few other people will spend so many hours examining the properties of these gems."

"Lenses such as the ones you wear now?" Elizabeth could not help but wonder if Mr. Darcy's spectacles had inspired his interest in the subject, or if it had been the reverse.

"These are not lenses in the true sense of the word," he replied in a voice that brought to mind a stern governess delivering a lecture on some obscure aspect of German grammar. "These do not bend light, for they are but plain tinted glass. I wear them for the benefit of the green colour, which helps to diminish the extreme brightness of the sunlight as it reflects off the water. When I heard of today's plans and saw the sky, I chose to wear them in an attempt to lessen the brilliance of the light, which can trouble me. I had this pair made by my uncle's spectacles-maker after the practice of the Venetians, who live surrounded by such reflections of light on the water, and after the style of the actor Carlo Goldoni. Signore Goldoni was..."

He seemed ready to engage upon another monologue, but Elizabeth stayed him with a touch to his arm. He turned to her, his mouth open to continue speaking, but then took a breath and paused. "Yes. I see by your eyes—how they flit away and then return in an unnatural manner, as if you are forcing yourself to maintain your regard—that you are losing interest. Your smile, too, is not the relaxed smile of true mirth, but is somehow stiff and forced. See, I am an adept student, am I not? Mild disinterest. I am learning this expression well. I have said enough to satisfy your curiosity, but any more would be excessive. May I continue in my explanation of what I have proposed to Samuel and his friend?"

Elizabeth nodded with a wide smile. He was an adept student! "Please, sir, my interest in that is genuine."

And continue he did. "Samuel, Robert, and I have discussed adding mirrors to lenses as well, to make spyglasses that can see around corners, or to use the properties of parabolic lenses to enhance one's vision at night or in dark spaces. I know full well that this is of limited fascination to many people. However, Samuel is as taken with such interests as lenses as I am. This is why I value his friendship. We understand one another."

"And I am most truly pleased, sir. He is a fine young man and I am glad he has a friend in you."

"Then," Mr. Darcy turned fully to face Elizabeth, "I hope you will join us when Samuel comes on Thursday to my work room to see my collection and to start construction on the periscope we have discussed. I have presented the invitation to your uncle and aunt, and through them to Samuel's friend Robert and his parents. It may not be of the greatest interest to you, but perhaps I can tempt you with a selection of books to read whilst we work." His voice was so serious and intent that Elizabeth had no choice but to laugh indulgently and reply that she would be most happy to accompany her cousin.

By now they had reached the pond, which was indeed brilliant with a thousand spangles of reflected light. As the children watched their boats sail across the sparkling water, Elizabeth began to wish that she, too, was in possession of a pair of tinted spectacles, for the glare off the water was distracting in its intensity! But the children seemed not to be bothered in the slightest, and even Samuel laughed and dashed about with a carefree smile upon his face that seemed quite unaffected by the brightness. His boat lost to his brother's, but he contented himself by holding onto Cabal's lead and scratching the hound's head at intervals, to the apparent pleasure of both boy and dog.

When the experiment with the boats was complete, Miss Pierce lived up to her promise and handed small sacks of seed to the younger Gardiner children. Lizzy and Mr. Darcy chatted lightly with the governess as the children tossed the seeds to the waiting pigeons and waterfowl, at first one piece at a time, and then as their excitement grew, in greater quantities. Through this, Samuel stood aside under the shade of one of the large trees, lush with the bright green foliage of ripe springtime, one hand holding Cabal's lead, the other resting on the dog's furred head, as the beast sat calmly at his side.

"How well they get along together!" Lizzy directed Mr. Darcy's attention to the pair—boy and dog—in the shade of the tree, just a step away from the noisy children and the hungry birds, and yet a world apart. "I must talk to my aunt again to see if a pet dog could fit into the household. Perhaps you will have some advice for her on the best breeds. I imagine he would do better with one that is large and calm rather than an active sort of a pet."

"Indeed, Miss Bennet. I have some definite thoughts on the matter, and if she wishes, can inquire about a pup from one of the breeders in Derby—"

His thought was cut short by a great cry from the direction of the pond. Little Julia, in her exuberance and joy, had flung a great handful of seed into the air whilst spinning on her feet as small children are wont to do. Instead of landing at the edge of the pond, as she had surely expected, some of the seeds fell instead by Samuel, and some even ended up in his hair.

The pigeons, quite unconcerned as to where their food landed, began rushing towards the pair in the shade in a flurry of feathers and beaks and loud caws. Sammy's eyes widened in horror as the birds descended upon him. Some landed inches from his feet, pecking at the seeds on the grass before him; others had seen or smelled the kernels in his hair and flapped about his head. "No!" he cried, waving his hands about him. "No, no, no!"

The wild motion of his hands scattered the flock for a moment, but the damage had been done. Samuel's voice rang with panic, and as Lizzy watched, his eyes lost focus as he continued to cry out against the aborted attack of feathered fiends. He continued to flail wildly as he shouted, seemingly unaware of his surroundings.

"Miss Elizabeth, watch the children." Lizzy barely heard Miss Pierce's voice. It had a been so long a time since last she had witnessed her cousin so distressed that she was quite in shock. Beside her, she sensed rather than observed Mr. Darcy's similar reaction. He stood perfectly still, eyes fixed unblinking upon her poor cousin and the effects of the trauma caused by the birds.

She blinked. Miss Pierce had spoken, had needed her. "Yes, yes of course! The children." She gathered the youngsters about her, all three of them wrapped within the circle of her arms. Julia was now crying as well. "I made Sammy sad! I didn't wanna make him sad. I'm sorry!" The little girl wept, leaving wet stains on Elizabeth's walking dress and tearing at the flowers on her bonnet.

Lizzy murmured soothing sounds and tried, with half her attention, to calm the children, whilst watching Miss Pierce with a combination of horror and awe. Mr. Darcy still stood as if in a thrall, watching the proceedings, and Cabal rose to his paws, moving just far enough from Samuel so as not to be hurt by a mindless swing of an arm.

Miss Pierce took two careful steps towards the distraught lad, speaking in a low and calm voice with words that Elizabeth could not hear. Now that she was recovered from her shock, she knew the routine and understood what Miss Pierce was about. The words that the governess intoned were of little import; the speaker and soothing tone were much more vital to the woman's purpose. As Lizzy watched, Miss Pierce continued to address Sammy in that calm voice until the swinging of the arms allowed her to approach more closely, but not once did she attempt to touch the youth. After what seemed a very long time, the restless arms fell to Sammy's sides and the boy began to keen in a high pitched voice. He wrapped his arms about himself and rocked from side to side, keening and whimpering, until Cabal took a step towards him.

Lizzy started. Samuel had taken a great liking to the dog, but he was as yet a novelty, something new and unknown. Would the presence of the large beast cause her cousin to revert to his tantrum? She fought the urge to rush towards him, mindful still of the three young children within her arms, and ever aware of Mr. Darcy, still standing as still as a statue, but with his eyes so very alert. This was not the man who retreated within his self-made shell, but someone painfully aware of what was happening about him.

To her alarm, she saw Samuel start to move, but now it was not with the wild motions he had used against the descending flock of pigeons. Rather, he held out one hand at the perfect height, and Cabal sidled closer, until his head was directly under Sammy's hand. His fingers clenched and unclenched in the thick fur on the hound's head, until he was petting and stroking it. Gradually the keening lessened and then stopped, and Miss Pierce stepped forward again, holding out her own hand. This, too, Sammy grabbed, and then they were gathered into a small knot, woman, boy and dog, until all was calm once more.

"Miss Bennet, might I ask you to take the children home," Miss Pierce asked at last. "Master Samuel and I shall join you shortly. Mr. Darcy, might we borrow Cabal for the moment? We shall return him to you as soon as we return."

"Yes. Yes, of course." Elizabeth looked around to ensure her three charges had all of their belongings and then began to lead them back through the park and towards the lane that would return them to Gracechurch Street, Mr. Darcy at her side. He had said not a word since the birds had started their unintentional attack upon Samuel, and she knew not what he must be thinking. Was he horrified at the association now? Had he seen an aspect to his young acquaintance which would make him wish to discontinue the friendship? Was he embarrassed to have any connexion with such a family that would allow a boy of twelve years—nearly a man!—to exhibit such untoward behaviour in a public park? Every doubt in the world assailed her, and Mr. Darcy's continued silence did little to ease her roiling sensibilities.

It was only after the three younger children had been delivered safely into the arms of their mother, along with an explanation of why Miss Pierce and Samuel were not with them, that Mr. Darcy spoke. "Miss Elizabeth..." his voice was low, his words uncertain. "I am sorry..."

"I am the one who is sorry, sir. You should not have seen that. I ought to have explained, to have warned you, that Sammy still has his difficulties and unexpected reactions to ordinary occurrences. He will never be completely unaffected by whatever makes him different. If you would prefer to sever the relationship..."

Now it was his hand upon her arm that stopped her. "That was not my meaning, Miss Bennet. Not at all. When I saw the birds begin to swarm towards him, I felt myself react just as he did. I have the years and practice to moderate my response, but I felt only the greatest sympathy and care for your cousin. I was only sorry that he should have suffered so shocking an event that brought him to that state. Believe me, what I saw does not alter my regard for Master Samuel at all. Neither does it change my regard for you... and your family." He added the final words after a slight pause.

Elizabeth felt her face grow red. Even Mr. Darcy could not mistake such a blush. She turned quickly towards the window and walked over to look out over the street to seek out Miss Pierce and Sammy.

"They are coming," she answered her own question. "Sammy will likely not know what to say..."

"Then you will allow me to speak instead." She turned to see a pair of warm eyes meet and hold her own.

Within moments the door opened and Miss Pierce, Sammy, and Cabal entered the house. Having discharged his duties, Cabal sniffed out his master and padded across the floor to Mr. Darcy's side. Sammy seemed much improved, but very quiet.

Elizabeth whispered her great appreciation to Miss Pierce, who took her leave to find the younger children and Mrs. Gardiner, leaving Sammy in the entry hall. His face was calm, but his eyes were red and fixed firmly upon the floor by his feet.

"Birds terrify me," Mr. Darcy tossed off the comment as if observing the weather. "They are so unpredictable." Then, without waiting for a reply, he added, "I hope to see you on Thursday at my house with your friend Robert, when we shall build our spying devices. Miss Elizabeth, the offer of my library stands, should you find little interest in my workshop. I do look forward to seeing you both then. Please offer my regards to Mrs. Gardiner. I must be going."

He offered his hand to Samuel, who shook it without looking up from the floor, and then took Elizabeth's hand to press a kiss just above her fingertip, before leaving with Cabal on his heels. Sammy still said not a word, but as he turned towards the stairs which would take him to his rooms in the nursery, Elizabeth was gratified to see a small smile spread across his pale lips.

Chapter Seventeen

The Workshop

In the end, it transpired that Elizabeth did not need the recourse of Mr. Darcy's literary collection, for she found, to her own surprise, the study of lenses fascinating. Perhaps it was the lenses themselves, the clear slips of glass and crystal, that had the intriguing ability to literally change how she saw the world; perhaps it was the overwhelming variety of them—convex, concave, parabolic—which when set up in concert with each other had such amazing properties; perhaps, she admitted only to herself in the most private recesses of her mind, it was the man explaining his collection to the small group gathered in his workroom.

Samuel and his friend Robert stood rapt as Mr. Darcy described some of the lenses he had in his possession, and then explained how to set them up in the tubes he had acquired for the purpose, along with some small and specially designed mirrors and prisms, to create the periscopes he and Samuel had been planning for some days. "We shall construct ours according to the plans described by Johannes Hevelius in his work *Selenographia, sive Lunae descriptio,* which he published in 1647." He spread some sheets of paper, covered with diagrams and schematics upon a worktable and pointed out various aspects of the device they planned to construct. Two young heads nodded very seriously at this directive and quickly settled themselves at the well-lit work table to get to their tasks.

Robert, a gregarious freckled boy with a gap-toothed smile and a mop of fair hair, seemed as enthralled with the task as his serious friend, but unlike Samuel, he was less willing to study the device for its own sake.

"What shall we use these for once they are complete, sir?" he asked of his host. "Surely they must be put to some practical employment!"

Mr. Darcy and Samuel exchanged a glance that admitted neither had considered applications for their toys, but Mr. Darcy was quick to consider Robert's question. "Why, Robert, I believe we may use these to engage in some sort of game. The lenses will magnify the images suitably that one may engage in sending messages to a partner. If she is so kind, at tea once we have finished our devices, Miss Bennet can assist us in devising rules and objectives for our game. A scavenger hunt, perhaps, wherein each party tries to direct the other to a secret object whilst remaining out of direct sight, using the periscope to transmit clues."

"A fine idea, sir!" Robert beamed. Elizabeth smiled as well. Robert, she considered, was to Samuel what Mr. Bingley was to Mr. Darcy: a good friend with all the natural social graces and innate good humour that would provide a nice counterpoint to the other's solemnity and lack of social ease. She hoped the two boys would retain their friendship through the difficult years of adolescence and into adulthood.

"I would be most delighted to help you design this game," she announced. Her enthusiastic smile was evident in her voice. "I shall consider some of the aspects we must decide upon whilst you construct your devices, and let us discuss and set out the rules at tea, as Mr. Darcy wisely suggests."

This was most agreeable, and everybody set to work. The boys quickly became completely engaged in building their periscopes, as Mr.

Darcy hovered near them like a mother hen guarding her chicks, ready for any question about the materials or problems with the construction technique. When not answering the boys' queries, he talked quietly with Elizabeth, further explaining the properties of different lenses.

The subject matter was of more interest than she had supposed, and she found the enterprise quite entertaining. It became even more so when Mr. Darcy took her to one side of the room to show her his smaller, but still considerable, collection of prisms and cut crystals. The boys by now were quite comfortable at their tasks and required almost no input from their mentor, leaving the adults to talk with little interruption.

"I am, for some reason, much less interested in the physical properties of prisms," the gentleman explained to his guest, "but even I must admit they are quite beautiful. Whilst I do not study them as I do lenses, they are very closely related in the realms of optical science, and they can be most useful when putting the lenses to practical use. However, I admit that my interest seldom extends to the useful! I am content to study my lenses for their own sakes. Nevertheless, I have a reasonable collection of these prisms, and I hope you will find some interest in them."

He opened the glass doors to a large cabinet that had been built to the specifications of the room, for it filled the space exactly and stood to its advantage in the full rays of the afternoon sun. On a set of shelves sat a bewildering collection of strangely shaped pieces of what looked like glass. Most were triangular or pyramidal of some description; others were the familiar tear-drop shapes found in the chandeliers of the finest homes. As the bright light streamed through the clear window, each beam filtered through the dazzling variety of glass and crystal and splintered into a thousand colours of bright rainbow light. The effect was marvellous and Elizabeth felt she had wandered into a magical realm.

As she gaped at the spectacular array of prisms, Mr. Darcy picked up one of the prisms and passed the precisely cut shape to Elizabeth. She held it in her hands and examined it. It was small—little more than an inch long—with a triangular base but square sides, and completely clear. "It's lovely," she whispered, watching ripples of light and odd half-reflections in the small facets of the item.

"Hold it to the window," Mr. Darcy suggested, "turn it so the light from the sun meets one of the flat edges.... Thus!"

And as her hand tilted the small object to just the right angle, a tiny, perfect rainbow appeared on the wall opposite. "Oh!" she gasped in delight. Whilst the array of splintered light in the cabinet was stunning, how much more exquisite was this one, singular and perfect spectrum upon the far wall, created for, and by, her. She raised her other hand and held it immediately behind the prism and laughed as the rainbow danced upon her own flesh.

"Beautiful, is it not?" he smiled in return. "Look at this one," he continued, handing her another, and then another, all of which she examined with delight as she turned them and tilted them in the sunlight, cooing at the variety of rainbows they produced on the dark walls and other surfaces of the room.

"The science of optics is fascinating indeed," Mr. Darcy told her. "Sir Isaac Newton was one of the first to describe the refraction of white sunlight into the multihued spectrum we see here on my carpet, and the flint glass, or lead crystal, we use today was developed here in London in 1673 by George Ravenscroft." She smiled indulgently as she recognised the tone of voice he used when assuming his professorial aspect. Oblivious to her thoughts, and blind to any intimations of disinterest, he continued his lecture. This was one facet of his personality that would never change, she knew. It must be inconceivable to him that not everybody held the same fascination for his personal interests as did he, and he seemed ready to speak endlessly on this chosen topic. Perhaps, at times, she should allow him to give voice to his interests; if she could learn something of his passions, and find her own interest in them, it would provide a safe topic for conversation; furthermore, the depths of his knowledge was formidable and most impressive, and she enjoyed the sensation of being the object of affection of such a learned and intelligent man.

Eventually, however, as his lecture grew confusing and a bit tiresome, she halted his monologue and suggested he continue his presentation at a later time.

"Ah. Yes, I see. I have spoken for too long." He frowned, then paused and asked his guest, "You have surely heard of the atelier in Waterford in Ireland, where some of the best cut glass and crystal are produced." Elizabeth nodded, unsure how this topic related to the previous one, if at all. "I travelled there two years ago, and commissioned a work for my sister, for her eighteenth birthday. It has recently arrived, and I have it safely at Pemberley, where I shall keep it for the next two years until she reaches that age, but I wish to show you something else." Elizabeth screwed her forehead in confusion, but said nothing. There must be a purpose to this diversion.

Mr. Darcy moved to the shelves at the far end of the cabinet, and opening the glass doors, removed a small wooden box from the top shelf. He handed it to Elizabeth. "Open it," he whispered.

Her hands nervously unhooked the hinged clasp, and she raised the polished lid to reveal a velvet interior, housing a small crystalline butterfly. "You may pick it up," he assured her. "I trust you to be most careful. I should not show it to you were I not to have full faith in that."

And there, in her hands, sat the most exquisite ornament she had ever seen. Each detail of the butterfly was a clean edge, cut from the clearest crystal she had ever seen. "It is most marvellous!" She hardly heard her voice as she spoke. "Truly, wonderfully marvellous!" Holding it now to the glass, she watched in rapturous delight as the multifaceted figurine captured the light streaming into the window and sent it exploding in a hundred different directions, lighting the butterfly from within and sending a myriad of tiny rainbows around the room. Even the boys looked up from their tasks to marvel at the display.

"The artisans used the same technique to cut the glass as they use in their drinking and display vessels. The idea for a figurine was my sister's although she does not know this exists. It was merely a musing of hers one evening. This particular piece was the first, small attempt on the part of the artist, to see whether he could complete the larger project. The one wing is chipped—there," he pointed to a minute irregularity in the edge, "and so it is not perfect. But it is too beautiful to discard, and so I keep it here to admire when I wish. It shows to its greatest advantage now, I see, being held by one as lovely as you."

Elizabeth did not know what to say and blushed before finding her tongue. "You seem to have acquired a facility with words, Mr. Darcy," she attempted to tease lightly.

"Perhaps I merely needed the right inspiration."

She caught his eyes with her own and felt drawn into their moss-green depths. "Oh," was all she was able to say as she stared, lost, unaware of time or the drawing of breath or the brilliant light-filled fragile butterfly she held in her hands.

It was only when the boys, who were completing a stage of their periscopes and needed assistance, began calling Mr. Darcy's name that the couple at the window recalled themselves to their senses.

"Um, well, yes, Miss Elizabeth, I shall return once I have finished helping the lads. Please feel free to peruse the rest of the collection, should you so desire."

"Thank you... I shall." She watched him return to his pupils with the rainbows dancing across his back.

By the end of the afternoon, two somewhat cumbersome but nonetheless utile periscopes sat atop the work table. The boys were justifiably proud of their hard and careful work, and had shown their creations to Elizabeth, who admired every join of heavy paper and leather and who crowed in wonder at the magic these objects could perform with their mirrors and lenses.

The boys insisted on demonstrating their periscopes to Elizabeth. "See here, Cousin Lizzy," Samuel gushed, "You look through this opening here, and the image you see will be something around a corner of some sort. The light from whatever it is you are seeing enters through the other end," he pointed, careful not to smudge the glass with his fingers, "and is reflected off a prism inside the tube, where it is magnified by a system of lenses. Then the light from the image reflects again off a second mirror at the bottom bend, and out through the eyepiece. And this enables you to see something that is not directly before you!"

This was intriguing, and Elizabeth was eager to see how the device worked in practice. She accepted her young cousin's periscope and held it up to her eye. It truly was a wonderful creation! By looking through the small eyepiece, and turning the top of the device, she was able to see around corners, read small (if backwards) print on a book on a shelf to her one side, and even see behind her if she raised the top of the periscope high enough. "They are marvellous!" She felt as excited as the boys and praised them again and again until they fairly glowed with the pride of their achievement.

At last the tea was brought in, along with lemonade and a wide selection of treats for the boys, and the four sat in earnest discussion over the objectives and rules of their game. It was Elizabeth's difficult chore to remind the youngsters of their manners, so excited were they at their new project, and once she even found herself about to scold Mr. Darcy himself for talking with his mouth full of cake. Of all his faults and difficulties, he had always shown the most fastidious attention to his manners, and this lapse, the first she had ever seen, only emphasised that he was as keen as the boys to engage in their game.

The objective was simple: to direct the other person to an object of the player's choosing somewhere within the park, while at all times remaining out of direct sight and earshot. Each boy would have half an hour to select his item and devise a system of twigs or stones or something else to direct his friend to the goal. Each clue would point to the next—perhaps an arrow of branches leading to a diagram made of pebbles. Ingenuity and interpretation were key, and everything must be around some sort of barrier from the preceding clue, so that the periscopes could be pressed into action. Written words were not forbidden but were discouraged. Mr. Darcy would locate himself in some central place where he could be found if needed, and Miss Elizabeth would, he hoped, deign to keep him company.

"I cannot wait to tell Mama and Papa what we have done today!" Samuel's words tumbled from his lips.

"I too!" Robert beamed. "Mother will not believe what we have made."

Sammy stopped and looked stricken. "Will they really disbelieve us? I would be distressed to be caught in a lie, and especially so if it is, in reality, true."

Grinning, Elizabeth explained the common idiom, and to reassure her cousin, confirmed that she would relate every detail to her aunt and uncle; She also promised to be most attentive in explaining the game. Rarely had she seen her cousin so enthused about something he had created. Theory often fascinated him, but hardly ever application. She was as pleased as he was. Now satisfied that his parents would not distrust his words, Samuel returned to the subject of the devices he and Robert had created. "Early uses of periscopes included watching public spectacles over the heads of the other people in a crowd! But if I hold it thus, I can see around a corner, or behind a chair. And hopefully, tomorrow, I shall peer behind hedges and over walls! Oh, this shall be the most wonderful fun, shall it not, Robert?"

Robert nodded vigorously, careful at last not to speak with a last piece of cake in his mouth.

"You have done a remarkable job, both of you boys, in constructing these devices," Lizzy complimented the lads. "Now, I do believe I hear our carriage." She turned to their host. "Thank you, on all our behalves, Mr. Darcy, for your time and for the means to construct these fascinating tools. You have been most generous and I believe we have all enjoyed ourselves."

The boys also thanked him quite properly and sincerely, and within moments, they were in their carriage, periscopes nestled safely in velvet bags and held close to excited chests, and heading towards home, with the promise of the most fun the following morning.

Chapter Eighteen

At the Park

T he following day dawned bright and clear, to everyone's satisfaction. Before Elizabeth entered the breakfast room, she could hear her cousins chattering with their parents in gleeful anticipation of the day's adventure. Young James, feeling rather left out of events, was to come along with his sisters for a quick demonstration of the periscopes, after which the younger children would return to the house for their lessons. Had Elizabeth not been well used to a house full of the hubbub and giggles of five sisters, she might have been quite disconcerted at the noise and energy in the room.

As it was, she was just as excited as her cousins, and it was with great satisfaction that Mr. Darcy arrived not too long after, followed in short order by Robert. "My brother Teddy wishes to meet us in the park for a few minutes," he sputtered, eyes wide, "and Francie too, even though she's sixteen and thinks herself much too ladylike for such games. Will anybody mind?"

Thus it was that a small army of participants and observers paraded to the park shortly after ten o'clock that morning. The boys proudly exhibited and demonstrated their periscopes to all, letting each try the devices. Robert's two older siblings expressed their admiration for the devices and asked several excellent questions, which Mr. Darcy answered with great patience, before they bid the company an excellent day and returned to their studies. Now the younger children spent a few minutes peering through the periscopes. "Birdies!" Julia cried in glee. "Birdies, upside down! Where are the birdies?" She spun around in circles looking for the birds she had seen and then asked Miss Pierce if she could have more seed to feed them. At this, Samuel inhaled sharply and his eyes went wide with alarm, but Elizabeth could see him shake off the memory of the recent ill-fated encounter with the birds and regain his ease. How proud she was of her young cousin! Such a response might be quite innate for someone like his friend Robert, but for Sammy, it was the culmination of a great amount of work, and the effort was now bearing fruit! She beamed at him and he, catching her eye, beamed back. He knew what he had achieved and was pleased with himself.

But there were other matters to attend now! There was a game to play! Mr. Darcy called the two youths to him to rehearse the aims and rules of the game and the three of them disappeared into the foliage to begin to set up their clues. The boys would head in separate directions, and Mr. Darcy, so they had planned, would visit with each to offer any assistance that might be needed until such time as the search would begin. Elizabeth sat conversing happily with Miss Pierce and the younger cousins whilst she waited, enjoying the fine day. With Samuel now occupied elsewhere and safe from assault, the governess handed both Julia and Helena small bags of seeds to toss to the birds, and they called after them, crying, "Caw, caw," and chasing the pigeons back into the sky. How different were these little girls from their older brother.

And then, at last, the game began and Miss Pierce returned to the house with the three younger children. Samuel and Robert reconvened, shook hands with the solemnity of two men about to engage in a duel, and disappeared once more in search of their quarries. Samuel would seek whatever object Robert had chosen, and Robert would seek Samuel's. The first to present his quarry would be declared the winner.

For some time, Elizabeth and Darcy sat on the chosen bench in the shade of some old oak trees, talking about the boys, their game, and various other topics as they arose naturally in the conversation, whilst watching the world unfold before them. First out to enjoy the park were the members of the wealthy merchant class, smartly dressed children accompanied by efficient and brisk governesses, marvels of efficiency and good breeding and the promise of a new future. These were the children not of privilege, but of hard work, and their guardians chosen for ability rather than suitable parentage. "This is the future," Mr. Darcy said. "These are the children who will grow into the leaders of tomorrow. Industry is changing the world, and our own pampered class will not fare well before their honest toil and superior education and training. Indeed. These are your cousins and their friends."

"I had thought you too fine to associate with mere tradesmen, Mr. Darcy!" Elizabeth teased. "I recall some rather cutting words upon our first attempt at playing the parts of pleasant company."

The gentleman blushed. "I am not too proud to admit where I was mistaken. I have learned a great deal since we first met, and my eyes have been opened not only to myself, but to the world around me."

Somewhat later came the children of the lower echelons of the gentry, families like Elizabeth's own, whose gentleman father might, but did not, have a house in London, but who were not considered quite of the right circles. Then the ladies, out for their morning walks, sometimes in pairs or small groups, sometimes on the arms of a beau or—shockingly enough—husband. Being close to the centre of town, smartly dressed members of the various branches of the military strutted along the paths, as did well-dressed lawyers and businessmen, foppish social climbers, pastry-sellers and the occasional elegantly clothed gentleman. It was a microcosm of London's society, and Elizabeth and Mr. Darcy observed it all as they sat happily in the midst of the action.

"We might be waiting for some time," Mr. Darcy stretched as he surveyed the park. "'Tis a glorious day and I would not wish to hurry the lads along, for they might well wish to enjoy the park. May I interest you in a game?" He reached into the bag he carried and withdrew a beautifully inlaid box, which, when opened, proved to be a chess board and which held a full set of miniature men.

"I am hardly of a mind to pay serious attention to such a game, Mr. Darcy!"

"I had not thought to engage in serious competition, merely to amuse ourselves whilst we wait. I shall not think for more than twenty seconds on each move, if that reassures you."

She had to laugh at his sincerity in his attempt to be frivolous. "Then I would be pleased. My father sends me puzzles to work out from time to time, on how to achieve mate within so many moves. I know that more accomplished players do not need the board, but can imagine the pieces with such clarity that they can achieve these puzzles in their minds. I am not of that calibre."

"One can," the gentleman offered in a wistful voice, "spend too much time in one's own head." He began to set up the board on the bench between them. "Shall we play?"

As they began the opening game, they talked of matters general and inconsequential. Mr. Darcy was becoming more comfortable with small talk, at least amongst those he knew and trusted. The air was fresh and the sun warm, and the general activity in the park gave them plenty about which to chat. Birds floated above them, then landed on the gravel path before their bench.

"Oh!" Lizzy chuckled. One flying creature strutted towards her and began pecking at her hem. "What can he want?"

"There must be some of your cousins' birdseed caught in the lace at the bottom of your frock." Mr. Darcy started to reach down, but then recalled himself. "May I?" The look on his face betrayed his conflicting wishes to rid them of the pest and maintain gentlemanly propriety. Was he, too, reliving the ordeal that Samuel had suffered only days before at the hands—or wings—of such flying creatures?

Lizzy kicked at her skirts and the bird scuttled off, and the chess game continued.

Of Samuel and Robert, there was no sign, until about an hour after they began their game, when Robert's fair head appeared from around a curve in the path.

"Mr. Darcy, sir, I am in need of help, sir! I was following Sam's signs and signals, and all was going so well, and then, well I just lost them! I looked everywhere, and not only did I lose the next clue, but I lost my previous position as well, and I am afraid I will never complete his game. Sir. I'm so sorry to bother you. But can you help me, please?"

Questioning green eyes met Elizabeth's amber ones and she smiled indulgently. "Do not worry on my account, sir. Go. The boys need you. I was expecting this, and have brought along a book, but if you would leave this board, perhaps I can attempt one of Papa's puzzles. I shall be most happy here until you return." At this assurance, Mr. Darcy rose and followed Robert back into the foliage in their attempt to regain the trail.

Elizabeth set up the board with the few men her father had indicated and began to search for the pattern that would lead to a checkmate in four moves. The pigeon, however, had returned and now would not leave her alone, hoping, perhaps, for some more seed from the lacy folds at the bottom of her petticoat, and failing that, from her hand or reticule. It hopped upon the small chess board, scattering pieces as it pecked at her hands and strutting around as if it had won the game.

"Checkmate, Mr. Pigeon. One move. My king is dead!" She giggled at the inanity of it and shooed the bird off, attempting her father's task one more time.

For a time, Elizabeth worked contentedly at her puzzle, not expecting her companion to return too soon, and thus she was rather taken aback to hear someone call her name.

"Miss Elizabeth Bennet! I am most surprised to see you here, but equally delighted!"

With alarm, she looked up to see none other than Mr. Wickham standing before her, elegant and handsome, dressed in the brilliant scarlet coat of his militia and looking nothing at all like the reprobate she now knew him to be. He dropped into a beautiful bow and rose again to bestow upon her a radiant smile. Quickly schooling her features, Elizabeth resolved to greet him properly but coolly, hoping he would not linger.

Not so long ago, she realised, she would have been rather pleased to see him standing thus before her, greeting her with such enthusiasm. She had enjoyed his cheerful manners, pleasing features and easy conversation. There had been such an expression of goodness in his countenance! such an openness and gentleness in his manner! How much had she anticipated those first few encounters, when he had favoured her and her alone, when his disparaging remarks about Mr. Darcy confirmed her imagined attraction to him, leaving her more confident in her supposedly unerring judgement of character! And now, oh how erroneous had that judgement proven to have been!

Those easy, smooth, and charming words that had danced off his tongue had beguiled her as much as his bright eyes, handsome face and elegant figure. He had flattered her, and she had succumbed. When compared with those awful, stilted attempts at conversation with Mr. Darcy, before she knew the man and what struggles he contended with, Mr. Wickham's conquest was assured. Now she berated herself: she ought to have been concerned at his flippant disclosure of personal relationships, of his willingness to speak so ill of someone immediately upon assuring her he would never do such a thing.

His exact words, unbidden, came to mind: *"Till I can forget his father, I can never defy or expose him."* And she had believed him. Flattered, reassured of her powers of observation and convinced of her infallibility, she had believed him. What a petty, unthinking girl she had been! How deceiving first impressions could be.

But that time had passed, and armed with better knowledge of herself, of Mr. Darcy, and of Mr. Wickham too, Elizabeth stared up into the eyes she had once found so appealing, but which now sent a slight chill down her spine. She returned his greeting, but with no warmth in her voice.

"Good day, Mr. Wickham." She inclined her head but did not invite him to sit. However, the officer did not seem to take note of her subtle cut and seated himself on the bench, regardless. Realising she had no recourse but to converse, or seem very rude—which would invite unwanted questions—she inquired after his health.

"I am most well, Miss Elizabeth, as are you, I do hope. We have missed you in Meryton these past weeks."

"Yes," she replied, "I have been visiting my dear friend Charlotte Collins in Kent."

"Ah, Kent. I spent many happy days there in my youth when I was in the old Mr. Darcy's good graces. He was wont to include me in many family excursions when I was a lad. Will and I were great friends, keeping each other amused until it was time for the heir apparent to appear before his relations. The cousin—Anne, you must surely have met her if you were at all about Rosings—was never at all amusing, and two young boys must have their merriments. Ah yes, Mr. Darcy treated me near on as a son." He paused dramatically, then added, "I was never so happy as to achieve that affection from his heir, I'm afraid."

Elizabeth said nothing, but smiled weakly, wondering what Mr. Wickham hoped to gain by reigniting her distaste for the younger Mr. Darcy. Did he hope to cajole her into some nefarious plot against the man? Or did he merely wish to reassure himself through association with like-minded people of his righteous dislike of Mr. Darcy? Whatever his motivation, Elizabeth was of no mind to hear it, and she mumbled something meaningless as she cast her glance around, hoping to find an excuse to leave her unwanted companion. But Mr. Wickham kept talking. "What do you now in London, madam? I ask, because I had not expected to be here myself, let alone find a familiar—and lovely—face."

"Do you flatter me, Mr. Wickham? The last time we spoke, you were to be married to Miss King."

The officer sighed dramatically. Oh, how good he would be on the stage, Lizzy thought. He had all the beauty and mannerisms of an actor. "Alas, that was not to be. My dear Miss King's uncle refused our union and took her to live with him at Liverpool. I confess, my heart was not quite broken, although my disappointment was great. And yet, I find I am quite recovered now. And so I find myself in London on a short leave from my duties to finalise the arrangements of the dissolution of our engagement with my solicitor. I expect to be here some days as he deals with these outstanding and rather dull details."

Needing to hear something of the truth from the man himself, Elizabeth asked sharply, "Should you have enjoyed such work yourself, Mr. Wickham? I recall someone once telling me you had chosen to pursue the law rather than the pulpit." She fluttered her eyes innocently at him. "I cannot recall from whom."

Mr. Wickham's face turned white. "Did you, perhaps, see Mr. Darcy whilst you were in Kent?"

A genuine smile now crept over Elizabeth's face. "Indeed I did. He and his cousin, Colonel Fitzwilliam, were both visiting their aunt. Do you know the colonel?"

Mr. Wickham looked at once surprised, displeased, and alarmed; but with a moment's recollection and a returning smile, replied that he had formerly seen him often; and after observing that he was a very gentlemanlike man, asked her how she had liked him. Her answer was warmly in his favour.

"He is a most charming man, of excellent manners and most a pleasant disposition. He is quite unlike his cousin is some ways."

Wickham concurred. Then, with an air of indifference, he added, "How long did you say that he was at Rosings?"

"Nearly three weeks. We saw him quite often—almost every day, I believe. He and Mr. Darcy were frequent visitors to the parsonage, when we were not invited to dine or take tea at Rosings."

"The colonel's manners are very different from his cousin's."

"Yes, very different. But I think Mr. Darcy improves on acquaintance." Elizabeth watched Mr. Wickham very carefully to gauge his reaction to this statement. He did not disappoint her.

"Indeed!" cried he with a look which did not escape her. "And pray may I ask—?" but checking himself, he added in a gayer tone, "Is it in address that he improves? Has he deigned to add ought of civility to his ordinary style? for I dare not hope," he continued in a lower and more serious tone, "that he is improved in essentials."

Ah, thought Elizabeth. *Now it is he who is hoping to learn something from me.* With the most pleasant and innocent smile she could manage, she replied, "Oh, no! In essentials, I believe, he is very much what he ever was."

Whilst she spoke, Wickham looked as if scarcely knowing whether to rejoice over her words, or to distrust their meaning. There must have been something in her countenance which made him listen with an apprehensive and anxious attention, as she added, "When I said that he improved on acquaintance, I did not mean that either his mind or manners were in a state of improvement, but that from knowing him better, his disposition was better understood."

Wickham's alarm now appeared in a heightened complexion and agitated look; for a few moments he was silent; till, shaking off his embarrassment, he turned to her again, and said in the gentlest of accents, "You, who so well know my feelings towards Mr. Darcy, will readily comprehend how sincerely I must rejoice that he is wise enough to assume even the appearance of what is right. And yet..." he drew his watch from its pocket with an elaborate show, "I find I must depart if I am to make my appointment on time. It was a pleasure meeting you here like this, Miss Elizabeth. Now I must bid you adieu."

And they parted at last with mutual civility, and possibly a mutual desire of never meeting again.

No sooner had Mr. Wickham disappeared down a winding path leading out of the park, than Mr. Darcy emerged from behind a nearby shrub. "Elizabeth, are you well?" he asked with greater alarm than the situation required.

Following Mr. Darcy's stare at Wickham's retreating back, Elizabeth perceived that Darcy had observed the interaction. "I was not happy to see him, Mr. Darcy, but as you see, I am quite well. He has no power to disconcert me."

Mr. Darcy closed his eyes and breathed out a sigh of relief. "I am most relieved to hear that, Elizabeth. I observed him walking towards you, but I did not dare to show myself. I thought it might provoke an unwelcome scene. Did he say anything to upset you? Your face shows signs of tension and displeasure. Your eyebrows are drawn in slightly and from the look of your mouth, you are chewing your bottom lip. As much as you attempted to maintain a neutral demeanour in his unwelcome presence, I am now sufficiently attuned to your expressions that I realised you were not at ease."

The concern in his voice was touching, and she felt all that aforementioned tension drain out of her brow as she grinned at him. "You are the most adept student a teacher might wish for, Mr. Darcy. You are correct on all counts and I thank you for you solicitousness at my well-being." She gestured to the bench beside her, where he sat once more. "In truth, though, I hope I did not reveal too much. Seeing him here infuriated me, as I recalled his lies and slanderous words, and I intimated that I knew, perhaps, more than he might have wished me to know. I also suggested that you and I were on far better terms than we were when Mr. Wickham last saw us together in Hertfordshire. Something makes me wonder if that was a mistake."

"Perhaps, Elizabeth, but what can the man do now? He can slander me all he likes. Those who are inclined to dislike me shall do so regardless, but what possible words could cause anyone to think ill of you? However, you are correct that he was hiding something as well, possibly thinking of something to further gain his revenge upon me, after I spoiled his plans last summer to elope with my sister. His face..." Mr. Darcy drew out of his coat pocket a corded velvet sack, about four inches in length and three across. Removing the items from the sack, he quickly fitted them together, much like a flute, and presented Elizabeth with the resulting item, a strangely bent tube no more than a foot in length. Elizabeth accepted the offered item, and quickly realised what it was.

"A periscope! I did not know you had your own, and so much smaller than what the boys made!"

"This was given to me by the glass master who creates many of the lenses I purchase. It is not very useful for most practical applications, being rather too small, but I thought it might be of use today with the boys. Although I did admonish the lads to respect others' privacy whilst engaging in their game, I admit to using it to observe Mr. Wickham's face whilst he spoke with you. I am disconcerted. As you know, I have perfect recall." She nodded, and at her invitation, he continued, "I have recently discovered something interesting. When I recall a specific occasion, I find I am able to replay in my mind not only the words used and the circumstances of the event, but I can also hear in my mind the tones of voice used, as well as the expressions that happened upon the various people's faces. It is like I am at the theatre, watching a performance. Every nuance is perfectly clear to me, as if it were happening at the moment.

"More interesting," he continued, "is that such nuances of which I was quite oblivious before are now more open to me. I find that, with my new abilities to analyse and interpret facial expressions, which you have taught me so well, I can revisit those incidents from my past and retroactively decipher what others were feeling.

"Whilst you were speaking with Wickham, I recalled several of our past encounters, most specifically ones in which I now know he had some nefarious schemes in mind. I analysed his facial contortions from those past events, and I believe that, in concert with your lessons on reading expression, I have found certain tics that he exhibits at those times. There is a half-smile, on one side of his face, that suggests he is devising such a devious or ill-considered plan, as well as a tilt to his head and a peculiar motion with his lower jaw and lip. As I recalled these past events, and as I watched him just these few moments ago, I noticed many of those same mannerisms.

"He is adept at schooling his features, as any habitual liar must be, but from what I have learned of late, his face does not betray deceit in the usual ways. Rather, these mannerisms are all quite benign and fleeting, at least to one who does not make a study of them. Since I have never commented upon them before, he must believe I am still blind to these things—or rather, I was blind! He cannot know of what I have learned, nor should he imagine you to have any such knowledge of his habits. You did not tell him of our exercises, I trust."

Elizabeth shook her head in alarm. "That, sir, is something I should never divulge to anyone not of your closest circle, and even then, only at your direction."

"I trust you, Elizabeth, believe me. But just now, when you were speaking to him, you must have said something that upset his equilibrium, if only for a moment. That moment was enough for his true thoughts to appear upon his face. I saw those same mannerisms. He has begun to think of some plans to cause further mischief, I am certain of it. I can only hope we discover what they are before he does anyone harm."

It was only a few short minutes after this pronouncement that the first whoops of joy were heard from the boys. Samuel was the first to appear, waving his periscope like a conqueror's sword, and holding his trophy high in the air with the other hand. "I found it, I found it! This is Robert's object. See—he wrote his name upon it with chalk! I found it some several minutes ago and have been waiting for Robert to discover my own. Oh, that was so much fun!" He turned back expectantly as his friend came running after him.

"Sammy, here it is! Is this your name in Ancient Greek? Whatever did you use to write it? Did you use a knife? Oh, Sammy, you did! You carved your name in Ancient Greek upon a stone! What if some archaeologist from the British Museum had found it? He would have rewritten all the histories, proclaiming that the Greeks were in London, and that they had sons named Samuel Gardiner! Oh, what fun that would have been!"

Elizabeth could not help but be cheered by Robert's irrepressible good humour and was thankful once again that he had chosen her quiet cousin as his friend. Almost immediately, the boys both launched into detailed descriptions of where and how they had discovered their clues. At length Robert ceased his part of the conversation and asked with some concern, "Is everything well, Miss Elizabeth? You look somewhat upset. Did something happen whilst we were searching to disconcert you?"

Elizabeth began to reassure the youth, when Sammy interjected, "It must have been that man."

"That man?" Mr. Darcy asked. Like Elizabeth, he appeared both alarmed and intrigued at what young Samuel might have observed.

"The man that sat with Cousin Lizzy for seventeen minutes and eight seconds and spoke with her." He then proceeded to give a most accurate description of Mr. Wickham, from the colour and shape of his eyes to the number and location of scuff marks on his boots. How strange,

Elizabeth reckoned for the thousandth time, that her young cousin could be so perceptive of these physical details, whilst so unaware of her own discomfort during the course of the conversation.

"When did you notice this man?" she asked gently.

"I found Robert's object quite a bit sooner than he discovered my own, and I was thinking to come here and rest with you, but as I walked near, I heard the man call your name and sit with you. I thought it would be more interesting to observe through my periscope than intrude on your *tête-à-tête*, and so I did just that!" He beamed proudly at his decision, and then, horrified, asked, "Did I do wrong? Oh, should I not have acted thus? Forgive me, Cousin Lizzy! I forgot my manners in my schemes."

"No, you acted rightly, Sammy," she assured him, "for Mr. Wickham had matters to discuss that were intended for my ears alone." Not wishing the conversation to veer towards Mr. Wickham and his questionable intentions, she redirected the discussion back to the hunt. "Now, tell me more about your game. How did you find your clues? Robert, I see you wish to speak. Pray, I am most interested in hearing it." And thus, the boys jabbered away thus through the afternoon and through dinner, until at last Robert's parents sent for him.

But always, at the back of her mind, was Mr. Darcy's dire warning of the troubles brewing in Mr. Wickham's head.

Chapter Nineteen

Letters from Jane

*D*earest Lizzy,

    How lovely it is to be home, in my own accustomed house, with my familiar bed and my giggling sisters, and yes, even Mama! It is hard to believe that a full week has passed since we arrived home, for it feels at once as if I only just arrived, and as if I never left at all!

Oh, Lizzy, I cannot hold this in any longer! You were right—we had not been home two days when Mr. Bingley came to call! He claimed he came to invite Papa to hunt with him the following day, but when Mama invited him to stay for tea, he accepted almost at once, and then he stayed through the noon meal and into the afternoon, returning home only for dinner, for he had an appointment that he could not change. And then, yes, he was back the very next day after the hunt, when he did stay for dinner, and the day after that.

We have had time alone, when Mary leaves to find a new book, or when Mama forgets her embroidery upstairs, or when we are out walking, and he has requested an official courtship. Oh, Lizzy, I am so happy! I shall only be happier should he, at last, offer for me, and I do believe he shall. He told me that he wishes only to assure me of his regard and faithfulness. He blames himself entirely for what transpired last autumn, although he has confessed Mr. Darcy's and his sisters' roles in convincing him to leave. He said he would never have left had he believed that I cared for him. Would you believe it, Lizzy, that when he went to town last November, he really loved me, and nothing but a persuasion of my being indifferent would have prevented his coming down again! I could hardly fault him, for I know that I am often too reserved for many people, and if he made a little mistake, it is to the credit of his modesty.

Oh Lizzy, if only I could see you this happy!

Elizabeth sat back in the comfortable chair in the parlour as she read Jane's letter. "Good news, Lizzy?" her aunt asked from her escritoire by the window.

"The best, Aunt. Mr. Bingley has returned to Netherfield and is courting Jane. I imagine it shan't be long before they announce an engagement. Perhaps this ill adventure has taught them that they must talk openly with one another. But Jane is happier than she has been these many months, and I am delighted for her. But there is more. By your leave, I shall leave you to your own correspondence and read what else she has to tell me."

Jane's letter concluded in similar happy tones, with only a few lines near the end that raised the mildest bit of concern. Lydia was indeed to go to Brighton when the militia encamped there for the summer, as the special friend of Mrs. Forster, under the guardianship of the latter's husband, the regiment's colonel. Elizabeth had written a series of letters to her father, vague entreaties in which she dared spell out no particular details but which begged him to put an end to this scheme. These, it seemed, had all gone unheeded; she had represented to him all the improprieties of Lydia's general behaviour, the little advantage she could derive from the friendship of such a woman as Mrs. Forster, and the probability of her being yet more imprudent with such a companion at Brighton, where the temptations must be greater than at home.

With what attention he had read her words, she never knew, but his reply, as conveyed through Jane's letter, was final: *Lydia will never be easy till she has exposed herself in some public place or other, and we can never expect her to do it with so little expense or inconvenience to her family as under the present circumstances.*

"If he were aware," sighed Elizabeth to herself, "of the very great disadvantage to us all, which must arise from the public notice of Lydia's unguarded and imprudent manner; nay, which has already arisen from it, I am sure he would judge differently in the affair."

Jane's letter concluded with a somewhat more sanguine thought on the affair, as her father had affixed a short note of his own to settle the matter.

We shall have no peace at Longbourn if Lydia does not go to Brighton. Let her go then. Colonel Forster is a sensible man, and will keep her out of any real mischief; and she is luckily too poor to be an object of prey to any body.

We can only hope, thought Elizabeth, that he is correct.

My Dearest Jane,

I knew he would come! I told you as much, did I not? I am so very happy for you, my Jane, and shall be even more so when Mr. Bingley makes you his wife. I do not think I shall have to wait so very long for that happy event!

In this vein, Elizabeth penned her reply to her beloved sister. She waxed enthusiastic about Mr. Bingley's return, the great fortune of his sisters not accompanying him on this trip (how fortunate that he expressed to them that he was merely returning to Netherfield to hunt), and the great benefit to Meryton's society now that the young gentleman had returned. She also wrote most enthusiastically of the experiment in the park with Samuel and Robert and their hand-built periscopes. She described the devices in detail, set out how they functioned, and outlined the nature of the game. She did not mention her encounter with Mr. Wickham, not wishing to bring any dark clouds into Jane's newly sunny world. Jane must be allowed to enjoy the first days of her courtship with Mr. Bingley unencumbered with news of the vile officer.

Mr. Darcy has been most attentive himself. He becomes more charming the more I know him. Perhaps I am growing accustomed to his slightly awkward ways; perhaps, indeed, I am beginning to find them endearing! Or, perhaps, as he grows more comfortable around me and our family, he sheds more and more of the stiffness and hauteur which marks his demeanour in unfamiliar circumstances. But Jane, I must admit to liking him more and more every day I see him.

Last night he invited my aunt and uncle and myself to his home, along with a married couple whom I met whilst in Kent. I believe I wrote to you once of Mr. and Mrs. St. Ives. Mr. St. Ives is a most accomplished violinist, and Mr. Darcy sat at the pianoforte to accompany him in some devilishly complicated works by a young Italian composer named Niccolò Paganini. Mr. Darcy hides a great many talents! I had no notion at all that he was so very accomplished at the instrument. I recall a conversation, whilst you were convalescing at Netherfield, in which he and Miss Bingley debated the requirements for accomplishment in ladies, but not a word was breathed about similar requirements in gentlemen. Perhaps, had we taken the discussion in that direction, the evening might have ended in a much more pleasant manner.

Our evening last night certainly ended most pleasantly. Mrs. St. Ives was as delightful as I recalled from our brief introduction at Rosings, and she seemed as genuinely delighted to renew the acquaintance as was I. Her husband, too, brings out many of Mr. Darcy's best characteristics, for when conversing on topics of interest to him, he is a most amiable and engaging conversationalist.

Oh, Jane, I do not believe I shall ever truly understand the man—sometimes so stiff and reticent, sometimes so free and friendly—but I do not believe I shall ever tire of him. And please, do not ever breathe a word of what I just wrote! I should cross it out now, but that would leave a large blot of ink on my page and ruin all the words I have just written! Oh, Jane, how I wish you were here to laugh with me, but in truth I am more pleased that you are where you are, for that is where your Mr. Bingley is.

Elizabeth took a deep breath before writing the last few lines of her letter.

I must ask, my dearest sister, what news you have from Lydia. You know as well as I how ill-advised our Papa was in allowing her to go; we can only hope that he was correct in his assumption that she will be too poor, and of too little real interest to any of the officers, to become anything of a temptation to them, never mind that she is the most determined flirt in all of England. If you hear news, I beg you to let me know as soon as is convenient.

For now, dearest Jane, enjoy your courtship, and I shall remain,

Your ever-loving sister,

Lizzy

When Mr. Darcy came to call the following morning, Elizabeth told him about Lydia's sojourn in Brighton with the militia. Although she attempted to adopt her father's devil-may-care attitude towards the situation, she had already confided in her aunt, and now hoped that Mr. Darcy too might be able to sooth her agitation.

"I should not speak ill of my parent," she told him ruefully as they took their tea with Mrs. Gardiner, "but he cannot know how poorly my sister's' behaviour reflects upon Jane and myself, as well as Mary and Kitty, of course. He believes that Lydia's exposure in Brighton will remain veiled from the eyes of society, but that can never be so. You, yourself, reflected upon the evils of family members run wild. Those things you said in Hunsford..."

"Are best forgotten, Miss Elizabeth."

"No, sir, they were all true." Shame tinged her voice although she suspected Mr. Darcy was unaware of that nuance. Still, she had to catch herself to stop from turning away from his beseeching face.

"Your sister, Jane, is most likely to become engaged to my friend very soon; Bingley has written to ask my advice on the settlement upon her. And you, yourself..." Looking up at Mrs. Gardiner, who sat staring intently at the pages of her book on the far armchair, he did not complete that thought, but said instead, "Wherever you are known, you must be respected and valued; and you will not appear to less advantage for having a very silly sister."

"Then you do not believe her to be in any danger, or of ruining the family with some terribly embarrassing scandal?"

"No, I did not say that!" he laughed. "I am certain she shall endeavour to bring upon herself all manner of scandals. However, perhaps your father is correct, and whatever occurs in Brighton will be so overshadowed by even greater follies involving better known people that none shall think on it after a day or two."

"I am hardly reassured, Mr. Darcy!" she scolded teasingly, but was somehow comforted by his indifference to Lydia's imminent misbehaviour. She realised now, sitting in this comfortable room with this unusual and enigmatic young man, how much his disparagement of her family had hurt her, not for the fact itself but because of the rift it had come so close to placing between them. If Lydia's behaviour should cause her to lose Mr. Darcy once more, she did not know how she would survive it. That he was now teasing her about this very matter set her mind much at ease.

He took a sip from his tea cup, and then said, "I may have yet another means by which we may assure ourselves of Miss Lydia's decorum." He looked up now and spoke loudly enough to capture Mrs. Gardiner's attention. "If you will do me the honour, Mrs. Gardiner, of joining me at my home for tea tomorrow? Hopefully I shall have some news that will soothe Miss Elizabeth's concerns over her sister. I shall send my carriage around. Miss Pierce and the children are also welcome, should they wish to explore a different park. I shall instruct my cook to have a basket ready for them for a special picnic, if they desire it."

The lady of the house inclined her head and accepted most graciously. She really was, thought Elizabeth, every bit as elegant and well-mannered as the high-born ladies who buzzed through the highest echelons of society, and she felt suddenly very proud to be related to her aunt.

"Then, if you will excuse me, ladies, I shall depart so I may make the connexions necessary for the information I wish to gather. I hope you will forgive my early departure." And with a bow to Mrs. Gardiner and a soft kiss on the back of Elizabeth's hand, he collected his hat and gloves and strode off to the mews to find his horse.

As might be expected, the children were thrilled to have an outing, and Miss Pierce was especially so when, later that evening, a note was delivered offering the services of Mr. Darcy's own former nanny so she might have some time to join the others at tea, or perhaps (if she wished it) explore the work room where Mr. Darcy kept his lenses, and which Samuel had raved about so enthusiastically. The boy's departure for Margate with the Harwin family had been unfortunately delayed due to the necessities of Mr. Harwin's business, and he too was eager to revisit the work room, should Mr. Darcy allow it. Such was requested of, and approved by, the master of the house. The same note which reiterated the invitation to tea indicated that should Mr. Gardiner wish to join the group after his day at his place of business, a good dinner would be available to him.

Mrs. Gardiner waxed enthusiastic about Mr. Darcy's fine manners and his thoughtfulness in including the children and their nursemaid, as well as her husband, and Elizabeth breathed freely in relief that not only had Mr. Darcy told her in the most definite terms that he would not hold her to account for her youngest sister's follies, he had reinforced his words with yet another invitation to his home. Consequently, a very happy and eager group from the Gardiner home gathered the next morning to await the arrival of the elegant carriage.

The ride was noisy, full of the chatter of young children. James attempted to be the young man he saw his brother becoming, but the little girls were too excited to contain their glee, and commented upon everything they saw or heard. They were not unaccustomed to travelling in the city by carriage, but being invited to a grand home with their mother was a great adventure, and one which required constant discussion. Every detail must be examined: was Helena's dress suitable for such an occasion? Should she have worn flowers in her hair even though Miss Pierce insisted they were not necessary? At what age should she begin to wear gloves with her dress? And what about little Julia's bonnet? Surely a child so young—only three years of age—could not be expected to keep her hair neat without it and yet she was still of an age where she sometimes took it off to pull at the ribbons. Could Mr. Darcy really mean to have such a messy creature in his house? Mrs. Gardiner smiled indulgently upon her children, confident that they would behave suitably under Miss Pierce's careful eye, and wondered in a whisper which Lizzy only barely heard, whether Mr. Darcy was hoping soon to set up his own nursery. Lizzy blushed furiously at the implication, but remained silent.

At last they arrived and out of the carriage they tumbled, some with greater grace and elegance than others; Julia decided at the last moment to become most nervous and it required a great deal of coaxing for her to be wrested out of her mother's arms. The promise of strawberries and ice in the kitchen at last convinced the little girl to go with her siblings and meet Old Mrs. Churley, who would help care for them that day.

Mr. Darcy himself had been waiting for their arrival at his front door, and once the children had been sent off to their activities, he escorted his guests to the sunny front salon. The room was not particularly large, but it was beautifully proportioned, with eggshell-coloured walls and soft blue draperies and carpets, focussed around a marvellous fireplace of carved marble. The furnishings, as were all those Elizabeth had seen in the house, were understated and elegant. It was a room in which she immediately felt very comfortable.

Initial pleasantries were exchanged, and after some minutes of polite conversation, the master of the house rang for tea. Samuel, who had elected to remain with the adults rather than joining the younger children with Mrs. Churley, seemed to steel himself for the inevitability of a long and rather boring tea with the tedium of adult conversation, when Miss Pierce, herself seeming to feel awkward in such fine company, suggested that the boy show her the work room, with Mr. Darcy's permission, of course. This was deemed a most suitable solution, and Mr. Darcy requested that a selection of tea and lemonade and biscuits be delivered to the two scientists.

Mr. Darcy then asked when the Harwin family expected to depart for their visit to the seaside. "The boys must be rather disappointed for the trip to be delayed thus."

Mrs. Gardiner chuckled. "You are correct, sir! We had spent much time preparing Samuel for the journey, and for the inevitability of unexpected events, and he was all anticipation. This sudden change in plans has been difficult for him, and it took some great efforts on Lizzy's and Miss Pierce's parts to calm him from his reaction. Once he was able to come to terms with the change, however, he has been managing rather well." Mr. Darcy nodded in understanding, and Mrs. Gardiner continued, "I do admit to being somewhat anxious about how he will fare on the journey. He finds sudden changes in plans difficult."

"He is," interjected Mr. Darcy, "a lad much given to routine and ill at ease with the unexpected, is he not?"

"Very much so," the boy's mother admitted. "We spent much time over the past several days discussing what he might expect, and discussing how he might prepare, if you will, for the unexpected. My son is very analytical about some matters, and if he expects to be assailed by all manner of new experiences and sensations, he does rather better than one might imagine. The planning for the unknown, however, is of utmost importance. And now, the unexpected has occurred, with the ironic result of more of his accustomed routine."

"An irony indeed. But he is doing well despite the change in plans, you say?"

"Yes," Mrs. Gardiner nodded. "He has found some other employment, I know not what, which keeps him busy and out of the house much of the day. I believe he is exploring the city with Robert, who also finds himself in need of amusement. They are good boys, and I do not worry after them, for Robert provides the common sense that Sammy often lacks. As much as my son is an unusual child, he has no malice in him, nor a desire to make trouble for himself, and he heeds his friend's wiser advice."

"Unusual, perhaps, Mrs. Gardiner, but no less delightful for it. His intelligence and passion for knowledge are remarkable attributes."

"Thank you sir!"

At this moment the tea arrived, wheeled in by a quiet housemaid, and Mrs. Gardiner asked whether she should pour, or whether Mr. Darcy wished to wait a while longer.

"I am expecting one more guest," he explained, "but that person is not entirely the master of his own time, and shall join us as soon as he is able. In the meantime, let us enjoy the scones and biscuits my cook bakes for me each morning. She is merely a Yorkshirewoman and not a trained French chef, but her baking, for all its simplicity, is exceptional."

No sooner had he said these words when a footman opened the door, admitting the expected arrival. In strode a gentleman—an officer, in fact—dressed in the brilliant scarlet and white of His Majesty's forces, his sabre hanging ominously from his side, his shining golden insignia indicating considerable rank. But instead of the stern and forbidding face one might expect from such a formidable looking man, his expression was one of the greatest pleasure at the sight of the company in the room.

Before Mr. Darcy could make the formal introduction between those who had not previously met, the officer beamed broadly and bellowed, "Elizabeth!" to which she answered with equal enthusiasm, "Richard!"

Chapter Twenty

Tea and Travels

A nd thus it was that Mrs. Gardiner made the very agreeable acquaintance of Colonel Richard Fitzwilliam.

"I cannot express my pleasure at meeting you here today, Mrs. Gardiner," he gushed. "Will has spoken so warmly of your son that I feel I know the boy; indeed, he sounds rather like Will himself as a lad. I believe he is somewhere hereabouts today and I do look forward to making his acquaintance, if he be so inclined. And Elizabeth has always spoken of you in such glowing terms I had thought to meet near on a goddess. But I do confess, I had expected a somewhat older woman, not this lovely young thing I see before me."

"Richard...." Mr. Darcy growled, but the colonel just beamed even more broadly and continued with his unabashed flattery. Elizabeth could not help but notice that the more extravagant and effusive his cousin grew, the more Mr. Darcy grew stiff and stony as he retreated behind his accustomed self-imposed barricades. Gone was the open, friendly man who had ushered them so graciously into his home for tea;

in his place was the haughty and cold creature who had so provoked the dislike of the society at Meryton those months past. Even his face seems changed, thought Elizabeth, as she watched his gentle eyes grow flinty and narrow and the planes of his face somehow flatten. She knew it was discomfort and not disapproval that engendered this remarkable metamorphosis, but it was disconcerting nonetheless.

Later on, when asked about it, Mr. Darcy confessed to her, "I do not know how to respond when Richard goes on like that. He says things which are not quite true—your aunt is an attractive and youthful lady, to be sure, but she must be two and thirty to have a son the age of Samuel, and she looks as a lady of those years should look. In retrospect I can rationalise that Richard is flattering and teasing, but at the moment all I can think is that I do not know how to interpret his words, for he cannot truly mean what he says, and yet everybody else seems to know exactly how to respond. Your aunt cannot really have believed him, but she laughed and teased back with such natural ease."

And he was correct. Richard had such a good-natured and open character that his shameless flattery was construed by its object exactly as intended, and whilst he bordered on flirtation, his obvious intention was never to cross the line of what was appropriate. Rather than supposing him to have improper intentions towards her, Mrs. Gardiner realised immediately what Richard was about, and within moments they were the best of friends.

Miss Pierce, when she reappeared some time later with Samuel in her wake, was afforded similar treatment, although Richard related differently to her somehow. He judged his approach with respect to the governess' position and more reserved personality, and with her, he spoke knowledgeably and intelligently about some matters of botany she had been studying to teach the children. Nor was his inherent likeability restricted to the women he flattered. To Sammy, he was most attentive, asking the boy after his experiments and interests with all due seriousness, and not verging into metaphorical speech. He treated Samuel as a worthy young man with interesting things to say and withstood the disjointed responses and lengthy monologues with a pleasant smile and an air of genuine interest. His manner to Sammy, thought Elizabeth, was similar to that towards Mr. Darcy, and she suspected he spoke to her young cousin similarly to how Richard might have treated his own cousin as a youth.

Later that day, when Mr. Gardiner joined the party for dinner, he too was met with Richard's genuine friendliness and happy manners, and was as charmed by the man's charisma as had been his wife, without once feeling any discomfort or awkwardness at the immediate familiarity between the members of the gathering. It was, Elizabeth realised, a gift, and she was thankful that the colonel used it well and honestly, rather than in the duplicitous manner of Mr. Wickham. She was struck again by the difference between the cousins, but observed that between the two, as greatly as she liked and admired the colonel, and was most proud to call him a friend, she preferred the quieter and more reserved Mr. Darcy.

During the afternoon, whilst Mrs. Gardiner and Miss Pierce went to look in on the children and Mrs. Churley, Mr. Darcy had raised the topic of Lydia and Elizabeth's fears for her deportment in Brighton. "Richard, I am hoping you may be of assistance here," he said.

The colonel nodded. "That I may. I am, Elizabeth, travelling to that location myself soon. My men, whom I am training now, will also be stationed there for the summer for manoeuvres, and I know of Colonel Forster. It would not be seen as unusual for me to make his acquaintance and be seen in his company. Your sister does not know me and I shall be careful to keep my connexion from her, but I shall be your set of eyes there, and shall endeavour to do what I may to ensure her appropriate behaviour."

Elizabeth sighed in relief. "Thank you, Richard! I shall sleep better knowing that you are nearby!"

"But what of Wickham?" Mr. Darcy added. "He is part of the militia under Colonel Forster's command, and he knows you all too well. He also knows Miss Lydia. Would he not relish yet another opportunity to slander me and all those I call dear? It might make your task that much more difficult."

"Never fear, Will. George Wickham knows me, but not some of my most trusted men. I shall endeavour to keep him under a watchful eye as well, never mind that the eye might not be my own. I shan't be able to keep him from talking to Miss Lydia, but I shall know what he says.

"Mr. Wickham?" a voice came from the doorway as Samuel entered the room most unexpectedly. "Is he the gentleman speaking with Cousin Lizzy at the park last week? I have knowledge of him."

"Sammy," Lizzy chastised, "you should not listen in on others' conversations."

"I did not intend to," the boy explained with an expressionless face, "but I came to retrieve my book and you were speaking. I could not help but hear what you said, for I did not know to cover my ears."

Shaking her head, she recognised the truth in the boy's words.

"What knowledge do you have, Samuel?" Mr. Darcy asked. "I am curious as to whether you might have discerned something from your brief observation during the game with the periscopes." He spoke with respect and Elizabeth noticed how his eyes did not flicker from Samuel's face.

"He has been around the house." Samuel's expression remained neutral, but Lizzy's displayed alarm and Mr. Darcy's displeasure. Samuel appeared to noticed neither of these.

"How interesting," Richard interposed. With as much quiet respect has his cousin had offered, he requested of the lad, "What can you tell us about this?"

Satisfied that he was not about to be scolded for his intrusion, Samuel spoke. "I have been playing with my periscope these last several days, since our trip to Margate was delayed, and I wished for some interesting occupation. I would hide around corners and behind barriers to see what I might observe through it. On several of those occasions, when it looked as if no one were about on the street, I noticed the man who spoke to Cousin Lizzy walk down the street. As soon as somebody appeared, he would turn his back or seek a doorway or tree, but when the street was empty again, he would resume his regard."

"Indeed!" Richard exclaimed. "Carry on, lad. You are most observant."

"It seemed an interesting diversion, to watch the man without his knowledge, and thus I conceived of a further plan. I contrived to follow him in a similar manner, to see how far I might get without ever being in direct sight of him, using the periscope. It seemed a great adventure and a good test of what the periscope might do."

"Sammy!" Elizabeth cried, but Mr. Darcy stilled her with a gentle touch to her forearm.

"How fascinating," Richard continued soothingly. He must be, Elizabeth noticed, most adept at instilling trust in his juniors and at encouraging the reports and observations of those whose information must be of use to him in his occupation. "Pray continue, lad, and tell me more of what you saw and how you proceeded."

Buoyed up by this most explicit encouragement by a man Samuel had come to admire during their very short acquaintance, he spoke on. "It was easier when the streets were busy, for I must have a place to conceal myself while using my scope, but the man was not hard to find. I do not believe he was expecting to be followed, for he did not turn around at all to see if anyone were behind him. This made my game much easier. The first two times I followed him, I did lose him, but the third time I succeeded in finding his ultimate destination."

"You did this more than once?" Elizabeth groaned. "How dangerous!"

But Richard silenced her with a quick glance and coaxed, "And where was that, lad? Your game sounds most very fascinating!"

Samuel described Mr. Wickham's rather circuitous route through London, including a visit to a cigar shop, where he purchased a carefully enumerated selection of the items, past a haberdasher, where he examined, but did not purchase, a rather elaborate dark green cravat, and past other establishments and buildings, at one of which he waved to a man watching from a window. The trip concluded at a rooming house in a less elegant part of town. Not quite dangerous, it was, nonetheless, not an area which those of the elite might frequent, nor those of the prosperous merchant class. In daylight hours, it might be safe enough, but once darkness fell, it would be less than savoury. "He knocked at the door and a lady let him enter, and I saw him remove his hat before the door closed. Then I decided my game was over for the day, and I returned home. The return was less interesting, for I had nothing to observe through my scope." He shook his head as if the use of the periscope were the only matter of interest in this tale.

"Well, young man," Richard smiled, "you are most resourceful! I am pleased your game was a success, and that your periscope proved so useful. Do you propose to use it thus again?"

"No indeed, sir," Samuel looked forlorn, "for Robert's father proposes to depart for Margate the morning after tomorrow, and I must oversee the packing of my trunks, and then Robert is coming over to discuss what adventures we may have on our journey."

Elizabeth sighed in relief. "Well," she uttered at last, "you had best run along to find your mother. She must be wondering where you have disappeared."

Samuel found his book, said polite words, and ran off as quickly as he had arrived.

"So, Wickham has remained in town?" Richard's eyebrows rose. "That is interesting news. I shall make discreet inquiries as to the nature of this rooming house. We cannot have too much information as to his whereabouts. The man disturbs me, for I never know what trouble he may be contemplating." He rose and strode to the window, where he spent a moment looking out over the street. "There goes Samuel now, running back to the park where his mother and siblings are. Yes, he is waving to them.

"I shan't use your cousin's tools of observation, Elizabeth, but I shall do my best to ensure that Wickham sees as little of me as he did of Samuel. I do not imagine that he will know that I am there, and thus will be unable to betray my presence to your sister. Now, about those berry tarts that your cook promised me upon my last visit... Might she be prevailed to equip a poor soldier with a basketful to tide him over a while?"

The following few weeks passed without incident. Samuel's holiday with the Harwins proceeded as planned and he returned from Margate full of tales and stories and pictures he had drawn of the town and seaside. Elizabeth was impressed with his natural, though untutored, skill with a pencil. He had captured the essence of the place so perfectly, she felt she had seen it herself. As well as drawings of street scenes and other locations, Samuel had also rendered quite passable portraits of the Harwin family, including their looks of delight at finding themselves at the seaside, although when asked, he had a most difficult time identifying the facial expressions he had captured so readily on paper.

Mr. Darcy had kept to his previous schedule of visits, but those were soon to come to an end, for he must depart for Pemberley to take care of matters there, and the Gardiners, with Elizabeth, were to travel north as well on a holiday. The children would stay at the Bennets for the duration of the holiday, although Samuel pleaded to be allowed to accompany the adults, since Mr. Darcy was his friend too! It was only when Mr. Darcy himself reminded Samuel how much his brother and sisters would need him—nearly a man—to be near to look after them, and that he might enjoy a longer visit the following year, that the lad ceased his pleading.

And so, within a short time, Mr. Darcy left London for his estate, followed by the Gardiners, who planned to travel in the area before spending a few days in the area where Mrs. Gardiner had lived as a child. Lambton, this small village, was only five miles from Pemberley, and the couple had happily accepted the master's invitation to stay at the estate whilst they were in the area. Although her aunt knew the area well and her uncle had travelled through it on many occasions for his business when he was younger, it was Elizabeth's first journey northward, and she found amazement and joy in every new vista, delight in every new estate they visited.

Yet there was one estate which lay most heavily in Elizabeth's thoughts: Pemberley. Mr. Darcy had invited them, expected their imminent arrival. He had mentioned her quite specifically when making his offer. Then why did her anxiety increase with every mile they traversed, drawing them closer and closer to the Darcys' ancestral lands?

As usual, it was her aunt who observed her discomfort and, when Mr. Gardiner slept against the cushioned side of his carriage, asked, "What troubles you, dear Lizzy?"

"I can hardly say, Aunt. I am most satisfied with this tour and am eager to see where you lived in your childhood. However your eyes are keen, and I am unsettled. I know not why."

"Are your thoughts confused at the prospect of seeing Mr. Darcy again?"

Lizzy sighed and stared out of the window for a long moment as she considered her reply. "I should not be! I was always most pleased to see him in London, when he came to visit, or when he invited us out. But the thought of seeing his estate terrifies me. Why should a building, some land, bring me more upset than the man who owns them? It baffles me, Aunt."

"In London, Lizzy, Mr. Darcy was just a man. An unusual man, perhaps; one who admires you, most certainly. But just a man. Here, in Derbyshire, he is more than that. He is the master, the principal landholder of a vast area. He is not just a man but an institution and a symbol, and you do not know what to expect from this facet of his character."

Elizabeth grinned at her aunt, feeling some of her ill ease lift. "You are one of the most perceptive people I know! I have been fretting and stewing for days, and you discern the cause of my worries in an instant."

"Ah, Lizzy, I am older and wiser, and I, too, have known people who exhibit different character traits in their various roles in life. But you will see—your Mr. Darcy is incapable of dissembling. He may put on a different mask, but the man inside will remain the same. You need only to find him."

Now the carriage at last turned off the lane at the lodge and drove onto the vast estate. They entered it in one of its lowest points, and drove for some time through a beautiful wood, stretching over a wide extent. "Remarkable!" she whispered to herself. "Oh, look at that view!" After half a mile, they found themselves at the top of a considerable eminence, where the wood ceased, and the eye was instantly caught by Pemberley House, situated on the opposite side of a valley, into which the road, with some abruptness, wound.

"What a lovely building, Lizzy!" Aunt Gardiner said in awe. "As much as we lived so near, I have never visited before. It is more beautiful than

I might ever have imagined." And it was lovely indeed: a large, handsome, stone building, standing well on rising ground, and backed by a ridge of high woody hills.

"That stream in the front," her uncle murmured in awe—for he had awakened upon turning off the lane and into the drive— "that is a stream of quite some importance, and look how it has been swelled into something even greater. What a vista that house must have. What fishing they must enjoy!"

"Is it done by man, or by nature?" his wife asked. "I see no artificial appearance at all. See its banks—they are neither formal, nor falsely adorned. Such sublime splendour can only be the work of the divine."

"It is delightful!" Elizabeth breathed. "I have never seen a place for which nature had done more, or where natural beauty had been so little counteracted by an awkward taste. It matches the man who calls it home, does it not, Aunt?" Then, to herself, she whispered, "Of this place, I might have been mistress!" Would Mr. Darcy ever risk his composure—his heart—to offer for her once again? Despite his attention to her and his invitations to events in Town, where their names were inevitably linked by the gossips, would he find the courage to propose anew? Moreover, did he still love her? Or had he supplanted that first, imagined, ardent passion with something more akin to friendship? Was this, perhaps, another cause behind her anxiety?

For she now knew, knowing the man, having seen the place he called home, that she might well be on the way to loving him. The next few days might see her as happy as Jane, or else they might break her heart.

Fortunately, Mr. Darcy was blissfully unaware of Elizabeth's contemplations, and the party could see him awaiting them at the front doors to the manor house, Cabal standing placidly at his side. As the carriage approached and slowed down before coming to a gentle stop, Elizabeth watched with warmth as he scratched at his pet's ears, smiling broadly. He had obviously been alerted by a signal from the lodge, for a small army of attendants was standing at the ready to welcome the guests and remove their luggage to their rooms.

Mr. Gardiner was the first to descend the carriage steps, followed by his wife, whom he handed down with a care and devotion that bespoke deep affection. He was ready to assist his niece when Mr. Darcy gestured him aside and assisted the lady himself.

"You came!" he spoke quietly, only for her ears. "As much as it had been planned, I could not believe it until I saw you here with my own eyes." Then, in full voice for all the guests, "Welcome, dear friends, to Pemberley!"

If Mr. Darcy had been a gracious host at his town home in London, he was even more so at Pemberley. "The house in town is where I dwell when I am there, but this," gesturing all around him, "this is my home," he told Elizabeth. He radiated a special pride as he led his guests through the grand foyer towards the wide stairs where the housekeeper was waiting to show the newcomers to their rooms. It was not, however, the haughty arrogance he had displayed in Hertfordshire, but rather that deep appreciative pride of a truly grateful man. "I have been fortunate enough to be born to this," his manner proclaimed, "and I shall strive to be worthy of it."

He was, at once, completely at ease in his country home, where he need be only himself with no need to strut and perform before the members of society, and more assured as well. This was his domain; this was his honour and his responsibility. The land provided for him, and in turn, he provided for the land. If the estate was wealthy and productive, it was because he had endeavoured through careful planning and hard work to make it so. Elizabeth knew that not all men were graced with land that could provide so healthy an income, but also that poor management could not compensate for the richest of prospects.

She recalled now his words from the drawing room at Netherfield when Jane had been so ill. She had spoken to him of pride and vanity, and he, in his literal and concrete understanding, had been careful to separate the two. "Yes, vanity is a weakness indeed," he had declaimed in his stiff and uneasy manner. "But pride—where there is a real superiority of mind, pride will be always under good regulation." At the time, she had thought him merely excusing his own sense of excellence, but now, seeing his genuine pleasure in his admittedly superior estate, she retroactively forgave his cold words. He was not boastful of his mental acuity, but was proud of the work he had done to bring himself and his responsibilities to the utmost of their potential.

Marvelling at her thoughts and at the grandeur around her, Elizabeth hardly realised they had reached the landing at the top of the staircase. A respectable-looking, elderly woman, much less fine, and more civil, than she had any notion of finding her, stood waiting for them. Mr. Darcy introduced her as Mrs. Reynolds, the housekeeper. Mrs. Reynolds greeted the guests cordially, announced that tea would be ready in an hour, after the visitors had a chance to rest after their journey, and offered any assistance that might be desired. Thereupon, she indicated that the Gardiners should follow her to their suite. At Elizabeth's curious glance, Mr. Darcy told her, "Yours is across the hallway from your aunt and uncle's suite, but I had hoped to direct you there myself." He offered his arm, which she gladly accepted, and led her in the same direction the others had just taken.

An hour was more than sufficient time to wash the dust from her face, change her clothing, and rest briefly. A young woman had appeared and announced that she would be Elizabeth's personal maid for the duration of her stay, and with young Sally's help, Elizabeth was soon ready to face company once again. Shortly before the appointed hour for tea, Elizabeth emerged from her room and sought the staircase once more. The stairs were easy enough to find, but once at the bottom, she realised she was quite lost. The entry hall, which had seemed grand and imposing upon first sight, now looked like the entrance to the Labyrinth. Doors and halls and wall niches presented themselves in a bewildering array before her, and she stood there, frozen to the spot, unsure which direction had been pointed out upon her arrival.

A friendly voice broke her concentration. "Miss Bennet, allow me to show you the way. This house can be quite the maze for those unfamiliar with it. I have sent a maid to your aunt and uncle's rooms. I hope young Sally was helpful? I should have requested specifically that she guide you to the appropriate room for tea."

She spun around to see Mrs. Reynold's smiling lined face. "Oh, thank you, Mrs. Reynolds. I had no idea there were so many exits from this entry space!"

"If you will follow me," the old lady invited. "Mr. Darcy wishes to give you a proper tour, but I will show you the shortest way to the tea room, through here." She led Elizabeth through the dining-parlour, a large, well-proportioned room, handsomely fitted up, with a bank of large windows through which Elizabeth could admire the prospect. The hill from which they had descended was a beautiful object. Every disposition of the ground was good; and she looked on the whole scene—the river, the trees scattered on its banks, and the winding of the valley, as far as she could trace it—with delight. Through a far door they passed, into a smaller passageway, and then into another series of connected rooms. From every window there were beauties to be seen; in every room, likewise. The rooms were lofty and handsome, and their furniture suitable to the fortune of their proprietor; but Elizabeth saw, with admiration of his taste, that it was neither gaudy nor uselessly fine; with less of splendour, and more real elegance, than the furniture of Rosings.

"The house is beautiful," Elizabeth praised. "It truly is a testimony to the care of its master and the good people who keep it."

"Mr. Darcy is the best of masters," came the response. "He is good and kind and cares most deeply for his tenants. He is a good tempered man too. I have never had a cross word from him in my life, and I have known him ever since he was four years old."

"Then you are lucky in having such a master."

"Yes, Miss Bennet, I know I am. If I was to go through the world, I could not meet with a better. But I have always observed that they who are good-natured when children are good-natured when they grow up; and he was always the sweetest-tempered, most generous-hearted, boy in the world. One can tell," confided the older woman, "by how a lad treats his animals. Mr. Darcy has always had the utmost patience with his dogs, no matter what the beasts destroyed of his prized possessions, even as a young lad. That, to me, marks a good soul from a bad. Aye, Miss Bennet, even as a lad!"

"I would like, very much, to hear about Mr. Darcy as a boy," she said to the other, not expecting a favourable reply, but Mrs. Reynolds gazed at her benignly and replied, "He was a most unusual child, and I should be happy to talk to you of him, should the master agree, but he was always a generous one, with genuine good intentions, that was the master! Now, here, through this door, you will find the room you seek. Mr. Darcy will show you the other passageways himself after you have had your refreshments."

Those few words from the housekeeper were not something Elizabeth had expected to hear about her host. So he had not always shown the cold and unyielding facade that had become his defence against the assaults of society. What a sad thing that he had found the need to erect such a barricade, when the man who cowered behind those stony walls was a man worth knowing. Her heart ached slightly for the torments that he must have experienced that caused him to slowly hide himself from the world, save for those lucky few who had the honour to truly know him.

Now, as she entered the room completely, she saw that the object of her musings was already there, seated in a wing-backed chair near the farthest window. The light streaming in from outside caught the highlights in his hair and illuminated him from behind, so for a moment, as he stood to greet her, it looked almost as though he glowed.

"Elizabeth!" He bowed quite properly, despite his increasing familiarity with her name, and led her to a comfortable sofa where she sat to talk in comfort for the few minutes as they awaited the Gardiners.

"Before your aunt and uncle join us," he inquired quietly, "I would like very much to know if I may... that is, will you allow me, or do I ask too much, to introduce my sister to your acquaintance during your stay? She is not at home now, but I expect her return tomorrow. If you are discomforted by this, she has already assured me she is happy to extend her visit with her friends."

The honour of this request was not lost on Elizabeth. Mr. Darcy had shown her his house in London, invited her to his estate, and now wished to introduce her to his closest relative, his sister. Perhaps, he was after all hoping to renew his addresses to her. She blushed slightly as she happily accepted his request. "I should be most pleased, sir, to know her."

Chapter Twenty-One

Pemberley

Miss Darcy, when she was introduced to the visitors the following day, proved to be a lovely young woman, some sixteen years of age. She was tall and well-made, not quite handsome, but with sense and good humour in her face. Where Elizabeth had, from Mr. Wickham's description, expected her to be very proud, she found instead that Miss Darcy was merely exceedingly shy. Her manners, however, were perfectly unassuming and gentle, and she exhibited a soft awareness of her companions and her surroundings that marked her as a very different sort of creature from her brother.

Elizabeth liked her immediately.

"How did you meet my brother?" the young woman asked as they ambled around the pond in the formal garden at the back of the house that morning. Mr. Gardiner had accepted the offer of a horse and guide to explore the estate and his wife was busy at her letters to local acquaintances informing them of her wish to visit, leaving Lizzy and

Miss Darcy to wander and speak in privacy. "My brother is an excellent correspondent," the young lady offered, "and has written of you often, but not once has he told me where you met."

"Ah, that is a story that should not be retold!" Elizabeth teased, "For it would not reflect well on him, and I have come to learn that he deserves better than to be judged on first impressions. Let us say it was at a dance, and leave the details for him to complete himself."

Miss Darcy had little to say in response to that. Elizabeth detected that the cause was not arrogance, but a deeply felt sense of unworthiness to reply with any semblance of wit. Contemplating her walking companion, Lizzy felt a sense of pity for the girl. She was taller than Elizabeth by a significant margin, and at just sixteen, she must have felt quite out of place amongst her peers. What was considered an advantage in a man was a disadvantage in a lady. Whilst she would no doubt grow into her statuesque proportions and become a rather impressive woman, bearing such height at such a young age must have been extremely uncomfortable; combined with a naturally shy character, her height must have been rather painful. She was also, in many ways, alone. With no parents and a brother very much older than she, there must also have been a desperate need for inclusion and love.

No wonder George Wickham had enjoyed such success wooing the girl. All he needed to have done was whisper to her of her loveliness, her grace, her importance to him. With the right words and the right gestures, it would be easy to convince an unconfident and awkward young girl that she was in love. If Elizabeth had not before marked Mr. Wickham as the worst sort of manipulative man, meeting Miss Darcy and seeing the deep need in her demeanour to be accepted and cared for, she would now have known the scoundrel for what he was.

But she could not, would not, speak of Mr. Wickham. Those memories were not to be rekindled by a stranger, no matter how well-meaning. Instead, Elizabeth asked after some of the flowers that bloomed in the carefully tended mazes of floral fecundity, hoping to find a topic upon which the young woman could converse with comfort and ease.

When they returned to the house, Mr. Darcy was sitting at his table in the salon reading a letter. "Georgiana, Elizabeth," he greeted them. After seeing to the ladies' comfort, he informed Elizabeth of the whereabouts of her relations. "Your uncle has returned from his ride and has now gone to explore the ponds, where I have offered him tackle to fish should he desire it. Your aunt joins him in the curricle. She insisted upon driving. I am just sitting down to peruse the latest letter from my cousin."

At this Miss Darcy brightened. "Not Anne, surely, or Alfred. Anne writes to me and not to you, so it cannot be from her, and Alfred hardly knows how to put pen to paper. You must mean Richard! Oh, I have not had a letter from him in an age; he writes so seldom. What does he have to say to you, Will?"

"Oh, mostly of military matters, dear one. He asked after you in town, and I know he wishes to visit as soon as he might."

The girl's eyes brightened at this. She clearly adored her cousin almost as much as her brother. "When, Will? It has been too long since he last was here. Perhaps I shall write to him and ask what his plans are. Now, where is my paper?" She bustled off in search of her materials, leaving Elizabeth alone with her host.

"Richard writes of more than just military affairs," he stated before Elizabeth had a chance even to sit. "I thought it best not to mention such matters in front of my sister."

"Indeed, sir, I believe that was wise."

Mr. Darcy paused. "I see things in her now that I never saw before," he commented abstractly. "Perhaps they were not there; 'tis more likely I was not looking and knew not what to see. She feels strongly, does she not? Her face is moveable, and now that I am observing her, I see there is a look about her eyes that I cannot quite identify. It is not sadness, nor is it despair. Have you seen it, Elizabeth? Can you tell me what she feels?"

"I believe, sir, it is loneliness."

"But she was so unhappy at school!" he burst out. "Her current companion is a good woman, but is she not what Georgiana requires? Did I do wrong by removing her from school and from her friends?"

218

"No, despite the consequences. But I believe she craves something that a paid companion cannot provide. She wants love and acceptance, true friends and a present family."

"I have failed her then."

"No you have not. You have other responsibilities, and you cannot be a friend to a girl—your sister—so much younger. But this, I believe, is what led her to be so easily seduced by Mr. Wickham. He offered her, or so she thought, all these things she wished for so dearly."

"I have failed her." He did not speak for some moments, and then changed the topic quite abruptly.

"Mr. Wickham features large in Richard's letter. He has seen nothing of any real concern in your sister's affairs. She is accepted as being loud and a flirt, and is happy to dance with any man who asks her at balls, but she has done nothing to garner true disapprobation. Mr. Wickham, however, has been a regular visitor at the Forsters, and thus Richard is unable to observe as closely as he wishes, for fear of alerting Wickham to our surveillance. He has sent three or four of his men to keep the eye out, on a varying schedule so Wickham should not think they are tailing him. There are no reports that incite alarm."

He spoke briskly, as if reading a laundry list. Elizabeth was relieved.

"Thank you. I have received similar impressions for Jane, although she has no spies to alert her to any trouble that might be brewing."

"What is brewing, brother dear?" Georgiana Darcy asked as she walked back into the room, writing paper in hand.

Mr. Darcy stared at her in alarm. He could not dare confess what Richard's letter included, and the thought of misleading her or worse—outright lying—seemed not to occur to him at all.

Elizabeth stepped in to save him. "Tea, Miss Darcy. We were contemplating having some tea, and wondered whether we should ask Mrs. Reynolds to start some brewing now, or if we should rather wait. Would you like a cup?"

Mr. Darcy's expression was one of amazement and gratitude. *Yes,* thought Elizabeth, *I understand you. You had no idea how to avoid telling your sister the truth and did not wish to alarm her. Deception is abhorrent to you, but harming your family is more so. You are a complicated, unusual, excellent man.*

Further speculation on Richard, his letter, or the state of the tea, was curtailed by the entrance of the Gardiners into the room. "Excellent pond there, Darcy," Uncle Gardiner raved. "Those waters look fabulously rich. If your offer of a morning with the fish still stands, I shall be most pleased to accept it."

"By all means, the offer stands. I shall join you for part of that time, but I do have business relating to my estate that cannot wait and needs my attention. Shall we depart right after an early breakfast tomorrow?"

"That would be most excellent, sir, most excellent indeed!"

By now, Elizabeth had rung the bell and Mr. Darcy requested the previously discussed tea, and the group sat amicably, discussing sights and activities on the estate until the tray was brought in. "These scones, Mr. Darcy...." Mrs. Gardiner's eyes widened as she took a nibble.

"Yes, indeed, Madam, the same as the ones we enjoyed in London."

"Does your cook travel with you?"

A very pleased look crept over his face as he nodded, "Indeed, madam. She hails from these parts, and asks to join me when I return to Derbyshire. She thanks me profusely for my magnanimity, but I am the one who ought to thank her, for I then benefit from her cooking."

Still curious, Mrs. Gardiner added, "You seem to have inspired much loyalty amongst your staff. The estate seems remarkably well managed, and everybody speaks well of you. Not just the words one expects to hear when asked about the master, but the enthusiasm, the looks of real respect and admiration upon their faces, those speak more loudly than the words."

"I try, madam. My father left me this estate in prime condition, and it is my honour and responsibility to maintain it. I do spend much time on its management. I have excellent people working for me, to be sure, but I feel I must be personally involved as well."

"But when do you find the time, Mr. Darcy?" Elizabeth asked. "My father has little interest in managing his small estate, but he spends many more hours on the books and in conference with farmers and managers than he would wish. Yet you, who are intimately concerned with the well-being of your land and tenants, have been entertaining us in London, and sitting here with us now, drinking tea and enjoying the prospect from your windows."

"I work at night, Miss Elizabeth. I am a man with little natural talent for the innate organisation of my affairs, and find many aspects of managing complicated operations difficult, but I have learned to become a master at planning my time and setting out my duties in small sections. My steward helps, of course. He sits with me as we plan what needs to be done. I have then set a schedule, in which I have allotted sufficient time—I hope—to be a gracious host, whilst still including the hours I need to complete my duties to my holdings."

"In other words, sir, you are a master at setting a schedule, and are pedantic about adhering to it!" Mr. Gardiner laughed.

"Guilty as charged sir! Guilty as charged."

It was decided over tea that whilst Mr. Gardiner and Mr. Darcy set off for their fishing in the morning, Mrs. Gardiner would be driven in the carriage to Lambton, where she had lived in her youth and where she wished to visit with acquaintances. Elizabeth was invited to join her. To this she agreed, since Miss Darcy quietly and apologetically mentioned her wish to spend the morning at the new pianoforte which had so recently arrived from London.

But when the morning arrived and the carriage drew up in front of the house, the footman announcing its arrival also brought in a salver of mail, including a missive for Elizabeth from Jane.

Seeing the letter on the table before Elizabeth, and seeing the look on her niece's face, Mrs. Gardiner quietly suggested that perhaps Lizzy might wish to stay at Pemberley to read her sister's correspondence. "It looks thick," she said with a lilt in her voice. "She must have much information to tell you about Mr. Bingley, perhaps?"

"Would you mind, Aunt?" Lizzy inquired. "I know I promised to accompany you, but..."

"But you would be spending the day with old ladies whom you have never met before, listening and trying to remain interested as we talk about people you never knew, when you would rather be here reading your sister's letter. I would do the same."

Reaching over to kiss her aunt on the cheek, Lizzy thanked her gratefully and wished her a marvellous day in the village. Then, taking the letter, her tea, and a small plate of sweets to the sitting room that opened from the breakfast room, she found a chair by the large window and broke the seal.

As Mrs. Gardiner suggested, Jane's letter was, indeed, filled with her thoughts and feelings about Mr. Bingley and their courtship. She recounted every visit, every gesture, every word he said. They had held hands as they walked in the wilderness behind the house, he had told her how lovely she was, he had made comments about how much she would love the theatre when they were next in town. Jane expected a proposal any day, and Lizzy agreed with her.

About the rest of the family, Jane had only a few lines to add.

Papa misses you very much, I believe, but he is resigned to your absence. He does implore you, though, to make an accounting of the extent and nature of Mr. Darcy's library. A listing of his catalogue would be welcome too, he says, although he cannot possibly mean that!

Mama is, well, she is Mama. Without Lydia always bustling in and out, she is, perhaps, slightly calmer than usual, and I have not heard her call for her salts once. But I believe she is bored without you and Lyddie to scold, and consequently she expends much of her energy upon poor Mary and Kitty.

Mary, of course, ignores it all and hides behind her pianoforte or behind a book, but Kitty does not know what to do, and often ends up running out of the room in tears. Oh, Lizzy, I do not miss being seventeen, and should not wish to return to that age for all the world.

We have heard very little of Lydia. She writes so rarely, we are shocked if a letter arrives at all, but Colonel Forster sends a note to Papa every few days to assure him of Lyddie's continued good health. From all accounts she is happy and all is well, but, well, he is a man more given to observing the marching prowess of his men than the fripperies of a silly girl with an eye for the officers.

Please, Lizzy, do not forget to send Papa some news of Mr. Darcy's books. I promised I should ask you, and I do think he wishes for some astounding news, if not the complete catalogue he requested.

Your loving sister,

Jane

After this page, another letter appeared. It seemed to have been written after the first and included in the envelope. Resolving to discharge her obligation to her father immediately, whilst the house was quiet, Elizabeth set down this second letter to peruse later. It could only be more news about Mr. Bingley. Perhaps he had, at last, proposed, and Jane had written down every word he had uttered for her sister's perusal. She would read it as soon as her task in the library was complete.

Once in the library, however, Elizabeth soon became lost in her task, and it was much later than she expected when she finally returned to her letter. She was surprised to see Mr. Darcy sitting in the chair opposite the one she had taken, dressed in the rougher garb of a sportsman and sipping from a cup of coffee, if she could judge by the rich scent that filled the air. Embarrassed, she admitted her recent errand, and when Mr. Darcy smiled, she allowed herself to laugh along with him. "Yes," she told him, "I was more than pleased to accept my father's commission. Your library is most impressive."

"I had hoped you might like it." Suddenly, he sat up a little straighter in his chair and set down his coffee. Some of his habitual rigidity overcame him once more and he stood stiffly, holding himself like a statue come to life. "Miss Elizabeth, I have only just returned from fishing and wish to change into something more suitable for the house, but perhaps you will grant me an interview when I return... I have something very particular I wish to ask you."

Her eyes widened, and she realised at once that he had noticed her reaction and had begun to work on what it meant. Attempting to remain calm, she nodded, feeling her cheeks flush and grow warm. "I would be happy to oblige, sir. I shall remain here, as I have the rest of Jane's letter to read."

Bowing, Mr. Darcy walked from the room, and then, from the sound of his footsteps, rushed towards the stairs which would take him to his rooms.

Opening the letter, Elizabeth tried to read, but she found her mind disturbed by Mr. Darcy's request. An interview, while everyone else was away or otherwise occupied. Could that mean...? That could only mean...

What would she say? How should she react? She knew her only answer could be to accept him, but would he expect a speech? Or would a teary nod be sufficient?

Squashing down these wild thoughts, she forced her eyes to Jane's words, and then gasped in astonishment and shock.

Since writing the above, dearest Lizzy, something has occurred of a most unexpected and serious nature; but I am afraid of alarming you—be assured that we are all well. What I have to say relates to poor Lydia. An express came at twelve last night, just as we were all gone to bed, from Colonel Forster, to inform us that she was gone off to Scotland with one of his officers; to own the truth, with Wickham!

What? Wickham! Lydia had eloped with George Wickham? How could that be? The man had never expressed the first bit of interest in her. Oh, the horror, the shame!

Imagine our surprise. But I am willing to hope the best, and that his character has been misunderstood. Thoughtless and indiscreet I can easily believe him, but this step (and let us rejoice over it) marks nothing bad at heart. His choice is disinterested at least, for he must know my father can give her nothing. Our poor mother is sadly grieved. My father bears it better. How thankful am I, that we never let them know what has been said against him; we must forget it ourselves. They were off Saturday night about twelve, as is conjectured, but were not missed till yesterday morning at eight. The express was sent off directly. My dear Lizzy, they must have passed within ten miles of us. Colonel Forster gives us reason to expect him here soon. Lydia left a few lines for his wife, informing her of their intention. I must conclude, for I cannot be long from my poor mother. I am afraid you will not be able to make it out, but I hardly know what I have written.

No! It could not be. For her sister to be married to a scoundrel like Mr. Wickham was bad enough, but no one knew how low the man could be, how he would lie to protect his name, how readily he would impugn the name of a good man. What would Mr. Darcy think? She must admit this to him before he spoke to her; he must not be allowed to make his offer without this knowledge. Tears sprang to her eyes. This would surely change his mind about her; his pride would never allow him such a close connexion to one such as Wickham!

But there was still more on the page. Reluctantly she lifted the sheet of paper again and began to read the words dated a day after the preceding note.

Dearest Lizzy, I hardly know what I would write, but I have bad news for you, and it cannot be delayed. Imprudent as a marriage between Mr. Wickham and our poor Lydia would be, we are now anxious to be assured it has taken place, for there is but too much reason to fear they are not gone to Scotland. Colonel Forster came yesterday, having left Brighton the day before, not many hours after the express.

The letter went on to explain that, although Lydia had told Mrs. Forster in her letter that they were heading for Gretna Green, one of Wickham's friends indicated that the scoundrel had never intended to follow through on a marriage. The couple had been heading towards London, but could not be traced past that point, and all evidence suggested that London was where Wickham had intended to remain, with Lydia or (heaven forbid) without her.

Our distress, my dear Lizzy, is very great. My father and mother believe the worst, but I cannot think so ill of him. Many circumstances might make it more eligible for them to be married privately in town than to pursue their first plan; I grieve to find, however, that Colonel F. is not disposed to depend upon their marriage; he shook his head when I expressed my hopes, and said he feared W. was not a man to be trusted.

My father is going to London with Colonel Forster instantly, to try to discover her. What he means to do, I am sure I know not; but his excessive distress will not allow him to pursue any measure in the best and safest way, and Colonel Forster is obliged to be at Brighton again tomorrow evening. In such an exigence my uncle's advice and assistance would be every thing in the world; he will immediately comprehend what I must feel, and I rely upon his goodness.

What could Elizabeth do, after reading such a dreadful letter, other than break down in tears?

Chapter Twenty-Two

A Disastrous Connexion

S uch was Elizabeth's despair that she did not notice Mr. Darcy enter the room. It was only when his hand settled upon her own with a butterfly's barely present touch that she came to herself and realised she was no longer alone.

"Elizabeth," his eyes betrayed his concern. "What ever is the matter? Even one such as I can easily discern that you are under great distress. Will you tell me what is wrong?" He glanced at the tear-stained letter in her hands. "It must be some dire news from home."

Sobbing, Elizabeth unburdened herself of the whole story in disjointed fits and starts. She knew this spelled the end of any intentions Mr. Darcy might have towards her, and her tears were for herself as much as for her sister; however, she could in no way conscience concealing the matter from him. He would find out soon enough. Better that she give him the opportunity to break with her now, before any words of love or the future were exchanged, when he would feel no obligation towards keeping an engagement, than to allow him to speak, to offer for her, and then to resent her for the rest of his life for trapping him so unjustly.

This she had to do; she had no option, no other choice. But how her heart broke. She could barely look at him as she choked out the words, "I have had a letter from Jane," she wept. "It cannot be concealed from any one. My sister, stupid, stupid Lydia, has left all her friends—has eloped! She has thrown herself into the power of..." she rubbed her temples as if in pain, "of Mr. Wickham! They are gone off together from Brighton. You know him too well to doubt the rest. She has no money, no connexions, nothing that can tempt him to—she is lost forever." She dissolved into another flood of tears, which not even Mr. Darcy's offered handkerchief could stem.

When, at last, she could speak again, she begged him, "Please find my uncle. We must be off immediately; his assistance is needed by my father in London. Oh, I could have prevented this, had only I spoken more openly to my father, but I did not wish to reveal too much." She stood suddenly, sending the pages of the letter scattering across the floor. She bent to pick them up and gave them to Mr. Darcy. "Read it if you will, for Jane tells the worst of it." She then hurried to the window and peered out anxiously, before pacing then back again. Her movements were skittish and nervous, her need to be doing something, anything, translated into physical agitation. Scurrying back to the window and peering out again, she asked breathlessly, "Where is my aunt? Oh, how shall I find her? We must pack; we must leave at once!"

When she looked up at Mr. Darcy through her wet and red eyes, she saw once more that stiff, haughty facade behind which the true man hid himself. He had closed himself off from her, and from the cold glint in his eye, he had no notion of relaxing his defences. He must be congratulating himself, Elizabeth thought, on having avoided so narrowly this awful connexion. How he must believe the whole family to be affected with this weakness of moral rectitude, a common disgrace; he would never wish any manner of alliance now. She fought for control over her features and battled to maintain her composure.

As if in response to her thoughts, he added in a voice edged with compassion, but imparting great reserve, "I shall call Mrs. Reynolds to summon your aunt and have your uncle recalled to the house right away. As soon as your relations have returned and the carriage is ready, you may be off. I shall see that your trunks are packed and sent along as soon as possible." He took a step towards her, then stopped and retreated, the walls around him growing higher and thicker. In a tight voice, he said only, "Now, I am afraid you have been long desiring my absence. This unfortunate affair will, I fear, prevent my sister's having the pleasure of seeing you later today. I shall summon Mrs. Reynolds right away."

And without a single backwards glance, he marched quickly and resolutely from the room, leaving Elizabeth to fight yet another wave of tears as she reflected that she would, in all likelihood, never see him again.

From this point, the point at which all her hopes had been dashed, events moved quickly. A flurry of action of the part of Mr. Darcy's household staff saw the hastily arranged plans set underway. As promised, her aunt and uncle were summoned at once and the carriage prepared, and they were on the road back to London within an hour of Mrs. Gardiner's return, with a promise of their trunks to follow. Elizabeth noticed almost nothing of the return journey, so wrapped was she in her own misery. All too soon, she was alighting from the carriage in front of her home at Longbourn, allowing the Gardiners to gather their children and continue the journey to London.

Samuel wanted only to talk about Mr. Darcy and his estate, but Elizabeth explained to him that due to circumstances that were no reflection at all on Samuel himself, their friendship might be at an end. If her sorrow for herself was great, how much greater was it for her young cousin, who would surely lose a cherished friend as a result of this awful happening. She searched for the worlds that might explain to the lad why a man such as Mr. Darcy could no longer associate himself with any one connected to Mr. Wickham. Nothing she could think of would suffice. At last, she simply told him, "My family has, I'm afraid, been touched by some news that will be distasteful to a man such as Mr. Darcy, and he may wish to distance himself from all of us. Never, ever, believe that you have done anything wrong, Sammy," she assured him. "You are a remarkable young man. Know that to be true!"

"I know nothing of the sort," the lad retorted in his guileless way. "Mr. Darcy cares not about the approbation of others. If he did, he should never have sought to befriend me! I am not of his class nor of any use to him. He was my friend because he liked me. Can that not be enough?"

Elizabeth could see his young heart breaking at the loss of his new friend, but she would not give her cousin false hope. "Mr. Darcy is an important man, Sammy, and whether he cares for the approval of others, he knows that the opinions of his associates matter, if not to himself then to his family and his sister. He moves in a world so different from ours. For his circle, appearances are so very important, and matters of integrity few. His world is not our world. I know that if he could, he would wish to remain your friend."

"If he wishes so, then he will do so!" Nothing could dissuade Samuel from his conviction, and Elizabeth hoped the reality of this disaster would not cause her cousin too much pain. Already, as the Gardiners' carriage was being loaded, she could see him wringing his hands obsessively, as he had done before Miss Pierce found a way to help him calm himself, as he still did when experiencing great turmoil. By the time the last of the trunks had been secured to the back, he was rocking backwards and forward slowly in place, a most sure sign of his distress. "I'm so sorry, Aunt!" she whispered as the carriage pulled away. "We have undone so much of what we have achieved." She wept now, for herself, for her sister, and for her young cousin as well, all of whom were to suffer greatly for Lydia's thoughtlessness.

The days passed slowly. Mrs. Bennet kept to her rooms, calling out incessantly for tea or her salts or some other anodyne for her nerves. Mary was all but invisible, and Kitty crept around shamefaced and horrified, for it seemed that she had had some notion of Lydia's plans. Jane looked almost as crestfallen as she had in the autumn after Mr. Bingley's first departure from Netherfield; only the fact that Mr. Bingley had not—yet—returned to town kept her from complete despair.

"And yet," Jane uttered quietly as they sat in the silent house, "he has not been to call since the news came. I know what I should think of that. I am steeling myself, Lizzy. This is the end for all of us." Having nothing to say to soothe her sister's fears, Lizzy just hugged her and fought back her own tears. It seemed that their fortunes had fallen greatly and irrevocably, and there was nothing at all to do be done but suffer for another's misdeeds.

On Tuesday, a note arrived from Mr. Gardiner. It read: *I have written to Colonel Forster to desire him to find out, if possible, from some of the young man's intimates in the regiment, whether Wickham has any relations or connexions who would be likely to know in what part of the town he has now concealed himself. If there were any one that one could apply to with a probability of gaining such a clue as that, it might be of essential consequence. At present we have nothing to guide us.*

Matters seemed increasingly dire: there had been no word from Lydia, no news of Wickham, and no reports of them past London. The crowded, teeming city was the best place to remain concealed, and hope was dwindling fast of ever finding them. Only the news that Mr. Bingley had still made no moves or comments about departing once more from Netherfield gave the Bennet family some faint hope for their future.

The following Friday, Mr. Bennet returned home, exhausted and pale, explaining that his presence seemed to be of little help to his brother Gardiner. Elizabeth was horrified at his words. Tired and drawn as her father was, he seemed satisfied to leave the recovery of his daughter to another. Once again, she observed, he was following the path of least resistance, much as he had when he had allowed Lydia to exhibit such improper flirtatious behaviour at balls or in town, and when he had permitted her travel to Brighton. Whilst she still loved her parent, she knew then she would never quite hold the same respect for him ever again. This saddened her, and brought to mind the men who were working ceaselessly for a girl so little connected to them, and she appreciated her uncle all the more.

Then, not many days later, shortly after the family had finished their breakfast, another letter came from Mr. Gardiner. The messenger was one of his own footmen, driving his carriage, and guiding two very tired horses to the stables. The letter was short and desperate.

Lizzy, please come. Sammy has disappeared. Your aunt needs you.

For the first time in her life, Elizabeth thought she might faint. Those words struck her to the quick, and the air around her threatened to darken as the floor tilted beneath her feet. Only with the greatest of effort did she remain standing, staring in shock at the footman whose troubled countenance surely mirrored her own.

"Yes, yes, of course, I must go!" she uttered at last, when the ability to speak was returned to her. "Oh Jane... Jane, come quickly. Mama... Papa...." She dashed upstairs to inform her mother of her imminent departure, then her father in his study, not waiting for permission. Taking charge of matters, in great haste she scribbled a note to be delivered to Mr. Bingley, begging him to at least ensure the family were as well as might be managed, even if he could not visit himself. A few necessary belongings were untidily stuffed into a bag, and within a half hour of the carriage's arrival, with fresh horses in harness, they were off once more to London at a terrific pace. The four-and-twenty miles seemed endless, and yet the journey was completed in an astounding three hours, such was the haste with which the driver sped along the roads, taking only one very short break to change horses.

As could only be expected, the Gardiner household was in a state of great disorder. The servants, usually so efficient and professional, were milling around like lost children, and more than one normally expressionless eye was wet. The servants clearly loved and were most worried about Samuel. The other children and Miss Pierce had been sent off to Aunt Gardiner's dearest friend Mrs. Dyson, and the lady herself was pacing anxiously around the salon, her eyes red and her lips pale. When Elizabeth was announced, she turned and caught Lizzy up in a hug as desperately as a drowning man might embrace a life preserver. "Lizzy," she sobbed, "oh Lizzy!"

"I came immediately upon receiving my uncle's note," Lizzy's voice was also raw. "I hardly packed a change of clothing, but I knew I must come at once. What has happened, Aunt? If you have the strength to talk?"

Aunt Gardiner mopped her red eyes with a handkerchief, and tried to settle herself on a sofa, although it was most clear she would find no physical comfort. "He did not come home last night, Lizzy. He went off yesterday morning, as he has done all the while he has been on school holidays, but before now, he has always been home long before the sun begins to set. Last night, he was not home for dinner, nor did he come home at night. Mrs. Harwin had no notion of where he might be, for Robert has not been on most of these adventures, and none of the servants has the first idea of where he might have gone. We have sent men out all over the city, seeking him, but there has been no word. None at all." Her face, normally so pretty and calm, was a mask of pain, and Elizabeth wrapped her in her arms.

"Have you slept at all, Aunt? Tell me what I can do."

"I am just so relieved you are here. Your uncle must be out, searching, finding anyone who might know where to look, and I must be here in case Sammy comes home, but sitting alone, all I can think of is every possible horror that might have befallen him. Oh, Sammy...."

A fresh handkerchief did little to dry her aunt's eyes, but it seemed to Elizabeth that the lady walked a little straighter now that she had someone in whom to confide. "Do you have any idea where he might have gone? Had he wished to return to Margate, where he enjoyed his time with Robert? Perhaps he bought passage on the new steam boats that travel the Thames, and he neglected to bring enough coin to return. Or did he set off for adventures elsewhere? He would not have tried to return to Longbourn, or heaven forbid, Pemberley, would he?"

Her aunt spoke with a voice thick with tears. "We have wondered if he decided to visit Derbyshire on his own. He has not stopped asking about the bridges since our return and he wished so much to see them, but we thought him to be satisfied with a promise to visit at some future time." She sniffed again and dabbed once more at her red eyes.

"Oh, Sammy! He is so curious, but does not always think of how his actions might affect others. Never fear, dear Aunt, we shall find him. He is most likely off having a grand adventure and lost his way when darkness fell. He is too smart a lad to come to trouble."

"But he is... He is different, Lizzy, and I dread to think what that might mean should he fall afoul of the wrong people."

"Be strong, dearest Aunt. He will be home soon, I feel it in my bones."

At this moment, the front door was heard to open and close again, and Mr. Gardiner staggered into the room moments later. He still had on his hat and his boots were dusty and soiled, their bedraggled state mirroring the man's exhausted face.

"Lizzy, dearest Lizzy," he breathed, as if too tired to speak aloud. "You came quickly. I sent my man off only this morning, and it is not yet time for tea. Thank you."

"Have you learned anything, Uncle?" She asked, trying to keep the worry out of her voice for her aunt's sake.

"Nothing. Nothing at all. This might be good news, for he has not been found de.... In poor condition anywhere." He would not speak the words, certainly not before his distraught wife, who sat still and white now by the window, but Elizabeth knew what he meant. No small bloodied bodies had been discovered lying in alleyways, no bloated corpses had been found floating in the Thames. Other disasters were, of course, terrifyingly possible, but every bit of good news was to be grabbed at whilst it could be.

"And whom have you contacted? Who is helping you?"

"I have sent word to the toll houses around London, should he attempt to travel out of the city, as well as express messages to my business associates around the country, in the chance he is seeking adventure further afield. In town, I have the fortune to have the same men seeking Wickham helping me search for Sammy," he sighed. "Better fortune would be that I no longer need them. But Colonel Forster's men have offered their assistance and I have agreed without hesitation. Even last night, they were here for our accustomed meeting about Wickham. That was when we realised Samuel had not returned home. They offered their services at that time, I was in no mind to refuse." He fell heavily into the closest arm-chair as if his legs could no longer support his weight. Elizabeth rang for tea and bread for the exhausted man, then returned to him, a notion coalescing in her head from what she had just heard her uncle say.

"These men—the colonel's men—have they been here often?"

"Aye, Lizzy, every night at nine o'clock."

"And you have discussed the situation with Wickham and Lydia with the colonel's men? Mentioned his name?" She tried to keep the agitation out of her voice, but the increasingly worried look on her uncle's face betrayed her failure.

"Aye... what are you getting at, Lizzy?"

"Uncle," she was half afraid to voice her thoughts, "Could Samuel have heard you? Could he have heard Wickham's name mentioned in your discussions?"

Her uncle thought for a moment. "No, he could not... he ought to have been above stairs in his bedroom, with the other children. Surely he would not have tried to listen in on discussions that did not involve him. Oh Lizzy, we tried so hard to keep all news of this affair from the children's ears. But Sam did ask, on several occasions, about the smart officers who came to call, hoping to meet some and maybe ask after their swords and pistols..." He broke off and breathed deeply. "Aye, indeed, he might have overheard."

"He has overheard conversations and observed people before and sought his adventures based on what he has learned. I fear he may have acted likewise now. Then, Uncle, I fear I may know where he is. But," she added quickly as her uncle began to rise from his chair, "I do not recall the details. I know who will, however. Can the men, the colonel's men, be in contact with Colonel Fitzwilliam? He will know. He and Mr. Darcy heard Sammy describe the place once."

She had never thought to utter Mr. Darcy's name again, and the pain it brought to her almost sent her into her own chair. The cold look in his eye at their last meeting rushed unbidden to her mind, and she could see, as clearly as if the man were standing before her, the stiff, haughty carriage of his shoulders when he said goodbye. He could not afford, for his own sake and for his sister's, to associate with the Bennet family ever again. They were all tainted, irredeemably damaged, by Lydia's foolishness and Wickham's attendant treachery. She had only just realised how much she loved him when circumstances had contrived to separate her forever from him.

From such a connexion she could not wonder that he should shrink. If only she had accepted him in April! She could not wish him obliged to her and resentful of it, but still, she was humbled, she was grieved; she repented, though she hardly knew of what. Perhaps, had she accepted him, she might have had more influence upon her father; perhaps Mr. Darcy himself might have had a word or two. But then, she had thought she had the better judgement. Now she knew better. At last, when it was too late, she knew she wished for his esteem. She was convinced that she could have been happy with him, when it was no longer likely they should meet. And now, when she at last knew her own heart, he was gone and his very name on her lips broke that heart anew. But Samuel's safety must take precedence over her heartache, and she would mention Mr. Darcy's name a thousand times over if it would bring her young cousin back safely.

How great, then, was her surprise when her uncle peered at her with an unreadable expression on his tired face, exchanged a strange look with her aunt, and said, "Colonel Fitzwilliam and Mr. Darcy have been party to these late-night meetings, Lizzy. I need not inquire after the colonel's whereabouts, for I know them intimately. He stays with his cousin. I shall send a boy over at once!"

She began to speak, but Mr. Gardiner suddenly jumped out of his chair, and began rushing around the room with an energy she did not believe his weary body possessed. "John!" he shouted from the doorway, "John? Prepare to send a message. Madelyn, help me change. I must be off again as soon as they arrive. Paper... I need paper and a pen. Where is my paper?"

The sudden rush of activity was almost as disconcerting to Elizabeth as had been the news of Mr. Darcy's presence in this very house each evening, and she felt herself incapable of finding any purpose, until she recalled the paper her uncle kept in his office. Needing some employment, she rushed from the salon, saying "I shall find your paper, Uncle. Do sit and take a moment to breathe. You will be of more use to Sammy if you are not falling faint from exhaustion."

Before many minutes had passed, the paper and pen had been retrieved, the note written and sent, and tea brought into the salon. It might have been the mud cakes her young cousins made by the banks of the pond in the park for all she tasted the food, but Elizabeth ensured that her aunt and uncle took some sustenance, and then encouraged them to retire to their suite to rest until a reply to the note arrived. "I shall wait here, and I shall summon you as soon as there is any news," she reassured her relatives and they grudgingly made for the stairs.

At last the salon was empty of all save herself, and silent. Elizabeth full well understood her aunt and uncle's reluctance to rest, for she too would have rather been doing something to help locate Samuel, but she doubted either had slept the previous night. Even a few minutes of rest would help them preserve whatever energy they might require over the coming hours or days.

She sank into one of the soft chairs and closed her eyes. The unexpected developments of the day—the messenger, the rushed journey into town, the notion about Samuel's whereabouts and the revelation about Mr. Darcy—all conspired to overwhelm her and she felt suddenly devoid of all energy. She let her head fall back onto the soft upholstery and her eyelids fluttered closed of their own accord.

She did not believe she truly slept, for she was aware of the quiet noises of the house—footsteps that thudded dully down the hallway, creaks from the opening and closing of doors, soft voices whispering information and directions—but the time passed quickly while she remained in her semi-conscious state. Then, a louder sound from the foyer brought her to greater awareness, and the definite click of the latch from the front door, followed by men's voices and the more definite tread of booted feet across the marble floor awakened her completely. She was, therefore, fully alert and standing when the door the salon opened and Mr. Darcy himself strode into the room.

Chapter Twenty-Three

Seeking Samuel

If Mr. Darcy were surprised by Elizabeth's presence, he did not show it. "Elizabeth," he offered in greeting, his voice low and rough. His eyes flickered to the side, and she could see the effort it took for him to bring his eyes to meet hers. In other aspects of bearing, too, Mr. Darcy had reverted to the stony automaton she had first met, but now she attributed this demeanour to physical exhaustion. Although he was not as ashen as the Gardiners had been, it was obvious that Mr. Darcy had also passed the night with very little sleep. Had he, too, been out all night searching for Sammy?

Resisting the urge to run to him and collapse against his chest—or possibly enfold him upon hers—she merely offered him a deep curtsey. "Mr. Darcy. It is good to see you again. I had not thought..."

This confession was interrupted by the sudden entrance of Mr. Gardiner into the room. "Darcy!" Mr. Gardiner exclaimed. "Thank God! I had not thought to see you so quickly. Thank you for coming. This is no time for social pleasantries, so if you will permit me to postpone such niceties for another occasion, I shall cut straight to the point. Lizzy here says that Sammy might have overheard us speaking, and might have gone off seeking Wickham himself."

Darcy turned to look at Elizabeth and blinked slowly, as if willing the world to come better into focus. "Yes. I had discounted that possibility, not realising the boy knew about the situation. Had he remained ignorant of the search, it would have made little sense for him to seek Wickham himself. However, if he had overheard us, it seems in keeping with other behaviours I have observed in him that he might have attempted some reconnaissance of his own. He followed Wickham once and therefore knew where to seek him out. We have had the boarding house where Wickham went under observation since first we arrived back in London and have seen no sign of him or the lad, but..." He paused for a moment, thinking so furiously Elizabeth could almost observe the ideas forming in his head.

"When he described the house which we have been watching," he continued at last, his eyelids blinking so quickly Elizabeth could hardly see them move, "he also described the entire route Wickham took that day. There was one house he mentioned where he waved to a man in the window. I am attempting to determine the location of that house from what I recall from Samuel's words."

Mr. Gardiner started, perplexed at what Darcy might mean, and Elizabeth rapidly explained about Mr. Darcy's remarkable memory.

When Darcy spoke again, he sounded quite confident. "I believe I have determined the exact situation of that other house. It is not far from the rooming house, and in fact, it likely backs onto it across the mews. The more I think, I can recall the directions he gave us precisely. Richard awaits in the carriage. We shall depart at once."

Mr. Gardiner began to move towards the door with the men. "Let me get my boots...." He stumbled and almost fell, retaining his balance only due to the arm Darcy had ready to support him, having anticipated his trajectory.

"No, sir. You need to rest. You will be needed later, and I cannot have you unable to move due to your exhaustion. Richard and I shall go, and we will send a messenger immediately upon discovering a need for you. But for now, you must stay and gather your strength. I insist upon it."

"But Darcy, this is my son! I cannot stay home like a weakling while others do the work. I must be there to help him."

"No, Gardiner, I must insist. You have been out all night and all day on the streets of London. You cannot have slept a wink in nearly two days. The boy knows me and I him. I care for him as a brother. Let me do this for him, and for you. You must sleep, and your wife needs you to be with her. Please, sir." The green eyes were soft but insistent, and after another desperate attempt, followed by the noticeable shaking of the desperate father's knees, he finally agreed to remain home with his wife.

"Then I must join you, sir," Elizabeth announced.

"Impossible!" both men spoke at once.

"No, imperative. If my uncle is here with my aunt, I am not needed in the house. I am better rested and able to function properly, and Sammy will need me. If he has been out all night, possibly hiding from or captive to Mr. Wickham, he will be most agitated, and his behaviour will be unpredictable. I know how to calm him. I have done so many times in the past, and he will respond to me. I must be there for him." The firm look that settled on her face brooked no refusal, and even Mr. Darcy seemed easily to discern her unwavering determination.

"I will not see you come to any harm, Elizabeth," he spoke directly to her. "You must promise to listen to me should we run into danger."

"I have no intention of being harmed, sir. I merely wish to be of assistance to my cousin. But I shall accompany you. Of that, there shall be no discussion."

Mr. Gardiner nodded his head. "Very well, Lizzy." He looked as if his legs would not bear his weight much longer.

Darcy echoed Mr. Gardiner's assent. "Agreed." He turned to the footman who was waiting in the hallway and bade him help Mr. Gardiner back upstairs to his suite. "I shall send a message as soon as we have word. You have my promise, sir." Then, to Elizabeth, "Are you ready to leave now? We might be out some time."

"I shall be ready as soon as I lace my shoes, sir, and prepare my reticule. And Mr. Darcy, thank you, for everything."

There was no time for further private conversation. No sooner were the shoes adequately laced and the reticule located and prepared with all her needs than the two were rushing out of the house and into the carriage awaiting on the street. Elizabeth and Richard greeted each other warmly, but such was the general level of anxiety in the carriage that little was had in the way of conversation as they moved through the streets of the city. The only sounds were Darcy explaining the situation to Richard, including their suppositions as to Samuel's—and possibly Wickham and Lydia's—whereabouts, and a quick set of orders from Richard to a boy riding with the driver who immediately jumped off the carriage to execute his task.

This was not, Lizzy realised, Mr. Darcy's usual carriage. This one was older, much less elegant, much more heavily used. The exterior was a scratched and peeling nondescript black with no insignia or emblem, the wheels slightly uneven and noisy. Inside, the leather was cracked and the paint was dull. Considering the area of town they were to visit, this was, she decided, a wise choice. The Darcy carriage in which she had previously travelled was very fine and obviously expensive, and it would be as out of place and remarkable as a ball gown in a rowboat. And what was imperative was that Wickham not know they were there. Elizabeth did not consider him to be a violent man, but desperation begets unforeseen behaviours, and she did not wish to rely on Wickham retaining his easy-going manner should he realise he was being trapped.

As they travelled, the buildings grew smaller and darker and the open spaces fewer and dirtier, until at last the driver, in the plain clothes of an unremarkable servant, stopped the horses at the side of a cobblestone street, near the door to a noisy establishment. The driver slowly unhitched the horses and made a bit of a show of asking directions to the stables and where he might put up for the night, not being needed until the following morning. He disappeared into the building, leaving the carriage looking completely abandoned for the remainder of the day, dull curtains obscuring the interior from anyone who might seek to peer through the dingy windows. With no light inside the carriage, one might look out, but not in, though the half-sheer fabric that hung untidily across the panes.

The building immediately to hand, into which the servant had disappeared, looked from the outside to be a tavern, with flickering light shining from the half-shuttered windows despite the faint sunlight that still stroked the street with its waning rays. The sounds of clanging flagons and drunken revelry also emanated from the establishment; Elizabeth shuddered to think what noises might emerge once full dark fell over the city.

The street itself was not too narrow for the carriage to sit without blocking passage for all others, but there was little space for more than one cart to pass, and what space there did exist was filled with dirty children, tugging at the sleeves of passers-by for extra coins, and women in somewhat unsuitable dress emerging from dark doorways. This was not quite the squalor of Whitechapel, not quite the depths of The Old Nichol, but it was also far from the cleaner and wealthier parts of London that Elizabeth knew.

But it was not the tavern that Mr. Darcy and Richard seemed to concern themselves about, nor was it the crush of unwashed humanity that slunk past the carriage. Rather, the men were staring across the street, four or five buildings further along, at a plain dark brick structure that stood four storeys high, with a heavy dark door in its centre, the exact colour of which was undetermined in the dying light of the day, and solid shutters closed tight on all its few windows. Elizabeth could barely make out the number plate at the door that read 132B.

"Is that the place?" she asked breathlessly, afraid to speak in more than a whisper. "Is that the building of which Sammy spoke?"

It was Richard who replied, his voice equally quiet. "I believe it is, Elizabeth. We have had the rooming house watched ever since we heard of Wickham's desertion, but none of our men have seen him there; we had not thought to retrace his entire route from what your cousin described. But from my faint knowledge of the area, this building is as likely a place for the rat to have holed up as any. And Will is correct; it backs onto the rooming house, and may even be connected through the mews." He had been consulting a map as they had travelled, nodding all the while. "Still, my men are here. The lad I sent will have seen to that." He pulled aside a chink in the sheer curtains that allowed them to see out but blocked the view of those seeking to peer in, and nodded to an old crippled man in rags, sitting against a building seeking alms.

"Captain Donnell," he murmured in explanation. "Injured on the Continent, lost a leg, but still a fine man and a good officer. Fear not for his appearance; he is pleased to be doing useful work, even after his injury. He is being well-compensated for his task."

Donnell, for his part, barely glanced up, but tugged his cap further over his filthy face and scratched an ear. Richard nodded and let the curtain drop. "No sign of Wickham today either," he sighed. "We have not been granted entry to the other building and have not wished to show our hand without knowing whether he is there. Should we enter and not find him immediately, it would not only alert him to our intentions, but would also present him with the chance to flee and hide more deeply. We have not wanted to take that chance. But now that Sammy might be involved, and now that we have located this other building, matters have changed. We will enter by the back after night falls whilst doing everything in our power to ensure Sammy's safety."

It was all Elizabeth could do to bow her head in acknowledgement of the colonel's statement. Suddenly she felt a touch on her bare hand—she had forgotten, in the rush to leave Gracechurch Street, to bring her gloves—and she looked down to see Mr. Darcy's hand gently resting on her own. "I care for the boy too," he whispered to her, "and would do anything to see him returned safely to his family. All will be well."

The three resumed their silent vigil as the last rays of daylight faded and were replaced by the uneven lights that shone through warped glass windows or that reached the cobblestones from the street lights on the cross street some several yards away. Shapes turned into shadows and shadows into gaping abysses, where light vanished into nothingness. Elizabeth shivered and found herself wrapped in a rough but clean-smelling blanket. Mr. Darcy reached for her hand again and squeezed it for a moment, then let his hand relax in hers, not relinquishing contact. For a very long time they sat thus, watching and listening, being silent and still, letting the world believe their carriage was empty of passengers.

Then, at last, a sound permeated through the shell of the carriage, rousing the three watchers from their trance-like states. The front door to the brick house opened slowly and a woman stepped out, looked around carefully, peering most curiously at the carriage. The three inside held their breaths, as if hoping to convince the woman by power of thought, that the carriage was indeed empty. At last, confident that she was not being watched, she then returned inside and called out in a relieved voice. "It's clear," the three watchers heard through the darkness. "Toss the garbage out!"

The next moment, a small shape was shoved out of that same door, and a man's voice snarled after it, "Be gone, idiot child. Whether you understand me or not, if I see your face again, I shan't be so gentle. Out!" Then, presumably to the woman, "The child is an imbecile, too feeble-minded to speak, should he even realise what he saw. I don't wish his blood on my hands. He shan't cause problems. He..." and the door closed on the rest of his words.

But the shape that now lay sprawled on the dark street began to move, and before she could comprehend what was occurring, Richard had darted from the carriage and scooped up the shape, rushing towards the door to the tavern. "Quick, Elizabeth, we must follow," Darcy urged.

As quickly and silently as they could, the two alighted from the carriage and hustled into the drinking house. Loud noises and the heavy smell of stale stew and yeasty ale assaulted her, but rather than being led into the main room of the tavern, Elizabeth found herself being pulled into a small room towards the back of the building. Three men whom she had never before seen stood around a table, poring over plans and maps, and the rough cot in the corner now held Richard and the dark shape from the street. The shape was shaking and mewling like a lost kitten, and Elizabeth immediately recognised her young cousin.

"Sammy!" She gasped in horror. "What have they done to you?" She approached slowly, knowing the boy's peculiarities, and examined him from a small distance. "Are you hurt? Did they injure you?" The boy did not answer, but merely stared into the air and mewled, his hands flapping before him, his eyes distant, displaying no awareness of the others in the room.

"I do not believe him to be physically hurt, Elizabeth," Richard said quietly, "but you see he is not himself."

"Alas, Richard," she explained to him, "this is what I feared we might find. I have not seen him in so bad a state for many years, but this is what we strove to overcome, Miss Pierce and myself. When he is badly upset, when he feels he has no control over his situation, or when events overwhelm him, this is how my poor cousin responds."

"He's worse even than you, Will," Richard smirked at his cousin, but Mr. Darcy did not grace him with even the hint of a smile.

"Let me near him, perhaps I can help calm him," Elizabeth suggested. "I have helped in the past. He knows me." Quietly and very slowly, she edged closer to the boy, now lying on his side on the cot. The three unknown men had moved to the far side of the room, and stood silently, watching the drama. "Sammy," Elizabeth whispered. "Sammy, everything is well now. You may return. You are not in danger. I am here, and Mr. Darcy. You are safe. Everything is well." She continued murmuring quiet words of reassurance to him, coming closer and closer, until she was sitting on the bed beside him. She reached into her reticule and slowly drew out a small object no larger than a grown man's fist. It seemed to be covered in dark hair, like a wig without a head. "Fur," she mouthed to the others in the room. The men all watched in silence as she placed the object in the boy's restless hands. At first he batted it away, his hands never ceasing their spasmodic motion, flapping up and down, but as she gently pressed the ball of fur to his hands again and again, the flapping slowed and at last he grasped the ball in one hand and the flapping of the other hand became a gentle stroking motion. Elizabeth continued her quiet monologue, her voice soothing and low, and after a great many minutes, the shaking lad on the bed stopped mewling and settled into a strange calmness. From the corner of her eye, she observed Mr. Darcy's own fingers flexing compulsively as if he, too, wished for something to worry at or stroke, and realised that for him, his dog Cabal was akin to Samuel's fuss toy that the lad used to calm himself from severe agitation.

"Sammy, you are well, all is well," she repeated again and again in a calm and soothing voice, and then asked, "Can you tell me how you are feeling?"

After a very long time—perhaps a quarter hour or more—the lad fell into a fitful sleep. It was another half hour before he awoke. The previously unseeing eyes blinked rapidly and then opened fully, focusing on the young woman on the cot beside him. "Cousin Lizzy," the boy breathed at last, his hands resuming their unceasing stroking motion over the ball of fur.

Seemingly from nowhere, one of the men produced a cup of hot sweet tea and some biscuits, which Samuel consumed hungrily, and at last he had calmed himself enough to relate his adventures, although he resumed stroking his ball of fur and at no point did he allow his eyes to meet those of anyone else in the room. His voice remained distant and emotionless, but he responded to his companions and Elizabeth smiled tentatively.

"Mr. Darcy," he called to his friend, "sit by me, please, so I can tell you what I did. Cousin Lizzy said you would not wish to be my friend any longer, but I did not believe her and you are here now." Darcy looked quickly up at Elizabeth, confused, but said nothing and perched himself on the edge of the cot, next to the boy.

"Master Samuel," he asked, "may the colonel also sit by us and take an account of your tale? It might be of great importance."

Nodding his acceptance, Samuel started his story, stroking the ball of fur all the while.

He had, he told the gathered company, overheard his father's discussions with the officers two nights previous, whilst heading towards the kitchens for something to eat. Intrigued by what little he had heard, he sat silently by the door until much of the situation had been revealed to him. He understood little of why Cousin Lydia should not marry whomsoever she wished, or why visiting London with Mr. Wickham were necessarily a bad thing, but what he did understand quite clearly was that the men were seeking Wickham, and he knew where Wickham was!

It had never occurred to the boy that Wickham might have chosen other quarters for his sojourn in town; once a behaviour had been settled upon, there seemed to be no need to change it. And so, the following day, as he had done before the holiday at Margate, Samuel walked the streets of London until he stood before the building he was certain housed the missing officer. He had, at first, made up games with his periscope, observing the street from behind carriages and around corners, but as darkness began to fall, he walked out openly into the street, and then, seized by some strange notion, walked up to the rooming house door and opened it.

The house, he informed them, was empty, but the corridor in which he found himself led past a staircase, past doors to rooms off the sides, and directly to another door at the back of the building, which was ajar. This, in turn, had led across the mews, directly to another door at the building behind it—the building from which he had been ejected so rudely not long before.

From that point, the tale became less clear; Elizabeth explained to the others that as the lad had become more agitated, his perceptions of events altered. However, a rough story emerged. He had entered this second building and, hearing voices, walked up the staircase to locate the source. On the second storey of the building, he found the appropriate room and opened the door without knocking. There was one occupant in the front room, whom he identified as Mr. Wickham, and he saw through a doorway leading into another room that there was a lady whom he thought might be Cousin Lydia, although he could hardly tell with her hair done the way it was.

Wickham had immediately grabbed him and begun to yell, which caused Samuel the greatest anxiety. Like Mr. Darcy, Sammy retreated behind barricades when greatly upset, but his defences made Mr. Darcy's seem like the walls of a sand castle on the beach. Sammy himself could not explain how he reacted under extreme stress, but his cousin explained to the others.

"He gets most extremely agitated, and loses the ability to speak," she told them. "He might make noises of the sort we heard when he first was brought in here, but he says no intelligible words. He stares into the distance, as if no one or nothing were in the room, and he sometimes spins in circles or rocks backwards and forwards, as if on a toy horse, or moves his hands compulsively and repetitively, in that flapping motion we all observed earlier. This is how he protects himself against what he perceives as an attack."

Mr. Darcy nodded. He clearly understood.

"To anyone who does not know my cousin," Elizabeth continued in a sad voice, "he would seem a feeble-minded halfwit, an idiot, the sort of child who should be in an institution or madhouse."

Samuel looked at her and said, "Those were nearly exactly Mr. Wickham's words. The lady who might have been Cousin Lydia asked what the commotion was, and Mr. Wickham told her not to worry and dragged me to another room on that same floor of the house where he locked me in. Every time he, or that horrible lady who lives on the first floor, would come to me, I found myself too upset to look at them. It was as if the waves we saw at Margate were all crashing down upon me and I could not breathe. I had to go somewhere safe, where I could not be hurt, and I went to my safe world behind my eyes. Then I awoke here, with my fuss toy." He held up the ball of fur, never ceasing to stroke it.

"It calms him," she explained unnecessarily. "The soft beaver fur is from his father's warehouses, a tiny remnant too small to use or sell, but soft and comforting. The motion of petting it calms him."

"So if I understand," Richard asked serenely, "eventually Wickham decided you were a mute idiot and posed him no threat, and threw you out of the house?"

The boy stared at him. It was the first time he had met anybody's eyes since he arrived. "I suppose so. I do not recall."

"What, then lad, do you recall?" The words were gentle and encouraging. "Surely a smart boy such as yourself made some observations before retreating to your safe world."

"I know," replied Samuel in definite tones, "the layout of the house, where Mr. Wickham's room is, how to enter from the back, how many candle sconces line the walls, and the colour shoes the lady was wearing."

Richard stood up and beamed at the other men. "Gentlemen," he announced, "General Samuel Gardiner is about to draw up our battle plans!"

Chapter Twenty-Four

Assault

From there, matters moved quickly. Samuel put his artistic skills to use and provided the men with a rather detailed plan of the house—much more detailed than even Lizzy believed was possible. The officers decided to wait until the dark hours of the morning before entering the house, so as best to catch Wickham unawares.

He also drew a sketch of each of the two women he had seen. Elizabeth identified the first as definitely being her sister. The expression Samuel drew suggested that Lydia was not being kept under duress; on the basis of his sketch, the only charges against Wickham would be desertion from the militia and kidnapping of a child, not the forcible confinement of a young woman.

The other woman Mr. Darcy identified as Mrs. Younge, late of his employ, and the woman responsible for leading his sister into the clutches of Mr. Wickham the previous summer. Her actions then had not been criminal. Now, however, she too was party to the kidnapping and confinement of young Samuel, and for that, he expressed satisfaction to believe she would see justice.

Shortly after these plans had been arranged, a noise came from a dark corner of the room Elizabeth had not previously examined in her concern and attention to her cousin. A small door, hidden behind a large cabinet against the wall, now creaked open from the alleyway behind the tavern, and through it stepped none other than her aunt and uncle.

"Mama! Papa!" Sammy cried when he saw them, and he rushed into their open arms. For the second time that evening, his eyes connected with another's as he gazed upon his parents. Mrs. Gardiner seemed too overcome to speak and was content to stand there with her arms wrapped tightly around her son, who seemed in no hurry to break the physical contact. Her husband, in a broken voice, thanked the colonel and Darcy profusely for their help, and commended the other men on their efforts in resolving the entire matter, before joining his wife and son in their embrace.

"In truth, Gardiner, we did little," Richard explained. "Samuel had already secured his own freedom. We merely happened to be present to help him afterwards. And he has provided us with all the information we need to trap this scoundrel at last and see justice done."

"And Lydia?" Mrs. Gardiner finally found her voice. "What will become of her?"

Darcy shook his head. "I do not know, Madam. Let us rescue her first, and see to Wickham, and then we shall consider her fate."

The Gardiners soon retreated to their carriage in the alleyway with their son, and thence to home, this time taking Elizabeth with them. She begged to be permitted to remain, to see to Lydia when the girl was brought down, but Mr. Darcy insisted that she return to the house with her family. Nothing would change his mind, and when Richard added his voice to his cousin's, only to be echoed by her aunt and uncle, Elizabeth knew she had little choice.

"We shall come to the house with Miss Lydia as soon as we have her," Mr. Darcy assured her in a formal voice. "But it shan't be before first light, if my guess is correct. You need to rest. Tonight has been long, and you have been of the greatest assistance, but I cannot, in good conscience, allow you to remain here, for there may be danger." He then dropped his voice and added, for her ears only, "Please, Elizabeth. Be safe."

And so she relented.

Sleep did not come easily to any residents of the Gardiner house that evening. Samuel was still too upset by his ordeal to rest and, in a manner unseen since he was a very young child, he begged his parents not to leave him alone. His mother was most happy to oblige, for she had despaired of ever seeing him again, and the two sat up late into the night in the sitting room attached to the bedchamber, drinking tea and reading to each other. The most severe symptoms of the boy's agitation had passed, and he was alert and communicative once more, but Lizzy felt it would be some days before he returned to the more sociable habits she and Miss Pierce had spent so many hours teaching him. Time and comfort alone would now help her cousin, and these she determined to allow him.

Mr. Gardiner seemed anxious to return to the tavern to assist the other men in capturing Wickham and rescuing Lydia, mumbling something about not being there to take responsibility for his own family—the contrast with her own father striking Elizabeth to the quick once more—but the thought of leaving his son so quickly upon the boy's return just barely overcame the need to depart again. And so he, too, stayed, periodically visiting his wife and son in the sitting room, and otherwise pacing up and down the hallways and in his office, eager for any word from the men and chastising himself for not being with them.

Elizabeth took herself to bed, too exhausted to remain upright; but although her eyes closed, her mind did not cease its relentless whirling. Had it only been that morning that she had awakened in her bed at Longbourn? The events of the day seemed something out of one of Kitty's dreadful novels, rather than events that she, herself, had been party to. She let her mind flit between her horrified apprehension upon learning of Samuel's disappearance, the tension-filled anxiety of the Gardiners' salon, the silent vigil in the carriage, and her desperate attempts to calm her young cousin and help him settle sufficiently to communicate with the gathering of men in the tavern. They had not known for certain, Richard had commented, where exactly Wickham had hidden himself, for there had been no sign of him at the rooming house the men had first discovered. That was the reason no attempts had been made on the building. To send armed men into a private house on the basis of a guess went against the King's Peace. However, after finding the proper locations, Samuel's report and the drawings he had made would be ample evidence against the miscreant and were more than enough for the soldiers to move on the building.

And then there was Mr. Darcy himself. How had he been party to this search? What had he to gain by helping retrieve her errant sister? She recalled his words, his face, on that last cold meeting in Pemberley when she had confessed her sister's sins to him. He could not leave her presence quickly enough, she had thought. He had turned and departed from her presence with scarcely a word. What, then, had possessed him to come to her uncle's house and offer assistance? Surely he had no further desire to associate with her! His reputation, and that of his sister, would surely be damaged by any connexion to Wickham. What could he be about? It must be the need to see Wickham finally called to account, to see justice done, to avenge his sister in some small way.

Images of his face raced through her mind behind her closed eyes. The haughty stare, the eyes that did not meet hers, the softening of those eyes and the beseeching plea to stay safe all paraded themselves before her, individually and collectively, melding into one. He was, of course, one man, the myriad aspects to his personality like the multiple facets on the prismatic crystals he had so proudly shown her so long ago, each unique unto itself, but each inextricably part of a larger whole. And, like the crystals, Mr. Darcy spread radiance and beauty around him, if only one were fortunate enough to see him in the right light.

She was lying there, still teasing out her thoughts when she heard a noise from the street below her window. Rising and pulling on her robe, she peered down through the sheer lace net curtains. The sky was still dark, tinged only with the faintest glow at the horizon, the stars pinpoints of light in the velvet sky, so unusually clear of fog and smoke. Down on the street, the light from the gaslights caught the outline of a carriage coming to a stop—the same carriage, she believed, in which she had sat those many hours by the tavern. The horses whinnied and snorted, to be quickly quieted by the driver, and a door opened, expelling a large man, a struggling bundle the size of her sister, and then another man, holding the girl in his control. She rushed down the stairs, forgetting her state of dress, arriving just as the sleepy footman opened the door to admit Darcy, Richard, and a very unhappy Lydia.

Within moments, both master and mistress of the house were present. Mrs. Gardiner began castigating her wayward niece the moment she entered the house, and then dragged her bodily up the stairs to the room she had set aside for the girl, ignoring the protestations of needing to go back to "Dear George" and complaints about people breaking into their rooms at such inopportune hours.

Mr. Gardiner, still dressed in the clothing from the night before, rubbed his red eyes and his stubbled chin and in a voice more cultured and polite than anything Elizabeth might have been able to manage, asked if the gentlemen needed to depart right away, or if they would appreciate a whisky, or perhaps a cup of coffee?

"Coffee, please!" Mr. Darcy responded, at the same time as Richard breathed, "Lord be praised, whisky!"

It was quickly decided that both would suit quite well. Mr. Gardiner led them into his study and produced a decanter of amber liquid and some fine crystal glasses, and after taking a quick sip, he disappeared into the kitchens to procure the offered hot beverages, not wishing to wake his housekeeper quite so early. "I am able to make a pot of coffee," he puffed out his chest. "I am rather self-sufficient when need be." Elizabeth then ushered the two exhausted men to the sitting room off her uncle's study, where the gathering of searchers had been wont to meet to discuss their strategy. Having finished their whisky, and almost oblivious to her presence—or, perhaps, quietly accepting of and accustomed to it—both men shuffled across the floor and pulled off their cravats and removed their coats before falling into two large chairs near the fireplace.

Elizabeth tended to the fire, and only after it was lit did she glance up at Mr. Darcy, now in his shirt sleeves. She gasped. Her shock was not at seeing him so unclothed before her, for her father had the habit of dressing only in his shirt and waistcoat whilst *en famille*, but at the stain of red that adorned one torn sleeve. "You're hurt!" she exclaimed in alarm, to which he merely grunted, his eyes closed and his head thrown back in fatigue. She knelt by his side and gently rolled up the ripped sleeve, ignoring his faint murmurs of protest.

"It is not deep, Elizabeth." It was Richard who spoke. "Nor is it serious."

"Was there much blood shed in the rescuing of my sister?" She was mortified at the thought that men might have been injured because of her foolish sister's antics.

At last, Mr. Darcy roused himself enough to speak. "No, very little. I believe that, other than Wickham himself, I received the worst of it."

"But what happened? Did he attack you with a knife? A sword? That cannot be from a pistol!"

Unaccountably, he laughed. "It is a sad and sorry tale."

"Well," she admonished him, "you may tell me as I tend to your wound." She dashed from the room to gather the supplies she required, then upon returning, led him to a small sofa and lit the large oil lamp on the side table, and finally settled next to him with a soft cloth and cool water to clean his injury.

Mr. Darcy spoke quietly, clearly embarrassed, as Richard strove to keep from chuckling. "Your young cousin's plans of the house were perfect. Such precision is seldom seen, even in the army, so Richard tells me. With men stationed at the front door and the back, to guard against Wickham's unlikely escape, the others managed to roust Mrs. Younge from her roost without the slightest disturbance, and then went up to capture Wickham and retrieve Miss Lydia. However, Samuel did not see the second door to the bedchamber, for he had not been in there, and so failed to indicate its presence on his plans. Whilst Richard's men were breaking down the main door to the suite, Wickham bolted, leaving your sister without a thought, and dashed down through the second doorway.

"I was not one of the men sent in to capture Wickham, not being in the military and not being recently trained in tactical manoeuvres or the most current techniques in wielding a weapon. I was, therefore, standing outside of the building, wishing I might be of more assistance. I also noticed a small door to the side of the building, most likely where deliveries of coal and vegetables were made. Of a sudden, this small door—a hatch, really—flew open, and who should I see dashing out of it, but George Wickham himself!" He spat out the man's name, as if it tasted foul on his tongue. "I had no weapon but my foot, and the cad was not expecting to see anyone there and did not notice me. As he ran, I tripped him. But as he fell, a sharp edge of his sword caught my arm. He had grabbed it as he fled, but had not sheathed it. Nevertheless, he fell, I immobilised him until the others arrived, and our mission was successful. And as you see, Elizabeth, it truly is only a scratch." He looked down to where her fingers were softly wiping the remains of the dried blood from his forearm. "However," he said too quietly even for Richard to hear, "I do not object to your ministrations."

To this, Elizabeth could say nothing, but she did not cease her task of gently wiping the injured limb, even long after her care was no longer needed.

If Mr. Gardiner noticed anything amiss when he arrived a short time later, carrying a tray of coffee and a plate of cheese, he said not a word. He merely glanced at his niece, sitting much too close to a partially unclad man, his bare arm in her hands, and asked if she, too, would take coffee or whether she would prefer tea. Then he smiled and asked Richard for his account of the assault.

Richard recounted the tale, then added, "Miss Lydia did not seem to appreciate her predicament, nor that her lover abandoned her at the first sign of trouble. She fought us the entire way here, demanding that we return her to him. You might wish to post a footman by her door should she attempt to escape."

Mr. Gardiner sighed in exasperation. "That child was always wilful and unthinking. My sister could not have done a worse job raising her... apologies, Lizzy. I know she is your mother too." He sighed. "I will inform my staff immediately to keep her under watch, until further notice." He stepped out of the room for a moment, presumably to confer with the housekeeper, who had awakened whilst he was bustling in the kitchen. He returned promptly, and asked what was to become of the unhappy pair.

"It seems, sir," Richard continued, his voice flat with fatigue, "that they must marry. They had been living as man and wife from the day of their... departure from Brighton. What will become of Wickham, we have not yet determined, but regardless of his eventual fate, he will meet it as a married man. A part of the decision rests with you, Gardiner, for it was your son whom he held prisoner. He faces stiff penalties for deserting his post with the militia; depending on your request, we can add various other charges to the pile. He might hang, or face transportation for his crimes."

"Leaving Lydia a widow at fifteen." The man shook his head. "I cannot think on this now. I must sleep, as I am certain you wish to do. Can I have my housekeeper set up rooms for you? No? Surely you are as dead on your feet as am I. Very well. I shall come by tomorrow, gentlemen, after conferring with my wife, and we shall talk more then." Whereupon, with scarcely a nod of his head, he stumbled out of the room and up the stairs to his bed.

This left Elizabeth alone once more with Richard and Darcy. Both men rose and reclaimed their coats, bidding the young lady a good night—or good morning, as the case might be. Before he departed, Mr. Darcy raised Lizzy's hand to his lips and bestowed a gentle kiss on her knuckles, but said not a word before leaving in his cousin's wake.

"And that," she whispered through the tears that flowed unbidden down her face, "was his final goodbye."

The morning—or, rather, early afternoon—shed its light on the state of affairs as they stood. Lydia refused to accept any responsibility for her wrongdoing and demanded again and again to be returned to "Dear George," and consequently, was locked in her room with a large footman standing duty outside. Escape from the window was deemed impossible although the possibility was checked quite thoroughly. Mrs. Gardiner, normally so calm and controlled, unleashed upon Lydia all the terror and anxiety she had felt upon the disappearance of her beloved son, leaving the girl in no doubt that had anything happened to the lad, it would all have been laid quite firmly at her feet. Elizabeth heard the haranguing from her own room, and wished, uncharitably, that only once her own mother might have taken the girl to task so severely.

Chastened, Lydia finally agreed not to try to leave again, but also seemed more than pleased to learn that she would, after all, soon be granted her wish of becoming Mrs. Wickham. However, Lydia also refused to see Elizabeth, unaccountably blaming her for the entire ordeal, and insisting that Lizzy leave the house.

"She is in no position to demand anything of me, Lizzy," her aunt assured her, "but should you wish to go home, I shall keep Lydia here under lock and key until the soonest day we can arrange her wedding to... that man." Her aunt then added, "If you do return home, would you consider taking Sammy with you? He is not quite returned to his accustomed control and might benefit from some time in the country, away from the places he associates with his ordeal."

And so it was decided that the following morning, Elizabeth and Samuel would travel to Longbourn, there to await news of Lydia and Wickham. Of Darcy, she expected to hear nothing. The man had seen his nemesis brought low and had discharged whatever duties he may have felt to her family; he had offered no words of expectation to her. The kiss on her fingers was one of tender parting, a memory of what they might have shared, but never could. Once more her heart threatened to break, but she was, she reminded herself, made of sterner stuff, and would overcome her heartache.

Mr. Gardiner had departed for Darcy's house, where he expected to remain for much of the remainder of the day, discussing Wickham's fate, and Elizabeth did not expect to speak with him about any such decision before her departure. And thus it transpired. By noon the following day, she and her cousin were enjoying the sights of the countryside near Meryton, and shortly thereafter were alighting from the carriage into the welcoming and very noisy arms of the anxious and inquisitive Bennet family.

Chapter Twenty-Five

All Good Things

Samuel prospered at Longbourn as his parents had hoped. He adored his cousin Elizabeth, and she was most competent at helping the lad deal with the consequences of his ordeal. She encouraged him as only she knew how and helped him discover ways to calm himself when he found his memories of his night of captivity too much to bear. She knew when to talk to him, when to leave him in peace, when to guide him to a quiet place to regain his composure, and when to offer him his fuss toy.

The doting affection of his Aunt Bennet—as kind-hearted as she was silly—and the cool and undemanding retreat of Uncle Bennet's study, where he might indulge in intellectual pursuits to satisfy his mind, also worked their wonders on the boy. Elizabeth was hopeful that when he returned home after the upheaval of Lydia's wedding, his parents would find him much the same independent and self-reliant lad who had so merrily gone off on holiday with his friend only weeks before.

News of Lydia's upcoming marriage spread swiftly through the neighbourhood, but the tale was managed with sufficient oversight that if people decided to believe that the couple were engaged in Brighton and had chosen to be married from London because of Mr. Wickham's military duties, they were not corrected in their assumptions. Gradually, the story became accepted, and the Bennets returned to their previous status within the community, although with the added advantage of having at least one daughter nearly married.

Even Mr. Bingley renewed his addresses to Jane, excusing his absence of the previous weeks as stemming from a desire not to intrude upon the family's distress at such a difficult time. He had never, he assured Jane, considered leaving again on account of Lydia's actions, whatever the result of those actions might have been. When asked what his sisters might have to say, he snorted and commented that he had placed too much reliance on their opinions before, only to be deceived. This brought a glow to Jane's eye and a smirk to Lizzy's lips.

Elizabeth's only true regret now was that Mr. Darcy should be lost because of the affair; there was no one else whose knowledge of a sister's frailty would have mortified her so much. But even had Lydia's marriage been concluded on the most honourable terms, it was not to be supposed that Mr. Darcy would connect himself with a family where, to every other objection would now be added an alliance and relationship of the nearest kind with the man whom he so justly scorned. No, he was lost to her, and lost forever. And whilst her heart broke, she could not blame him. He had not only himself of whom to think but also of his sister, whose marriage prospects might be harmed by a connexion with such a man as Wickham, and whose heart and sensibilities might be damaged as well.

Of an evening, when all else was silent, she would dwell on what might have been, had only she accepted him when he uttered his first odious proposal at Hunsford. However, the reality remained that he would have honoured his commitment but resented her for it forever, and that was something she could not bear to contemplate. To have him thinking ill of her was worse than knowing he cared, albeit from afar. She must, she schooled herself, grow satisfied in the notion that of all of her family, she would be the only one to suffer for Lydia's foolishness, and that the stain of a connexion with the vile Mr. Wickham would not touch her sisters, would not damage the long-sought happiness of her dearest Jane.

And yet in her deepest heart, she lamented her loss. Mr. Darcy was everything she could want in a man. He was intelligent and caring, and although he had his faults, he was aware of them and strove to become even better than nature alone had allowed him. She was convinced that she could have been happy with him, when it was no longer likely they should meet.

At last, the pall lifted from Longbourn. One morning, not too many days after the news of Lydia's forthcoming marriage had been received, Mr. Bingley came to call and asked to speak privately with Jane. The entire household was, of course, all aflutter at this request, and when Elizabeth entered the drawing room some time later in search of some paper, she saw she had interrupted a most private conversation, for there were Jane and Bingley standing together over the hearth. They hastily turned round and moved away from each other, but the looks on their faces told it all.

Bingley whispered something into Jane's ear and quickly left the room, and Jane fell into her sister's arms with a glorious smile upon her lovely face. "Oh, Lizzy! I am the happiest of women! Oh, why cannot everybody be this happy?" Jane then rushed off to tell her mother, and when Mr. Bingley returned a few minutes later from his meeting with Mr. Bennet, Elizabeth congratulated him most warmly. At least one of the Bennet sisters would be happy! Her sacrifice was worth the cost, and she delighted in Jane's joy. She resolved to be the best possible aunt to Jane's children, feeling certain that no man other than Mr. Darcy could ever tempt her into matrimony now.

Letters of congratulations arrived, of course, from all quarters. Charlotte Collins included a lovely note alongside her husband's scolding missive about Lydia's moral failings, which he must have learned from Lady Catherine, who in turn must have had it from her nephew. Aunt and Uncle Gardiner wrote variously to the different members of the family, with well wishes, invitations to visit, and news of the other Bennet sister, so imminently to wed. They would, her uncle wrote, journey to Longbourn the day after Lydia's wedding, to see their relatives and collect their son, hopefully now much recovered.

As for Wickham himself, Mr. Gardiner, in consultation with his wife, had decided not to charge Wickham with the kidnapping and imprisonment of his son. Such a charge would almost certainly carry a capital punishment, and as much as they deplored Lydia's thoughtless actions, neither aunt nor uncle wished to see her a widow on their account. His ultimate fate was still undecided, for having deserted his post in the militia, and during a time of war at that, his punishment must be decided by a court martial.

In a private note to Elizabeth, Uncle Gardiner wrote:

We had not known before, but this was not Wickham's first stint with the militia. It seems that he took a similar commission four years ago under a false name, presumably after accepting Mr. Darcy's payment in lieu of the living at Kympton, of which he has spoken. At this time, he used the name George Younge, which was his mother's name. He deserted that position after six months and was never found. His former colonel recognised him when he was brought to the prison in London where he is being held. A first desertion is treated lightly; a second carries a much more dire consequence.

Colonel Fitzwilliam is speaking to everybody he can to avoid the almost inevitable sentence of a death by shot for this second offence, with your poor sister's welfare in mind. He has made mention of, perhaps, demotion to the lowest ranks of the regulars and a posting to mosquito-infested Jamaica, or to the Canadas, where tensions are rising and the threat of invasion grows daily. If the colonel is successful, Lydia will surely accompany her husband. I hate to offer this thought, but I cannot believe he will survive long enough to return. His commanding officers will have little goodwill for a repeat deserter, and will give him the worst tasks. Perhaps a firing squad would be a kinder fate for which to wish.

There was one last note in Mrs. Gardiner's letter, a small package written in a neat and familiar hand, directed to Master Samuel Gardiner. Elizabeth stared at it, savouring the sight of the handwriting she had never again expected to see. Mr. Darcy might have repudiated her and her family, but he would not cast off his friendship with her cousin! The notion that he held the concerns of a young boy so high endeared him even more to her, for Darcy could have nothing to gain from the friendship but the esteem of a young boy who regarded him as only slightly lesser than a god. For some reason, this sign that the great master of Pemberley wished to continue his association with her young cousin touched her heart more deeply than had his efforts to rescue her sister.

Oh, how could she ever thank him? He had saved her sister, saved the family's name, to be sure, but he had befriended and encouraged a boy who, teetering on the brink of manhood, sorely needed a role model such as he. For one so insecure in society as young Samuel, to know he might succeed as Mr. Darcy had succeeded was more valuable than any lessons she or Miss Pierce might teach. She so wished she could express her gratitude to the gentleman. But she was still quite certain that Mr. Darcy would never wish to see her again, that all he had done had been for her aunt and uncle, whom she knew he held in great esteem, and for her young cousin. She, herself, was tainted with her sister's sins, and not even Jane's engagement to Mr. Bingley could erase that stain from her reputation.

Still, events had settled much better than ever she might have dreamed, and despite the great pain in her heart, where her soul lay quietly bleeding, she knew she must be forever grateful. And, not being formed for melancholy or distress, grateful she resolved to be!

Soon enough, the Gardiners saw Lydia safely married to Wickham. Richard's entreaties had been successful, and in lieu of a sentence of death, the former lieutenant was demoted to common soldier, before being publicly flogged. In his new and unwelcome post, he had been assigned to a regiment bound for Jamaica, with no hope for return to England for seven years. Immediately upon making their vows and signing the register, therefore, the couple had been loaded onto a ship bound for Kingston. If Mrs. Bennet bewailed not being allowed to see her favourite daughter happily wed, she was reminded by all who could manage to be heard that, by this very fact, she had the privilege of overseeing the wedding arrangements for her second-favourite, Jane.

Having seen to this unhappy duty of sending their youngest niece to the West Indies, the Gardiners were, at last, at liberty to return to Longbourn to retrieve their son. The boy was much improved, and excitedly told his parents of what he had read in Uncle Bennet's library and what he hoped to tell his friend Robert of his ordeal, now seen as a great adventure. The Gardiners all happily returned to London, to see the entire family reunited in a peaceful home once more.

In the great excitement of Jane's engagement to Mr. Bingley, Mrs. Bennet had insisted on hosting a celebration for the couple, in honour of their betrothal, and she convinced Mr. Bingley that the ballroom at Netherfield was the perfect location for such a gathering, never mind that there was no hostess at the house. She would do all the planning and she would act as hostess, she promised her future son. Not even Caroline's precipitous arrival from the north would deter Mrs. Bennet from her task, and Lizzy now threw herself into that project, hoping and trusting that occupation would be the best balm for her broken heart.

And solace was there, in the form of writing up lists for invitations, meeting with the cooks, visiting shopkeepers in the village, and a hundred other small tasks that needed doing. Jane was too busy being in love, and Mary and Kitty too serious or flighty to be of real assistance. In truth, she was thankful to be kept so busy, and when she fell into her bed at night, she was relieved that her thoughts revolved around procuring ice and the necessary quantity of ham and bread for the celebrations and not around a certain enigmatic man with a poet's soul beneath his stony exterior and moss-green eyes.

At last the day of the party arrived. The dresses had just arrived from the dressmaker, with ribbons and lace and pearls, and dancing shoes accompanied them, one pair for each sister. Hill had brought in her niece to assist with the Bennet sisters' hair and toilette, and before long, the family were gathered in the salon, awaiting the carriage that would carry them to Netherfield. Jane, as always, was beautiful in her soft pink gown, the darker rose ribbons swirling gracefully down her skirt from the high waist, pearls glowing softly in her hair. No one would look at anybody else, Lizzy reckoned, although she admitted that Mary was in particularly fine looks this evening. The dark yellow that suited no one else rather became her! Kitty seemed to disappear in comparison to her sisters, having lost so much of her erstwhile high spirits after Lydia's unhappy marriage, despite her new light blue gown. "As for me," thought Lizzy, "I have no cares how I look. I shan't embarrass my beloved Jane, but that is all I care for my appearance."

With these musings, she watched her sisters descend from the carriage in front of Mr. Bingley's grand house. Bingley himself was there to assist Jane, after which Mr. Bennet helped down his wife, then his two younger daughters, leaving Elizabeth as the last to exit the conveyance. She checked her reticule and ensured that she had her wrap with her, lest it grow chilly during the evening, and at last, with a sigh, moved to the carriage door.

A hand reached up to help her descend the short stairs. Not her father's hand... but...

"You came," whispered a voice she thought she'd never hear again, and she looked up in amazement, wondering if she were imagining things.

"Mr. Darcy!"

The evening passed in a blur. There were scores of people—friends and relations—coming to congratulate the happy couple. Elizabeth noticed none of them. Not even Mr. Bingley's objectionable sisters could disturb the serene joy she felt at being, once more, in Mr. Darcy's company. Although he had not been on the list of friends Mr. Bingley had given her, he had come (invited personally by Bingley himself, she later discovered) and had sought her out, had honoured her by awaiting her arrival and handing her out of the carriage himself.

He danced with her, happily, proudly even, not once, not twice, but three times, and danced with no one else, not even Miss Bingley who hung at his elbow like a lost puppy when she was not otherwise engaged. That stiff rigid mask he donned when uncomfortable threatened to slip over his handsome face from time to time, but Lizzy noticed that each time the sights and sounds of the room grew too great for his senses and his composure began to slip, he took her lessons from

Rosings to heart and excused himself from the room. And when he returned, the smiles he gave her outshone all the chandeliers that hung from the ceiling of the grand room. He left no doubts in the minds of the others at the ball as to his intentions with regard to Miss Elizabeth.

It was only towards the end of the evening, when guests were beginning to depart and the crush lightened, that he had the chance to draw her away from the ballroom where she had been standing with Jane for so much of the evening. "Come with me, Elizabeth, come to the balcony," he urged her. "The moon is wondrous tonight, the breezes warm and the air fragrant with the late roses." Excusing herself from Jane's side, she gladly followed.

Standing outside a few moments later, she was forced to agree. The party had been a brilliant success, and all the guests raved over Jane's beauty, good fortune, handsome husband and excellent cook. She would be very well-settled woman, they all concurred. But it had been hot and noisy and very crowded, and the chance to stand outside, in the fresh evening air, admiring the silver sheen on the fountain in the garden just beyond the balustrade was so very welcome. "Ah," she sighed, "This is lovely indeed."

"Not as lovely as you," came the unexpected reply. She turned and saw that Mr. Darcy was close, much closer than she had expected. He raised his hand to her cheek and held it there, softly, as if caressing the wings of a butterfly, hardly felt but excruciatingly sensed.

She had to say something, offer some words of gratitude for her sister Lydia's deliverance.

"Mr. Darcy," she said at last, stepping back so slightly from him, "I am a very selfish creature; and, for the sake of giving relief to my own feelings, care not how much I may be wounding yours. I can no longer help thanking you for your unexampled kindness to my poor sister, and more so, to my young cousin. Your friendship means the world to the boy. I would have understood had you decided to break with the entire family, as would my aunt and uncle, but Samuel... he sees life through a different lens, and might only have seen your abandonment without reference to my sister's misdeeds."

He cocked his head and blinked, stationary as a statue for a moment, but without the air of impenetrable hauteur he so often carried. "Ah, a metaphor. Yes, indeed he does see life through a different lens than most, as do I. But in one respect my vision—if I may continue that metaphor—is quite clear." He fixed his remarkable eyes upon Elizabeth's own as he continued speaking.

"I confess I did not think immediately of your cousin, Elizabeth, for such is my limited understanding of the world as well. I recollected him only after a word on his behalf from Richard, and for that I am ashamed, for I truly like the lad. But rather, if you will thank me," he said, staring into the darkness, then deliberately moving his eyes to capture hers in his view, "let it be for yourself alone. That the wish of giving happiness to you might add force to the other inducements which led me on, I shall not attempt to deny. But in truth, at the heart of matters, I thought only of you."

He paused to consider his next words. "I am the one who ought to offer an apology," he stated at last. "Had I been more vigilant, more careful, this elopement should never have taken place. I was concerned about Wickham's need to take his revenge, but I never imagined it would be in the form of eloping with your sister. Richard's men did not consider that he might abscond in the middle of the night, and since he had been seen to pay little particular attention to your sister, they thought nothing of abandoning their surveillance when the company retired for the evening. If I had been more adamant, they might have watched him more carefully, at all hours."

Suddenly Elizabeth felt her eyes flood with tears, and she quickly turned from her companion, unwilling to let him see this unexpected weakness.

"What is the matter, Elizabeth?" he asked with the greatest concern. "I need not examine your face for minute nuances of expression to perceive that you are distressed. What have I said, what have I done, to occasion this? I know I am not always the most perceptive of men, and might have inadvertently said something to injure you."

Unable to stop herself, she blurted out, "I had never thought to see you again! I believed you to be happily rid of my whole, indecorous family, with our horrid manners and moral lassitude and shameful connexions. When we parted at Pemberley, you seemed to have decided to close yourself off from me, and in London, when you departed, you said nothing at all. It seemed the veriest of adieux. And now I see you again, and I cannot control my tears."

He gently grasped her elbow and led her further into the shadows where they might not be seen nor interrupted.

"It was never my intention to abandon you, Elizabeth. At no time did the thought occur to me, not when Wickham absconded with your sister, nor when he married her. I hold my friends more dearly than that, and you are the dearest of all."

He handed Elizabeth a linen handkerchief with which she daubed at her eyes, mopping tears that were of relief and thanksgiving rather than of bitter grief.

"But when you read the letter, that awful letter from Jane, you could not leave my presence quickly enough! I thought you might..." she broke off. It would not do to utter her thoughts, even at this time when his intentions once more seemed clear.

"If I seemed to withdraw, it was my unthinking retreat behind my fortifications, where I hide when I am unsure of how best to act. You had need to return as soon as you might to your family who depended upon you, and I had need for solitude wherein I might best ponder how to proceed. My thoughts were to assist, never to forsake."

"I thought I had come to know your ways..."

"I was more distressed at that moment than ever I had been since rescuing my own sister from that same wastrel. If my retreat was sudden and inexplicable, all I can do is apologise, although I am not able to promise it shall not occur again. But believe me, Elizabeth—for deception is anathema to me—I never have, and never will, wish to desert you."

He moved two fingers to her chin to raise her face to his until their eyes met, hazel and green "Do you believe me?"

She lowered her eyes. "It appears, sir, that I have little choice."

"No, you are an autonomous creature with free will... oh. Another idiom." He offered her a brilliant smile. "There, I made you laugh."

She answered his smile with one of her own. "Aye, sir, you did! But I still do not understand why you acted as you did."

"I knew there was no way to remove the pain of your sister's unfortunate elopement, but there were surely ways to ease that pain. I did what I could for you. I needed only to think of what might be done. I wrote to Richard, of course, and together we met with Colonel Forster, and we gathered in your uncle's sitting room each evening to exchange whatever news we had discovered during the day. It was no more than any man would have done." He paused and examined her face. "You are chewing your bottom lip and your eyes are cast down. What troubles you?"

"You cared more for my sister than my own father did." She took a deep breath and released it, allowing her regret to escape with the air. "But when we met once more at my uncle's house, during all that time we were together as we sought my cousin, you said not a word of this. How could I believe you did not intend to discharge your duty and appease your conscience and then depart again? In truth, I would not have blamed you, for you have your own status and your sister's future to consider."

"You are my future, Elizabeth!"

"But after we rescued Samuel and discovered Lydia and brought her to safety, you just left! You said not a word to me. What was I to think?"

Those beautiful moss-coloured eyes clouded in regret. "What could I say, with Richard at my side to hear every thing I uttered? And if I departed without a word, it was because my heart was too full for my brain to form thoughts. I knew your family required time to recover from the consequences of Lydia's actions, and Richard and I had much to do in town to ensure that Wickham's punishment was suitable without being excessive. I could not send him to his death, nor to the Antipodes, and leave your sister a widow or an abandoned wife. The separation was necessary, but I had every intention of it being short in duration. I could not count the days quickly enough before I might see you again. I always intended, without regard to your sister or Wickham or my relations, or anyone else unconnected with us, to return to you. Believe me in this."

"You are," she looked directly into his eyes, "the very best of men."

He said nothing, but raised her hand to his lips and kissed it reverently, then after a short pause, stiffened and stepped away from her.

"Why do you shy from me?" His behaviour left her confused, but his words gave her hope.

His eyes opened as he caressed her with his gaze, and he breathed deeply. Elizabeth watched in wonder as the gentleman before her slowly eased himself out of his barricades, to become once more the man she had grown to care for so very much. At last he spoke. "You are too generous to trifle with me. If your feelings are still what they were last April, tell me so at once. My affections and wishes are unchanged, but one word from you will silence me on this subject for ever."

"Oh, Mr. Darcy!" The words came out in a rush of emotion, barely considered, flowing of their own accord. "Can you doubt me? How can I express how greatly my sentiments have changed since that awful day? How embarrassed I am to even think on it now. How badly I abused you, and how unjustly! Can you not believe that I have amended my opinions so entirely?"

"There was nothing you said, dearest Elizabeth, that I did not deserve. I have learned more about myself than ever I had known, and I hope I have become a better man for it, one deserving of you. Will you, Elizabeth? Will you relieve me now of my suffering? Will you agree to marry me?"

"Mr. Darcy.... Fitzwilliam... Will" His eyes lit up as she, at long last, gave voice to his name, "There is nothing that would make me happier!" Then, drawing closer to him in the privacy borne of the darkness, she lifted his hand to her own lips and kissed it. Then, with more daring than she had known she possessed, she leaned forward to touch his lips with hers. When she looked into his green eyes, she saw nothing but radiant happiness.

Not wishing to make their announcement at Jane and Bingley's party, they agreed to keep their engagement secret for a few days. Those days were both excruciating, for they wished so much to share their happy news, and exhilarating, for there is something magical about enjoying a shared secret, but at last they deemed enough time to have passed for them to reveal their engagement to the world. Will was now staying at Netherfield, and would remain there until Bingley and Jane's wedding, three weeks hence, by which time he hoped to have enough of his own affairs in order to finally marry Elizabeth forthwith.

If the Bennets were surprised at the engagement, they said nothing of it, and Mr. Bennet gave his permission for the union readily enough. Once Mrs. Bennet managed to overcome her professed dislike of Mr. Darcy, based so heavily on his behaviour of the previous autumn, she found herself sufficiently in awe of his status and wealth that she was rendered almost mute, a circumstance which satisfied both Elizabeth and her betrothed.

The moon was a sliver in the sky one night, after a well-appointed meal at Longbourn, when the couple were walking in the gardens before Darcy returned to Netherfield. They talked of those matters which engaged couples talk about, and when sure that no one was watching, held hands and dared to exchange the sporadic chaste kiss. Just before turning back to the house, Darcy cast his eyes again on his bride-to-be and leaned forward to kiss her forehead. "Your eyes, your beautiful eyes, are wide tonight, my lovely Elizabeth. They are wide and soft, and whilst your face is relaxed and easy, there is still an intensity about your gaze which puzzles me. It is not a look of worry, nor of despair; I am ready to believe you happy to be with me. Can you tell me, dear one, what that look indicates?"

With a gentle smile she leaned forward and returned his kiss, pausing to brush his lips with her own. "This look, Will, this expression, is one you must learn well, for it is the look of one who is deeply in love."

Epilogue

Six years later...

The late summer sun flooded into the bright morning room at Pemberley, treating its occupants to some welcome warmth after several days of rain. Two large glass doors, banked by large windows that extended the width of the room, stood open to the terrace beyond, and from her seat on the sofa, Elizabeth Darcy could see across the beautiful gardens and the gentle valley to the hillside that rose up at the distant end of the park. The leaves of the shrubberies on the terrace still shone wet with the moisture from the recent rains, and the entire view fairly shone with suppressed radiance in the early morning light.

So taken was she with the beauty displayed before her that she had all but forgotten the pile of letters that sat on the small table beside her until a rustle from across the room drew her attention back to her task.

"Is everything well, Love?" How she had come to adore that rich voice. Even after six years, it had the power to make her heart sing. She turned to her husband to reply, but he stayed her with a hand.

"No, no, allow me," he smiled. "Your beautiful eyes are wide and focused afar, there is no tension in your face, and your lips," he rose from his own chair as he spoke and walked to her to place a kiss upon them, "are settled in a soft smile. You are wool-gathering, although there are no sheep in here, and feeling content." He kissed her nose and added, "Your nose, as always, is perfect," before returning to his chair and his own stack of correspondence. "Did I do well?" He chuckled.

"Always, my love. You have long since proven yourself a most adept student in all things related to me. And yes, you are correct. How can I devote myself to these letters when such magnificence beckons my eye? Here is an invitation from Mrs. Ellings at the vicarage, and another from the Bancrofts, and here are some petitions from various ladies for my time or contributions towards their worthy causes. And each is due its consideration, but..." she waved her hand at the scenery outside. "I shall never be inured to this."

"And this is why you married me. For my scenery." Darcy chuckled again.

"Indeed, my love. For that and that alone."

"You delight in teasing me, Lizzy. What ho? A letter from Richard? May I?"

"Yes, read it and tell me what he says." She ruffled through her own stack. "I have one from Jane, and what is this? From Lydia? It is six months or more since she has written! But I shall read Jane's news first; I must hear how she is getting along." She broke the seal on Jane's letter and began to read.

Jane's news was good. She and Charles were still looking for a suitable estate to purchase, and had begun to make inquiries into some land near Pemberley. The Bingleys' two children were growing well and Charlie, the elder, was insisting on exchanging his petticoats for breeches. There would be a breeching ceremony after Michaelmas. "We are invited. It will be grand cause for a celebration after what heartbreak they suffered."

She had no need to elaborate; her husband knew of the babe that was born too soon and was lost, and of the pain the Bingleys still felt, no matter how common such events were.

Darcy's moss-green eyes met hers. "Will you be fit to travel, Love? It is a long distance."

"I am perfectly well, husband, and you know it! Little Anne will be three months old by then, and can travel with us in the carriage with her nurse. I know Jane would want both children to come, and Tommy can ride with us, or with Jones and Cabal in the other carriage, as he wishes." Thomas George—Darcy had refused to burden his first-born son with his own name, and consequently had opted for the names of the boy's grandfathers—was four years old and as smart as his father, with the same grey-green eyes and dark hair, but with his mother's smile and sense of humour. He was a delight to his parents, and—thus far, at least—a doting brother to his infant sister.

"He will wish for breeches too," Darcy cocked an eyebrow. "Shall we suggest a double ceremony?"

Lizzy laughed and returned to her letter. "There is little else of news, merely sisterly chatter. I am so pleased to see Jane returning to her accustomed self. What of Richard? What does he write?"

She watched Darcy's eyes flit back to the paper on his lap. He had become much improved at looking into her own eyes with little discomfort, but she knew he found relief in those moments when he might look elsewhere.

"He is well. His leg is quite healed now from his fall last winter, and he reports no lasting ill effects at all from the accident. Anne has opted not to return to Rosings after helping nurse him through his recovery, but has formed an attachment with the doctor who tended his leg! Aunt Catherine will never approve."

Elizabeth broke into a wide smile. "Then we shall support Anne if her mother will not. I am pleased for her and wish her happy. What does he write of Mrs. Fitzwilliam?" Two summers before, Richard had been pushed into matrimony at last by his mother. His bride had a large dowry, a small but profitable estate in Buckinghamshire willed directly to her by her late grandfather, and a caustic sense of humour which Elizabeth rather enjoyed but which left her husband very confused. Despite it being a society marriage for the usual reasons of wealth and connections, the couple seemed very well suited and quite taken with each other.

Darcy raised his eyes from the letter to meet hers again. "His wife is well, and they are looking forward to visiting us at Christmas, if the roads allow the drive from Matlock. It is only twenty miles, but the snows can be heavy in December." He paused. "Lizzy, I do not understand Harriet at all. She says one thing, but her face, from everything I can determine, tells me something quite different. Her words suggest mirth but her features speak of tragedy, or worse, she recites tales of gloom with a bright smile upon her face. Whatever shall I do when she is here? I know I shall say something to offend her terribly, but I cannot make her out at all."

Now Elizabeth rose from her chair to walk to her husband. She settled herself upon the arm of his chair and fell into him, pressing her own kiss upon his forehead, and then upon his lips. "She is an unusual woman. We will decipher her together, my love."

"Did Lydia write as well? Did I hear you correctly?" Darcy wrapped an arm around his wife and pulled her tight before letting her rise to return to her sofa and her letters.

She read for a few moments more and then looked up.

"You have bad news. I do not need special skills to recognise tears. What does she write?"

"Wickham is dead. Oh, my poor sister! She wrote this three months ago, and it happened a month before that. How horrible, and I never knew! How troubling that it takes so much time for letters to arrive from the Islands." She sniffed in a very unladylike way and dabbed her eyes with a lace-trimmed handkerchief. "It is hard to determine the exact matter of things from what Lydia writes, for she has always been blind to his faults and to the truth, but it appears that he was the master of his own demise. From what I can understand from her strange tale, he engaged the wrong sort in his gaming and wagering, and when he cheated them of their money, they attacked him and left him dead behind the tavern. Oh, Lydia! Now she is alone in Kingston with three babies and no money."

Darcy did not move as she told the sad tale, and for a moment she could see him returning to the statue-like man she had first met. These moods did not bother her now, for she understood him to be reflecting on what he had heard, and considering how best to proceed. He might remain thus for a few moments, or a few days, and whilst she could never be pleased to see him so, neither was she concerned. This reaction was as much a part of him as his green eyes and his loving heart, and she would not part with it.

"I shall provide her with a small income," he said at last. "When she returns to England, I shall arrange for a small cottage near Meryton and shall ensure she has enough to live respectably and raise her children properly.

This was more than Elizabeth had expected. "You are, and always have been, the best of men." Now her tears were borne of gratefulness and less of sorrow.

"Cousin Lizzy! What is the matter? You are crying."

A young man stood in the doorway. He was eighteen years of age, with a mop of sandy hair and bright eyes set in a face that was just now losing its boyish contours and that was a masculine version of his mother's. He was not particularly tall, but he had grown much over the past several months and he was certainly above average in height. He was, in all, a pleasant young man to look upon.

"Sam, come and sit with us a while." Over the past six years, Sam Gardiner had grown in maturity of manner as well as height, and he had requested this nickname as more suited to that of a man than the diminutive Sammy. "I am sad because of unhappy news from Lydia, but my tears are for her and not for me."

Her cousin cocked his head and furrowed his brow. "Are not all tears the same? How can one be crying for another if one is not sad oneself? If I am sad, I find myself tempted to cry, although I know this is something men must not do. And yet, if something sad happens to another person, I might expect that person to cry, but why should I cry, or be tempted to do so, on his or her behalf? If there is something I am able to do to assist, I can respond that way, but to cry when another is sad does not make sense to me." He looked over to Darcy, who shrugged his shoulders, and Elizabeth smiled despite her sympathetic tears. These two men were so similar in many ways, and she would never tire of trying to understand them.

She looked on in pleasure as her cousin took a seat beside her husband and proceeded to open the newspaper that sat atop the side table. He would, Elizabeth knew, be reading as much about the races as the news. That interest had never changed over the last several years. He cared just as little for the horses as ever he had done, but the betting and the odds still fascinated him as an intellectual game. From time to time, he mentioned something to Darcy, who responded in a cryptic language she only half understood, and the two would nod as if they had jointly solved all the problems of the world. This had become their way of late, and it had never ceased to amuse her, for all that she would never truly comprehend it.

She would miss this. Sam had been at Pemberley since the spring, working alongside Darcy, whom he idolised as much now as when they first become acquainted. Sam was eager to learn about the proper management of a large estate, and spent hours with Darcy both in his study over the ledgers, and in the fields and amongst his tenants. For his part, Darcy had all but adopted the lad as a brother. They shared an understanding that Lizzy could only grasp at, and they were as comfortable in each other's company as ever she had seen either.

It was Darcy who had suggested Cambridge to Uncle and Aunt Gardiner the year before. Sam was as smart as any boy she could imagine, and he had expressed a wish to continue his education past the schoolroom. Darcy had insisted upon paying Sam's way— "I would do as much for my own brother, and he is as a brother to me"—and refused to be swayed from his position when Sam's parents resisted. He did, however, allow that Oxford or St. Andrews would be acceptable alternatives. Furthermore, when Sam's friend Robert began to ponder his own future, it was Darcy who suggested the two friends take rooms together, which he would fund.

Robert's parents naturally demurred, but Darcy had replied, "Robert has been such a stalwart friend to my cousin. I know that friendship is its own reward, but if I may be so selfish, I would wish to assist them to continue together, for Robert can ease Sam's way where he might otherwise struggle. It is no hardship for me, and would ease my mind." And consequently both lads—now young men—were preparing for their first term at Cambridge immediately after Michaelmas.

Elizabeth's eyes fell upon her husband's handsome face once more. How this man had been a blessing, not only to her but to all her family. Whatever had she been thinking when first she rejected him? She had been so blind! The notion that she might have lost his goodwill forever, have forsaken the joy of being his wife and partner, was too horrible to consider.

These self-recriminations were cut short with the sound of rapid footsteps and a babbling voice, followed by the sound of a woman urging calm and a baby's coo, and almost at once, the door opened again. In flew a bundle of curls and energy which threw itself upon Elizabeth as she sat upon her sofa.

"Mama! Mama!" the whirlwind cried and wrapped chubby arms about her neck.

"Tommy, my darling! And here are Miss Roth and Annie. Come here, my sweets!" She took the baby from the nursemaid's arms and stared into the beautiful little face with its midnight-dark blue eyes and wisps of flaxen hair. Then she lifted her head to kiss her wonderful young son who looked so much like his father, and turned so she could see Darcy and Sam as well, all of her family in a single view.

The gardens, with their sun-drenched radiance and lush foliage, under clear blue skies and rich with the promise of a prosperous and glorious autumn, no longer called for her attention. They were no match for what she saw before her now. Her children, her husband, her cousin: these were the most wonderful things in the world to her now. No, she decided, as beautiful as the view through the windows, this sight before her was far more precious still.

Fin

Afterword

Many readers will recognise that the different lens through which Mr. Darcy and Samuel Gardiner see the world is that of the autism spectrum. Mr. Darcy is lightly touched by what a lot of people know as Asperger's Syndrome; Samuel is a bit further along the spectrum. They both have challenges and difficulties with social interactions, albeit to very different extents, and they respond to the world in different ways. However, autism was not a known condition during the time of the regency, and depending on the severity of the individual's symptoms, they were tolerated as eccentrics or treated as lunatics, and in the worst cases, were sent off to private institutions to be forgotten by their families.

Today, Autism Spectrum Disorder (ASD) is recognised as a complex developmental disorder that affects social interaction and communication, with a vast range of types and severity of symptoms. At the mildest end, people with ASD might have trouble with nonverbal communication or social skills. At its most severe, people with autism can be completely non-verbal and unable to communicate.

Despite the great number of symptoms of ASD, most people on the spectrum do not exhibit all of them. As the saying goes, if you've met one person with autism, you've met one person with autism.

Mr. Darcy's primary challenges include his difficulty in maintaining eye contact, his trouble understanding non-verbal communication such as tone of voice, facial expression, and metaphorical language, and his oversensitivity to sensory stimuli. For example, whereas a room full of chatting people might be an ignorable hum to many, some people with autism cannot filter out the background noise. Each sound fights for attention, each voice is part of an overwhelming din, and the person has to find some means of dealing with this assault.

Samuel shares some of Darcy's challenges, but has some of his own. He has difficulty maintaining the usual back-and-forth of conversation and exhibits the repetitive mannerisms often associated with autism, such as rocking back and forth when under stress. He relies on rules and routines to guide his way through the day, and has a hard time adjusting when plans are changed suddenly.

Both Darcy and Sammy also have fixed interests in unusual topics and are not easily able to see things from other people's points of view.

But along with the challenges autism brings, it can also carry with it great strengths, especially at the milder end of the spectrum. Both Darcy and Sammy have above-average intelligence, as well as unusual talents, such as Darcy's perfect recall and Sammy's mathematical skills. For this reason, many people consider 'high-functioning' autism not to be a disability at all, but a difference in ability, and speak proudly of neurodiversity, referring to the acceptance of people whose lenses are different and welcoming their strengths while supporting their challenges.

There are many organisations worldwide supporting autistic people and their families, and where you can read more about the condition. One such site is autisticadvocacy.org.

About the Author

Riana Everly was born in South Africa, but has called Canada home since she was eight years old. She has a Master's degree in Medieval Studies and is trained as a classical musician, specialising in Baroque and early Classical music. She first encountered Jane Austen when her father handed her a copy of *Emma* at age 11, and has never looked back.

Riana now lives in Toronto with her family. When she is not writing, she can often be found playing string quartets with friends, biking around the beautiful province of Ontario with her husband, trying to improve her photography, thinking about what to make for dinner, and, of course, reading!

If you enjoyed this novel, please consider posting a review at your favourite bookseller's website.

Riana Everly loves connecting with readers on Facebook at facebook.com/RianaEverly/

Also, be sure to check out her website at rianaeverly.com for sneak peeks at coming works and links to works in progress!

More from Riana Everly

Teaching Eliza

A tale of love, manners, and the quest for perfect vowels.

From a new voice in historical romance comes this sparkling Regency tale, wherein the elegance of Jane Austen's Pride and Prejudice and the wit of George Bernard Shaw's Pygmalion collide. The results are clever, funny, and often quite unexpected....

Professor Fitzwilliam Darcy, expert in phonetics and linguistics, wishes for nothing more than to spend some time in peace at his friend's country estate, far from the parade of young ladies wishing for his hand, and further still from his aunt's schemes to have him marry his cousin. How annoying it is when a young lady from the neighbourhood, with her atrocious Hertfordshire accent and country manners, comes seeking his help to learn how to behave and speak as do the finest ladies of high society.

Elizabeth Bennet has disliked the professor since overhearing his flippant comments about her provincial accent, but recognizes in him her one opportunity to survive a prospective season in London. Despite her ill feelings for the man, she asks him to take her on as a student, but is unprepared for the price he demands in exchange.

"With her clever mash-up of two classics, Riana Everly has fashioned a fresh, creative storyline with an inventive take on our favorite characters, delightful dialogue and laugh out loud humor. Teaching Eliza is certain to become a reader favorite. It's a must read!" – Sophia Meredith (author of the acclaimed On Oakham Mount and Miss Darcy's Companion)

Teaching Eliza is a full-length JAFF novel of about 110 000 words and is available in eBook or paperback format from your favourite bookseller.

The Assistant

A tale of love, secrets, and adventure across the ocean

When textile merchant Edward Gardiner rescues an injured youth, he has no notion that this simple act of kindness will change his life. The boy is bright and has a gift for numbers that soon makes him a valued assistant and part of the Gardiners' business, but he also has secrets and a set of unusual acquaintances. When he introduces Edward to his sparkling and unconventional friend Miss Grant, Edward finds himself falling in love.

But who is this enigmatic woman who so quickly finds her way to Edward's heart? Do the deep secrets she refuses to reveal have anything to do with the appearance of a sinister stranger, or with the rumours of a missing heir to a northern estate? As danger mounts, Edward must find the answers in order to save the woman who has bewitched him . . . but the answers themselves may destroy all his hopes.

Set against the background of Jane Austen's London, this Pride and Prejudice prequel casts us into the world of Elizabeth Bennet's beloved Aunt and Uncle Gardiner. Their unlikely tale takes the reader from the woods of Derbyshire, to the ballrooms of London, to the shores of Nova Scotia. With so much at stake, can they find their Happily Ever After?

The Assistant is a full-length JAFF novel of about 90 000 words.

Recipient of the Jane Austen Award from Jane Austen Readers' Awards.

"With a poignant storyline and colourful array of characters...Ms. Everly's work demonstrates a commanding hold on narrative and history..."

Excerpt from

The Assistant: Before Pride and Prejudice

Prologue

Autumn, 1799

The rains had come in a deluge the previous night, with thunder and lightning, frightening horses and sending young children into the arms of their anxious parents. A storm this heavy could cause damage to homes and bridges, could knock down trees and block roads. Such heavy rain was unusual for the early days of autumn, but not unheard of, and consequently the servants at the estate were prepared for the worst when the first crash of lightning lit the midnight sky as bright as noon.

They were prepared when a subsequent bolt struck the stables, setting them afire despite the torrential rains. One small crew worked fearlessly to bring the terrified horses to safety under the portcullis of the old buildings, whilst another strove to douse the flames that licked at the hay stacked under the peaked roof. The work was exhausting and all-demanding, and when, after some time, the fire was extinguished and the horses returned to the slightly charred but otherwise undamaged building, the servants gratefully retired to the kitchens for some well-earned tea and cakes, and perhaps something stronger to ease their nerves. The storm had abated now and lightning no longer split the air, and in the aftermath of their exertion and the lessened sense of urgency, the men and women took their ease, resting before the demands of another day of work.

No one noticed the small figure that crept its way out of the kitchen door, which had been left ajar to allow men access to the warmth and sustenance.

The ground was wet and spongy underfoot, and the passage of two feet left small puddles in their wake, grass-covered indentations filling with water before slowly releasing their liquid back into the rain-soaked earth. In the heavy cloud-laden darkness, still hours before dawn, the slight figure picked its way tentatively down the edge of the hedges that rimmed the long drive, ducking into the foliage wherever possible so as to avoid being noticed by any who might still be awake and watching. The figure hefted a small bag onto one shoulder and wrapped the greatcoat more snugly. At long last, upon reaching the road at the end of the property, the tense shoulders relaxed just a bit, the first ordeal having been survived. One step closer to freedom!

It was a long walk to town, near on ten miles, but the traveller did not seem to be in any hurry. Although the road from the estate ran straight into the town, it was too well traveled for the fugitive's peace of mind. A little known path through the woods that bordered the thoroughfare would provide better protection. Keeping to the bushes, the rough-clad wanderer crept slowly onward through the wet undergrowth, anxious of unseen stones or slippery patches in this darkest of nights, stopping every now and then to assess location and direction. In the woods ran a stream, surging from the recent downpour, which fed the river that flowed through the city, and the traveller carefully and slowly followed the sound of the rushing water. There was no need to hurry. There was no one waiting. Brushing dirty hands on rough woolen trousers, the wanderer adjusted the much-worn coat atop thin shoulders and moved on, towards what, heaven only knew.

Made in the USA
Coppell, TX
23 June 2020